DATE DUE

JUN 6 2000

OCT 0 6 2008

OCT 3 1 2013
JUL 0 9 2015

PORTRAIT OF
THE ARTIST'S WIFE

ALSO BY BARBARA ANDERSON

I Think We Should Go into the Jungle

Girls High

PORTRAIT OF
THE ARTIST'S WIFE

BARBARA ANDERSON

W·W·Norton & Company

New York   London

Printed in the United States of America

Manufacturing by The Maple-Vail Book Manufacturing Group.

Library of Congress Cataloging-in-Publication Data

Anderson, Barbara, 1926–
Portrait of the artist's wife / Barbara Anderson.
p.   cm.
I. Title.
PR9639.3.A536P67   1993
813'.54—dc20   92-27676
ISBN 0-393-03489-5

W. W. Norton & Company, Inc., 500 Fifth Avenue, New York, N.Y. 10110
W. W. Norton & Company Ltd., 10 Coptic Street, London WC1A 1PU

1 2 3 4 5 6 7 8 9 0

For Piers, Sally, Sam and Harry

ACKNOWLEDGEMENTS

The author gratefully acknowledges the
assistance of a travel bursary from the Literature Committee
of the Queen Elizabeth II Arts Council of New Zealand,
and the 1991 Victoria University of Wellington
Writer's Fellowship

An extract was previously published in *Metro*

PORTRAIT OF
THE ARTIST'S WIFE

I

There was a large crowd in the auditorium. Sarah made a quick guess as she stepped onto the dais beside the Minister. Three hundred at least. How amazing.

Jack had taught her as a child how to get a quick tally on a mob. 'Blocks of ten, Sal,' he shouted through the choking dust of the yards. 'Get a block of ten in your head then multiply.' Sarah and her brother Dougal had practised for hours, bare legs pressed hard against the yard rails for balance, eyes narrowed against the glare.

The guests stood close together near the top of the stairwell, their feet shuffling, their eyes glancing from side to side, a wary flock released into a fresh paddock. The area was not large and the ceiling was low but dignity had been achieved. A series of large portrait photographs of men and women whose endeavours had furthered the cultural life of New Zealand lined the walls. The heart rimu floor had been donated by Forest Enterprises, according to a brass plaque. Two metres in from the walls a narrow inlay of matai provided visual interest. No member of the crowd gathered together to honour the memory of Jack Macalister at the posthumous launching of his last book strayed beyond this line. If they did they would fall off the edge of the world, hurtle through space, be lost to the flatlands of post-colonial culture.

Smiling and gentle, her brain ticking with rage, Sarah stared out over the sea of faces. I hate the lot of them. No I don't. I'm not a hater any more than Jack. Never have been, why start? But there is not one, not one I would trust. And that's a lie too. I'm getting hysterical. There's nothing wrong with Desmond O'Reilly and his

7

fluff of white hair and his dear little pot belly. Never has been. An honest man, an honest broker. Why *should* he have taken the risk to publish Jack when he began writing. Who would have bought it. If people write weird stuff what can they expect. There's a guy at Harvard writing funny stuff, wrote Ezra Pound about Eliot. Imagine when they met. What joy to discover there's another guy writing funny stuff. That yours is not the only funny stuff in the whole flaming world. Sarah's eye met Charles Bremner's. One thatch of eyebrow climbed his forehead as it had done through the years, the rages, the turn ups and the roll ons of Sarah and Jack's thirty years of matrimony. She smiled at him, calmed.

He had been her lover many years ago. A man blessed with a strong face which Sarah could never decide whether he had earned or not. He was not smiling; his face was grim, a grim dig. Smile, she wanted to hiss at him. Smile, you dumb bum. You don't have to like them. Just smile.

Nicola Bristowe wasn't smiling either. She looked a mess. A deliberate mess, so she said. She had explained her reasons to Sarah at some length. Her spiked black hair, her purple T-shirt and khaki bush-jacket indicated she was anti the whole thing. Not Jack of course.

'No,' said Sarah.

'You know I worshipped Jack.'

An acolyte. A devout follower. Sarah nodded. 'Yes,' she said.

'And you of course,' said Nicky, one boneless paw on Sarah's arm. If you ran a hand through that hair it would be lacerated. The red hand by Bristowe.

One face. One loving face. Sarah's daughters Dora and Emily scowled from the edge of the crowd. Not at her: at the academics, the published, the funded and the funders, the multinationals and the small. Selwyn Dempster, who had published Jack after Charles dropped him, beamed at her. Kindly, avuncular and drunk as a skunk. How had he managed to achieve that, the clever old sot? By making preparations in advance, presumably. Sarah's white wine was warm and tasted of sour apples.

The Minister was speaking, had probably been speaking for

some time. His jaws were moving, a stream of spittle attached his upper-left molars to those of his lower jaw. Some people have stronger, more viscous spittle. Sarah had noticed this before.

'. . . the untimely, indeed tragic death of New Zealand's most venerated writer. The whole nation rejoiced,' lied the Minister, 'when Jack Macalister won a Commonwealth Prize for Literature with his novel *Kereru Pie*. The very title was typical of the wit, the satire of the man. Jack Macalister was known to all as a dedicated conservationist, one of the first back in the days before selective logging, the nuclear free zone, waste disposal clean up and the like. All those things we take for granted now, Jack Macalister fought for with his pen. You would never have found him, as a Pakeha, shooting a native pigeon for the pot,' cried the Minister. 'No sir. The title was satirical, like I said. Jack Macalister was a passionate lover of his country, its people'—Charles's head lifted—'its flora and its fauna and yet he lived for his art: the art of the storyteller, the committed writer, the whole man. It is fitting,' cried the Minister waving one arm in a sudden sweeping gesture, 'that we should meet here to honour Jack Macalister because we have to admit,' the deep voice dropped, ' we have to admit that we lack the cultural heritage of five or six centuries like the rest of Europe.' Emily's smile combined delight and astonishment. The Minister swept on. 'So, as I say, it is fitting that we meet in this venue among the portraits of so many of his friends and mentors, those who have left their mark on the cultural life of our land.' The photographs of the wise gazed down, the faces of the crowd gazed up. The eyes of the photographed among the audience flicked to their images, as dismissive of alternatives, as unheeding of the rest as a mother who waits by a circling merry-go-round for her own babies to reappear. They were good photographs, they captured the essence. Strong black-and-white images gave each face the attention it merited. An intense Maori face was draped by hair. You couldn't tell of course that the eyes were a blaze of blue. Or that one jokey face scarcely ever smiled in real life. A photograph of a man with a beard, thought Sarah, is all beard. Nothing else shows, well, not much. Concentrate you fool. She stared at her feet. A patch of

9

crushed chips reduced to golden dust lay beneath them.

'She looks good, doesn't she,' muttered Emily. Dora nodded. They were both tall, far too tall, their bones showed, they ate like horses and their hair shone. Emily, aged sixteen, spent a considerable amount of time training her red-gold hair into horizontal ripples. Dora's thirty-six-year-old face was chalk white, her mouth scarlet, her black hair so long she could sit on it and sometimes did. How does she cope with that hair! people asked nervously. She's very striking, isn't she? They couldn't take their eyes off her, her swinging stride, the set of her head. She cared for nobody . . . no, not she, except for her lover, Eddie, and Emily and Sarah for whom she fought like a threatened tigress. This infuriated Sarah and made her feel guilty. You could never say to Dora, 'Shove off,' as you could to Emily. Everything concerning her mother mattered, was magnified, became a heartbreak to be resolved or stowed away till it could be used as evidence for the prosecution at a later date.

Sarah's daughters stared at their mother, the movements of her hands, the gleam in her eye. She wore Great Aunt Patricia's velvet bridge coat over a black shirt and trousers. They don't make fabrics like that now: purple flowers, brick-red flowers, green and black leaves of velvet melded together, sumptuous and splendid. 'All I want when you snuff it, Mum, is the bridge coat,' said Dora and Emily on frequent and separate occasions. They never mentioned her paintings—well, not to her.

Sarah's head lifted. She caught Dora's eye and smiled. Her dark hair flicked back, an acknowledgement intimate as a wink that they were on the same side, that they knew how phoney the whole thing was, but never mind because they also knew that Dad was good, that drunken, whoring old Dad was a good, a great writer. They knew that. It was the mainstay of their lives, something to cling to, a fiercely guarded possession. And anyway he wasn't as drunk as all that and he hadn't whored for years and his writing got better and better and he'd died last year aged fifty-two. Dora's eyes filled with tears. Emily wiped the back of her hand against her nose. Her leather miniskirt kept riding up.

'So it gives me great pleasure,' said the Minister, 'a pleasure tinged with sadness that the author cannot be with us today, because . . .' How on earth was he going to finish the sentence? Sarah's mouth dropped, Emily snorted, Dora scowled. Because he's passed over? Away? Beyond? Completely unfazed, the Minister gave another expansive sweep of his right arm. 'He cannot be present at the launching of his last book *Emotion on the Page*,' he cried, 'because he is no longer with us. I will ask his wife, his loyal wife of over thirty years, Sarah Macalister, to launch the book.'

The Minister bowed to Sarah and moved two steps to the left and one backwards. The loyal wife nodded at him and moved to his recently vacated space. She had a long neck, her head was high.

'I have never,' she said in clipped tones, 'been present before at the launching of a husband's book by his relict.' She glared at them, daring them to disagree. 'Wives, as we know, are often acknowledged by their author husbands in print. These thanks range from the fulsome to the idiotic, "To my wife without whom this book would have been finished in half the time," et cetera.'

There was a ripple, less than a ripple, a smiling nudge from the audience. It was all right. Sarah was not going to come on strong. Jack was going to stay safely buried, for which we must all be devoutly thankful. Turbulent widows may have their place but not, please God, while I'm at the party. The relieved audience smiled and swayed together. Charles drained his glass of tepid wine and waved it at a waiter, who ignored him. No topping up during speeches.

'I think,' continued Sarah, her eyes on the furthermost line of photographs depicting the great and the good and a dedicated bookseller, 'that it is safer to wait for a posthumous launch such as this before inviting a wife to speak.' She smiled; a crack which had started life long ago as a dimple appeared in her right cheek. 'Not in fact that Jack did ask me. But then, of course, he didn't know he was going to die.'

Not so good. Eyes viewed the heart rimu with interest. Feet shuffled. Pointed fashion toes were inspected from on high.

'But he should have known! What did he think would happen to someone who smoked and drank as he did? Whose idea of exercise was to heave himself up from the typewriter to crawl around the chair once and collapse on it again? Who regarded sleep as an intrusion and food, in his latter years, as a waste of time?'

Reactions varied from a few 'How interesting's to many 'Christ, how appalling's. 'Some loyal wife,' sniffed Nicola Bristowe. Perhaps the widow was joking. How to know? Smiles, nervous, diffident smiles, were tried out on a few faces. Most remained serious, stern even, as though present at an extermination order. Charles still glared, Nicky was outraged, Dora and Emily smiled. Well, well well, they thought. Good old Mum.

Sarah's hands were clasped together. She had no notes. She spoke from what the paper would describe as her heart. 'But none of this would have mattered,' she continued. 'Men have smoked and drunk and died and worms . . .' Her hand fanned out at them, palm upwards, fingers outstretched. 'But not always at fifty-two. Men have smoked and drunk and lived pink-cheeked and crisp for ever. Jack made two mistakes. He chose the wrong parents . . .'

'Why drag in his unfortunate parents?' muttered a small publisher.

'History of infarct,' replied his wife, who was a doctor with a large practice and a nose for facts.

'. . . and he lacked recognition in his own country.'

Eyes back to the heart rimu. 'What is the point of the Commonwealth Prize for Literature?' cried Sarah, hunting down the members of the audience who were game enough to meet her rhetoric eye to eye. 'Of course it's an honour, a great honour and recognition. But it's the reaction *here* that matters. *Read* his books. Read them. I don't mean buy them. Who buys books? A few harmless nutters, born and bred in an alcove. People with storage room and bookcases and eyes which move from left to right and back again. Read his books! Beg them, borrow them, get them from the library. They will tell you all you need to know. About here. About now. About how it has always been! Read them.'

Mad. She knew it was mad. Her heart was thudding beneath the bridge coat. The few people who 'believed' in Jack Macalister were present in the auditorium. Why lambast Anthony Bannister who

12

made his pile in underwear and spent it on Art. The small worried eyes of Ewen Stotter met hers. He loved his cats and his books and nothing else. Elsie Smith had dragged her withered leg from Petone to honour her brightest pupil, the only one she had ever sent to the Head to be caned she told Sarah every time they met. She leant propped on elbow crutches on the littoral zone beyond the matai inlay looking puzzled and unhappy. She had come to praise. I am behaving, thought Sarah, like clergymen who harangue the congregation who have come to church for the sins of omission of those who haven't. There are not many believers here. But some. Stop before they cry.

She tugged the quilted collar of purple and rusty red against her neck with both hands.

'*Emotion on the Page*,' she promised, 'is different from Jack's previous work. It is much more accessible. It stands alone in his oeuvre.' The corners of her lips pulled downwards at the unaccustomed word. 'It may be described as a full-frontal confessional. I think you will find it interesting.' She paused, daring them once again to disagree. 'I certainly did.' She swallowed. The back of her throat felt damp. Not now, especially not now to bawl her head off. She concentrated on the black-spotted tights of a wide-legged woman in the front row. 'It gives me great pleasure,' said Sarah, smiling radiantly at the lost audience so recently cupped within her hands, 'to launch this book and may it always be as becomingly clothed as it is in this, its first edition. Thank you.' The applause was loud with relief, but not long.

'I thought it was one of the wife's paintings on the cover,' muttered a literary editor called Macy to her new lover Geraldine who wore an enormous red jersey, red plastic earrings and little else.

'It is.'

'What a skite.'

'I believe she's quite good,' said Geraldine, inspecting her thumbnail. 'Sarah Tandy.'

'Is that *her*! Well, well.'

'Their marriage was a disaster, of course,' sighed Geraldine, shaking her head at a tray of proffered canapés. A ring of dark grey surrounded the yolk of each half-egg. Her hand indicated to her lover the scattered black grains which decorated each one. 'Lumpfish,' she said.

Patrick Wheeler moved towards them, his hands making small flipper movements through the crowd, an endangered species on the move. 'Good turnout,' he said. He glanced towards the table piled with copies of *Emotion on the Page* and smiled. 'Odd not being able to get your copy signed.'

Geraldine hugged her jersey, red plastic banged her cheeks. 'Patrick!'

Sarah stood beside the table, a copy of the book in her hand as she explained its cover to Charles. 'It's me,' she said.

Charles's face sagged, the grooves deepened from nose to mouth as he stared at the dust jacket. 'You?'

The painting depicted a small flat-roofed bach of vertical weatherboards painted with what looked like used engine oil. A spray of red-tongued flax-flowers brushed against a faded green water tank set on a rickety stand. The two small windows of the bach reflected a bleached sky. Seed heads and stalks of long grasses, dead daisies and flattened kikuyu grass were depicted with precision.

'I didn't know you were into photorealism,' said Charles bleakly.

'I'm not. Just this one.'

'Why?'

'Because it's me. I told you.'

He looked at her. His eyes would soon be rheumy. What a word. She laughed up at him, patting his arm with quick good-dog affection. 'It's called *The Rover's Return.*'

She had always overdone a joke. Thrashed it bare. Rubbed your nose in it. Like Jack.

'We're past the bach myth,' said Charles.

Sarah's head snapped back. 'No, no we're not.'

'There are too many myths. We make up too many myths to comfort ourselves.'

'We Pakehas have not enough myths, not of our own.'

'The little grey hut in the bush built by man alone. Home is where the bach is. We're past all that.'

'But that's just why we need the myths!' Her brisk anger about things that didn't matter had always intrigued him. 'It's when things have nearly disappeared that myths become necessary. They have to import cowboys now from Mexico. Did you know that? The indigenous ones are almost extinct. The myth is more essential now.'

He laughed, moved his head in defeat and changed the subject. 'Anyway, why you? Why's it you?'

'It is a portrait of the artist's wife.'

His face was serious once more. 'You can be so infuriating.'

It was not the moment, it never was the moment for Charles to understand. 'Come and tell me who they all are,' she said, nodding her head at the black-and-white photographs, offering him a way out. 'Do you know them all?'

'Yes.'

Of course he did.

'I've gone off the idea,' she said. 'I need a drink, a strong drink.'

'How many are going to eat afterwards?'

'About eight.'

'Eight,' said Charles, taking two glasses from the tray. He nodded at the waiter. 'Thanks Tom.'

Tom was fresh-faced and jaunty and took pride in his work. He was employed by a firm called Boys and Girls who charged too much for their less-than-expert services but at least they didn't actually throw the stuff around like some.

Tom smiled and moved away to succour the next group.

Charles watched Sarah. She should be surrounded by enthusiastic crowds, by crowds determined to honour both Jack and herself. He noticed how people melted away as she moved towards them in the same way groups of people who had no burning desire to meet the Governor General dispersed as he and his handlers circled around a reception. People who had nothing against the Governor General, but what the hell. Why bother and what would you say? What would you say to Jack's widow? Well done mate. A patient sufferer at rest.

15

And anyway her speech hadn't helped.

The Minister and his wife, a cheerful woman with purple lipstick and large white arms, appeared beside Sarah.

'Mrs Macalister,' said the Minister, 'I don't think you've met my wife, Eunice Leadbetter.'

'How do you do.' The hand was unexpectedly cool and dry. 'My name is Tandy, in fact. Sarah Tandy. I paint,' said Sarah as though that might account for it.

'I was so relieved when Ross asked me to marry him,' said Mrs Leadbetter, 'that I'd've changed my name to *anything*.'

'Call me what you like,' cried her husband, 'as long as it's not late for breakfast.'

Eunice laughed, a friendly chortle as though she had never heard the joke before in her life.

Nice lady.

'Why?' said Dora, who had appeared to peer down at the pretty plump face, the pink-blonde hair. 'Why were you relieved?'

'Things were different in my day,' smiled Eunice. 'There was nothing else to do except get married.'

'Why not?' demanded Emily, draped like a question mark a foot above the interrogated.

'It's difficult for you girls to understand.' The lady was completely unruffled. She loved the young. She was good with them. She never judged and was a leavening influence on her husband, who never stopped for a moment. She thought Dora and Emily were lovely. Different perhaps, but lovely. Imagine being able to wear your hair glued, literally glued, to your scalp then hanging for miles and still look as good as Dora did.

'I'll never forget the day I signed my first housekeeping cheque,' she said. Bubbles of mirth surfaced from stained lips, one heavily ringed hand fluttered in front of them. 'I signed it Eunice Belton, my maiden name, instead of Leadbetter.'

Dora and Emily stared at her blankly.

The Honourable Mr Leadbetter's shoulders moved. He was getting bored. 'I think we can all fit in the car. It's not exactly a stretch limo but . . .'

'What about Charles?' said Sarah in sudden panic.

'Charles?'

'He's coming isn't he? He said he was. Charles Bremner.'

'Oh. Oh yes. But there'll be another car. The Literary Fund man, Highgate, and his wife are coming as well. What's her name, Eunice?'

Mrs Leadbetter whipped out a diminutive red book with gold corners. She riffled the pages. 'His first wife was Janine.' She paused. 'But she's dead. I've crossed her out.'

This was much better. Dora and Emily looked almost cheerful. 'Her name,' said Sarah, 'is Penny Broad. And she's not his wife. She's his mistress.'

'Ah,' said Mrs Leadbetter. Her head moved down and back in stately tolerance.

'Oops,' yelped Tom, manoeuvring between them with a sloping tray. One lone grey half-egg dropped at Emily's feet. Tom dropped to his heels and stared. Emily smiled and trod on the egg.

'It's so interesting,' beamed Mrs Leadbetter, 'how lovely you girls look when you're cross.'

It was getting hot. The few smokers present lurked on the outskirts, their puffs guilty as their first attempts behind the bike-sheds of their youth.

'Ah, there you are,' cried Mrs Leadbetter to the Literary Fund man and the woman beside him. 'Simon Highgate isn't it? And Penny? You all know each other, of course.'

'Of course.'

Sarah looked at the small nuggety figure, the eager animated face, the bush of black hair. She had found her husband and Penny locked together at the bottom of a cliff at Anawhata in 1969 just before she and Jack went to England.

'Your frock's the colour of artichoke soup,' she said.

Penny clapped her hands. 'That's your colour sense! I couldn't remember what it reminded me of. I've always been so grateful to Sarah,' she told Mrs Leadbetter. 'It was she who said they don't have to be peeled for soup.'

'Olga Becker told me,' said Sarah.

'Oh.' There was a moment of silence as cue-boards of memory clicked into place. 'Your benefactor?'

'One of them,' snapped Sarah.

'Don't you?' said Mrs Leadbetter, still with the artichokes. 'You learn something every day.'

Sarah glanced around, her eyes hunting for Charles. He was by the lift talking to Miss Smith. He had found a chair for her. 'Excuse me,' murmured Sarah. She moved quickly to the lift doors to embrace the woman who had taught English to both her husband and Charles. 'How good to see you. I should have come over before.'

'Nonsense.' Miss Smith clambered to her feet. 'This is your night. Jack's night.'

'"Nor Spring nor Summer beauty hath such grace / As I have seen in one autumnal face." Jack used to quote that about you.'

Miss Smith grimaced, the lines round her mouth deepened. '"Autumnal face." Not one of Donne's best efforts. Jack always had to watch his sentimental streak.'

'I can't say I ever noticed it,' said Sarah, irritated at the blatant honesty of the rejection from someone Jack had christened 'Old Corn is Green'.

Simon Highgate touched Sarah's shoulder. She jumped. 'Don't ever, ever, do that again,' she gasped. 'I can't stand "boos".' He was long, grey, the colour of melting putty. God in heaven, behave yourself woman. 'I'm sorry,' she muttered. 'Miss Smith, this is Mr Highgate. Mr Highgate is on the Literary Fund. I understand,' she said politely, 'that the Fund is soon to become part of the Arts Council?'

Simon Highgate opened his mouth to reply.

But Miss Smith was not pleased. She began a concise summary of exactly what was wrong with the Arts Council, where the money was squandered and where funds should be rechannelled. Charles and Sarah stood warmed by her presence. Sarah's heartbeat slowed, she took a deep breath. Simon Highgate wriggled on his pin, his limbs twitching.

'If you'll excuse us,' he said finally, 'the Minister is waiting.'

'The Minister?' said Miss Smith moving her weight to the other elbow crutch.

'Our host.'

'Ah,' said Miss Smith. 'Host. Well, off you go.' She waved a crutch. 'And good luck.'

Charles and Sarah kissed her.

'I'll go with Howard,' said the Minister, who always travelled in the front with his driver because he wished to demonstrate his egalitarian convictions. He climbed into the Ministerial LTD. 'If you ladies just like to . . . I'm afraid it'll be a bit of a scrum but . . .'

Howard held the door wide. He sucked his belly into an almost forgotten Gaylord Hauser stomach-snatch as yards of Dora and Emily jackknifed themselves in to perch alongside Mrs Leadbetter and Sarah. They sat with their four knees together, straight-backed and eager.

Emily's face fell. 'There's no flag.'

'Oh no ma'am,' said Howard, now seated behind the wheel and tugging at his safety belt. 'Just for official occasions, the flag.'

'I thought there'd be a flag,' said Emily.

'Where's Charles?' said Sarah, straining her neck to peer out the back window. She saw him laughing with someone unknown as he hobbled down the steps. His arthritis was getting worse.

'After dark,' said Howard, four fingers on the wheel and their lives in his hands, 'it has to be receptions for the Queen, Governors General, things of that nature.'

'What a bummer,' said Emily.

Sarah refrained from nudging her. The why-are-you-kicking-me gleam was visible in Emily's eyes, the set of her mouth. 'Never mind,' she said, patting her daughter's knee. 'We're in a limo, that's something new.'

'It's nice to think someone your age cares about the flag,' said Mrs Leadbetter.

'Oh, I don't,' said Emily. 'It's not that.'

'I care about the flag,' said Dora.

'Well I don't.' Emily's pout equalled Brigitte Bardot's in her pre-seal days.

Sarah stared at the harbour. The wind had got up. Yachts yawed at their moorings, slapped by dark waves. A man jumped ashore, slipped on the hard and scrambled upright. Jack had cared about the flag. It was all very odd. The whole thing.

The car swept into the forecourt of the Plaza Hilton. They could easily have walked, have blown the launching out of their hair, tossed the memory out over the harbour, up, up, and away.

Brigitte Bardot perked up. 'Are we going *here?*'

The Minister nodded. His voice was solemn. 'The venison is very good.'

'Chrissie says,' muttered Emily into her sister's ear, 'that this place is all hair oil and no socks.' Her smile at the top-hatted concierge was radiant. 'Hi,' she said.

'How did Chrissie get here?'

'Her new guy brought her. She said the breakfast was the best bit.'

Let it rip, thought Sarah. I am proud of them. Sarah Tandy and her daughters sailed into the foyer and kept calm.

But it was not easy.

'Not a Maori in sight, of course,' said Emily as they sank into the dining chairs indicated by Mrs Leadbetter after consultation with the plan from her clutch bag.

'There's one over there, dear.' Mrs Leadbetter indicated the wine waiter. Emily's smile was pitying.

Charles, whose courtesy was usually infallible, refused to play. He disliked the Minister, he loathed Highgate, he was puzzled by the insistence with which Penny Whoever's thigh pressed against his. His deep rumbling voice was not heard for some time. He leant across Sarah who was puddling about with her avocado and kai moana.

'What is your lot going to do about Fiji?' he asked the Minister.

The Minister's face was startled above his soup spoon. He gave a short wounded yelp. This was dirty fighting from a guest of Literature. 'Government's policy is quite clear,' he said. 'Non-intervention.'

One hand touched his designer spectacle frames. 'You'll have to ask the Minister of Foreign Affairs for details on that one. It's not really my area. Not in depth.' His forehead glistened as he leant forward to impart more information.

'You know Government is changing its name.'

'What?'

'Foreign Affairs is about to become,' the Minister's hand executed a quick ally-oop, a triumphant rabbit-from-hat gesture, 'The Ministry of External Relations and Trade. As from Christmas.'

'Oh.' Charles leant back feeling even more depressed; the ludicrous place, the waste of the taxpayers' money, the shame of being here.

'I'll never forget the first time I was called Mrs Leadbetter properly,' said their hostess. 'It was the grocer who said it. I looked behind me, you know how you do. Over my shoulder. For Mrs Leadbetter, I mean.'

Emily was still staring. 'Oh.'

'And then, do you remember, Roger? The very next week my housekeeping cheque bounced. Well, not bounced exactly. The bank had put Roger's cheque into another Leadbetter's account, see. Someone said we could've sued. I'll never forget, though. Standing there scarlet from head to foot in the Four Square. You can imagine.'

Sarah looked at the dusty pinkish curls, the soft unlined face. You are a good woman and I like you. Generations of good women have raised you. Your children, if they have any sense, will rise up and call you blessed. She leant across the table. 'Do you by any chance know how to remove ballpoint stains from material, Mrs Leadbetter?'

A challenge. Mrs Leadbetter was away. Charles's knees jerked against Sarah's in retreat from Penny. The Minister was bent over his plate, his face serious and responsible as he stowed away overpriced food for which he would not be expected to pay. He was now on to Conservation, the central theme of the biennial Conference of Cultural Partnerships from the Commonwealth Arts Administrators' Conference. 'Of course in today's climate you can

21

imagine,' he said after a good chew on his vol-au-vent. 'Weren't you there as an observer?' he asked Simon Highgate. 'Terrific concern about conservation of indigenous art forms, wasn't there?'

'Yes,' said Simon.

'All the convening countries face almost identical issues of cultural identity of the indigenous,' glared the Minister. 'That was my impression.'

Simon's tongue was busy on a food trap between his right-side back molars. He nodded.

'We mustn't get bogged down in negativism though.'

'No.'

'But I felt, personally, that the overriding mood of the conference was positive. Did you feel that?'

He'd have to leave it till later. 'Yes,' said Simon, recentring his tongue. 'Yes, I did. Most strongly.' He paused. 'I liked the idea of the cultural charter.'

'Exactly,' said the Minister. 'Absolutely.' He glanced around the opulent gilded room. 'Where's the wine waiter?' He lifted a hand. 'And I feel we should be working already towards giving a cultural identity to the 1990s.' He nodded, a quick dip of affirmation to his own statement. 'A lot of people,' sighed the Minister, 'haven't any sort of a feel for the nineties as yet.'

'Possibly,' said Charles gloomily, 'because they haven't arrived.'

'Round the corner though, aren't they. Just round the corner. Almost there. Three years is nothing. Not even three; just '88 and '89 to go and we're in business,' cried the Minister, pink with excitement at the prospect.

A camp young waiter with white gloves and delayed adolescent acne stood at the end of their table. 'Good evening,' he said, in love with himself and the excitement of his job.

'See what I mean,' hissed Emily to Dora. 'White gloves!'

'I'll just run through the menu for the main course,' said the young man.

'Why?' asked Charles.

The shining face made no pause. 'The fish of the day,' he

intoned, 'is hapuka served with a plum coulis draped with fennel and served with ratatouille-garnished zucchini.'

Details of the preparation of *Coq-au-vin à la Beaujolais* were described in detail. *En chemise* was explained, the young man's eyes sparkled with joy, his hands rolled as he encased fantasy fillets in wrappings of invisible pastry.

'Why do they do it?' moaned Charles.

Mrs Leadbetter patted his arm. 'They just want to help. And it's friendly.'

Dora was happy with her snails. 'They're tinned of course,' she told Charles. 'All they taste of really is garlic. But I'm mad about garlic.'

Charles blinked. He saw himself and Sarah side by side in the Loire Valley almost twenty years ago. Saw the shimmering heat haze as they stood arm in arm gazing across the river to Chaumont. 'It's just like the Tukituki with castles,' Sarah had said, turning back to the hired Renault. Garlic had been their own discovery, their secret ingredient, their elixir.

Dora stopped digging at her snail shell for a moment. 'You were the first to publish Dad's stuff, weren't you?'

'Yes.' She was astonishing-looking, her face chalk white. 'How old are you now, Dora?'

'Thirty-six. Why?'

He shook his head. 'Nothing.'

'My boyfriend Eddie wasn't asked,' she said.

He recognised the quick derisive tone and laughed. 'Good God no. I didn't mean . . .' He glanced across the table. 'And Em?'

'Sixteen. How long have you known Mum?'

Charles looked at Sarah. His leg banged against hers as he swung it away from Penny's yet again. The corners of Sarah's mouth lifted with surprise before she turned back to Mrs Leadbetter. 'Yes,' she said. 'Normally I wouldn't give it a thought but it's on a rather nice white cotton bedcover. Jack always wrote in bed if he thought of something in the middle of the night.'

'Did he?' said Mrs Leadbetter, intrigued by this glimpse of the writer at home. 'Meths is the answer for ballpoint, but it does weep.

Personally I'd leave it.'

Emily smiled at her. Her steak knife moved slightly to indicate the zigzag muscles of the fish on Mrs Leadbetter's plate. 'They're called myotomes,' she said. 'Those zigzags. We had it in Bio. Myotomes are fish muscles.'

'Is that right?' replied her hostess.

'How long have you known Mum?' asked Dora again.

'Oh, forever,' said Charles. 'Forever.'

Mrs Leadbetter gazed at her plate. A narrow hapuka island draped with fennel lay in a sea of puréed Satsuma plums, a zucchini dug-out canoe laden with ratatouille was beached alongside. There was a fuchsia.

'They make everything so pretty here,' she said happily.

She poked the island with her fish knife and fork. The flesh separated into firm white zigzags. 'It's a pity to disturb it, isn't it? Myotomes, you said, dear. I'll remember that.'

No one spoke. Mrs Leadbetter reverted to her original theme. Her chuckle was fat, deep-seated and endearing as a baby's. 'Occasionally, you know,' she said, her fork poised above the wine-dark sea, 'I still wake in the night in a muck sweat with a nightmare. That I'm not married, I mean.'

2

They all grew up in the Bay: Nigel and Jack Macalister; Dougal, Sarah and Sybil Tandy; and Charles Bremner who was an only and therefore envied. Whenever they met in later years the topic would always crop up. 'The Bay! Live in the Bay again? God no. Imagine.'

'How did we stand it?' Dougal Tandy asked his brother-in-law Jack twenty years later. He removed the horn-rimmed glasses he now wore, scrubbed his eyes with the heels of both hands and replaced them.

'We didn't.' Jack added more whisky to his melted ice and rolled it around the bottom of the glass. 'Sarah and I shot through pretty smartly.'

'Well you had to, didn't you?' replied Dougal.

Jack laughed, a crow of pleasure and achievement. 'True,' he said. 'But I wouldn't have thought Otago would be much better.'

'Another world, man,' said Dougal. 'Another world, the South.'

Their mothers were old friends. Laura Tandy, Maggie Macalister and Prudie Bremner had trained as nurses together. They spoke with reverence of the work of Sir Truby King, of sterile swabs and foments and old-fashioned splints. Laura Tandy had been a voluntary aide at the makeshift hospital at the Racecourse after the '31 earthquake. Responding to the call like a moose to the tundra she had dumped baby Dougal with her mother, who happened to be staying at the time (his sisters Sarah and Sybil did not yet exist), and worked with the wounded till she dropped. Maggie Macalister and Prudie Bremner, trapped on their respective homesteads by slips and crevasses on the back country roads, were deeply envious though generous in their praise. A newspaper clipping from the *Daily Telegraph* labelled 'Post-earthquake birth' shows Laura Tandy with a baby in her arms, the Sister's veil resurrected from a bottom drawer low on her forehead, her face aglow. There is no sign of the mother but Dr John Tandy who delivered the baby also looks pleased.

Laura's, Maggie's and Prudie's babies were born within a few years of each other. The mothers shared a maternity cloak, a green wool velour designed to hide their shameful shapes in turn. Laura owned it originally for Dougal, a Depression baby who was tossed from his pram by the big earthquake and narrowly missed by bricks cascading from the living room chimney. He was found by his distracted mother still smiling, flat on his back beneath the walnut tree. Laura lent the cloak a year later for Nigel Macalister's arrival to Maggie, who passed it on to Prudie Bremner to hide her vastness caused by the unborn Charles and his twin, Henry, who died shortly after birth. Prudie, said Maggie and Laura sadly, had never completely recovered, not completely, and there were no more Bremner babies.

Frank Bremner and Nelson Macalister managed to cling onto their farms during the Depression of the '30s. There was no money but they could kill a sheep, eke out somehow, survive. As did Dr Tandy, despite bad debts which he knew could never be paid because there was no money. All three of them were lucky, they knew this, much luckier than most.

Maggie Macalister had no qualms about asking Laura for the cloak before Jack was born in 1934. She had little imagination and no superstitions about ill luck and dead babies. The green cloak hid her stomach, made her look 'decent in town' and she was grateful.

'I'll have it back when you've finished,' said Laura and Sarah was born, followed three years later in 1938 by Sybil. The green cloak was mothballed for some time then handed on to John's surgery nurse whose husband had joined the Navy as soon as war was declared.

Laura said they should have burnt it and danced around it like witches. Maggie was faintly shocked. Prudie's expression didn't change.

Nelson Macalister, John Tandy and Frank Bremner were the husbands, the winners or the losers, the hangers-on of this deep friendship. Nelson, a large amiable man with a red face and a good dog-trial record, liked them all. Frank Bremner, a sharp-featured ex-polo player who bred Aberdeen Angus, hated the situation. Dr John Tandy scarcely noticed. He drove his family in whichever direction his wife suggested: out to the Coast if they were bidden to the Macalisters at Glenfrae; in the opposite direction if it was to the Bremners at Waikeri where they usually spent Christmas Day.

On Christmas Day 1943 Frank Bremner lifted his glass of Vidal's white and glared at the assembled company. His wife Prudie's face was scarlet with Yuletide effort, his son Charles sat pale and miserable in his steel-rimmed glasses, his shoulders hunched beside Dougal Tandy. Sarah and Sybil Tandy, aged eight and five, were attempting to kick each other's legs, their dark and blonde heads bent in silent concentration. Nigel Macalister was fresh-faced and cheerful. His brother Jack looked slightly vacant. A blowfly, trapped on the fly paper which hung from the orange silk lampshade above the table, buzzed its death throes.

'We should all be at the war,' cried Frank Bremner angrily to his male guests. 'All of us. Every man jack of us!'

How could they be? Farming, like medicine, was a reserved occupation. Not all of them could go, were even allowed to go. Someone had to run each farm. Dougal aged twelve knew this. He also knew from conversations overheard in the back of the Buick as its lights swung around the shingle curves on previous drives home (always shorter than the drive out) that Frank Bremner had a short fuse, but you could have guessed this without being told. Dougal watched the eyebrows, the sharp blue eyes, the small mouth puckered as a duck's arse.

Prudie, Laura Tandy and Maggie Macalister sank onto their appointed chairs looking flustered. Her friends had helped Prudie with the complicated Dish Up. Had strained the peas, buttered the new potatoes, and stood by looking anxious as Prudie tottered backwards from the Aga weighed down with the Christmas turkey collected the previous week from the cool store, though fortunately she'd cheated and made the gravy ahead. As she said, enough was enough at a time like this. Maggie leapt to her feet. 'I've forgotten my apron,' she cried, whipping off the red-checked thing and sitting on it.

Frank Bremner carved with skill and speed, the blade of his horn-handled carving knife honed by endless sharpenings to half its original breadth. Plates were passed up the table for vegetables, passed back, inspected closely by the young. Sybil opened her mouth and shut it again at the shake of her mother's head. Frank selected choice pieces of white meat, dug deep and wide for stuffing and passed his plate up. The carver is either a fool or a knave.

'Happy Christmas,' snapped Frank Bremner on its return and fell upon the mounded heap of food before him.

The sun streamed in through the slatted wooden blinds throwing slices of light and shadow across the white damask cloth, the large scaly hands and horny fingernails of the men, the bemused faces of the women. 'Look,' said Sarah, 'we're all in slices.' Her mother glanced at the bright eyes, the excited face. The child was too quick, too sudden and unpredictable.

'I'm not in slices,' said Sybil.

'You are.'

Sybil shook her head. 'And anyway I don't like turkey.'

'Honesty,' crowed Frank. 'That's what I like.'

'Don't encourage her,' said Laura.

You never knew with Frank. He was liable to tease and tease and be enraged at the result.

The room was quiet except for the clatter of knives and forks and the death throes of the blowfly. Heat steamed from the turkey, the gravy, the vegetables. Faces were mopped. A faint breeze from the tall open windows made little impression. The meandering river, diminished by lack of rain, glinted its way across a wide bed of shingle; silver paddocks melted in the haze. A cattle beast lowed.

Frank and Nelson bemoaned the lack of feed resulting from the near drought. They spoke of falling prices at the yards. Frank's two-tooths had been a disaster. As for the cattle. He'd have to start feeding out any moment. Their wives were silent, their faces serious and attentive as their men droned on. John Tandy resisted the temptation to wink at his wife. War was good for wool prices but farmers always moaned. Every non-farmer knew that. Laura caught her husband's glance and smiled a townie's knowing smile. John Tandy loved his wife. He liked her small neat head, her bright eyes. He wished she wouldn't smoke so much. She had money too. Old money. South Island money.

'We haven't sold our two-tooths yet, have we Dad?' asked Nigel Macalister with his mouth full.

'Not yet son,' said Nelson, proud of the interest, the straight glance and the strong eye.

Jack yawned wide and long. Plain in the head, thought Nelson sadly, not enough width between the ears. Narrow in the head and skittish, eyes all over the place. And a romancer. Given to romancing, which is another name for lies.

Maggie tried to catch her younger son's elusive eye, holding one hand in front of her mouth to indicate the correct procedure while yawning.

'What's wrong?' said Jack.

Maggie smiled bravely. She was a loving mother but Nigel had been no preparation for Jack. 'Yawning,' she hissed.

'What?'

John Tandy, wearied by stock prices, was extolling the virtues of his new Buick. He had been to Taupo and back in top and regaled them with the finer points of the trip, the steep pinch at Titiokura, the tricky curves at the base of Turangakuma. They all had occasional petrol to spare despite rationing because of being farmers and a doctor.

Frank Bremner stowed the last of his chestnut stuffing inside his cheek and leapt at him. 'Buicks! Gas guzzlers.'

'No worse than your Snipe! Better.' Prudie stiffened. Her hands gripped damask.

Frank lifted his glass for a quick swig. 'A man,' he said, replacing the glass and banging the starched napkin at his moustache, 'is entitled to the car he can afford. And I choose a Snipe.'

'Can I get down?' Jack's feet were already on the floor.

'Not yet dear.' Prudie's laugh was nervous. 'You haven't had any plum pudding.'

'I don't want any plum pudding.'

'Nor do I.'

'Nor me!'

Threatened by mutiny, Prudie glanced at her husband.

'Nobody,' said their host, 'gets down till I say so.' He gripped his knife tight. 'Nobody.'

Charles felt odd, his hands sweated. 'If I have any pudding, Dad,' he said, 'I'll be sick.'

'Then go!' shouted Frank, suddenly changing tack, his arm flung straight, pointing to banishment. 'The whole bloody boiling of you.'

'Frank,' said Prudie nervously.

Bottoms slipped from hard shiny leather, feet scuffed the carpet square, faces were torn between relief and apprehension.

'But I want some pudding,' whined Dougal Tandy.

'Me too,' said Nigel, who didn't really but wasn't going to be stuck with the little kids.

'You two can have some. The rest of you go. Go! Not further than the plantation.' He pointed to a large tiger skin which hung from the far wall, the head and front paw supported on a small stool with a woven seagrass top. Its open mouth, filled with enormous fangs, was locked in an endless snarl.

'That's where Grandpa shot the tiger. In the plantation, so watch out.'

Sarah, Sybil, Charles and Jack ran the length of the haircord-covered passage, tumbling and pushing, crowding outside into heat and silence. The sun pressed down on their heads. Sybil put one hand on her cap of hair. Her stomach bulged beneath her smock with red rabbits on it. 'It's hot,' she said.

Sarah was drawing a face in the dust where the concrete had crumbled by the steps at the back door. She used a clothes peg, a broken one with only one leg. The face in the dust had small eyes, the mouth was a downward curve. Sated with food, Sybil and Charles watched her from the bottom step. Jack stood higher up, leaning over the white-painted banister. Charles's white face stared at them. 'Do you like your fathers?' he asked them. 'You lot?'

It had never occurred to the girls. Sybil tugged at one white sock. 'Do you?' she said.

'No,' replied Charles.

'Why not?'

Sarah chucked away the peg. It clanged against the silver separator bowl in the nearby shed and fell to the ground.

'I just don't,' said Charles.

'You don't have to,' said Jack. Charles smiled at him, acknowledging sense from one a year younger.

Sarah was thinking hard. She saw herself beating Sybil to the door to welcome their father when he came home. Smelt the sickly sweet scent of ether as her nose pressed against his waistcoat. The last time she'd jumped into his arms he had dropped her. She was too heavy, though Sybil wasn't. Did she like him? Or not?

Golden and fat as a butter ball Sybil had no qualms. 'I love my Daddy,' she said.

Jack leapt over the rail. Dust puffed about his brown sandals. 'Come on,' he said.

'You haven't said whether you do or not, Jack.' Sarah was always conscious of fairness.

'You've got to have them,' said Jack, bored with the whole thing, 'otherwise you wouldn't be here.'

'Why not?' said Sybil, but Jack had disappeared, leaping down the track through the pine plantation, arms wide and stiff for aeroplane wings.

'The light's in stripes here too,' said Sarah.

No one answered. The sheep dogs (Wag, Sky, Reef and Laddie), secured by long chains, ran yelping across the bare dirt in front of their half-water-tank kennels, their legs all over the place with excitement. They crossed and recrossed each other's paths, their chains making wide arcs across the baked ground. They leapt at the ends of their chains, barking hysterically, their sleek pointed heads thrown back. Sybil moved behind Sarah. '*Shuddup*,' yelled Charles in imitation of his father's roar, but the dogs took no notice. 'Can't even shut y'own dogs up,' muttered Jack as they ran on. Charles said nothing. The sun slanted through the pines onto deep drifts of fallen needles, good tight pine cones and dozy half-open ones which were no good to collect for the fire because they burnt too quickly. Some mothers, not Prudie, pushed bright cotton material between the bracts and made pin cushions with painted owl faces for Christmas and school fêtes.

One track led to the meat safe which stood high above them on four solid legs. A cloud of blowflies swarmed around the wire gauze which separated them from dismembered slabs and hunks of meat, red with solid white fat which you had to eat as well as the meat when it was cooked. Sarah stood on her toes. 'There's blood,' she said staring at the congealed crimson jelly on the tin tray.

'Dad only killed yesterday,' said Charles.

Jack was standing on one skinny leg, the other clutched behind him, the sandal in one hand. 'Does he let you watch?'

'Yes.' Charles paused. 'Sometimes he makes me.'

'Come on,' yelled Jack once more leaping down the river track. He was not supposed to watch Ernie the shepherd kill and had fainted last week as Ernie sliced the ewe's throat and blood spouted. Ernie had jumped at the thud as he fell.

'I near as a whisker cut my thumb off, y'little bastard,' he muttered to Jack over mugs of hot sweet tea in his whare afterwards. 'If your Dad says no, it's no, right.'

Jack nodded. 'Don't tell, Ernie.'

'Not this time.' Ernie's hand enfolded his mug. 'All kids like to watch. I did myself at your age and got a helluva belting.' His thumb moved. 'But if it's no, it's no, like I said.'

The four children stood in a row watching the creek. Edged with watercress it ran deep and clear past the empty pigsty. Bernadette had turned into ham the week before Christmas. Only a few whiffs and ringed cabbage stalks remained. A narrow two-board bridge led to the shearers' quarters and the rust-red woolshed on top of the mound opposite. The last two planks of the bridge had rotted and fallen into the creek, two wooden arms snagged by mud and cress.

Sarah stepped backwards into deep pine needles. A length of discarded fencing wire beneath her sandal leapt upwards, thrashing and unravelling. She screamed as its end struck, a steel snake whipping round her leg.

'Tiger!' yelled Sybil and ran waddling up the track in fat-bottomed terror.

'It's all right.' Charles unwound the wire. Squatting on his heels he coiled it and held it up. 'It's only a bit of old number eight.' Sarah's heart was racing, banging inside her. It was the most sudden thing that had ever happened.

Jack was laughing so hard he nearly fell in. One hand was spread on each knee. He laughed and laughed, pointing at the wire, pointing at Sarah, pointing at Sybil, who stood frozen, open-mouthed, halfway up the track.

'Sookies, sookies,' he gasped. 'You lot should be in the paddock with the rest of the sucking calves.'

Sarah leapt at him, her hands tearing claws. He jumped away holding out a hand to Charles. 'Give us that, Charlie. Chuck it over.'

Charles handed over the wire. He didn't want it.

'Right,' said Jack. 'Now you're all going to walk the plank.'

What did he mean? He was always the one to think where to go and what to do when they got there. They stared at his tight brown curls, his quick dancing eyes, the length of wire in his hand. He could hardly keep still. His eyes were gold in the sun.

'I'm the pirate king, see, and you lot are captives.'

'I don't know about captives,' said Sybil, who had trailed down the slope again.

'Prisoners.'

'Oh.' Sybil sounded doubtful.

'I don't mind walking your silly plank.' Sarah ran onto the quaking board, pirouetted around at the end with her arms up like her friend Maxine at ballet, stuck her tongue out as far as it would go and ran back. 'See!'

Both Jack's hands gripped the wire.

'Charlie!'

Charles shook his head. 'No.'

The wire twitched in Jack's hand. 'Now.'

'No.'

'This is a cat-o'-nine-tails.'

'I don't give a shit what it is.'

'Ooh.' Sybil had her hand at her mouth. Jack was dancing now, jigging from one brown school sandal to the other. 'Don't give a shit, eh? You will when you feel it.' The stiff wire waved in his hand.

Charles's head dropped as he charged. His glasses were crooked, his arms whirling. The wire lashed snaking through the air. The blood was beads at first, then a stream dripping, pouring onto his blue Aertex shirt. Charles tugged a handkerchief from his pocket and held it to his cheek. It was red in seconds. His astonished eyes were fixed on Jack's white face. Sybil was wailing and wetting her pants. The noise changed to sobbing hiccoughs, tears streamed past gravy traces on her cheeks. Sarah snatched Charles's free hand and started up the track. 'Quick! Dad'll fix it. Come *on*.' The chained dogs began their sharp yelping tumult once more. No one spoke. Halfway up the track Sarah turned. 'You're a little, you're a little . . . *shit*,' she told Jack, who was last.

'Sarah,' moaned Sybil. 'Sarah, you are *aw*ful.'

The Girls had just finished the washing-up when the procession appeared around the separator shed. The large scrubbed deal table had been wiped clean of food droppings. Charles now lay upon it.

Jack was somewhere being dealt with by his father. Dougal and Nigel had disappeared long ago to the river. Sybil sobbed occasionally in Prudie Bremner's arms on the deep cretonne-covered sofa beside the tiger skin. Sarah had crept back from the living room to hide behind the open kitchen door. Her mother was being second nurse in the kitchen. Through the slit above the middle hinge

Sarah could see everything except Charles's head which was hidden by Maggie Macalister's broad back. She could see his feet pointing to the window, the brown sandals splayed wide apart, his grey shorts with their snake-buckle belt, the blood on his Aertex, his brown arms. Sarah's father was now The Doctor, his spectacles high on his forehead as he bent over Charles. His stiff-sided doctor's bag was open on the floor beside him, the side bits hanging. One of the bottles, the one with a yellow wooden cover over its stopper like the top half of a faceless Russian doll, stood on the table by Charles's knee. The left hand lid of the Aga was upright; steam rose from a white bean-shaped enamel bowl on the quick side of the stove.

'It'll need at least two stitches,' said Dr Tandy. Maggie's back stiffened. 'Much better done now.' Maggie nodded. Sarah's mother stood behind her husband, her eyes bright.

'Forty miles over that road!' Dr Tandy shook his head and turned to the Aga but his wife was before him to tip out the water at the sink by the sash window. She held the bowl in a sacking oven-cloth bound with blue gingham and presented it to the surgeon.

Dr Tandy threaded the needle with catgut from a sealed cellophane packet which Laura had opened for him using sterile technique. He held the gut with one set of forceps and the curved needle with another.

His mouth smiled at Charles beneath his moustache. 'I'll try and be quick Charles, but you must be brave.'

Maggie took Charles's hand and squeezed it tight. Laura clamped his arms as Dr Tandy bent over. Charles's sandals leapt in the air and banged back. The noise was a gasping yelp, a quick strangled shriek of terror. 'I said *hold* him,' snapped Dr Tandy.

Sarah's feet scudded on the haircord. She raced along the corridor and fell onto the sofa beside Sybil. Prudie leapt up, seized her shoulder, shook her. 'Where've you been?' She guessed. Shook harder. 'Tell me what's happening. Tell me!'

Prudie had wanted to be there. To hold her son in her arms. Maggie and Laura and John said no. Mothers get in the way at such times. Prudie realised that. It was part of her training. 'Leave it to us dear,' said Maggie. 'You mind Sybil.'

Sarah stood and tugged at the cretonne cover on the arm of the sofa. 'I wanted to say hello to the tiger,' she said and walked carefully to bury her face on the wide head which smelt as old and sour as Granny Tandy's wardrobe in Otane. She lifted her head and stroked the tough dead hair. Mr Bremner stood looking out over his burnt flats, his hands clasped behind his back.

'Charles!' cried Prudie and ran out the door.

Mr Bremner didn't turn. His hands clenched. 'Sit *down* woman!' Prudie had gone.

On New Year's Day a week later the Tandys' Buick swept forty miles out of Hastings in the opposite direction from the Bremners, out through the hills to the coast to visit the Macalisters. The Bremners didn't come. 'A hundred and twenty miles is too much for that lot,' Frank said to his wife, 'after that little bastard's effort at Christmas. You realise it's going to leave a scar?'

'Yes,' said Prudie.

Dougal and Sarah sat in the back and Laura in the front with Sybil because she got carsick. She was liable to throw up without warning, a sudden convulsive heave of disaster. Every ten miles or so their father pulled the Buick onto the grass verge, stopped the car and sent Sybil ahead for fresh air. She mooched along in front of the stationary car with frequent pained backward glances, a cloud of small blue butterflies about her martyred head, tinker-tailor and barley grass brushing her chubby legs. Laura, who seldom accompanied her, always became anxious after she disappeared around the first corner. 'Now,' she said peering along the empty road, both hands clutching the enamel sick bowl. 'Go now, John.' The answer was always the same. 'She hasn't had long enough,' replied the doctor, turning on the ignition.

The road was much worse than that to the Bremners' station: longer, with tighter bends which looped and curved and looped again enveloping the Buick in its own dust as it swept over the dry bony hills.

'Rape,' muttered Dougal as they passed a paddock of bright green beyond a wire fence. He nodded at the choumollier in the next paddock. In winter it would be nibbled to the ground by the sheep which raised mild enquiring heads momentarily before resuming their cropping. 'Chou,' said Dougal. He longed to be a farmer and not a townie, but how could you if your old man didn't own any land?

It was more fun at the Macalisters'. They were a happy family, except of course for Jack. Maggie ran out the back door to meet them as the Buick drew up, laughing and eager. She ran everywhere, her square body balanced neatly on trim legs. She ran to meet Nelson each afternoon when he appeared at the kitchen door with the day's eggs rolling in the bottom of the billy or hidden in one vast hand if there were only a few. They were his daily gift to his wife, the result of her loving kindness to him and the hens. The egg money was Maggie's pin money, all for herself, no strings attached. 'You've got to love them,' she had insisted over Prudie's Christmas cake last week, 'or they won't lay. Hens are very temperamental. And each one's different.'

'I hate the bloody things,' said Frank relighting his pipe yet again, 'but Prudie can suck up to them if it means more eggs. Hear that Pru? What Maggie says?'

His wife had nodded, her eyes on Charles who lay white-faced beside her on the sofa, two tufts of black catgut sprouting beneath his right eye.

Maggie's perm bounced around her earnest face. 'They'll know. They'll know if you're just pretending to like them. You can't fool hens.'

Prudie had to mark the number of eggs laid each day on a slate which Frank hung on the wall of the fowl house. If the hens had achieved less than two eggs she was not allowed to let them out, to let them rush squawking into the paddock bounding from one leg to the other, flinging their weight from side to side before settling down for a good scratch.

'How do they know?' Sarah had asked Mr Bremner years ago. 'How do the hens know that's why they're kept in? Because they haven't laid, I mean?'

'They know,' said Frank.

The legs of the white leghorns were scaly as dragons'. Sarah's favourites were the Rhode Island Reds with their padded behinds frilled and ruffled like Sonja Henie's skating pants. They lurched towards Sarah at feeding time, leaping across the grass as she flung the wheat from the rusty old Bournvita tin to entice them inside the fowl house at dusk. They made her want to laugh, to clap her hands, applaud. The boys thought she was mad. Sarah drew lots of hens. Hens in action were hard to draw, hard enough when still. Horses were easier. All the girls in Standard Two drew horses. A lot of them drew nothing else. The foals all had long lashes like Bambi. They didn't draw stallions unless they were standing on their hind legs pawing the air with their front ones, which made them more interesting as well as easier.

Nelson Macalister, like Maggie, was always pleased to see his guests. He ambled out of the dark little room at the back which he used as a farm office, his good brogues crunching the shingle sweep of the drive, one bone-crusher hand extended to John Tandy, his lips smacking in rampant hospitality. He clasped Laura to his chest, flattening her nose against his Aertex, scrubbed Dougal's head, which the boy hated, and laughed down at Sarah and Sybil. 'How many times did you throw up this time?' he asked. Whatever the reply—two, three, four—his reply never varied: 'You can have a real tuck-in now you've got rid of that lot.'

It was years before Sybil could reply with wide eyes, 'I wasn't sick once.'

Nelson Macalister, confronted by loss of innocence, had nothing to say.

The homestead was old, single-storeyed with wide verandahs on three sides. Tall windows faced the sea. The silver birches around the tennis court had been planted by Nelson's grandfather who had walked up the coast from Wellington and been befriended by the local Maoris and bought his land from them. He had no exact idea of who the rightful owners had been originally, but how could he have found out, he asked himself once, and never again.

The air at Glenfrae was still, filtered through birches, oaks, elms, and the wide encircling pine plantation. You would expect to be happy at Glenfrae. Good, even.

There was always tennis, the court mowed by Nelson and marked by Nigel while Jack hid in the woolshed loft writing stories, an idle romancer in love with words.

The parents played till tea-time, slamming and banging, the women shrieking but not Maggie who was good, or Laura who wasn't bad either. She looked as if she knew what she was doing in her short flared skirt and had a strong serve.

Macalister friends and relations came as well on New Year's Day. Lean men with faded blue eyes and thoughtful faces whose sudden guffaws of laughter seemed unexpected to themselves as well were accompanied by fresh-faced wives with white teeth and blond children who clung, their brown faces flattened against their mothers' skirts. 'He's shy.' 'She's shy.' 'They're shy,' explained their mothers.

Two large golden retrievers milled about the group attending the arrival of the Buick; Basher and his son Chris, who had been born on Christmas Day two years ago. Chris's head yawed from side to side, his mouth wide open to swallow a child's arm with hopeless love. This mouthing, as it was called, was discouraged by roars from Nelson or Nigel. Chris opened his mouth and released the arm, shaking with silent mirth, his head bent backwards, his jaws gaping. Basher raked the silver-gilt banner of his tail from side to side, sweeping the smallest blond relative onto its padded behind. The child was calm, bucolic even. They had labradors at home.

After afternoon tea, the second tuck-in of the day, came charades. This was organised by Nelson as a treat for the merry laughing children who now stared at him in sullen dismay from one end of the dining room. Sarah hid behind a brown velvet curtain and wondered if she could make a bolt for it across the verandah to the plantation. A rooster crowed, trumpeting advice to the negative. The curtain smelt of dust and meals long past.

Nelson was up-ending a Moses basket full of discarded After Five garments: lace, chiffon, delicate silky things cascaded into heaps. Beaded tarnished bodices which smelt funny on your fingers lay with striped velvet waistcoats beside a top hat. There was one buttoned boot, scarves the colour of damson plums, Golden Queen peaches and greengages, elderly cracked handbags and rusty black trousers.

The colours cheered Sarah. She reached out her hand for a long scarf of tawny reds and deep greens. Jack hissed in her ear, 'Look at the old man.' Nelson was at work, his hands busy as he chose with care and placed his selection on the sideboard. The top hat was there, a long black coat, a waistcoat. 'That's mine,' he cried, snatching a walking stick from Nigel's hand.

'Look at him!' Jack's hazel eyes snapped. 'He's meant to be giving us kids fun! He just pinches all the best gear. That's all he does, eh.'

Sarah stared at kind Uncle Nelson. His son was quite right. The pile on the sideboard was growing as Sybil and the other little blond kids rooted among the diminishing heap on the floor, heads down, busy as Bernadette at her pig-bucket but with less result.

Sarah turned to smile at Jack. His sharp elbows moved against his skinny body, his hands tugged at the snake clasp of his belt, his feet moved. He laughed back at her. Momentarily at ease, his smile stretched wide across his face, he felt happy.

3

Sarah was pleased with herself. The world of '52, you could say, was her oyster. She was going to Elam Art School in February, was Jack Macalister's girl and had painted her toenails for the first time. She lifted one foot in greeting to her mother as she came through the back door. Sarah's decorated feet pleased her. Four novice nun toes in descending order of height were ranged beside one wide-girthed mother superior, their faces shining and pink with *English Rose*. Sarah wiggled her toes. The four novices prostrated themselves, the mother superior stayed upright.

'Nice,' said Laura. 'My polish, I suppose?' Sarah nodded. Laura collapsed on a chair at the kitchen table and stared at her elder daughter, who remained prone on the ancient sofa in the sun porch, a copy of the *New Yorker* flat on her stomach. Dark eyes, curved mouth, good skin. Laura lifted her right arm and sniffed. 'I smell,' she said thoughtfully. 'And my hair's so sweaty it itches.'

'What do you expect if you're going to go crashing about on a tennis court in this heat?' Sarah was still inspecting her toes. 'How old are you?'

'Forty-four.'

'So you were twenty-seven when I was born.'

'Mmn.' Laura was stuck to the chair; every ounce of energy had melted down her legs to the soles of her tennis shoes and disappeared through the floor. 'It's funny how you sweat more afterwards.'

'I don't.'

'Because you don't play.'

'Painters don't play tennis, for God's sake.'

'And don't swear.'

Laura had kept her figure and was thus envied by her contemporaries. 'You've kept your figure,' Maggie had accused last week in Roach's fitting rooms, as though Laura had cunningly not discarded some artifact undervalued at the time, a marble-stoppered bottle say, which was now no longer available and therefore much sought after. 'It's all right for you.' Maggie had handed back the flowered Horrocks cotton to the black-gowned Miss Dwyer and smiled sadly. 'Have you anything . . . ?' Her hands had moved. Miss Dwyer had nodded and moved to the 16s. She had been in Ladies' Mantles for ever.

Laura had kept more than her figure. She had kept her hair black with a little help from Miss Gill at Villa Ariadne. She had maintained an amiable bed with her husband and the affection of her children. She smoked continually, coughing occasionally, a dry honk from deep inside her chest. She and her clothes smelt of Blue Grass and nicotine, the scent of comfort since her children's babyhood.

Sarah waved the *New Yorker*. 'I never get the point of these little pictures. They've got nothing to do with the contents.'

'I must go and have a shower,' said Laura, still sitting.

'This one, say.' One finger tapped a tiny drawing of a man in a riding helmet astride a horse with its legs crossed, presumably in some dressage manoeuvre. 'Or this.' The finger tapped impatiently at an outline of two backs, a bereted woman and pig-tailed child before a For Sale notice. Sarah peered. 'They're all signed.'

'Mmmn,' said Laura, remembering with relief that there was enough cold meat left for tonight. And some Spanish cream, which she had read somewhere was an excellent culture medium for the summer-sickness bug if left unrefrigerated. It could be disastrous at weddings.

'I used to think when I was a kid that they were jokes. Unknowable jokes for Americans.'

Her mother nodded.

'But they're not. I don't suppose I'll ever know.'

'That should be down at the surgery,' said Laura. 'That's why Dad gets them, not for you.' She ran her hand through her hair and yawned. 'Maggie rang this morning.'

'I'm not going,' said Sarah. Nothing in fact would keep her away; the thought of Jack clenched her with excitement but the usual response could still be made. She would go. She would sit beside him. Slide his tongue against hers. Eat him. I am in love thought Sarah. I am melting with desire. That is what I am doing. Melting.

'Nonsense. We're all going except Dougal who's doing overtime at the cannery.'

Sarah's feet were jammed hard against the end of the sofa as though gravity was attempting to dislodge her.

'Lucky old Dougal. The pea-viner'd be a treat.'

'Don't be childish. And we're giving Charles a lift out to save Prudie and Frank having to come all the way into town to pick him up. They'll take the back road out to Glenfrae.'

'No!' Sarah's face was a mask of horror. Charles Bremner's hands sweated through his white gloves at dances. He was the only boy who wore them. You could see him a mile off, standing tall and hopeless, a gangling heap in steel-rimmed glasses. Or circling the floor, working his way through his mental list of girls with whom Prudie had instructed him to dance. He looked like a crane, a stork, something that perched on steep tiled roof tops thousands of miles away and was equally out of place at the combined High Schools' Dance in the Assembly Hall of the Hastings Municipal Buildings. He always asked Sarah to dance. She always did, revolving slowly around the greenery-laden walls of the room if it was a waltz, shuffling clenched in his arms for a quickstep, her eyes focused past his right ear hunting for Jack, who was usually drinking with the Chapman boys in their father's ute.

Sarah avoided the tango with Charles. It was too much. His flailing arms, his anguished unhappy grin, his embarrassing sweaty worry about it all.

Jane Atwood quite liked him, which was surprising. She thought he had got something but was unable to say what in answer to Sarah's hooting mirth. Jane was Sarah's best friend and responsible for a lot in Laura's opinion. She was small, bright-eyed, her face framed by a pageboy of rich mouse hair, a medieval youth with a message. 'Sire, my liege, the French are but two leagues distant.' That sort of thing. Her success, her integration with those who mattered at school, was remarkable as she had not arrived till the Fifth Form. Usually girls to whom this happened were regarded with suspicion bordering on distaste. They were different, the worst thing that could befall an adolescent in the Bay. There was nothing for them to do but turn into swots and be disliked still more. They learnt work habits and were often successful in later life, but their school years were blighted.

Not so Jane's. She knew exactly where she was going, which was out of Hastings and that smartly. 'And,' said Jane, 'I won't come back.' Her bank-accountant father Cyril Atwood and his wife Beryl were proud of, though rather startled by, Jane, who was always top of everything and had every intention of winning a university scholarship because she couldn't get there otherwise and this was her first step on the road from the Bay.

At the final school dance Sarah drank beer with Ewan and Jock Chapman and Jack in the ute behind the Muni. They crammed into the cab, Jane and Charles in the gutter alongside keeping an eye out. They were rewarded with mean stealthy sips from yellow plastic mugs. Jane's face was puffy, her nose streamed, she shivered in her pink taffeta. Charles took off his Donegal sports jacket and placed it round her shoulders. 'She is heavy with cold,' he told the squashed occupants of the cab. Sarah stared at the long solemn face beneath the street light. Just what he would say. Funny but not quite.

'No!' cried Sarah once more, waving a fine foot. 'Charles is the cloaca.'

Laura, who neither knew nor cared what the word meant, dragged herself from the chair and leant both hands on the kitchen table. Her arms were smooth and firm; nothing about her had flopped, unlike some of her contemporaries. The roll of flab above the back of Maggie's strapless bodice at the Hunt Ball was almost as exuberant as her overflowing breasts in front.

Laura's voice was sharp. 'We always go to the Macalisters' at New Year.'

'They're so dull!' Sarah's legs kicked in emphasis.

'You left school three weeks ago!' snapped Laura. 'You're a snippy spoilt little . . .'

Sarah lifted one leg. She could see why stocking advertisements often showed legs upside down. The placement of curves is better.

'You brought me up.'

'Oh shut up,' muttered Laura and moved to the bathroom for a shower.

She changed her mind and turned on both bath taps. A soak might help. A soak with lavender-scented bath salts. Pain dragged at her lower back. Laura inspected the handle of the ancient back scrubber.

How typical of life, fate, the dictates of cantankerous gods on mountains that menopause and adolescence should appear in tandem. She abandoned the back scrubber which was a present from Maggie's sister Mary in Camberley and had lost most of its whiskers. She threw in a handful of lilac crystals and stirred the water in viscous swirls. The smell had overtones of napthalene as well as lavender. Laura disliked bubble-baths, the latest excitement for the pampered. The bubbles were icy, their chill unexpected. Bath bubbles should be warm but they are not. Laura turned off the taps and clambered in with stiffening legs. She'd forgotten her smokes. 'Sarah,' she screamed.

Sarah handed the Capstans, matches and ashtray around the door.

Sarah watched Jack. She watched him as he sat beside his father on the verandah, his face blank, his hands hanging, his eyes following the passage of an armour-plated slater as it toiled across the wide scrubbed boards.

'It was last Tuesday, no no I'm wrong, it was Wednesday,' said Nelson, fixing his audience with an eye as strong as Jip's, his best heading dog. 'I can remember now. It was Wednesday and we were loading the wethers. You were there weren't you, Nigel?' Nigel nodded, he could remember quite well. He nodded again; sun-bleached hair fell across his eyes.

'Jack? Were you there Jack?' Jack scowled. 'Yes, yes of course you were, and Ernie, he was there too and the shearing gang were still there packing up. They'd cut out in the sheds the day before. We'd been lucky with the weather. Very lucky. Hadn't we, Nige?'

Nigel nodded. 'You can say that again.'

'Very lucky. Day after day. Not a drop. I was worried on Sunday night. Great black clouds over Porongahau way. I thought, oh my God, no. Rolling down, really sweeping in they were, but it held off and we had a straight run through. He's a good worker, Hori Baxter. Got a good gang. Ever tried him, Frank?'

Frank shook his head. He moved to the edge of the verandah and tapped his briar against a post. Pipe dottle sprinkled the heads of Maggie's pale buff-coloured stocks. She had raised them from seed. You had to to get them true, the buff ones.

Frank refilled the pipe, his quick angry fingers pressing, tamping down the threads of tan and black tobacco.

'So like I was saying,' the voice continued, 'we were all there, the whole lot of us and this rooster from Walters Carriers arrives for the wethers. Ever use Walters, Frank?'

Frank's head moved. His mouth was busy sucking.

'No? Well you're not wrong. By God I never will again. Not after this lot. Wait till I tell you. This goon, big man, beer gut, know what I mean, cocky-looking bastard, he backs right up to the race and he leans out and he yells . . .'

Children for whom life is easy don't think much about individual adults. Adults are members of a different tribe. Some are better than others. Grandparents possibly. Mothers for temperatures and comfort, fathers to be avoided or adored, uncles and aunts who may be present. Bores go unnoticed: adults who are just around until you are old enough to analyse what the stifled yawn in the back of the throat indicates. Sarah was fourteen before she realised, sitting beside Uncle Nelson as the waves rolled in at the beach at Glenfrae and he told her the saga of the new cattle stop, that Jack was right about his father. She was surprised at her discovery and shocked that his own son had known this startling fact, had recognised this truth for ever. Now Nelson paralysed her, reduced visits to Glenfrae, except for Jack's presence, to slumbering torpor.

Jack was on his feet, one hand stretched down to Sarah. 'Come on.' This was what she came for. This was the other side to Glenfrae. Sarah stretched, giving fulfilment to her yawn. Her bra strap tugged her shoulder. 'Drop the bust forward, dear,' Miss Acherson the corsetière had told Sarah's pink face several years ago. She had demonstrated behind blue curtains, her trim corseted shape bending and snapping upright. 'Bust right forward then flick the fullness like this.' The back of her fingers flicked at Sarah, her eyes narrowed. 'No, I think you could fill a B already. Fancy that.'

Sarah held one hand out to Jack. He tugged her upwards, a quick, vicious one-hander. She fell against him.

Sybil was de-fleaing Basher. She liked the hunt, the quick snap of carapace between thumb and mid fingernail. 'I put my money on the sandhills,' she murmured.

Laura hoped Maggie hadn't heard. Maggie, who had, wondered how anyone who looked like Sybil could think of such a thing, let alone come out with it. Sybil often did. Fourteen years old, round, cuddly and adorable, she came out with anything liable to land her siblings up the creek, preferably without a paddle.

Maggie converted her sigh into a puff of expelled air.

'Doesn't anyone want a four?' she called to the departing backs.

Jack and Sarah didn't look back. Their steps lightened, they practically skipped around the corner past the scented jasmine falling from its frame against the weatherboards, their tennis shoes making quick skidding streaks in the shingle.

Maggie didn't know what to do. She was sure, almost sure, that Jack had been drinking with the Maori shearers. An unslept bed discovered at two a.m. one night last week when she trailed the length of the corridor to the lavatory, the sound of the truck clanging over the cattlestop while Nelson's snores echoed in the dark at four a.m. More worrying even than this was the distancing Jack practised from any comment, decision or thought Nelson or Nigel expressed.

'I like the Maoris,' he had shouted at Nelson last week, legs wide apart, hands on hips. Of course he liked the Maoris. Especially Hori's gang. Nice boys, Maggie liked them all. 'I was brought up with the Maoris on the East Coast,' she said frequently, which was not strictly true but she thought it was. Their laughter, the voices of the shearing gang, their songs, had all been her lullabies, her girlhood memories. She liked the romantic American ones best. She could still hear the plangent chords of Andy Ropata's guitar echoing across the paddocks as he sang 'Ramona'. 'I'll see you in my *dreams*,' they sang, their voices harmonising. Maoris have good voices, everyone knew that. But you didn't drink with them. Not even if you were a man and welcome in the pubs. Some men, perhaps, would call in at the pub by the bridge over the Tukituki on the way home if they'd had a good day at the saleyards, but not Nelson, not ever. And not Nigel. But she was almost sure Jack did, even though he was under legal age. It wasn't just a generation thing. It was something inexplicable in a Macalister but present in Jack since birth. The word tearaway surfaced in Maggie's mind. Her hands clasped. She could never tell Nelson. She looked at her husband, large, sunburnt, at ease on his broad pastures with his family and his friends and his faithful hounds. Maggie heaved herself up from her striped canvas deck chair, leant over the rail by the steps and blew hard at the black dottle on the frilled buff petals below her. She chose her moment before Frank appeared back from the lavatory by the back door where her husband and sons removed their work boots, if she was lucky, before entering the kitchen.

Charles Bremner sat on the middle step. He moved politely as Maggie's bulk loomed over to puff the dottle, his eyes on the sand-hills. I am never coming here again. I am over eighteen. I can die for my country. I am not, his hands clenched, ever coming here again.

Sarah and Jack sat in the shearers' cookhouse. The rouseabout had swept the place before leaving. Nothing remained of the gang except an empty De Reszke packet in a corner and a torn black-and-white Dalgety's calendar depicting rolling country. A small flock of Romneys ambled through a gate covered in lichen. Vast kahikateas leapt at the sky. The focus was soft, heaped clouds sailed high, the land looked good. Someone had added fat ballpoint nipples to a pair of mounded hillocks in the middle distance.

Jack leant forward on his hard chair, jabbing the air with one finger. He was explaining why he had to get out of the Bay, how he couldn't stand it another minute, how he really thought he'd been swapped at birth, fair go. His other hand was a manacle clamping her wrist as she laughed. 'No bull.'

'You look like your father.' Her finger stabbed back at him. 'He does that.'

'Christ! Don't give me that.' He was on his feet storming around the dusty space. A long table filled its length, a backless bench stood at each side, two chairs at each end. There was a kitchen beyond a wide counter. A faint echo of mutton fat lingered in the still air. The coal range stove was dark with grease, twenty-man saucepans with blackened bases hung on nails. Jack prowled around the table, his arms waving, emphasising his insistence that she understand. He was too tall, too skinny. ('Raised on dog tucker country,' sighed Nelson.) He stopped in front of her, glaring, hands balled on his hips.

'If I tell you something . . .'

The shadow from the open door lay diagonally across his face. There was quite a lot of green, she noticed, you'd need green in the lower half. But his face was moving all the time, his expression a combination of sharp fleeting frustration and rage. She'd never get it.

'Don't you ever sit still?' she said.

He squatted on the bench beside her.

'I've never told anyone else.'

She took his hand, his skinny freckled hand, and turned it over in hers. One finger traced the sloping crease from wrist to index finger. 'I never know which is which,' she said. 'Life line and Health and all that stuff.' He tugged the hand away.

Sarah inspected the palm of her own hand, bending it at the wrist and dropping the straight fingers. She pointed with her other hand. 'Those lines beneath the little finger . . .'

He glared down at her, his body tense. 'Listen!'

Sarah seemed really interested in her hand. Her head was down, her hair forward as she peered, her heart thudding. 'They're meant to be children but I can never work out which lines you're meant to count. And who wants to?'

'I'm a writer,' said Jack. His eyes were cat's eyes, his chin thrust out. 'That's what I'm going to do. Be a writer.'

Sarah smiled. Her smile told you it would be all right, or better anyhow. 'I'm a painter,' she said, flicking her nose with one finger.

'Yeah, but I mean really. I write all the time. Up in the woolshed loft. That's all I'm going to do. All I want to do is write what I like when I like.' And fuck when I like and drink when I like, he could have added but didn't.

'Me too. Paint I mean. I'm going to Art School. Elam, in Auckland.'

He sighed. It was too much to expect the first time perhaps, but he thought she might have got it. Realised he wasn't fooling.

He clamped her wrist again and pulled her out the door. The late afternoon light was golden, drenching the hills, the dry grass, the woolshed. Bellini light, Miss Pritchett called it, handing around her Art History postcards. 'By the edges girls, by the edges. They are very precious, my cards, very.'

'I'm coming,' said Sarah. Nothing would stop her, no power in heaven, or on the earth beneath, nothing could stop her now.

Jack's left leg shot out as he kicked the unlatched door alongside the cookhouse. He burst his way into the stillness like a gunman with both hands full.

A dog barked a single sharp yelp and was silent. A skylark sang, a torrent of runs and trills falling from a sky hazy with too much sun. It was very hot. Well into the nineties.

Sarah rubbed her wrist in silence. There were four bunks, a few four-inch nails hammered into the back of the door, a sash window and nothing else. The sacking of the bunks sagged in deep curves; the end of one had torn slightly leaving a flap hanging at the top.

They stood blinking at each other, smiling. They knew what they were doing.

Jack touched her face with one hand.

'Hello,' he said.

Dr Tandy's elder daughter sprang at him.

They stared at each other in the Doctors Only carpark, eyes wide, two guilty kids who've copped it, who know they've got it coming to them. She saw him aged nine at the Bremners' the day of the number eight wire, legs braced, head back in outraged innocence as he tried to convince the adults it was an accident, that Charles had moved, that he couldn't know he was going to move, how could he? None of them believed him. Least of all his father. Not even his mother, try though she would to understand him, to make allowances. What they were she couldn't imagine but there must be something. Some reason for his difference.

He glanced at the hands lying in the lap beside him. The bright nail polish seemed incongruous, make-believe, a child clomping around in high heels and her mother's discarded finery from the After Five section of Mantles.

'How old are you?' he asked.

'Seventeen.'

'Shit.'

Her voice on the telephone the day before yesterday had sounded like an anxious eleven-year-old's. 'You'll have to come in. I've got to talk to you.'

'What?' It was a party line and Mrs Bradley at the Bailey bridge over the river eavesdropped. People had heard her hall clock chime. 'Remember the clock.' Jack's laugh had sounded very loud.

'I mean it. You'll have to come in.'

He had managed to wangle the extra trip into town. He couldn't even remember what lie he'd told Nelson.

Sarah had insisted. He was not to pick her up. They met by the parrot cage in Cornwall Park. Side by side on the scarred grey trunk of a dead plane tree one rosy-pink galah and one sulphur-crested cockatoo peered at them through the netting, blinking occasionally with ancient wrinkled eyelids which came up from the bottom of the eye as well. The cockatoo fanned its sulphur-yellow crest and cranked deep within its throat. 'Welcome,' it squawked, a mechanical croak of doom. They stared at it in horror. The galah turned its back on its fellow captive, huffed its neck feathers and shuffled sideways to the end of the branch. On the concrete below traces of oily lysol lay on puddles on which floated peanut shell boats. The stench was unforgettable, known for ever, specific and evocative as that of the local freezing works.

Sarah's fingers, still tipped with *English Rose*, clutched the strong, wide-meshed netting.

'I think I'm pregnant.'

Jesus. Jack wanted to run, to bolt screaming from the park on legs of melting wax, away from the parrots, the stench, the sun. He saw his woolshed hideout, his pad, pen, everything. A kid rode past whistling 'You are my sunshine' off key. Jack clung to the netting. 'You can't be.'

She was calm. 'Why not?'

'Because I didn't stay in you, that's why,' he shouted.

'Shut up. I'll have to see a doctor.'

'Doctor?' he yelped.

She inspected her watch strap. It was striped, red, black, green. 'That's right. Doctor.'

He had to say something. 'Your father . . . ?'

'Are you *mad*? I've made an appointment with Dr Cunliffe in Napier.' Dr Cunliffe was a general practitioner with a special interest in obstetrics who was disliked by Sarah's father. He was unctuous and wealthy. A roly-poly man with wispy black hair and pink hands, he had the reputation of being kind. Women flocked to him.

'You can drive me in this afternoon,' continued Sarah. 'The appointment's at two.'

Jack was silent, his eyes on the netting, the way the loops of steel held, the way they were attached to the poles. The parrots were a blur of out-of-focus colour. He leant his forehead against the cool mesh. 'OK,' he said.

Dr Cunliffe recognised Sarah. Mrs Cunliffe gave parties for their daughters Meryl and Andrea in their Bluff Hill home, which was full of overstuffed armchairs and cut-glass vases. Mrs Cunliffe did the cooking (which was a lot) herself because the girls were as useless as bandicoots. She was invariably exhausted and her daughters crippled with guilt by the time the festivities, which were minor and embarrassing, began.

Dr Cunliffe was kind. He patted Sarah's bare shoulder. She stared at an advertisement on the back of a medical journal for an emergency laryngoscope. 'Reliable! Robust! Economical!' it cried.

It was too early to tell yet, said Dr Cunliffe after the examination, but he would give her a form for a test at Outpatients. 'We must consult the frog, my dear.'

'What?' The Cunliffes always had poinsettias at Christmas, masses of sharp red-leafed things in pots on an oak sideboard.

Dr Cunliffe's moustache moved. 'A pregnancy test.'

'Oh.' Stunned with shame and rage at herself (what on earth did she expect) Sarah grabbed her white plastic bag and fell out the door; past the receptionist Miss Reagan with her fluffy champagne-coloured perm and her neat white cap who was in love with Dr Cunliffe and had been for the last twenty years, past the toddlers with oozing noses who rolled about on the floor among coloured blocks of wood, past the mothers and the occasional father and the old and the hopeless, back into the sun. She climbed into the cab of the Bedford. 'I've got to go to Outpatients.'

He turned to her, his face shadowed by the brim of his brown pork-pie hat. 'Why?'

'For a pregnancy test of course.' The phrase had the same effect on him, she was glad to see. He threw his cigarette out the window as though it was about to explode. His hand fumbled with the ignition key, his foot over-revved. The truck shot out from the kerb in front of the surgery like a joke car, a Keystone Cops take-off.

Sarah felt cold, cold as she'd ever felt in the icy corridors in the winter term at Girls' High with their useless sausage-shaped heaters which didn't do a thing except burn your ankles if you got pushed against them. She wrapped her arms around herself and shivered in the hot cab. Spider webs filled the bottom corners of the front windscreen, decorated the rear vision mirror. The truck leapt up Hospital Hill. 'Families waited on for orders' said the sign above the store on the corner. It must have been there a long time. Nobody delivered now.

Jack parked the clapped-out Bedford by the sign 'Doctors Only' painted in large black letters. White lines divided the space. The view over West Shore to the mountains was spectacular.

'Why park here?' asked Sarah from a thousand miles away.

Jack had parked here when he'd been invited to a party in the House Surgeons' quarters last year by his cousin Ted. They had drunk Vat 69, the Pope's telephone number Ted called it and everyone laughed because it was so funny. Jack spent most of the night in the cab of the ute pressed hard against a chubby girl with curls and a lisp. 'I'm in Men's Thurgical,' she said. 'I'm in Midgley.' She told him they had to be careful to label the falth teeth when they collected them pre-op otherwise it was chaoth later.

Jack stared at the sign. I lost my virginity in Doctors Only. Only a year ago. Jesus.

'Why not?' he said. 'Stuff them.'

Sarah shrugged. A man on an aluminium elbow crutch inched up a sloping ramp beneath a sign labelled Fracture Clinic.

'What's the time?' said Jack. He never wore a watch. His father, wedded to pips and time checks, found this incomprehensible. Nelson had never owned a watch without a sweep second hand to reassure him, to make time certain and keep it in its place.

Sarah glanced at her seventeenth birthday Seiko. 'Five to. I'd better go.'

He took her hand. 'Do you want me to come?'

'No.' She snatched her hand away and ran in the door saying 'Outpatients'.

Jack gave a quick soundless puff of relief. He pulled out his squashed packet of Camels from the back pocket of his khaki drill trousers and ran one finger down the knife-edged pleat. Maggie ironed sharp creases even in their working pants. She had an old ironing machine in the laundry for flat things. Two magpies, Sidney and Florence, hung around the grass patch by the laundry even though Maggie took pot shots at them with the loaded .22 she kept in the long broom cupboard by the door. Jack had named the pair after the Prime Minister and his lady wife. He could never understand why the birds stayed, strutting about as though they owned the place. You'd think they would have caught on.

Jack lit his cigarette and inhaled. What the hell was he going to do? After a few more drags he jumped out of the van and loped into Outpatients. Sarah was sitting staring straight ahead with her white sandals together, not reading or anything. A little girl at Sunday School.

She glanced up. 'What're you doing here?'

'Nothing.'

She smiled, a slow smile which lasted some time.

'What are we going to *do*?' said Jack.

'Have a baby.'

'You don't know.'

'Yes I do.'

He shook his head. 'You can't. I can't. No. Not get married and stuff. No!'

She was calm, cool as a water lily on ice. 'You should've thought of that before.'

'Mrs Tandy?' called the nurse, one hand holding back the green curtain, Dr Cunliffe's form flapping in her hand. Dr Cunliffe was being kind.

Sarah leapt up. 'Miss,' she said. Jack stared at his boots in silence.

OK, he hated the farm, but did he really? He was a good stockman, better than Nigel, to Nelson's surprise. He liked the space, the hills, being alone. His father and Nigel were morons but that didn't matter. You didn't have to talk to them or anything. All Jack's living except for pubs and girls and food and the sea was done inside his head with its own people and his own world of words spinning. He had been careful ever since primary school to hide this world. To disguise the astonishment, the secret delight when the words came together the right way, knocked against each other and took off. It was the best drunkenness. Why did he bother with booze when he could be drunk this way, which hardly ever happened? He had never read a New Zealand writer except Katherine Mansfield, who made him toss, until Miss Smith at High lent him Frank Sargeson's *A Man and His Wife*, and he wasn't sure about him either. Some of the stories, yes, you could see what he was on about but did the people he wrote about . . . did they talk like that? Jack knew they didn't and he'd show them one day but not yet. He'd always known it would take time. He didn't expect anyone to understand, let alone share his excitement. Nelson and Maggie had been proud of him in primary school when he was dux of the local country school and won the medal and an eggcup-sized silver cup for English. Jack had been so appalled at the thought of going up in front of the other kids to collect the dolly little thing that he'd pretended he had a guts-ache, writhing about in simulated agony in his cool high-ceilinged bedroom with two disappointed faces staring down at him. 'Do you think he's swinging the lead?' Jack heard his father mutter as they left the room. 'Why on earth would he do that?' asked Maggie.

At high school his real life remained hidden until the Fifth Form when Miss Smith took them for English. He had until then assumed the protective coloration of anyone with sense and a secret at Boys' High. He lay low and said nothing. His marks were good, he was not bad at sport, he shally-humped and shally-hooped about comparatively cheerfully in prickly khaki serge in the blazing February heat of Cadets' Week while the staff organised the timetables. His leadership qualities were poor, he was informed by the explosive sergeant major. Jack was not surprised.

His best camouflage was his ability to make the other kids laugh. He achieved the reputation of a wit, one who could put the boot in verbally and did so if given a chance. The rest of the class left him alone.

Nigel and Jack boarded in town with Gran Macalister during the week. All country pupils at Girls' and Boys' High had to board by the week in flat-as-your-hat Hastings with its grid-like arrangement of streets, its only diversions the Ngaruroro river, the Cosy, State and Regent for flicks and Rush Munro's Ice Cream Garden which was justly famed throughout the land.

Before the Fifth Form his essays had come back marked in red: 'Highly unlikely', 'Spelling atrocious', and, worst of all, from smart-arse O'Connell who should have gone to the war but had weaselled out of it as everyone knew, 'The Danube is only blue when you're in love.' Jack developed his double life early. He wrote stuff for school essays and his own stuff at home hiding in Gran's woodshed.

Miss Smith wrote 'Free up' in his margin at the beginning of the year. 'Excellent!' she wrote later, underscoring her surprise in heavy black ink. 'Please see me,' she wrote.

She lent him books of poetry: T.S. Eliot, Hopkins, Dylan Thomas and Auden, who was the best. And Shakespeare's Sonnets.

He handed back her *Penguin Shakespeare* as she stood on the dais at the end of a double English period. His guard was down, his hazel eyes glittered. 'That "When, in disgrace with Fortune and men's eyes" is the best, you know, love one I've ever read.' Jack's sharp features were transfigured by excitement. He beamed at Miss Smith and told her,

'Haply I think on thee, and then my state,
Like to the lark at break of day arising
From sullen earth, sings hymns at heaven's gate.'

Miss Smith nodded. She paused, scratched her head briefly and inspected her fingernail. 'Yes. You realise the early sonnets are thought to be written to another man?'

'Yeah,' lied Jack. 'Sure.' His head whirled; poofs, queers, brown-hatters and left-footers—or was that Catholics—were the only words he'd heard in the Bay. And this, this amazing thing, had been written by one of them.

Jack's world tilted.

'It's a good poem,' said Miss Smith. 'A great poem.' She rubbed the chalked words 'metonymy' and 'synecdoche' from the black-board and turned to him again. 'Do you know Charles Bremner in Six Professional?'

The child looked almost shifty. 'Yes.'

She banged the blackboard cleaners against each other, averting her face from the cloud of dust. 'He enjoys reading. Writing.'

Charles also boarded with his grandmother, a small intrepid woman who had brought up four sons at Waikeri after her husband had been killed in a farm accident. She did have a very good Maori shepherd, but still. She was now old and fragile and farted at each step like an elderly draught horse as she clomped down the steps from her verandah to sit alfresco beneath the pepper tree. Charles loved her dearly.

'Did you know that?' asked Miss Smith.

'No,' said Jack and departed quickly with *Portrait of the Artist as a Young Man* clutched to his chest.

'I hope you're going to keep writing, Jack,' Miss Smith said to him in the Upper Sixth Form.

He looked at her with affection, wondering if her metallic black hair was dyed. 'Yes, Miss Smith.'

Both shiny-knuckled arthritic hands tugged at her gown as she considered. 'Good. How will you manage that?'

'I'm going to be a writer.'

'Yes, but you'll have to do something else as well. Earn something to live on.'

'No.' Jack was quite sure. 'I'm going to be good see. Every-where, I mean. Not just here. That's all I'm going to do. Write. I'm not going to do anything else.'

Miss Smith smiled and patted his arm. Muscles too. They all had muscles, her Sixth and Upper Sixth Formers sweating in their flannel shirts and navy-blue pants, hairy legs kicking and being kicked, tripping and being tripped as they clattered up and down the main stairs.

Miss Smith had lent him *Enemies of Promise* in the Upper Sixth so he knew about the debilitating effect upon male writers of prams in halls. A high English baby carriage thing it would be, beside steep stairs going up and up for ever and ending in the attic with a dormer window where the maids slept. He knew this from the illustrations in Maggie's childhood copy of *The Little Princess*, which came with her from the East Coast when she married. That and her other book, called *Bobbie* (red with gold printing on the cover and a spirited heroine within), had to be read in secret in case Nigel saw him reading girls' books. Nelson's and Nigel's sweep second hands left little time for books. They read each word of the paper, which was a day old by the time it reached them, and not much else.

Jack came to, blinking. On the wall by the receptionist's desk Donald Duck sat in the curve of an upside down rainbow. On the opposite wall Pluto leered from a similar curve. Jack leant his naked elbows on his knees and covered his face with his hands. He was still like this when Sarah, having produced a specimen as directed by straddling over a lavatory with bent knees and piddling into a plastic jar one inch in diameter, came through the green curtain.

The test was positive. Sarah concentrated on Dr Cunliffe's striped tie. Designed for the exclusive use of the officers of an infantry regiment raised by a Duke in Somerset in 1749, it had been purchased at Napier Menswear last week by Dr Cunliffe's wife, Blanche. She liked the quiet authority of its striped diagonals.

'I don't want to have a baby,' said Sarah.

Dr Cunliffe smiled. 'You should have thought of that before, my dear.' Rage at hearing her own words churned back at her stiffened Sarah, found her the impossible words.

'I want to get rid of it.'

Dr Cunliffe leant back in his revolving chair. He looked like a frog, a frog with huge jokey black-rimmed glasses, a greeting card frog from the section marked Humorous with a daisy in its mouth and an obscene message within.

He sighed heavily. 'You girls are all the same. You get yourselves pregnant and then you come running to me to get you out of it. There's no way you can have a termination of pregnancy unless I and two of my colleagues recommend it and that would only happen if all three regarded your condition as a threat to your life.'

She saw the power seeping from him, oozing from his pink fingers, haloing his pink and black head. Years later when she heard about auras she thought of Dr Cunliffe, felt again the creeping chill of her despair.

He licked his lips, a quick flipping slide of his tongue. His fingers pressed his blotter. 'Dyazide cuts strokes by half,' it said. A jar of jelly beans for the kiddies sat alongside.

'And that will not happen. You are in perfect physical and mental health, my dear.'

I am not your dear, shrieked Sarah in silence.

'I'm not going to die or go mad, if that's what you mean.'

'Exactly!'

'I'm not mad or ill. I'm just desperate.'

'Now, now.'

A framed photograph of a fat waxen baby, presumably Andrea or Meryl, stared from the wall.

I will not tell him about the pictures, what I can see, what I can do. None of that will I tell this man. 'The man's a sod and that's that,' she heard her usually tolerant father mutter beside the garden tap as he mixed the rose spray the day after the arrival of the last invitation to a Cunliffe party. 'Ssh,' said Laura as she picked up the handles of the wheelbarrow and trundled round the front. They always gardened together. Sarah had never thought of that before.

Why on earth had she come to the man then? Because he was in the next town, far away and kind to women.

'I'm seventeen.'

He leant forward, hands clasped with excitement. 'That is the very best time to have your babies!'

She had a sudden glimpse of Jack and herself gardening together, herself picking up the grass clippings, following behind with the wheelbarrow as Jack whizzed up and down shaving the lawn in narrow vertical stripes. She almost laughed, her eyes on the glass shelves which carried the blood pressure thing, a cream plastic model of vertebrae linked with red blood vessels and a rubber hammer for testing knee jerks.

The pink hands clapped together. 'That's better. I'll look after you. And I'd like you to have a blood test.' He scribbled on a yellow form and handed it to her.

She stood up with it in her hand, turned on her heel and walked to the door.

Sarah found every aspect of her own behaviour inexplicable, her refusal to confide in Laura the weirdest thing of all. She liked Laura, admired her even and had kept silent when the other girls at school had sat around in each other's bedrooms hissing details of their parents', especially their mothers', iniquities, meannesses and antediluvian expectations. Laura had taught her the facts of life, smiling at her daughter's startled face as she stood naked with a pad between her legs demonstrating the fun way to deal with menstruation and explaining how this was a good thing as it would enable Sarah to have babies later on—a thought which had never occurred to Sarah, who had never glanced at a baby in her life unless pressed. Laura had explained sexual reproduction, the delights of married sex. The perils of the other sort were known to all at Girls' High. Occasionally a girl left, Linda Barr for example, and had to get married. Or worse, was unable to get married due to circumstances beyond her control, such as a married seducer or a lover who had shot through—in which case the girl left the district to hide with relatives in the country or at a far away Salvation Army home for unmarried mothers. The resultant baby was put up for adoption, or sometimes the grandmother, if gallant and caring enough, took it as her own. But everyone knew. The phrases were well known: 'Had to get married', 'Left the district', 'Put up for adoption', 'Took it as her own'. The life and death of Sorrow Durbeyfield made more impact on the girls of Six Classical than did that of Little Nell.

Sarah had biked over to see the fallen Linda and her baby in their rented villa by the Showgrounds. She had stared at the crumpled old face in the bassinet furbished with layers of hailstone-spotted muslin for baby Linda's arrival sixteen years before, at Linda's pale face, her nervous gratitude. 'None of the other kids at school, you know, none of the others have come.' 'Jumped up little shits,' snorted her husband Owen, who worked on the night shift at the gasworks and pedalled home each morning smelling of coal dust. Sarah turned to the baby once more. He seemed alien, out of place, unexpected as a buttercup on a moon crater. Sarah left her shop-bought blue bootees and departed as quickly as possible, ashamed of her relief but wow. She leapt on her red bike and pedalled home shouting, 'Frankie and Johnnie were lovers, oh lordie how they could love,' which her parents sang at parties when they'd had a few drinks but not at the Macalisters or the Bremners.

So why did she not tell her mother? Dr Cunliffe had assumed she had already done so.

'You're lucky,' he told her, his amphibian gums chomping. 'Your parents will stand by you.' Another of the phrases. Sarah's sense of fairness prevented her telling Laura. As the man said, she had got herself into this mess, except of course that Jack had, but why had she let him? Because she wanted him, because nothing could have stopped her, and, of course, she had thought she'd get away with it. 'The trouble with you, my dear,' Granny Douglas had told her on their last visit to Dunedin, 'is that because you have been fortunate you think it will last for ever.' Sarah saw herself leaping at Jack across the bare boards of the whare, flinging her clothes off, grabbing at him as they fell onto the lower bunk with the unripped sacking which soon ripped. He'd been astounded at his luck. He had promised it would be all right in her one lucid moment when she remembered Linda and Sorrow and all the phrases and dragged herself off the sacking onto the floor. He seized her, pulled her back, one naked foot braced against each side of the bunk for purchase. 'It's OK. It's OK. I'll come out.' She knew about that too. A phrase of a different sort. Startled by reality, she lay beside him once more, her head hidden against his chest.

There was no point in trying to work it out. It was her business. And Jack's.

She walked across the shiny blue vinyl of Outpatients after the blood test and sat by him. He glanced at her, his face faintly surprised.

'Hello,' he said.

'It'll be all right,' said Sarah.

'It bloody well won't!' He glared straight ahead. 'I'm a writer. I haven't a bean.'

'We'll live on the dole. And I'm a painter.'

'You can paint anyhow.'

If you turned the cartoon cutouts up the other way, he thought, the curved boats would become real rainbows. But then Donald Duck and Pluto would be standing on their heads.

'We'll get married at the Registry Office straight away,' said Sarah. 'And go to Wellington.'

He looked at her in amazement. 'Wellington! And what'll we live on?'

'You can get a job in the woolstore.'

'Oh great. Great! It was the dole a minute ago.' A morphine addict in dark glasses who had called for his legal amount from the Pharmacy window in Outpatients jumped in fright. He shuffled his grey tennis shoes, stamped each foot once, reached in a trouser pocket for the makings and rolled a cigarette with shaking fingers.

'We won't tell our parents until we're married.'

'I don't want to get married, for Christ's sake.'

'And I don't want to have a baby, for Christ's sake.' She was still calm; the most sought-after girl in the Bay, black hair, brown skin, white teeth. His girl.

She laid her hand on his thigh. His skin tingled.

'I'm not coming here again, or to Dr Cunliffe. Dr Cunliffe,' said Sarah, 'is a swine.'

He laced his fingers in hers and rolled their hands palm upwards on the shiny wooden bench. They stared at the cupped fingers, the lines.

'I could shoot through,' said Jack.

'No.' She shook her head. A hank of hair dislodged itself, fell across her face.

'Why not?'

'You couldn't live with yourself,' said Sarah. She had heard this one too. He couldn't have lived with himself, they said, if he hadn't married the girl.

'I wouldn't bet on it!' Jack leapt to his feet and stared about the waiting room, his eyes darting around the place. There were not many patients left; only four remained to stare at nothing, to await their call.

'Where's my hat?' he said.

'In the truck.'

'Oh. Come on then.' He held out his hand to her.

Six Classical had had a film entitled *Gorillas* last term with Miss Glenhorn, who was useless at Bio and thus showed as many films as possible (though the projector was a hazard as she was no good at that either). Eventually the film had flickered into focus. A male gorilla strode through rain forest, head lowered as he climbed. A female followed with a baby in her arms. At a steep part of the track the male paused, turned, gave one sharp grunt and offered the female his hand. She took it with a small answering grunt. He heaved his family upwards and they slogged on. Sarah and Jane thought it was sweet.

Sarah gave the outstretched hand a quick dismissive shake of her head and strode ahead.

She paused briefly on the ramp and stared at the mountain ranges beyond the white-frilled curve of the Bay, instinctively counting the different depths of blue in the lines of hills which stretched away to infinity. Six, there were. No. Seven.

Jack was loping across the asphalt to Doctors Only.

'I'm still going to be a writer,' he said. 'You know that, don't you.'

She nodded.

He stopped abruptly, so unexpectedly that she trod on his heels. He gave an odd little skip to one side, an instinctive retreat from danger.

'We're too young,' he said.

Her face was puzzled, eyes narrowed against the sun as she squinted up at his. 'What?'

'We'll have to get their permission. Our parents! God in heaven!' He dragged a clammy hand down each leg of his trousers. 'We're under age, see, to get married without,' he swallowed, 'parental consent.'

She was still staring, her eyes wide, vulnerable as a bobby calf's. She blinked several times.

He put his arms around her, held her tight and changed tack. 'It's all right,' he said. 'It'll be all right. Don't worry about it. OK? All we've got to do is tell them and they'll say yes. What else can they say? And then we'll get married and then . . .' He propped his chin on the top of her head and gazed at the sweeping azure curve of the Bay, the endless creaming surf. 'Then God knows what happens.'

She made a muffled sound against his chest which he hoped was laughter.

4

They were married at the Registry Office three weeks later, the only other people present their parents, the Deputy Registrar and their witness, Ernie Waihi—Jack's confidant since Sarah's first telephone call. He had begged them to tell their parents at once, his face anxious as he held Sarah's hands. 'What will she think, eh, your own mother? Why? Why don't you tell her, Sal? Why not?' Sarah shook her head, touched his arm. 'You don't understand, Ernie.'

The Deputy Registrar was a large woman in a beige linen suit, beige cubans and a kingfisher brooch made of paua shell. 'There's a mirror over there if you want to touch up,' she told Sarah. Sarah glanced at the coffin-shaped glass etched with a spray of lily-of-the-valley. 'No thank you.'

The Deputy Registrar wriggled her shoulders and got down to business. There were several rows of chairs. You could have had a real wedding here, a party. Laura stood very straight, her eyes fixed throughout the brief proceedings on the kingfisher brooch. Halcyon days indeed. She clenched her hands tight. John stood completely relaxed beside her, a faint courteous smile on his lips, his eyes glancing around the bare room with mild interest before returning to rest on Laura once more. She had never looked better, he thought happily; the navy-and-white suit made by Miss Grant, Hastings' dressmaker of choice, suited her, a straw boater sat rigid on her head. She didn't return his glance. She was concentrating. Holding on.

'I didn't know you were going to wear a *hat*, Laura,' Maggie had gasped on arrival. Her pink linen was crumpled but what could she do. It crushed as soon as you sat down and she had been sitting in the Holden for forty miles. She felt crumpled internally as well. To think that a son of Nelson's could get any girl into trouble, least of all a nice little thing like Sarah. Maggie was weepy: large, pink, and weepy. Her hands shook. Nelson, who was leaning stiff-armed on the back of the wooden chair in front of him, staring at the floor, his sunburnt face impassive, reached out a mammoth hand and enfolded his wife's in his.

A notice framed in black begged from the wall, 'Please! No confetti.' The bottom panes of the old sash windows were painted, for privacy the Deputy Registrar informed them.

She told them they had terrible writing. 'All you kids have but, boy, you should see the doctors'.'

'Now,' she said to Jack finally, her face pink with satisfaction at a job well done. 'Now you can kiss the bride.'

Sarah burst into tears and flung herself against Ernie's blue-suited chest. He held her, stroked her, murmured gently.

'It's all right Sal, it's all right. Don't you worry Sal. It's all right.'

Jack, his defeated arms hanging, his wrists protruding inches below the cuffs of his herring-bone jacket, stared at the distraught child sobbing in the arms of the old man. Jesus. The Deputy Registrar reassured him, hitching her shoulders into position once more.

'Don't worry son. It takes brides like that sometimes. Nerves. Just nerves. You'd be surprised.'

Ernie was right about Laura. She couldn't understand it; not being told first, confided in by her worried child. She never understood till the day she died and was deeply hurt, which she tried, not entirely successfully, to hide. Laura had no particular wish to be 'mother-of-the-bride', an honourable estate much desired by many of her friends. She had no wish for the exhausting but stimulating challenge of masterminding a lavish production to be remembered with pride by its comptroller and admiring female guests. 'Remember the floral garlands in the Caldicott marquee? White hydrangeas and shasta daisies with Constance Spry trim?' Laura did not look forward to the obligatory drives along the dry ruts of shingle roads to the outlying homestead gardens of her friends, which waited to be denuded of their begged-for lilies, their dewy glads, their copper beech for background foliage; to laying them tenderly on tarpaulins in floraceous heaps in the back of the car and returning with all possible speed to soak them overnight up to their necks in nice warm water with an aspirin. She had never anticipated any particular pleasure in rising early on her daughter's wedding day to deliver this booty to her distraught friend Sheila Macready and her secateur-armed helpers so they could transform the naked church into a bower, could encircle the ends of the pews with ivy (preferably variegated) and attach the pew posies before concentrating on the chancel. Weddings in the Bay were hard work and not worth the effort, in Laura's opinion. 'I hope Sarah and Sybil elope,' she said to Prudie, who smiled.

But she felt she had not been trusted, relied on, treated like an honourable mother. She had no way of knowing that Sarah scarcely understood herself, that her daughter's real reason for her steely fixation on independence, her insistence that she and Jack get out of the Bay, have the baby and get on with it, was not to save her parents embarrassment, not to avoid the breathy interest of the bridge ladies at Dr Tandy's daughter's precipitate nuptials, not even to escape Sybil's golden scorn or Maggie's tiny garments, but to keep her painting self intact. She could do it. She knew she could do it even now. If she got away.

Laura's mother had been a painter, rather a good painter. The only daughter of a wealthy tea importer in Christchurch, she had attended the same sketching class as Frances Hodgkins in Caudebec-en-Caux and been inspired. But she left France and dear dirty old London and came home, married Laura's father and went to Dunedin. She did what she could. She was a pillar, a leading light of the Academy. She painted serious women in large hats seated in comfortable chairs in green and blue rooms, but occasionally she knocked off one of her 'little things', as she called them; delicate red chalk sketches of dreamy nudes, intimate drawings of the inner workings of a flower, the underpinnings of a toadstool. Her reputation in the twenties and thirties was that of a gifted amateur and had lapsed completely at her death. Her work, in 1952, was much sought after. A Douglas, particularly an early Douglas or a 'little thing' of red chalk, was highly prized by those who knew.

'Frances loved little things,' she told Laura once. 'She called them "tender silly little rearranged things". She always fell for them.'

'But yours aren't arranged.'

Laura's mother laughed. 'One mustn't be too derivative,' she said.

Laura had many of these small treasures, salvaged on trips with the children to Granny Douglas in Otago. Trips which were not undertaken lightly nor wantonly. The journey involved two long days in the train and a night on the inter-island ferry coping with Sybil's seasickness which startled even the stewardesses. 'Poor little sparrow,' they said, dumping yet another strawberry box and departing at speed. 'And it's flat calm. Tsk, tsk,' they said. Sarah read the *Reader's Digest* 'It pays to increase your wordpower' on a top bunk and thought of her biscuit labelled Wine which would be delivered in the morning by one of the grey-haired ladies. Dougal slept.

But it was worth it to be with Granny Douglas, who made no fuss about anything and gave Sarah stubs of red chalk, scraps of charcoal, proper paper and her serious attention to every line.

Sarah overheard her in the kitchen banging pots about with Laura, while her granddaughter stood in the wide hall staring at the unblinking brown eyes of the wapiti shot in Doubtful Sound by Grandad Douglas, now equally dead.

'The child might have something. I think she has.'

They said so at school too, right from the primers. Whenever grown-ups asked bumble-footed Dougal what he was going to be when he grew up and he hung his head with shame at having no land, Sarah would answer, 'I'm going to be a painter like Granny Douglas.' Even though they hadn't asked her first because she was a girl.

'Just tell them,' said Laura to Maggie who sat opposite her, hunched and damp across the Tandys' kitchen table, 'that Jack and

Sarah were married the other day. That's all you have to say.' She leant backwards, one hand reaching for an Agee jar with a brown top from the bench behind her. 'Thanks so much for the cream,' she said briskly. 'Take this jar instead of yours.'

'Thank you.' The faintest possible shadow of disappointment flicked across Maggie's face. Her jar had had a nice red lid. She wrung her hands, turned one balled fist inside the other. Her eyes were red, she sniffed. Any moment soon she would start keening. 'I don't know,' she said, 'I just don't know.'

Laura leant over the table, one arm brushing the floppy red felt comb of the rooster tea cosy Maggie had knitted her last Christmas and she had remembered to use. 'Look, it's done. All you have to do is look everyone straight in the eye and say, "They're married." Nobody's going to have the nerve to say "Why?" to your face.'

'But they'll . . .' Poor soggy Maggie; the best theatre sister in twenty years, the gastroenterologist Dr McIlroy had called her. Cool as a cucumber in a crisis.

'Of course they'll talk, but so what?'

'But don't you *care*?'

'Yes,' said Laura, swatting a fly which was cruising across the table. Its corpse lay in the centre of her black rubber fly swat, a squashed currant fringed with thread-like black legs.

Their parents presented Sarah and Jack with wedding cheques in two awkward ceremonies at their respective houses.

Laura was determinedly bright, brisk, laughing beneath a grey pottery jug on the mantelpiece filled with zinnias the colours of pastels on dark paper: hot pinks, chalky whites and strong acid yellows. John Tandy looked shy but amiable as usual as he handed over the slip of paper to Jack and shook his hand. 'Yes,' he said. 'Yes, well. All the best to you both.'

'For the future!' yelped Laura. She gave a sharp gasp. 'Why did you give it to him, not Sarah?'

The cheque hung from Jack's fingers. 'Well,' John laughed nervously, scuppered by his loving wife. 'He's the man of the house now! The breadwinner.'

Jack's face was blank as he folded the piece of paper and handed it to Sarah. She took it, folded it again and shoved it down her front. 'Thank you, Dad.' She walked the couple of paces between them and put her arms around him. He touched her hair helplessly.

The Macalisters were even worse.

Sarah had spent the previous weekend at Glenfrae but returned to town under the pretext of packing her things. There was little to pack. A few clothes. 'For later,' as Laura said. Her paints. Art book prizes, a few other books. She bequeathed the minute milky glass animals with blob noses and speck eyes, which Granny Tandy had given her for years and she had never really liked, to Sybil, who, thank God, was staying with her horsey friend Dorothy at Tiokino. Dorothy fascinated Jack. He doubted if she could be more horse-like and retain her human form.

Maggie had rung again, mindless of the party line. 'Do come out this weekend, dear,' she said, 'we have so much to sort out.'

'What is there to sort out?' Sarah asked the mouthpiece, her eyes on her mother's watchful face above the Shacklock.

'Please,' begged Maggie.

'All right.'

Maggie had made up the two beds in the spare room after the wedding. Jack and Sarah fell into one of them, eyes wide with licence, regardless of the bedsprings and Maggie and Nelson next door. Jack's arm was still around her as Sarah woke next morning to the warbling tuis.

'Listen to the tuis,' she whispered as his eyes opened. He rolled over, turning his back to her and the light. 'Nnn.' Sarah lay on her back, her eyes following the patterns of light on the high plastered ceiling. It was so weird. A piece of paper, a form and then you were allowed to do it. To fuck this man and lie in peace. In lassitude. Perhaps it would be OK. Even the baby.

Her hand stroked the muscles across his shoulders. He was asleep again already. The grey light fell on the bowl of Shot Silk roses placed on the dressing table by Maggie as part of her pretending game, her signal to herself and the world that everything was all right.

The following weekend the roses were still there, brown, rotted and dead, welcoming as bolted shutters. Maggie wouldn't have meant to leave them. Sarah gave her that.

Since her sons had become adult and lived at home, willing and able to defeat the impossible perfection of her previous house-keeping standards, Maggie had become more troubled, more petulant and incompetent. Her pleasant face sagged, the crease between her eyebrows was constant, her run became more clumsy. Plaintive hand-printed notes were tacked to painted tongue-and-groove walls. 'Please clean this basin after use. Other people are busy too!' cried the bathroom. 'Lift the lid!' yelped one above the lavatory. Jack thought his mother was a silly old bat. Sarah agreed.

The presentation was made in the drawing room, the French doors open to a still Sunday morning. Nelson made a speech, his hands tugging at his belt, his back to the fireplace, which was filled with Maggie's dried arrangement for the summer.

Maggie and Sarah sat side by side, one on each fitted cushion of the two-man sofa. It was covered in Sanderson linen in corn-flower pinks and blues, an all-over pattern chosen by Maggie with an eye to wear and tear and work trousers. (Put a newspaper down first!) There was a lot of piping. Piping edged each cushion, each scroll of the arms, ran along the back and edged the base above the pleated frill. Yards and yards of piping.

Jack lay sprawled in one cornflower-decked chair, Nigel in the opposite one, their long splayed legs encased in tight moleskin pants. Nigel, red with embarrassment, shoved his yellow hair back continually with quick raking gestures. Jack's face was tough beneath his tight curls, his lower jaw thrust out. Sarah's longing for him localised into a bruised ache, her hands plucked the piping. Jack's right eyelid, the one away from Nelson, dropped in a half wink. She beamed at him.

Nelson was well away, Sarah realised, blinking. She tried to concentrate. '. . . I can't pretend,' he continued, 'we can't pretend, your Mother and I . . .' He nodded at Sarah's face, which hadn't caught up and was still smiling. 'Auntie Maggie and I, we can't pretend we're happy about this. We're not happy, by crikey we're not. Not by a long shot. Who would be? To think that a son of mine . . .' He paused, his eyes on Jack, who lay more horizontal than ever, his eyes on the long cord of the central light, the scuffed toes of his elastic-sided boots reaching for the sky. '. . . should get the daughter of one of our oldest friends . . .' Words failed him. Sarah's smile disappeared.

'It takes two to tango,' Jack told the ceiling.

'What?'

'Nothing.'

'Sit *up* can't you!' Jack sat up. Slowly, deliberately, he reassembled his limbs, his eyes fixed with calm attention on his father's scarlet face. The rims of Nelson's eyes were bright pink, the irises sky blue, he was breathing hard. 'That's better! As I was saying.' There was a momentary pause. What was he saying? Maggie's chest tightened. She felt she was going to cry. To cry for Nelson, for dear old Nelson who should never have been landed with this mess but then nor should she, but perhaps it was her fault—but what could she have done?—and anyway look at Nigel, who had never put a foot wrong, not ever.

'As I was saying. We're not happy, we're not happy, my word. But this doesn't mean, mind,' Nelson had warmed up again, was on track once more, his eyes glistening, 'that we won't stand by you. No. Blood is thicker than water, my word. You're our children, both of you. If you want to stay here with us, both of you, you too, girlie, till the . . .' his voice cracked, 'till the baby's born, then that's OK by us, isn't it Maggie?'

Maggie nodded, speechless. They had lain awake night after night, side by side on their backs in the darkness, discussing the situation since Jack had dropped his bombshell over the bacon and eggs placed in front of him by Maggie. 'Sarah and I have got to get married. She's pregnant.'

Nelson had overcome Maggie's terror of what the district, especially their Road, would say. 'They're our kids, Maggie,' he had said, his hand on hers. 'Yes,' she whispered. 'Yes.'

'But I understand,' continued Nelson, 'I understand from what you say Jack, that that's not what you want. You don't want to stay here.' Jack nodded, his eyes on his father's face. His expression had changed. Nigel crossed one leg tentatively over the other and ran a finger down the side seam of his bleached moleskins.

'No. No, well if it's not what you want we don't want to force it on you. No. That's not what families are for, parents I should say. That's not what parents are for. I understand you want to leave the district.' Nelson shook his head. 'I can't think why. What're you going to live on, for God's sake? But that's your decision. Now we respect that decision, your mother and I, even if we don't understand why you've made it. It's your decision.' His head moved again, sparse strands of tow-coloured hair lifted on his scalp. His hand reached in his trouser pocket and pulled out an envelope. 'This is for you both and for the baby with all our love,' said Nelson.

Jack was on his feet. Within seconds, the movement invisible, he was in his father's arms.

Nelson held him awkwardly for a moment then slapped his back. 'There y'go, lad, there y'go.'

Nigel dragged himself to his feet holding out another envelope. 'And this is from me,' he said, the words dredged up through depths of shyness, 'with all the best for the future.'

Maggie smoothed her skirt and smiled a moist forgiving smile at Sarah. She had bought some one-ply in secret last week from a little shop in Stortford Lodge where she wasn't known. The lady had been very helpful, and you couldn't always get one-ply.

5

Sarah and Jack rented a cottage in Wellington, the cheapest they could find. Land agents refused to deal with them. 'Your only hope is the paper,' advised Trev Haden of Haden Homes. 'Or word of mouth.' Whose mouth, thought Sarah, hating the black hair between the knuckles, the equine teeth and the man himself. 'And you can wipe Wadestown, Khandallah, Oriental Bay, the prestige suburbs for a start,' said Trev, reaching for his telephone in dismissal. 'You've no hope of a view. You can wipe a view for starters.'

The cottage was around the harbour on the road to the Eastern Bays, its back hard up against a high rock cliff covered in ice plant. It was damp and smelt of age and wear but it had a bed and a sofa, a chair or two and a geyser Sarah refused to light which belched either scalding or tepid water into the stained bath beneath or sulked completely, huffing and wheezing to itself above its ring of flickering blue flame. The front door and two windows opened onto a six-foot patch filled with the fleshy triangular leaves of ice plant surmounted by pink and lemon flowers. Beyond lay a picket fence and the curve of the main road.

On the other side of the road the sea crashed and slid across sharp black rocks. In a nor'westerly storm breakers swept across the road sheeting the cottage, the cliffs, the whole world in spume and spray. The windows leaked, it was a fight to get out the door, condensation trickled down the walls, life became a survival course in a leaky boat. 'I promise we'll leave if the B goes mouldy,' said Jack.

The house got little sun but you could dash across the road to the rocks in good weather, timing it carefully to avoid the traffic sweeping around the curve. There was a sign nearby, 'Caution. Penguins Crossing'. Sarah had never seen one, which was a pity, but it slowed down an occasional bird lover.

Every morning when the weather was fine and she could get out the front door with ease, Sarah assembled her sketch pad and her watercolour kit, her Windsor and Newtons which she had bought with money from a school art prize, her screw-top water jar and a fold up canvas stool she'd pinched from the garage at home. She clutched them to her expanding stomach and headed for the beach, walking on the seaward side, her thumb raised to hitch each likely vehicle. Truckies were the best, leaning over to open their passenger door, one hefty arm outstretched to give her a heave up when it became necessary.

She established her patch on the beach, moving nearer the lavatories down the far end as her bladder became less efficient. Like all the regulars she became proprietorial about her beach, gracious to the grey-haired woman in the purple beret and her clutch of decrepit fox terriers in tea-cosy vests who tottered along the sand each day, friendly to the old men with sticks and the bent-crone driftwood collectors, dismissive of spoilt kids and their feeble mothers. She worked till hunger drove her home. She had never been happier or healthier in her life as long as she didn't think.

The weather was getting colder, which was a problem. Early May had been very mild. 'Real Indian summer, isn't it?' the beach regulars said to each other smiling, pleased with the phrase and the weather and their cordiality.

But this morning the temperature had dropped, a gust of wind and sand swirled around Sarah's feet. She wiped her dripping nose against the back of her hand.

The four woolly-jacketed fox terriers looked cold and miserable as they skittered around the flannel trousers of the old man standing in front of her. He wore a peakless woven hat embellished with prancing reindeer; the long ear flaps were tied beneath his layered chin. White hair escaped around his purple face. He didn't look very well. He walked behind her in silence to stare at her wash of Somes Island and the light on the hills across the harbour. 'That is very good, I think,' he said in heavy careful English.

Sarah knew it was. She wiped her nose again. 'It's usually a lady with the dogs,' she said finally.

'My wife is unwell so I am, shall we say, dog boss this morning.'

'Oh.' He obviously wasn't going to move.

'Have you ever had any lessons?' he asked.

'Oh yes.'

'Where?'

'At school.'

'Ah. Ah ja.'

She picked up her brush.

He almost jumped at her. One of the dogs yelped in fright and retreated with its tail between its legs. 'No more. It is finished.'

She looked at him, shook her head. 'No.'

He put his mittened hand gently on her arm. 'I promise. Come.' He slapped his hands together. 'I will buy you a coffee.'

What a bit of luck. Sarah packed up and they moved, escorted by the four shivering stiff-legged terriers, to the Esplanade Coffee Lounge. They had to sit outside because of Flops, Mops, Cotts and Peter—'They are my wife's names, not mine'— but it was warmer than the beach.

Sarah's hands were wrapped around her mug. She smiled at the old man with gratitude and sipped her hot chocolate.

'May I see the rest of your sketchbook?'

She handed it over in silence and concentrated with dreamy pleasure on her drink. Flops, or maybe Mops, gave a brief yelp of request for food. She broke off a small piece of lamington and dropped it on the ground. A whirling frenzy of black-and-white rear-ends was followed by more silence. The old man took no notice. One hand untied his Laplander's hat; the strings fell either side of his scrawny neck, his lower cheeks hung in folds. Sarah remembered a phrase from Miss Glenhorn's Bio. 'Pendulous drupes.' At the time she had thought of Granny Douglas's breasts, glimpsed once by accident in Dunedin and a nasty surprise.

The four dogs gave up on food. They circled several times then lay coiled at their minder's feet, their sharp noses hidden from the gusting wind.

Eventually the old man shut her sketch book and sighed. 'I could give you lessons,' he said.

How did she know he was any good?

He smiled. 'I taught at the *Kunstgewerbeschule* in Vienna until 1937. After the war I taught at Elam for several years before I retired.'

Elam she knew about.

'I haven't any money,' said Sarah.

His eyes were pale, almost watery blue. His bulbous nose was still purple, the rest of his face had faded to a dull rose.

'I have enough money. You can repay me when you are . . .' he bowed, a quick dip forward, '. . . when you are rich and famous.'

It would be warm too, at his house. And she couldn't go to the beach in the winter.

'Thank you very much,' said Sarah. 'That would be wonderful. My name is Sarah Tandy.'

He heaved himself from his chair with an old man's bent-kneed lurch, bowed again and shook her hand. 'Otto Becker.'

It never occurred to Sarah that Olga Becker, whose rounded shape, long nose and spikey hair suggested an upright hedgehog in a butcher's apron, might be bored by her husband's generosity to a complete stranger. She simply moved in smiling and was rewarded by affection. Olga and Otto's open-plan exposed-beam house, designed by another refugee from Austria, delighted her. She had never seen anything like it. Art magazines, foreign newspapers and piles of books covered every horizontal surface. Hanks of golden wool dyed from lichens in black saucepans smelling of mushrooms were draped over rafters to dry. There were paintings, real paintings: a small ornately framed one of fruit glowing on a table, an even smaller highly-glazed portrait of a pale face above a needle-point collar hung on large nails banged into the pine wood walls, a red and orange mobile drifted far above beside the hanks of wool,

a large white monochrome without a frame leant against a book-
case. There were old frayed rugs of terracotta and rose-pink, other
rugs woven by Olga from undyed fleeces, battered chairs of
enormous depth covered in blue rep. There was nothing shiny,
flowered or new within sight. Coffee was brewed in a battered
aluminium percolator which overflowed each time it boiled,
hissing onto the flame beneath and startling the dogs. A large
honey-coloured spinning wheel sat alongside Olga's weaving
loom, which occupied almost half the living space. Otto's easel
stood in front of the sliding windows which looked out onto the
bush above Muritai Road. All was profusion, nothing was restrained. There were no holds barred. Nothing matched or toned
or picked up a colour note throughout the whole house. It was
another world.

'We like it,' said Olga when Sarah tried to express her pleasure.
They had escaped from Austria in 1938 and lived for many years
in Auckland. They had no children. They were loving to each
other, attending to each other's comfort with cushions; a wrap
perhaps? Nein? They stirred sugar into tea or coffee for each
other, patted each other in passing, murmured soft endearments,
none of which Sarah recognised except liebchen. They were
fascinating.

'What will you do after your baby comes, Sarah?' asked Olga
as Sarah packed her gear after Otto had departed to the beach in
a sulk at her stupidity, her resistance to using enough water, her
drought-stricken brush. He had slammed on his funny hat and
huffed down the steps without even a kiss for Olga.

'Do?' Sarah was angry too. The silly old poohbah. She sucked
her number five brush in rage.

Olga was on her knees on an old sheet sorting her latest Romney
fleece. Her hands moved quickly, cardboard boxes labelled 'Good',
'Average' and 'Compost' awaited her decisions. There was a strong
smell of woolshed. Olga lifted her mild face, her tough grey hair
stuck straight upwards. 'What will you do with your baby when
you come to lessons here with Otto?'

'Oh.' Well obviously she'd bring it, wouldn't she? An alternative had never occurred to her. Tricky. 'I thought,' said Sarah smiling, 'that I could bring it with me.'

Olga's lips, rosy pink without lipstick, shut tight. She shook her head. 'No.'

'But . . .'

'We are not used to babies.' Olga's hands, made shiny by the oily wool, tugged off a hank. She held it to her nose and sniffed it with pleasure. 'Especially Otto.'

'But it wouldn't cry or anything. It'll just be in a . . .' Sarah's hand moved.

Olga laid the hank in the box marked 'Good' and smoothed it. Her face was solemn. 'You expect too much Sarah,' she said. 'From other people, I think.'

Sarah did no housework. She ironed Jack's shirts until she discovered him one morning throwing them in heaps on the woven bed-cover handed on by Laura as he hunted for a decently ironed one. She told him he could iron them himself, which of course he didn't. Each evening as he fell off the bus with every muscle sore and shoved his shoulder against the warped door for access Sarah greeted him with sensuous delight and strange messes of mince and herbs. 'Any fool can cook,' she said happily, forking withered black slices of Otto's home grown eggplant into her mouth. 'Why do women go on about it? Your mother, say. I suppose she had nothing better to do.'

Jack thought of Maggie's table. Groaning, groaning was the word. Laden with succulent golden-skinned joints and hunks of meat, vegetables which gleamed and dripped with butter, deep puddings with cream. Trifles, say, with little purple sugar flowers on the solid whipped surface beneath which lay fragrant sponge slices steeped in sherry by Maggie's heavy hand. There was jam too. And slivered almonds. His mouth watered.

Jack had never analysed his commitment to Sarah. He loved her. Oh God yes, of course he loved her, but it had all happened so quickly, the pram in the hall bit. He was glad to get away from the Bay, that was no problem, he had been planning to shoot through to Wellington anyway but not till he'd saved some money so he could get a part-time job, anything, what did it matter as long as he could get on with writing his book which was all that mattered. He hadn't even shown it to Sarah yet, she'd never asked to see it, his mad whirling *Ulysses* of the South and what could be more derivative? Part pastiche, part childhood idyll, part self-indulgent corn. Even the working title, *Ultima Thule*, was pathetic. He knew that but the thing was just to get it down, it was only the first draft and parts of it were good. He knew that.

The woolstore had nearly killed him when he started. He had had no idea it could be so hard. He had thought most of the moving of bales would be done by fork lifts but he landed up heaving the 300-pound things beneath the high skylights of the cavernous store with a hand hook, just as he'd done at Glenfrae. He listened to the other men talking, committed the rhythms of their speech and their idiom to memory. They seemed to Jack to have an exaggerated respect for anyone who had served in the war as most of them had; the RSA badge adorned most of their wear-home jackets. They seldom spoke about their experiences except for an occasional story of a wild night with a bint in Cairo or a heavy session with a booze artist named Arnold in Noumea. Any crime, misdemeanour even, from one of their own saddened them. 'He's a Returned Man too,' they told each other gloomily at smoko, shaking their heads in sorrow at anything from minor pilfering to violent rape, '25th Battalion.' They were strong hard-working men except for one little shit called Boyd who pinched anything in sight if you weren't careful, even your hook, for God's sake.

The third week he was there Jack found two bales from Nelson's main clip. He stared at the black stencilled GLENFRAE, put out his hand, touched it, heard the magpies yodel, felt the dust and heat of the yards, saw Ernie's muscled thigh moving beneath his ripped khaki shorts. Ernie was a Returned Man too, from the 14–18 War.

Jack had removed all trace of his life in the loft at Glenfrae before he left. He now wrote at night, doggedly, stretching his eyes wide when the eyelids drooped, his back against the streaked wall of the musty bedroom, a stiff-backed red exercise book propped against his knees. Sarah crawled in beside him and lay silent and still.

'If I don't do at least four pages a day I'm done,' he said.

She nodded.

'I'll never do it otherwise.'

'No.' She knew he was right.

'It's so fucken easy to give up.'

'Yes.'

He swung around to her in rage, his body slewed across the white bedspread, his boots banging the baseboard. 'Especially now.'

She nodded again. She lay flat on her back, her stomach belling the sheet into a mound.

Jack leant his head against the wall again.

'Oh Christ, I don't know.'

She heaved herself onto her elbows.

'It'll be all right.'

'Oh sure, sure.' He slammed the book shut, held it a moment between both hands then put it on the floor. She shut her eyes.

They never talked about the baby, made no plans. Maggie sent matinée jackets with frilled edges, small Plunket pattern night-gowns feathered with white stitching. 'I hope you like the feather stitch,' she wrote. 'It's such fun to do. Fondest love to you *all*.' Sarah rewrapped the things in tissue paper and put them in a suitcase under the bed.

'Your mother sent some stuff,' she told him, propped against the doorway of the dank little bathroom one evening in August. Jack lifted his dripping face from the handbasin and blinked at her.

'Stuff?'

'You know.' Her head moved. 'For the B.'

'Oh.' Oh Christ. The muscles of his neck clenched as he stared at her. 'That's decent of her.'

'Yes.' She smiled, put her arms round him, licked his ear.

*

Laura was appalled at their lack of preparation. She had no idea of the situation till she and John arrived a few days later to stay at the Eastbourne pub. 'Who's your doctor?' she asked.

'I haven't got one.'

'For heaven's sake, child!'

'It's all right. I'll get one later.'

Laura fixed that with some help from John who rang Nev Braithwaite, whom he hadn't seen since Medical School but who was happy to recommend a new man in the Hutt.

'You have booked in, I presume,' Laura said next morning.

Sarah pulled three minuscule black balls of wool from the underside of her jersey sleeve and placed them on the arm of the sofa. She lifted her eyes. 'What?'

'Booked *in*. At the Hutt Hospital.'

'Oh.' Sarah rearranged the balls into a triangle. 'No. Not yet.'

Laura was deeply worried by her dreamlike inertia. It was so unlike her quick, infuriating child. 'It won't go away, you know. This poor unfortunate baby. Just because you refuse to think about it.'

Sarah smiled. 'No.'

'You must *love* this child.'

'Yes.'

'Both of you.'

'Oh hell, yes.'

'Oh, Sarah.' Laura tried to take her daughter's hand. Sarah heaved herself off the musty sofa. 'Instant, OK?' she asked.

Her parents had driven down, their car laden with produce from the Bay. Things Sarah had almost forgotten about, which were devoured with enthusiasm by Jack and ignored by her. Hokey Pokey biscuits, afghans, banana cake, chutneys and pickles (Alison's Sweet, Maggie's Mustard). To Sarah the car was a caravan manned by emissaries from a foreign land, laden with gifts from another country distant as Sinkiang. Jack liked the tuck-ins.

John regaled them with his car-packing problems. 'Every time I turned round your mother'd got some other tin or something sitting up on the balustrade of the verandah! The frost was inches thick, we've had some snorters lately.' He paused, enjoying the farm hogget from Glenfrae which melted in the mouth. 'She had all this stuff . . .' His arm encircled the piles of produce about the hutch-like room, rickety piles of biscuit tins depicting the Queen crowned and sashed and smiling, Milford Sound, or puppies with flopping ears and soulful eyes. There was a string bag of passion fruit, a small box of lemons and a large one of apples. Mounds of meat and vegetables were stowed in the fridge. 'Every time I turned round there was something else, something that had to come and what do you think she said?'

Sarah shook her head, wondering about her father. Always there, always pleasant, he toddled along glancing at Laura occasionally as he waited to be told which foot to put forward next. He laughed, flinging his neat grey head backwards at the joke. 'She said, "Don't worry. It will all go under my feet!" Every time she put another thing up there that's what she said.' He laughed again. '"It'll go under my feet."'

Jack put down the knucklebone he'd been chewing. 'Hh.'

They were perched around the rickety card table sent by Maggie, which Jack had placed in the middle of the ten-by-twelve living room. His chair was jammed against the fireplace, John's against the furry sage-green sofa. Laura and Sarah sat on round-topped stools either side of the men. This place is only a temporary refuge, Laura told herself, a shelter beneath an overhang visited by nomads. Her eyes swam with sudden useless tears for her daughter who had been such a fool, who had no idea in the world about matrimony or motherhood, who was a spoilt child about to give birth. Laura stared at the ugly brown of the painted fireplace, her gaze intense as one searching for cave drawings, as she tried to suppress her unwanted concern.

She rubbed her fingers briskly on her handkerchief and laughed at them.

'Well!' she said.

Sarah glanced at her. Jack and John continued to munch with slow, ruminant efficiency, their eyes on their plates.

'Did you know Charles Bremner is in his second year at university here? At Victoria?' said Laura.

Jack sat up. 'What's the weirdo doing?'

'English. And Charles is not a weirdo. His mother,' said Laura as though they would be fascinated to hear it, 'is one of my oldest friends.'

Sarah winked at Jack. Laura intercepted the wink and flushed with rage. 'And,' she said, 'Dad and I have invited him for a meal at the Eastbourne pub with us tomorrow night but you needn't bother to come if you don't want to.' Appalled at herself, her platitudinous prissy self, she plunged on, fulfilling their expectations and hers. Charles was a nice boy. Charles was very intelligent. Charles was very good to his mother. Charles, she almost screamed at the two mocking faces, would never have got you in this mess, Sarah. And they knew that too. They entirely agreed. Their faces became solemn. Their unspoken thoughts filled the hateful little hole, banging and flapping against Laura's flustered face like giant moths shedding dust.

No, he wouldn't. You bet your sweet life he wouldn't. He wouldn't know how to start.

Jack forgave her first. He put his freckled hand over hers, his heavy-knuckled fingers pressed in comfort. 'I'd like to come, thanks, Laura.'

'Me too,' said Sarah. 'I'm mad about the carpet.'

'Don't let's talk you into it,' said John, who had been shelling out pounds, shillings and pence ever since the Buick headed down State Highway 2 to Wellington and was suffering an attack of the deflation, the self-dislike, the accidie known occasionally to the one who marshals, the one who packs the car, the one who picks up the check from the crumb-laden cloth beneath the fingers of his laughing guests who have practically forgotten the existence of the bore who will foot the bill.

'Mean,' signalled the eyes of the young to each other across the table. 'Mean as shit.'

Charles was leaning forward in a tartan chair talking earnestly with her parents when Sarah and Jack arrived at the Eastbourne pub.

The carpet was mock tartan, a tartan which had never kilted the knees of a shepherd, nor been flung over a soldier's head when the crash of his fallen body exposed buttocks white and naked as a wanton girl's.

The colours were purple, red and blue on an emerald ground, the lines were thick, the pattern decisive. It surged up the cumbersome wide-armed chairs as well.

'Isn't it marvellous?' cried Sarah. 'I've only seen it from the door. I didn't know it had eaten the chairs as well.'

She refused to wear the fashionable maternity garments of the early fifties, the straight skirts with a scoop removed to accommodate the belly hidden beneath vast smocks. She tied her gaping trousers together with string, wore a checked shirt of Jack's and washed her hair each day. Her cheeks glowed with health. Charles felt the familiar clutch in his groin.

'Hello,' she said, kissing him to cover her surprise.

For Charles was a surprise. Charles was an astonishment, made over and born again. When on earth had this happened? It couldn't be a year since she had seen him—nine months at the most. She laughed at the thought and kissed him again on the lips.

His steel-rimmed glasses had been replaced by something with dark frames which looked as though he meant to wear them. His face was very thin, his cheekbones stood out, his straight hair hung across his forehead from a cowlick the existence of which she had never noticed before. He wore a dark green woollen shirt with a red scarf at the neck, a dark jacket and pale trousers. The leather belt had been tugged two holes tighter. He looked like a Tartar, for Heaven's sake, a marauder even, someone who knows what he's doing, if Tartars do.

'You're thinner,' said Sarah.

He was very calm, serious as usual. He didn't make the obvious crass comment. Jack did, slapping her rump.

'Not like some.' He shook Charles's hand. 'Hi.'

Laura glanced away blinking. Irresponsible, arrogant, troublemaking and always had been. Mothers, it is well known, have no favourites among their children and Laura worked hard to hide the intensity of her feeling for Sarah.

86

But the evening was a success. Conversation expanded, lifted and soared above the tartan.

Charles and Jack got on to books with the soup. What they were reading, writers they couldn't stand, newly discovered heroes. They became heated, they ignored their hosts, they had a wonderful time. Wordsworth cropped up somehow, was torn to shreds and flung to the tartan.

'Why go on about him then? If he's so useless.' Sarah moved on her chair, readjusting her belly after the conversation had been going some time.

'He's everything I despise,' yelled Jack.

'Oh sure, sure. Except for the words occasionally,' said Charles leaning forward, 'and what he has to say. You know he wrote a sonnet in praise of Toussaint L'Ouverture.'

'Who?'

'The black leader of the slave revolt in Haiti.'

Jack didn't care. 'I'm talking about poetry.'

'So am I.'

'No one who wrote "The Thorn" could be genuine.' Jack leant forward to demolish, eyes snapping with derision, lips moist with excitement as he declaimed:

'No leaves it has, no prickly points,
It is a mass of knotted joints,
A wretched thing forlorn.
It stands erect, and like a stone
With lichens is it overgrown.'

'Why did you learn it then?'

'Because it is such irresistible crap!'

'Language, Jack,' murmured John Tandy.

Jack scarcely glanced at him.

'But the bad ones are a fraction of the rest,' cried Charles. 'Look at the man's output.'

'He wouldn't have let them be published if he didn't think they were OK.'

Charles's mouth opened and shut.

'And how are your studies going, Charles?' asked Laura, taking advantage of the pause. Prudie would want to know and Frank would insist on an answer.

'Oh. Oh, OK I think thank you, Mrs Tandy.' He had always rejected the honorific Aunt and Uncle titles children in the Bay were expected to bestow upon their parents' best friends. So had Jack, who called them nothing at all.

'What are you doing?' he asked belatedly, still astonished to think that he had been talking about anything of interest to Charlie Bremner.

'Dad'll never accept the fact that I've refused to take over Waikeri. He insists I do Law as well as English.' Charles stared at his hand on the dining table. 'I don't want to do Law. I don't want to do anything where I can't read. That's how I'm going to make a living.'

'Reading?' enquired John mildly. He had decided with a stab of relief that they wouldn't need another bottle. The boys were talking so hard.

'Reading. Working with books. Publishing, whatever.'

'Well that's peachy,' said Jack after a pause. 'I'll write them and you publish them.'

Charles didn't smile. 'What are you writing?'

Jack glared at him. 'A novel.'

'Not poetry?'

'No.'

Sarah raised her eyes from a bon chrétien pear which was her 'Fruits in Season' from the end of the menu. 'He can't,' she said, turning to Jack. 'Can you?'

Jack's snaking glance, the glimpse of gold beneath the pale eyelashes, was pure venom. He couldn't write poetry and he knew he couldn't and he hated the knowledge.

'Can I read it?' asked Charles. 'The novel?'

'No.'

'He hasn't finished it,' said Sarah.

Jack was silent. Sarah glanced at him calmly. 'He's got a job at the woolstore,' she told Charles.

'Hard yakker?'

'Yes.'

'Why don't you have a go at School Publications? The School Journal.'

Jack's face changed. The mouth twitched, tightened. 'I don't want to write for bloody kids.'

Charles was unimpressed. 'It's a proofreading job. I saw the ad yesterday, that's all.' His shoulders moved. 'I suppose they want someone experienced.'

There was a pause as both men thought the same thought. The shit hadn't changed after all.

6

'Guess what!' Jack burst in the front door assisted by the nor'-westerly and the usual thump of his shoulder. He grabbed Sarah and attempted a joyful skip or two but gave up when she instinctively shielded her stomach with splayed hands. 'Charlie Bremner's lent us his car!'

'What!'

'Yeah! Till after the B comes.' Jack abandoned her blundering shape and danced solo around the smelly sofa. He kicked it once, collapsed on it and pulled her onto him. He kissed her, beginning with a gentle exploratory movement of his tongue and continuing for some time. 'You know something,' he gasped. 'I quite like you like this.'

She kicked his shin. 'Why's he lent it?'

'I saw him on the Quay and he said, "Come and have a beer," so I said, "OK," and he said, "Where?" and as we were outside de Bretts I said, "Here," and he said . . .'

'Spit it out! You're just like your father.'

Jack leant back with his arms behind his head, beaming at the flyspotted white porcelain lampshade above his head and continued. 'When we'd had one or two, he said suddenly, "How are you going to get Sarah to the hospital?" and I said, "God knows, taxi I suppose," and he said, "You're too far away," and I didn't say anything and after a bit he said, "You can have my car if you like till it's come," and I said, "Gee thanks," and he's bringing it over on Saturday.'

Sarah was silent. She sat very still, staring at the hands folded in her lap.

'So! How about that!' He pushed her hair back from her left ear and nipped it gently.

She moved her head. 'It mightn't come for weeks.'

'So much the better! We'll have it for longer. A *car* for God's sake.'

He was on his feet again, tense, tough, strong as a whiplash snaking about the grotty dump. She couldn't move. She was rooted to the sofa, weighted and bulbous as a Cranach Venus.

'You had a nice easy time last night, I hear,' said the staff nurse as she picked the bundle name-tagged Macalister from the two-tiered trolley and handed it to Sarah. 'Good on you.'

Sarah was still dazed. Jack had not yet seen his daughter. He had been told to go home by the staff on duty last night and had done so with relief.

'The female sea-louse explodes when she gives birth,' murmured Sarah, her eyes on the baby's sleeping face. It really was shaped like a heart. Extraordinary.

'Come again?' Staff Emerson's smile was friendly. Her boyfriend was a tearaway. A real heller. They were getting married, she'd told Sarah, when she'd finished her six months' passion fruit picking, get it.

Sarah got it.

'She's a birthday present for Mum, I hear.'

'Yes.'

'How old are you then?' continued Staff.

'Eighteen today.'

Staff's tongue smacked, a wet cluck of pleasure at the wonder of life in the Maternity Annexe. 'And what's her name?'

'Dora.'

'Dora!' The sun-tanned face was startled. 'Was there an aunt or something?'

It rhymed with Laura and Flora was too twee. Sarah moved her head. She wanted to weep with exhaustion.

Staff Emerson's head gave a sideways jerk at the curtain drawn around the next bed. 'Next door's called hers Heaven.'

91

Sarah's smile was non-committal. She could see Staff's cheerful moonface, lower lip caught beneath top teeth as she hissed at the mother of Heaven, 'Next door's is called Dora, would you believe.'

Staff presented her starched behind and headed back to her trolley with its cargo of swaddling-clothed cocoons. 'Well, get on with it,' she said over her shoulder.

She was shocked to discover when she returned that Sarah had not unwrapped Dora.

'Whyever not?' she asked. 'They all do, or mostly.'

Sarah, who was both sore and incompetent, realised she had failed another arcane test. She looked at the older woman blankly above her screaming child. 'Why?'

'To see if they're all there of course. All the bits and pieces.' Staff picked the scarlet-faced arch-backed heap from the bed and held it against her chest.

'Now Macalister,' she told the clenched waving fists, the anguished blind mouth, 'we'll have another go. You and me, Mac,' she crooned, 'are going to lick your Mum into shape.' Dora was now silent. Staff looked at the wide-open eyes with infinite tenderness. She raised the chin with one finger. 'Eh? Unbutton,' she said to Sarah, who already was.

Laura arrived by Newmans the day after mother and daughter came home, bearing messages from everyone, especially Sybil, who couldn't wait to get her hands on the baby.

'Can't you come the day before, Mum?' Sarah had begged down the hospital telephone.

'Why?'

'How'll I keep her alive till you get here?'

'They're hard to kill,' replied Laura, hoping she meant it.

Charles had lent Jack the car again to collect his family from the hospital.

The baby lay sleeping in its carrycot as Jack drove home through the manicured glades of Lower Hutt. Sarah looked at each house, each verge with the intense interest of the temporary car owner and prayed that Dora would not wake till they arrived home.

Jack drove with arms straight, a cigarette drooping from his lip, his hat on the back of his tight brown curls. 'D'y'reckon it's still breathing?' he said.

Dora was a contented baby. 'You don't know you're alive,' said Laura, her wrist under the doll head, her hand supporting the pink kewpie body in the plastic bath. Dora's limbs moved, her expression was serious, almost stern. She was doing very well according to the Plunket Nurse, who told Sarah she was a lovely little mother for one so young. 'Some of them,' she rolled her eyes in despair. 'You'd hardly credit. But Baby's happy as a clam now you've let down. Like I said,' sighed Miss Jenks, 'you're a lovely little mum.'

Sarah was bewildered by the monstrous regiment of women who assumed her reaction to this solemn infant would be as milky and madonna-like as theirs. Her honesty rebelled, she longed to shout at their besotted faces, 'She's here because we fucked!' She had assumed that maternal feeling would descend upon her, would flow in draughts like that to which Miss Jenks referred as 'Your lovely supply dear'. So far it hadn't. All right. She would mind Dora and love Dora, of course she would love Dora, her hopeless sense of fairness demanded it. She traced her daughter's face with one finger. 'It's not your fault.' Dora's kitten mouth yawned. 'I'm probably too young or something.' But was this a factor? Sarah was not convinced. She was not a recruit in the army of motherhood. She had been press-ganged. The thing now was to ensure survival for her daughter and herself.

'Never complain, never explain,' Granny Douglas had murmured when Sarah had once stormed at her in a passion over Sybil's latest sneakiness: pretending to eat all her Jaffas then waving her full packet triumphantly in Sarah's face when she'd motored through hers to make it fair.

She would assume the motherhood persona when required; she would let things ride. She would not waste her energy feeling guilty at her lack of rapture or attempt to fight the impossible odds staked on the side of woman-fulfilled-as-mother. She would keep her energy for painting and her bewilderment at the puzzle to herself. Why did no one expect Jack to change, to undergo automatic metamorphosis into a father? He liked the baby. He was tender, pragmatic about sick and shit, did his stuff. Pulled his weight, as Nelson later noted with pride. 'Shall we dance?' he asked his daughter the day she and Sarah came home. They blundered around the card table, Dora clasped to his chest, one tiny hand held high in his.

But no one expected that paternity would alter him in any fundamental way, would enrol him as a life member in a world-wide organisation in which he had no wish to serve. There were many clubs for fathers. No one assumed they would all join the same worshipful company.

Sarah pondered these things.

Sybil arrived panting with excitement a few weeks later. She took the baby over completely—bathing, watching and applauding every vague waving movement of a hand or leg. 'If you'd wean her I could do the lot,' she begged.

But that bit was now easy. Her sister leant forward on the green sofa to watch as Sarah held her breast back from the snuffling nose with one finger. Sybil was still chubby, rosy, almost edible in appearance. Grey eyes peered from between masses of heaped straw-coloured hair. She sounded quite breathless as she confided, 'You know, all I want to do is to find some nice kind man and marry him and have lots of babies. That's all I want to do ever. I don't want to paint or have a career or any of that stuff.'

Sarah said nothing. She and Sybil had never been friends, had barely tolerated each other, had fought and snarled and niggled from earliest childhood. To Laura, who was devoted to her sister Pat, this was surprising and painful. Sarah knew that nothing she did or produced apart from this baby would ever be of the slightest interest to her sister. Why should it be otherwise? She saw this now. Why should anyone expect their sisters or their brothers or their cousins or their aunts to take the slightest interest in whatever was really important to you, in what kept you ticking, ensured your breathing in and breathing out? Sarah felt 150. I am wise beyond my years, she thought smugly. She touched Sybil's hair with one finger. 'That shouldn't be too much of a problem,' she said.

Dora sniffled. 'I'll burp her!' Sybil flung the spit rag over her shoulder and held out her arms for her niece. 'Here.'

'I've been thinking,' she said later as Dora operated on the other side. 'I think I'd like to marry a high country farmer in the South Island.'

'Good thinking,' said Sarah, her eyes on Dora's face. She was frowning. She looked furious.

'Yes.' Sybil pulled her legs up and sat cross legged, her thighs flat on the sofa. She patted the green surface, as denuded in patches as Mine, the teddy bear of her infancy. 'This thing smells, you know that.'

Sarah sniffed. 'Does it?'

'When I lie on it at night I can smell cat pee,' said Sybil with certainty.

'We haven't got a cat!'

'A previous cat then. It really pongs.'

'Mum didn't say anything.' Dora's eyes closed. Individual dark lashes fanned her cheeks. She burped, puffing one milky bubble at her mother.

'Well Mum wouldn't, would she?'

'Probably not. Oh dear,' said Sarah, secure in the thought that there was nothing she could do about an ancient nebulous smell of cat.

'You get used to it,' said Sybil graciously. 'As I was saying, I like the South Island. Wanaka, say. Round there.'

'Why not?' said Sarah again, wondering if she'd get away with sliding Dora into her carrycot without de-burping.

Sybil's lips were damp, her eyes on the faraway peaks and valleys of a fine skelp of land with good steadings owned and farmed by a gentle man.

'I'd love a lilac bathroom,' she said.

Sybil was appalled by the Beckers' house. 'It smells of toadstools and dags,' she told Dora as they waited for the bus home. 'And those skittery little dogs, they smell a bit too.'

'Oh, you are hopeless.' Sarah stormed onto the bus with her ticket held out. 'Come on! Two please,' she snapped at the driver.

Sybil comforted the man with a smile and sank down beside her sister, arms outstretched to take Dora.

'Leave her!' Sarah was hot with rage. Her eyes snapped.

Sybil pouted. 'I was only *saying*. And anyway,' she whispered to the pink ear sticking out from the lopsided bonnet knitted by Maggie. 'It does pong.'

Nelson, like most farmers, could seldom get away. He was lambing, or he was docking, or he was dagging. He sent the bus fare and the family progressed overland by Newmans hung about with baby clobber. 'God, look at all your gear!' yelped Nigel, who picked them up. They fell off the bus, the baby screaming, both parents harassed and defeated by the effort required to keep a fractious baby quiet for eight hours of public transport.

But the visit was worth it. Dora was exactly like Jack as a baby, said Maggie, though perhaps there was a hint of Sarah about the eyes, what did she think? Sarah, who thought the baby was exactly like her mother, smiled politely.

Prudie came out with Laura to pay her respects. She seemed more vague than ever, her hair more wispy, more collapsed, her large eyes guarded behind the pink-rimmed spectacles she now wore. She took Sarah in her thin arms and held her close. 'Dear child,' she murmured. 'How good to see you. Are you as well as you look? I mean, is life . . . ?'

'Life's great,' said Sarah. She bent to reroll Dora, whose salamander movements had taken her to the edge of her spit rug on which blue bears played leapfrog.

'You're painting?'

Sarah glanced up. 'Of course. I'm having lessons from a really good man in Eastbourne for free.' She sat back on her heels. 'Because I'm good. He wants to teach me.'

Prudie shook her head in surprise at both the lessons and the lack of modesty. The breeze from the French doors moved the strands of hair around her long face. El Greco madonna, thought

Sarah, remembering Miss Pritchett's card of his *Nativity* and the scent of stale apples and tennis shoes in Six Classical.

'It was very kind of Charles to lend us his car,' she said. She paused. 'Very.'

Prudie leant forward. Her wrists and hands were slender, attenuated, the fingers unnaturally long. She revolved her wedding ring round and round, round and round.

'He would be happy to. Charles,' said Prudie, 'has always been very fond of you.'

Sarah picked up her daughter and kissed the top of her head. 'Oh well. It was very nice of him.'

'How is he?'

'Charles? I haven't seen him lately. Jack sees him quite often at the pub.' Sarah's glance was sidelong. 'He looks different now, Charles, doesn't he?'

'Yes,' said Prudie, leaning back on Maggie's canvas-work cushion, which depicted one very large dog called Dignity and one very small one called Impudence. 'He looks beautiful.'

Maggie was in her element, her arms round a baby, her tins filled, her heart assuaged. It was as though someone had taken her poor swollen nettle-rashed heart and soothed it with unguent, anointed it with balm. She gave thanks. It was all right now. It had come right. She was a grandmother and it was all lovely.

Nelson was also happy. He nursed his granddaughter when he could get a look in, one giant finger in her mouth as though he was training a bobby calf to suck the bottle. 'Go away in,' he had said to Maggie outside The Baby Bonnet in town last Wednesday. 'Go away in there and buy something for the wee girl.' He dragged a fistful of crumpled notes from his pocket. 'Here.'

Jack spent most of the weekend in the woolshed loft except when they went to Ernie's whare. He made tea for them in the green thatched-cottage teapot Maggie had given him many years ago for Christmas. He took the baby in his arms, talked to her in Maori, gave her the old carved kauri spoon from his Granny's Lord Kitchener tea caddy to suck. Michael Joseph Savage gazed from one wall, Private Eru Waihi, killed in action, Galatos, May 1941, from the other. The same bright hussif crocheted by his Aunty Kura before the war still covered the bed. It was all just the same.

Jane Atwood was not in Hastings when they returned to Glenfrae. She had won a university scholarship as planned and gone to Auckland. A demure blurred photograph headed 'Top Scholar for the Bay' had appeared in the *Hawke's Bay Herald-Tribune*. Her parents were spellbound, Girls' High delighted, Jane calm.

Jane's pragmatic lack of interest in Sarah's pregnancy had been a help at first. It was bloody bad luck, she agreed, but Sarah had always been mad about Jack and what the hell.

'It's not like Uni, say. You can still paint,' she had told Sarah, resiting the whipped cream and nuts which had slipped from the chocolate half of her Rush Munro's Maple Walnut Sundae. The tables and uncomfortable wooden chairs, made and painted by Mr Rush Munro, had been splotched with separate brushes, red, green, orange and blue; you could see the brushmarks. Bull-necked goldfish swam languorous and graceful in the pool in front, their drifting tails glimpsed between the lily pads.

Sarah moved her buttocks on the painted wood and dug deep into her banana ice-cream soda with the long spoon provided. 'That's what Jack says. But I was going to Art School. To Elam. I'll miss all that.'

Jane paused with her spoon in the air. 'Why do you always have sodas instead of sundaes? Especially when it's my treat, for your leaving the Bay.' She scraped the last traces from the amber glass dish, licked the spoon three times, sighed and thought of Auckland. Her bare arms reached for the skies then flopped back. 'You've never been there, have you? To Auckland?'

Sarah was still sucking. She shook her head.

'It's marvellous! Quite different from Wellington, and as for *here*. It's got all these Arcades and Speciality Shops and things. There's one that sells only blouses, and there's imported shoes and masses of coffee shops with real coffee, some of them are under the ground and you go down and you could be anywhere in the world. It's all so cosmopolitan.'

Sarah nodded. The last of her soda sucking made a satisfactorily loud squelch.

'You'd never do that in Auckland.'

'I would so. Don't be nuts.'

Jane's smooth head flicked to one side and back. 'It just wouldn't occur to you. They're all so sophisticated. They've got better tans than we have even, and they're all beautiful, well, the young ones, and so smart.' Jane glared at the fish pond, the bright plastic streamers fluttering above the Used Car lot across the road, the cyclists pedalling home to tea against the endless head wind. A truck hurtled by, its tray laden with an assortment of children, who waved. 'We're all so hick here,' snorted Jane as they waved back.

'Mmn,' said Sarah, still sucking in token defiance.

'In the coffee shops they have salads with pineapple and cottage cheese for people who're fat and brown bread sandwiches with bacon and lettuce and salad dressing and chicken, say. Nothing like the dead egg ones here turning up their toes in the Tip Top.' She grimaced.

Sarah sat silent. Her face was expressionless as she stared at the contorted face of her best friend. She knows I can't go to Art School in Auckland. She knows I'm bloody pregnant. If she's so clever why doesn't she belt up? And why, she asked her red and white straw in silence, is she my best friend?

She knew, of course. She and Jane shared a common interest. They wanted, they had confided to each other endlessly, to 'do something', to achieve something, to live their chosen lives free as air and happy as birds with handsome devoted men as optional extras. They even enjoyed, they confessed in whispers in the locker rooms which smelt of feet, the steely joys of hard work.

Jane's mind was rigorous, she would never let Sarah get away with such burbling guff and yet here she was bleating on like a surrogate Sybil. It was one thing to hide any brains you happened to have from boys, that was one of the prerequisites of having them, but why act the dumb bum with me? Perhaps, thought Sarah sadly, twiddling her straw between both palms, she thinks I've sold out.

'And the buildings! Some of them are so high you leave your stomach behind in the lift as you whizz up.'

Sarah felt sick. She marched with head held high to the cloakroom behind Mr Rush Munro's trellis, which was painted white.

Horizontal rain flung across the harbour often flooded the letterbox. Jane's first lilac-coloured message from beyond, fortunately written in ballpoint, was dried by Sarah in front of the one-bar heater. Anglo-Saxon was the cloaca but Jane really liked Middle English. The other kids in the hostel were OK but some of them were really stinking about answering the phone when it was their turn. Her roommate was OK. She was called Oriol and came from Taumarunui and always wore her stockings inside out. She said they weren't so shiny that way and Jane had worn hers like that to the Freshers' Hop and had a really good time so maybe that was why, ha ha. She hadn't met anyone she liked as much as Charles. She would like to talk to Sarah about the course but it would have to wait till they met up because it would take hours. Remind me to tell you about Courtly Love. How are you all?

The letters became less frequent, largely due to Sarah's lack of enthusiasm in replying. She couldn't think of anything much which would interest someone deeply involved with *Sir Gawain and the Green Knight*. Otto Becker's insistence on a wet brush? Dora's diarrhoea?

She did tell Jane months later that Jack was going to chuck his job at the woolstore before Christmas. That he had a job at School Publications, which was great. The money was less but they could manage as long as they could keep Dora in the cot. Sarah had sold a watercolour of the harbour, how about that? Mr Becker knew the lady at the Esplanade Coffee Lounge, which was only a milk-bar really, but she let local painters hang things on the walls and Sarah's had sold in two days. The framing was a problem. Mr Becker was going to teach her how to do her own because it cost the earth professionally. You had a little mitre thing. It took time more than anything.

Sarah changed her grizzling daughter, dealt with the used

nappy, washed her hands with Dora horizontal under one arm, applied the anti-rash cream to the naked behind and blew on Dora's stomach to cheer her up. It worked. Arms and legs motored at twice the rate, the face beamed, the chortle was throaty. Dora was easy to love.

Sarah propped her daughter beside her on the sofa and continued answering Jane's letter. The rain flung itself against the rattling windows. Dora clamped her left foot in both hands. 'Have you seen a photo of Charles since he's been down here?' wrote Sarah. 'He looks quite different. Hunted and haunted and sexy. When are you coming to see us? Won't suggest you stay here because, (a) The sofa/bed smells of cat pee according to Sybil, (b) We heave the cot into the living room when we go to bed.'

Jane answered promptly. She'd love to come before Christmas. She had a second cousin in Eastbourne who'd give her a bed and she could come round every day. The cousin worked at the Turnbull Library so that was all right. 'She wouldn't get po-faced at me using the place like a boarding house, as Mum would say.'

'But that's the week I start at School Pubs,' said Jack as he spooned puréed vegetable into his daughter's mouth that evening. Dora spat it out and ground a starfish hand into the resulting mess on the tray of the high chair.

'It's the silver beet,' said Sarah. 'Dodge round it.'

'Why did you do it then?'

'She's got to try new stuff.'

'Jesus wept.' Jack tried drafting the green specks to one side. Dora remained unconvinced at first but eventually resumed her open-and-shut feeding action.

'What difference does that make? Jane's coming, to your starting at School Pubs?'

'There's going to be a party. A Christmas party.'

Sarah sat at the kitchen table beside him. A smile spread across her face. 'A party?'

'Yup.' Jack spooned in the last mouthful, operated on the wastage on cheeks and chin, ate the rejected silver beet and scrubbed Dora's face with a bib appliquéd with a sailor dancing a hornpipe. He undid the strap of the chair and heaved his daughter onto his knee. 'A real party eh,' he told her. Dora was pleased.

'What'll we do with her?'

'Take her with us.'

'Oh, break it down.'

'Well, what're we going to do otherwise? Unless you don't come.'

They stared at each other. Babysitters cost the earth. Jack re-adjusted Dora on his lap and placed one hand on Sarah's leg.

'Look, it'll be OK. You put her in the carrycot. Get the four-thirty bus. I'll meet you.'

'Mmn.' Sarah nodded, smiled once more, tucked a strand of hair behind one ear. Her hair was long now, down to her shoulders to save the expense of cutting. 'Mmn. OK.'

They made love in the musty bedroom that night. They gave each other a great deal of pleasure. They were both good at it; they knew each other very well.

Jack fell into the cottage next day clutching the yellow telegram from his father. There was no telephone in the house—the landlord, a vast slab of a man from Naenae, wouldn't hear of it —and anyway they couldn't afford it. Tears fell down his face. 'It's Ernie,' he said. He gave a great shuddering sigh, searched for a handkerchief in both pockets, gave up and let them stream. 'Oh Christ, oh Christ, it's Ernie,' he said again, collapsing onto the sofa.

Sarah tried to comfort him, held him in her arms, wept for Ernie and for him. Ernie was getting old, she explained. He'd had high blood pressure for years. Ernie hated taking his pills. They saw Ernie demonstrating how he disposed of them, a quick decisive chuck with one hand, a chain pull with the other. 'Straight down the toilet, man, straight down the toilet.'

Jack stared at her. 'He's dead,' he said. His sniff was long, deep and loud. 'How the hell are we going to get to the tangi? We're skint. Completely bloody skint.'

'You can have the five pounds I got for the watercolour.'

His face was shocked. 'Don't you want to come?'

'Of course I want to! But it won't buy two tickets.'

'No.' He stood up, put his arms round her, kissed her hair.

'Will they let you off School Pubs when you've only just started?'

'They'll have to.' Jack tugged at his belt, his face thoughtful.

He might get some good stuff at the tangi.

Sarah had arrived at the Beckers' for her Tuesday lesson with Dora aged three weeks in the carrycot; the baby virtually invisible, her mother smiling as though both had been warmly invited. Olga was spinning her new Merino fleece. Otto was seated at the table studying a new book on Kandinsky. Sarah had observed this process several times. Otto didn't merely look at the reproductions of the paintings. He absorbed each one with intent concentration for at least half an hour, waiting to find out what it would tell him, how it would increase his understanding, what it had to say. 'They are a poor alternative for the paintings,' he had told her once, his chins moving. He glanced at the cabinet which contained his meticulously cared-for 78s. 'Records also.' He paused. 'They are a very poor substitute. But they are the price we pay for being alive, is it not?'

Otto and Olga both glanced up at her knock, their eyes wary. They shuffled to their feet. 'You have come with the baby for your lesson?' said Olga.

'Yes.' Sarah placed the carrycot on the rose and terracotta rug and extracted the sleeping Dora.

'She has hair,' cried Otto. 'Black hair!'

'Yes.' Sarah remained cheerful and calm. 'It'll probably all fall out, they say.'

'Fall out,' yelped Otto, more alarmed than ever.

They continued to stare for some time, standing side by side, their faces solemn. Olga extended one finger and touched a cheek.

'I'll just put her on your bed, if that's all right,' said Sarah brightly.

They exchanged glances, eyes wide, necks stretched, two small threatened animals of the same species. 'She will fall off, perhaps,' said Olga.

'Oh no, not for months. But perhaps it'd be better to start off with her on the floor,' said Sarah. 'I'll do that.'

'There's a sheepskin,' said Olga. 'But it must be cleansed.'

'Good heavens no. It doesn't need cleaning.'

Olga's head was up, her hair stiffer than ever. 'We do not enjoy babies,' she said, 'Otto and I. If she cries, Sarah, you both go.'

'If she cries,' said Sarah, her smile radiant, 'I feed her.'

Otto looked green.

He taught her so much, Otto. Sarah's dull ache of rage (admitted to no one) about missing out on Elam had dissipated. Otto had no other pupils. He was generous with every ounce of his knowledge, he insisted she explore, experiment, see. 'That is all you have to do, child.' He slammed a hand against his forehead. 'Of course it's not all you have to do. You need talent, you need technique, you need luck. Ah yes, luck you will need always, but first you must see. The worst thing of all is someone with talent who will not see. Who thinks he can skid along.' Otto's spatulate fingers made a straight schuss downhill then braked stiffly upwards. 'Psch!' His eyes glared, his attendant chins shook once more. 'It is not so! And work, work you need always. Talent you have and work you have but you must see harder. You look, but still yet you don't see. An artist is someone who sees. I,' said Otto standing ramrod straight, 'will make you see.'

'OK,' said Sarah.

Otto inspected her latest sketches of the baby asleep, a charcoal head of Jack writing.

'Do you think they are good?' he asked.

'The head I do.'

He nodded. 'You must love your work. To insist to the world of its excellence. To fight! It will be more difficult for you.'

'I can fight.'

'No, no, no! You will be . . .' his fingers waved, 'fragmented!'

She smiled at his hands, the explosive puff of air from his lips, his intensity. 'No, I won't.'

'Babies. Husbands. Lovers maybe.'

She shook her head, smiled into his anxious eyes. 'No more babies.'

He sighed. 'Soon we start oils. Oil painting is another world. It takes concentration, hours of concentration. Where are you going to get these hours? You can paint only from what grows inside you, from the spirit! What grows inside you? Babies! Not paintings. Not great paintings.' His face sagged more than ever. He looked desolate. 'I am wasting my time.'

Sarah was still smiling. Indulgently.

Otto's hands hung dejected between his knees. He placed the sketches on a nearby table and called, 'Olga!'

'Ja?' answered a voice from the kitchen.

'Coffee?' He paused. 'Olga used to paint,' he said thoughtfully. 'She was very good once.'

Olga appeared with two pottery mugs on a painted tin tray. Her feet trod carefully between the four sleeping dogs. She blundered around the easel, manoeuvring her bulk to avoid the splayed legs.

Otto took his coffee. 'Danke, danke,' he murmured and turned to Sarah.

'I still believe in life work also. Do you paint your husband nude?'

'Yes. Well, sketches.'

'Has he a good body?'

'Yes.'

'It doesn't matter, of course, but it's easier to understand the anatomy, how the muscles work, if they're not hidden by fat.'

Olga gave a loud sniff. She turned to pad back to her apfelstrudel.

'He could pose for us both.' Otto was delighted with his happy thought. 'Here!'

Jack's reaction swam before Sarah's eyes. Her laugh was nervous, phoney. 'Well.'

Olga balanced her flower-painted tray on the back of Sarah's chair and exploded. Quills of grey hair quivered in outrage. 'No!' she cried. 'Enough is enough. More than enough! The mother, the baby, and now the nude husband, is it! No!'

Her back was straight as she departed.

Otto was astonished. He dragged himself from the depths of his blue chair and followed her to the kitchen. 'But lieb-chen . . .'

Sarah drank her coffee, which was delicious as usual, and continued her sketch of the puriri tree outside the window.

'I can't ask you round tomorrow,' Sarah explained to Jane, who had arrived the day Jack went to the Bay for Ernie's funeral. They were sitting on the rocks opposite the cottage. Dora lay on her back on a tarpaulin, her hand reaching for the sand available. The wind was freshening, whipping short choppy waves into action across the harbour. 'It's my art lesson day.'

'Can't you skip it?' said Jane.

'Pooh! Dirty!' said Sarah, removing sand from Dora's mouth with one hooked finger then wiping her face with several. 'Here.' She handed Dora a Mickey Mouse rattle which was inspected briefly then tossed aside. 'No,' she told Jane, 'I can't.' She paused, glanced at Jane. 'You can mind Dora if you like.'

'No thanks.' Jane wrapped her Mexican print dirndl tighter round her knees. 'When're we going to see Charles?'

'When Jack gets back, I suppose.' Sarah stood, retrieved the Mickey Mouse from a nearby rock-pool and made another scoop of Dora's mouth. 'Come on, let's go home. This is hopeless. Bad babies,' she told Dora as she clamped her beneath her arm, 'get rabies and have to be shot.' Dora yelled briefly, a handful of sand secreted within a balled fist for future use.

Otto and Olga had a plan. They made many plans, discussing expeditions to the city in their Morris Minor for days in advance. Making plans was one of their shared interests. A grocery list was carefully calibrated, checked and rechecked, nothing was left to chance, everything was talked through. This particular plan was a major one. Otto and Olga had been bidden as usual to their friends

Clara and Hubert Bechstein's house for a pre-Christmas party. 'They are not Christians, of course, any more than we are,' said Otto, 'but then neither are we good Jews. We are just ones who survived and we meet each year before Christmas because after Christmas in Wellington it is a morgue while everyone lies on the beaches, is it not?'

The daring plan was the Beckers' request, granted with enthusiasm because the Bechsteins loved the young, that they should bring Sarah and Jack to the annual party. 'Two birds with half a stone,' cried Otto. 'We meet your Jack, you meet our friends.' His voice dropped. 'Clara,' he said, 'is very gifted.'

'In what way?' asked Sarah rebalancing Dora on her hip.

'In every way. Clara and Hubert are both what we call *Schöngeist*.' His fingers snatched the air for meaning. 'Untranslatable. Art lovers, music lovers. But more than that.' His face was earnest. 'Much, much more.'

This party sounded better than the one they'd missed at School Pubs. 'When is the party?'

Side by side, twinned by thirty years of matrimony, they beamed at her. 'Tomorrow!'

Sarah plonked down on the blue rep. 'Oh no!' Dora dribbled curdled milk. Otto averted his eyes. Olga handed a tissue. 'Jack's not here. And my friend Jane is.'

Explanations could perhaps be made to the Bechsteins. A tentative alternative plan was rethought, a new campaign mounted in depth. There was much discussion. 'Perhaps, after consultation with Clara of course,' Otto explained to Sarah (one always had to check most carefully any change of plan with Clara), 'the friend, your lady friend, might come instead of Jack. It might be possible, might it not?'

'If, of course,' Otto and Olga glanced at each other, two small grey planners for the common good, 'Clara is prepared to have the baby in with the coats.'

She was.

Jane was unimpressed. 'But they'll all be a hundred and ten, for heaven's sake.'

'No, they have lots of young friends and anyway they're so amazing, you must meet Olga and Otto.'

It was better than hearing about staff problems at the Turnbull all night perhaps, but not much. And conceivably there could be someone interesting.

Clara Bechstein was larger than life. 'Larger than life' was not a compliment in the Bay. 'She's larger than life. She terrifies me,' Maggie had told Sarah apropos of the new Bishop's wife. It was a euphemism meaning 'I dislike her but I am too nice to say so'.

Clara boomed at them from the top of the stairwell on their arrival, 'Gute Nacht!' she cried, her arms wide to embrace five people, three of whom she had never seen before in her life. She held her arms outstretched, peered at Sarah and Jane in turn, clucked with approval at Dora, clutched Olga and Otto to her once more, murmured something to them in German and tossed the young aside. She swept off with the proud Beckers, still shouting. She wore a long embroidered shift thing of purple velvet, a tabard, or was that shorter? Her red hair was piled high, her lipstick was bright orange. She was magnificent.

It was her husband Hubert who showed Sarah a quiet room in which to hide the baby. 'Not with the coats, goodness me no,' cried Hubert. 'Anything can happen with the coats. See, here there is a cot, even. For our granddaughter Sophia when she visits from Melbourne.' Sarah saw Sophia trailing an infant nightgown across the Tasman like Popeye's Sweetpea on the scoot.

Hubert was smaller than Clara and had no hair at all. 'I do not know you,' he said later, offering white wine in long glasses to Sarah and Jane, who had waited in the living room, 'but I am pleased to see you because you are young and beautiful but then so are all the young, are they not? Come and hear Albert, who recites poetry.'

Albert was interesting. He was tall, fresh-faced, chestnut curls fell about his forehead. He waved his arms, he declaimed.

'When them golden trumpets sound,
Where will *your* soul be found!' he demanded.

Sarah stiffened at his stare.

'Oh, standin' around,' he sighed. 'Standin' around.'

Her heart sank.

'But, when them golden trumpets sound,' the voice soared,

'Where will *my* soul be found?' Albert leant back, his face beatified, his hand high.

'With the crowned, with the crowned.'

The applause was considerable.

The worst thing that could happen at parties in the Bay was Items. 'Will there be Items, Mum?' begged Dougal in agony when yet another invitation arrived from the Cunliffes. Items were clammy hands, recitations, pianoforte pieces and despair. And yet surely this rapture, this melting weakness in the gut, had been occasioned by an Item, within the meaning of the act.

'Who is he?' gasped Sarah.

Jane shook her head, her mouth open.

'He's a poet,' said a man in sleeveless fair-isle jersey. 'Albert Belisle.' The man put down one of the two glasses he was holding and held out his hand. 'And I'm Scott Bruce. I paint.'

'Paint.' Sarah smiled. What a bit of luck. 'So do I.'

'Are you any good?'

'Yes.'

He hitched up his trousers, picked up the second glass again and took a long swig. 'You're very young.' He clutched her hand. 'Never, never be a painter unless you can do nothing else.'

She disengaged her hand. 'I am a painter,' she told his glazed eyes.

Jane had disappeared. Sarah glanced around the room while Scott Bruce described to her how impossible the art scene was in New Zealand. He told her of the pressures, the pain, the immensity of his soul-destroying struggle to maintain artistic commitment in a nation composed of fools and dolts. He licked his lips, a quick anteater flick, before spitting out the words once more. 'Fools and dolts!'

Jane was across the room talking to Albert Belisle. The stiff white broderie anglaise frill of her petticoat was visible. Her hands moved with animation. She had beautiful hands.

'Give me one name, one decent name who sells!' demanded Scott, his fair-isle jersey wrinkled with emotion.

Sarah shook her head.

The Bechsteins' house in Roseneath was different from the Beckers'. It was not only the evidence of money spent. 'He has done so well, my friend Hubert,' Otto had told her with pride. 'He has built himself up from scratch. He had nothing when he came. Nothing at all and now you see how well he has done with his nuts and bolts. He is a scholar also. He gives lessons in German Language Reading at the university. A professor, he was before.'

The gold lamp fittings, the mini sconces, the shiny silken rugs on the walls must all have been imported, which indicated time and effort as well as money. There was no effort obvious in the Beckers' house; it grew and flourished, nourished by the eclectic tastes of Otto and the enthusiasms and bowerbird instincts of Olga.

Sarah felt faintly depressed. Although completely different in style, the atmosphere of attentive care, the matching of colours and the picking out of high-notes, the knee bent to the gods of decor, reminded her of Dr and Mrs Cunliffe's gracious home on Bluff Hill.

Sarah was bored by Scott's moaning, his two-armed drinking habits and his hopeful hands. She had well-developed instincts of survival. She smiled and moved away.

Albert was in full flight again. Jane stood beside him, looking faintly proprietorial.

'Oh, Sister Catherine,' he begged,

'Send me a husband!

Tall, Sister Catherine,

Rich, Sister Catherine,

Soon, Sister Catherine.'

Jane laughed, flinging back her head in praise, clapping her hands with delight.

'At the time of your birth,' a voice confided in Sarah's left ear, 'it was expedient for us both that we should part.' The speaker was a small man, his face eager. He wanted to tell her all about it. 'My

God, how I agree with that!' He clutched Sarah's hands to his chest. He was slightly drunk. Beer, it must have been; a sharp yeasty smell puffed at her in breathy waves. 'Don't you?' he begged.

'Who said it?'

'Lady Bessborough. Eighteenth century, nineteenth. "I have never been of the opinion that children owe their parents anything. At the time of your birth it was expedient for us both that we should part." I think, I think,' the man panted, 'that that is one of life's most beautiful statements. I may be misquoting slightly.' He hiccoughed. 'I probably am.' He thought for a moment, considering the pros and cons. 'Almost certainly I am, but you get the gist. And that statement is definitely, categorically, without any doubt whatsoever, the most beautiful statement ever made by a mother.' He mopped the end of his nose, gave it a quick scrub and restowed the handkerchief to seize her hands once more. 'Any mother.'

He dropped her hands, discarded them, left them to their own devices. His face was bearded, his shoulders sloped. He changed tack. 'No strings and no connections, no ties to my affections,' he crooned, a smile vacuous as Fred Astaire's leering at her through his beard. 'Why can't every mother see that,' he demanded, 'instead of lumbering us all with loads of shitty guilt?'

'Mine didn't.'

'I must meet her.' The egg-shaped head dipped. 'Bernard Long. School Publications.'

'You're a poet.'

'Well *done*.'

'My husband's a fan of yours. He knows your stuff by heart.'

'That pleases me. Thank you.' His shoulders straightened, he glanced about him, a furry animal sunning itself outside a burrow. 'Manna,' he said. 'Manna to the ears, if you follow me. And what about Hardy?' His face darkened. 'What does he think of Hardy, your husband? His poetry, of course.'

'He likes him.'

'Good. Good.' He glanced around the crowded room once more. 'I must meet him too. Even before your mother.'

'He's not here, but he's starting work with School Publications when he gets back from a tangi.'

Bernard Long's hands sprang apart, fingers stretched in excitement. 'Not a Maori fan!'

She shook her head, smiling in commiseration. 'A friend of ours has died in Hawke's Bay.'

'Ah,' he said, 'the Bay. That explains it. You come from the Bay.' She nodded.

Albert Belisle and Jane had disappeared. There was music. People—unknown, interesting people—were dancing.

'Sarah!' The voice achieved delight and astonishment in the one word. Charles embraced her. They stared at each other. They were pleased to meet.

Bernard Long's small hands were scrabbling at Charles's waist beneath the overhang of his cotton shirt. Charles, startled, clutched his belt. Bernard, still burrowing, dragged the buckle into view. 'What a magnificent thing!' His lips, made pinker by the proximity of his black beard, pouted in petulant envy. 'Where did you get such a thing? Here, for God's sake?' His eyes narrowed. 'Overseas?'

The oval buckle was black enamel rimmed with gold. The words Harley Davidson were also in gold. The wide tongue of the belt hung across Charles's body. 'I made it from an old advertising thing I found in a junk shop.' Charles undid the buckle, his hands demonstrated the reverse side, how it was attached to the leather belt.

Bernard was hopping with excitement. 'I'll buy it. Name your price! Prices.'

'No.'

'It's so fucken sexy,' moaned Bernard.

When Charles laughed, which was less often than a lot of people, the rumbling mirth welled up from below. It was a large laugh, which took some time in coming.

Hubert appeared at Sarah's side, touched her arm. 'Your baby,' he said, 'is weeping.'

'Oh, thank you.' Sarah turned to follow her host, who was not larger than life and probably never had been.

'I'll come too,' said Charles, detaching Bernard from his belt with difficulty.

'I'm going to feed her,' said Sarah.

No other living soul had a smile like that.

'I don't mind.'

She acknowledged the mini-joke with a movement of her head. Strands of hair fell about her face as she laughed. 'What would your father say?' The outraged moustache, the enraged popping eyes appeared before them. Charles lifted her hand and held it.

The party grew better and better. 'Clara's parties,' Otto had told her, 'are a bang.'

People danced in the dining room, talked in the living room, listened to Beethoven quartets in Hubert's study. Clara dispensed white plates piled with sauerkraut, unexpected sausages and sharp pickles. There was bread made by Clara, chocolate truffles made by Clara, strong black coffee brewed by Clara. Clara sang lieder by Schubert, she told them. She was cheerful and relaxed, doing what she was designed to do, being larger than life and making people happy through planning, hard work and sheer insistence. There was no sense of struggle, no martyrdom. Her hair collapsed to one side. She was having a ball. She directed people, dark intense people and lazy people, carefree people and people virtually unknown to her, to eat their food seated on the stairs—why not?—to fill their glasses, see, see, there is more. Much more.

It was a beautiful night. You could see the lights of the city traffic, the Hutt, the western hills. The stars. Charles and Sarah sat side by side on the balcony as they ate, their legs stretched in front of them, their eyes bright. They smiled at each other, conspirators who had infiltrated, God's spies on duty at an interesting assignment, their ears straining to eavesdrop on each of the conversations which ricocheted around them.

A small woman with eyes red-rimmed and round as a herring gull's was insisting to a man in a cardigan, 'I have never heard of a woman psychiatrist sleeping with a male patient. Never! The reverse, yes, certainly. Many, many cases I have known.'

The man's reply was drowned by a higher voice from a man

with a ginger moustache. 'That was his trouble!' he cried. 'He could've been right up there,' he demonstrated, one hand ascending layers of strata. 'Top, top, top! But he liked the boys and the good life and that's what he got.'

'Then he was lucky,' replied a woman in black. She shoved her long hair back with fingers sinuous as a Balinese dancer's, the nails sharp and pointed.

The moustache dipped in acknowledgement. 'Ja, ja, but the war is over now. I mean. Top, top, top! World class he could've been and . . .' The hand chopped, undercut. 'Pff!'

The woman's hands slammed together at the base of the palms and sprang apart. 'He is alive! Let him live his good life!'

'No,' cried the moustache. 'No. That is *why*. It is *because* he survived that he should insist on excellence.'

Olga was being adamant about Cio-Cio-San. 'So many people get her wrong,' she insisted to a large man covered in cigarette ash. 'They think her kindness and gentleness is weakness. It is power! That is her strength.'

They argued about gramophone equipment, became heated about Thomas Mann, Nijinsky, Schumann, synchronicity. A woman in emerald green had tracked down a small butcher who made salami in Johnsonville. 'We must support him,' she insisted. 'All of us. Otherwise he will sink.' She paused. 'He has several varieties already.'

'Kosher?' asked an anxious man with spectacles.

Her large shoulders shrugged. 'Ask him, Simon. Ask him yourself.'

Jane, followed by the chestnut-haired Albert, tripped over Sarah's feet. 'Where ever have you been?' she cried. She leant forward, one hand on Sarah's shoulder to steady herself. Her grip tightened. 'Charles!' She handed Albert over to Sarah on a plate and sank down beside Charles. Sarah rubbed her shoulder. She wondered if she was slightly drunk. She gave a loud burp and beamed up at Albert. 'What a bit of luck I've fed Dora.'

'Pardon?' He was all attention, undeterred, in fact pleased by the unexpected change of partner.

They danced in the dining room, slinking and sliding, their thighs locked together in propinquity undreamt of at the Assembly Hall of the Hastings Municipal Buildings. I need more of this, decided Sarah. I am sorry Jack is missing it. He would have liked the people. But he can't dance and I can and I find it agreeable.

It was even more agreeable dancing with Charles, who must have had lessons or something. Or perhaps he had just relaxed when he got away from Prudie's list of girls to be danced with. That was it. They smiled at each other.

Otto came tramping across the floor in pursuit of her and Jane, navigating with difficulty between entwined couples with their heads thrown back. 'Sarah,' he cried. 'Girls! Now we must go. Olga is waiting to drive us home.'

'If I had a rose from you, For every time you made me blue, I'd have a room full of roses,' sobbed the gramophone.

'This noise,' moaned Otto. 'This horrible, horrible noise.'

He clapped his hands. 'Now. Now we go. It is already one a.m.'

Albert was distraught. 'They can't go now! The night,' he whimpered unexpectedly, 'is a pup.'

A woman with lipstick painted on with a brush nodded her head in agreement. She and her partner swung into a complicated manoeuvre of dips and slides which beached them against the sideboard against the opposite wall. The food had been served from Clara's kitchen.

'I'll take them home,' Charles said to Otto. Albert and Sarah, Jane, Charles and Otto formed an island; an island lapped by drifts of tango and tides of dance.

'You are not her husband,' Otto huffed at Charles, moving his left leg in the nick of time to avoid a sideways swipe from a three-inch heel. 'You are not either of their husbands.'

Jane's hand had not moved from Charles's arm. 'He is a very old friend,' she murmured.

'Our mothers nursed together,' cried Sarah, her wish to stay at the party and ride home in Charles's pumpkin coach transcending sense. 'In Hawke's Bay.'

Otto bowed and retreated amid smiles and waves. The party

rolled on, inexorably, wonderfully and for a very long time. Eventually Albert was dumped at home in Thorndon.

Charles drove around the harbour at four a.m. very, very carefully. Sarah lay in the back with Dora in her arms. Jane's head was on Charles's shoulder. He escorted her up the librarian's drive and ran down again, jumping in giant leaps across the dark asphalt.

Sarah and the baby were both asleep.

He woke her when they arrived at the cottage, stroking her face with one finger. She blinked and surfaced with reluctance. 'Thank heavens you didn't go "boo",' she yawned. 'I can't stand "boos".' She looked around her. 'Oh shit,' she murmured and began the organisational regrouping required. Charles took Dora from her arms, the key from her hand and headed up the track through the ice plant. The flowers were closed, their tentacles folded inwards like threatened sea anemones. Sarah trailed behind him clutching the carrycot, an old Chinese shawl of Laura's tugged around her shivering body. 'The thing about babies,' she told his back, 'is that they're always there. They never shove off.'

Charles said nothing but handed Dora to her, unlocked the door and gave it its obligatory shove with his shoulder.

The place smelt as uninviting as usual after an absence of some hours; traces of damp and whiffs of gas filled the air. Charles stared down at them both, his face unhappy. 'Will you be all right?'

Sarah grinned up at him. 'Of course.'

Dora was now awake. She gazed around the room with interest, wide-eyed as a daisy and ready for action. 'Go to sleep,' Charles told her. He embraced them both, kissed Sarah and departed quickly. His feet squashed the ice plant. *All I want is here. All I want in the world, sweet Christ, lies in this dump.*

Sarah was in bed twenty minutes later when the ding-dong doorbell sounded. She was not alarmed. She wrapped the Chinese shawl over her nightgown with blue forget-me-nots on it, crept past Dora, who was asleep in her cot in the living room, and tugged open the door.

Charles stood backed by ice plant, his feet close together, his arms by his sides. His face was unsmiling as he held up one hand to display his car keys. 'The car's conked out,' he said. 'Just round the corner.'

The corners of her mouth lifted. 'By "Penguins Crossing"?'

He smiled back at her. Vertical lines appeared either side of his mouth. 'Yes.'

Sarah tugged the shawl tight. 'I believe you,' she said. 'Come in.'

7

The office where Jack was interviewed for the job with School Publications was small and tidy. Two dim prints of English countryside depicted in watercolours so delicate as to be practically invisible hung either side of the woman's desk. Jack sat before her. His hands, to his surprise, were sweaty.

The Editor glanced at his application. 'You're very young for the job, Mr Macalister,' she said. 'Only twenty?'

Jack gave a slight cough. He wasn't quite. 'Yes.'

'A proofreader at School Publications, you see,' her eyes were steady above half-moon spectacles, 'is expected to understand, even evaluate the work. It's not just correction of mistakes.'

Jack's behind moved on the hard chair, a small self-congratulatory wriggle. 'I can do that. My English is very good.'

'Yes. Yes, I see that. And so are your testimonials.' She picked up the Headmaster's and Miss Smith's hand-written one from her desk and held them in both hands. 'And you write yourself?'

'Yes.'

Her smile broadened. 'We have several writers here. The poet Bernard Long for example.'

Jack nodded. 'I know.'

There was a small cactus in a pot on her desk. Someone (the Editor herself?) had pinned two round black cardboard eyes in position. It looked debauched, an irresponsible cactus letting the side down.

'I think,' said the Editor of School Publications some time later, after they had discussed salary and conditions, 'that we should give you the job. Proofreader and librarian it is, Mr Macalister. I'm sure you'll do very well.'

Jack's face crumpled with relief. He beamed at her, loving this wise ex-Principal, her small office, her drunken cactus. The prospect of no more shitty woolstores, of a world of words and books, smiled down on him. He looked at the unaccustomed shine on the toe of his boot, saw it nudging an opening door. He stood up and reached for his hat.

'Thank you,' he said. 'Thank you very much.'

'You come from Hawke's Bay?' said his beautiful middle-aged saviour.

He didn't remember putting that on the application.

She shook her head, smiling at his surprise. 'No, no. I recognise the pork-pie hat. I taught there for many years.'

'Oh,' said Jack and left. He loped down the corridor, jumped down three flights of stairs two at a time and tossed his hat beneath a bus thundering along Customhouse Quay.

'I don't want to talk about it yet,' he said to Sarah when she asked him about Ernie's tangi on his return from the Bay the night after the party.

Normally she would have put her arms around him, comforted the man, grieved for Ernie and her absence from his tangi.

I am a slut and I am not good at deception. 'Charles stayed here last night,' she said.

Jack glanced up from his tea mug, his blank eyes still focused on the carved face, the open coffin, the sound of the women wailing.

She told him about the party, how she was sorry he had had to miss it, how he would have loved the people. How Bernard Long looked forward to meeting him. How Charles had driven them home and the car had gone phut at 'Penguins Crossing' and he had come back and stayed the night.

He took a long swig of milky tea. 'How did he like the cat pee?'

Her head was down, her hands busy as she folded the dry washing. 'He didn't make any objection.'

'Good on him.' He stood up and pulled her hair back from her face with both hands. 'Good old Charlie,' he said. 'He told me about School Pubs, remember?'

She twisted her head. 'Stop calling him old Charlie. You'll be calling him old young Charlie in a minute. Like your father. "I saw old young Bailey at the yards."'

He gave her head a quick tug back into position. 'And how about Jane?'

'She's all right. She's coming for a meal tomorrow night.'

He nodded. 'Charlie fucked her yet?'

'Don't say that!'

What does it matter, saying it? I am not only a slut, I am a phoney slut.

Jack stretched his arms to the dirty ceiling. 'I'll have to give him a few lessons.'

Shame and rage engulfed her. 'Oh shut up! You cocky little . . . !' She fought her way up, her hands beating against tides of anger to release her trapped hair. 'What are you!'

'I'm a writer.'

'Well, you don't sound like one.'

'You don't have to sound like one.' He kissed her mouth. 'That's the whole point.'

He was happy with the new job. Some of the stuff was pretty boring, especially some of the Bulletins—*The Dairy Farm, Our Timber Industry, Our Coal Mines*—but what could anyone do with that sort of thing? Proofreading was pretty mechanical but he was good at it.

'And a lot of the writing is excellent,' he said in surprise. 'Even some of the Bulletins. They're keen to get away from all that bluebells and pirates and pantomimes crap we had in the Journals. They want to have stories about here, for Maori kids as well as Pakeha. About things we know.' He paused. 'The library's full of New Zealand books, imagine. Bernard Long says our Englishness hangs over us like a pall. They're great guys the lot of them.'

'And the women?'

'They're all right. The boss is a woman. I told you.'

She nodded.

'I mean there aren't any women inspectors and hardly any women principals in schools even,' he continued.

'And what's Bernard Long like?'

'Great guy. Bit of a boozer. Talk! He's mad about Kafka. "Any conversation that is not about literature bores me." How about that? In the tearoom.'

Sarah stared out the small salt-stained window at the bus shelter across the road. An old Maori woman seated on the bench removed one white shoe, shook it, peered in it, felt in it with outstretched fingers, replaced it and stared straight ahead, both hands clutching her kete. The rain poured down.

'Mmn,' said Sarah. 'I'd better get Dora.'

'Where is she?'

'In the coalshed.'

He glanced at her through mists of Kafka. 'What?'

'She was in the pram and I wheeled her into the coalshed when it started to rain.'

'Why not in here?'

'I was working and she was asleep.'

Dora lay talking to herself in the dark. She welcomed Sarah with outstretched arms. 'I'm not going to start getting guilty,' Sarah told her. 'About anything. OK?'

Dora's eyes were round. She emanated slight whiffs of coal dust like Linda Barr's husband Owen.

'Men don't feel guilty,' Sarah told her firmly.

Dora peered back at her from beneath a white knitted cap which Jack said made her look a dead ringer for the Pope.

Which is one of the reasons I like him. He is unexpected and irreverent. And I don't know what he is going to say.

I know what Charles is going to say. I have loved you since I was ten years old. I will love you till I die.

'We could ask old Charlie, if Jane's coming tomorrow,' said Jack later in a pause from chewing his way through sausages anointed with carrots and garnished with reconstituted peas.

Sarah banged her fist against the end of the tomato sauce bottle

121

and was punished by excess. 'If you're a writer you should listen to what you say. Old Charlie!'

'I'm demotic. I refuse to be crippled by expectations of failure.' He glanced at her. 'And I'm good in bed.'

She had nothing to say.

After a pause he dabbed one exploratory finger at the corner of her left eye then licked it. 'What's up?'

Her head was bent. 'I'm a bitch,' she muttered. He shoved his stool backwards, grating against the uneven tiles of the mini-kitchen.

'What the hell? Why wait till now to decide?' He held out one hand.

She shook her head. 'Don't be nice to me,' she muttered, the words so soft he could scarcely hear.

'How are you going to paint all this stuff, all this colour and light you say you want to paint? How can you paint that if you hate yourself?'

Her eyes were huge and dark.

Jack folded his arms, stretched and aired a new word he'd heard last week in the tearoom. 'It's probably,' he said, 'something to do with menstruation.'

Her laugh was a hopeless noisy hiccough. 'Where on earth . . . ?'

But he was bored with the subject, finished with the word. 'Any more food anywhere?'

She shoved her plate with its abandoned curve of sausage, its half-eaten potato and hectic peas across the tiny formica table. 'I don't want it.'

'Thanks.'

Grease slid down the sausage casing in tiny runnels as his fork stabbed.

'Dougal'll be here too,' said Sarah suddenly.

He was still munching with enthusiasm. 'What?'

'Tomorrow night.' Sarah sat up straight. 'I'll get some fish from the fish lady.' She was now an incipient hostess, her angst evaporated for the moment. Jack watched her with interest, noting the sudden swing of mood for future use. He was having trouble with his heroine.

'He wants the sofa tomorrow night,' continued Sarah. 'I had a card yesterday. He's on his way to North Otago to work for the Potters.'

There was no need to elucidate. Jack knew about the Potters. The Potters were North Otago and North Otago was the Potters. The family owned many thousands of acres of good sheep-grazing country and had done so for almost a hundred years. Fifty years ago Lookout Station had been self-supporting with its own school, blacksmith and over thirty station hands. The original holding had been divided between Potters and the sons and daughters of Potters who still flourished, buoyed up by the good wool cheques of the fifties. All the Potter men had to do to maintain their desirable existence, muttered disgruntled small run-holders nearby, was to sit on their wide verandahs with a whisky in one hand and watch the wool grow. In fact the Potter men were excellent farmers who worked hard and their wives equally so. If you asked any Potter wife how she was she would invariably respond with a quick smiling intake of breath. 'Busy,' the questioned Mrs Potter would gasp, 'very busy.' Busyness, to a Potter woman of middle age, was both a physiological condition and a state of grace. They cooked and cleaned and sewed and gardened and were endlessly hospitable. Important visitors to New Zealand, if they ventured as far south, invariably lunched with a Potter and often stayed the night. Nobody, except the Potter women themselves, could understand how they coped, which was by working like slaves for a week before the event, to appear gracious and smiling at their own tables, to glance at the superbly orchestrated chicken with faint surprise as if they had never glimpsed it before, let alone disembowelled it and plucked it before moving on to haute cuisine. They were of course always extremely grateful to Mrs Pitt, the head shepherd's wife, who saved the Potter bacon on many occasions by helping out in the kitchen.

Large diamonds in need of cleaning decorated the Potter women's hands, pearls of rare lustre hung around their pleated sun-tanned necks. They went on trips Overseas occasionally but not often because their men hated leaving their farms. They had a lovely time over there but were always glad to get home, to breathe the hill country air and pick their roses barefooted in their nighties before the sun was up. They were no fools, the Potters, and their daughters were more beautiful than the dawn.

Any Potter in London at the time of a Royal Garden Party was invariably presented to the incumbent Sovereign. Penned up for their briefing beforehand, they waited 'with one or two other culls', as Tim Potter muttered to Helen when the Queen advanced unsmiling in pistachio green.

Tim's father had had a new morning suit made for the occasion. The one he had owned since his youth, despite the gusset inserted by his wife in the waistband at the back, was no longer man enough for the job. Grandfather would have been happy to have hired the coat and waistcoat, Tim told his daughters, but he wasn't going to wear another man's trousers.

Dougal was going to work for Tim Potter and knew he was lucky to have the chance.

'Five's too many for the bridge table so we'll have it on our knees OK?' said Sarah.

She's like Mum, thought Dougal, who had never noticed it before; she was bright, smiling, caring for her guests' needs. She avoided Charles's eye and hoped Dora would be good.

She had quite a lot to do and felt hot. She declined a seat beside Charles on the sofa. She insisted Jane sit there, laughing and patting a couple of deceased grey cushions behind her back.

Charles's hands clenched. He was anguished by the loss of her behind beside his, anguished at another rejection. He had begged her to leave Jack after the Bernsteins' party and she had refused. She told him she loved Jack, that she was a tramp; tried to explain, couldn't explain, made love to him with passion and fell asleep. Charles, after an hour staring at the dark and listening to the sea roar, slept beside her, their bodies curved together, till Dora's squeaks announced another day.

Sarah had attempted once more to explain before she fed Dora but it was useless. She would need another piece of paper, another licence, a licence which did not exist. There was no piece of paper which allowed you to love two men, let alone fuck them both. Her lips brushed the pale skin beneath Charles's eyes, which was usually hidden behind glass. He was lost without his spectacles. She kissed the faint white scar high on his right cheek. 'I wanted you,' she said simply. 'When I saw that man's hands at your belt I nearly kicked him out of the way.' His penis dug at her belly as he seized her again and Dora gurgled at the mildewed ceiling next door.

'Leave him!' he shouted. 'Leave the sod. You and Dora. Leave him now.'

'No.' She heaved herself upwards and mopped one leaking breast with her discarded nightgown. 'I told you. I love him. And he doesn't need all of me. He doesn't want it. I don't mean,' her hands sprang apart above the ruined bed, 'this. He'd kill me for this. But I can work, see.'

She jumped out of bed, almost tripping on a trailing sheet as Dora's sudden wail became insistent. 'Coming, Dotty,' she called. 'Hang on.' She came back with Dora already at her breast and climbed in beside him.

It is physical, this ache of longing and self-loathing. 'I'll have to go,' said Charles.

She watched him in silence. You wouldn't do it to a dog, what I have done to this man. 'Wait,' she said. 'Wait. I won't be long.'

He lay back then rolled on one elbow to watch. One finger touched Dora's cheek.

He climbed out of bed later and stumbled into his trousers. 'Wordsworth had a daughter called Dora.'

'Is that right?'

'Yes.'

'I didn't know. I didn't know that.'

Charles wanted to scream in their faces, to shout something wild and dangerous at her across the tiny room. They must know—how could they not know?—his rage, the aching despair of his loss. It was a taste in the mouth, a kick in the groin. He moved his buttocks, Jane rolled nearer. The springs of the sofa had gone and he was heavier.

Jack was now in full cry. He told them about School Pubs. He related a couple of anecdotes about Bernard Long, his poetry, his drinking habits, his generosity of spirit.

'I might get a chance to drive him round the South Island some time. He was talking about it the other day. He doesn't drive but he wants to revisit some of his favourite country pubs. Combine it with a few readings. Only in the main centres of course. University students.' He laughed. 'God knows what they'll make of him.'

'You'd like that?' said Charles, inspecting his thumb nail. He wondered how long Jack had been at the public bar of de Bretts before catching the Eastbourne bus.

'Sure. Wouldn't you?'

'No.'

'Why the hell not?'

'He reminds me of Dad.'

Jack was outraged. His shoulders twitched. 'Your father!'

'They both seem to regard their brains as some sort of sanctuary. If an idea ever gets in no one can attack it. It's sacrosanct.' Charles leant back, wriggled his shoulders against the soggy green of the sofa. Jane watched him. 'Or else they don't think at all,' he continued. 'If something doesn't interest them it doesn't exist. What did Long think of the situation on the wharves last year? Lock-out or a strike?' Charles's face was tight with anger. 'Ask him. Dad, of course, knew it was a commie strike designed to ruin the farmers and topple the government. I'm still fighting him. I remember last New Year's Day at Glenfrae . . .'

There was a pause, quite a long pause, while they remembered last New Year's Day at Glenfrae. Jack glanced at Sarah who had her head down and was busy.

'Why should Bernard think about the bloody wharves if he doesn't want to?' he demanded. 'He's a poet.' Jack drew himself up, the open bottle of beer sweating in his hand. Like most people he was unable to pour and talk at the same time.

'All I want is to find a corner and puddle about in it and write my head off. What's wrong with that?'

'Because you're not going to write about anything that matters.'

'How do you know?'

'Well show me then,' dared Charles, loathing the man's guts, his weasel eyes, his self-sufficiency. 'Show me your stuff.'

Jack's shoulders dropped. His vaunting self-confidence seeped through his fingers on to the dripping bottle. 'Later,' he said.

'It's very good,' said Sarah, avoiding everyone's eyes. Jack had shown her the first draft the day she and Dora came home from the hospital, dumping the MS beside them on the sofa. For the rest of her life Jack Macalister's first novel, the turbulent, aggressive *Ultima Thule*, would be linked in her mind with maternal nourishment and the sleepy contentment of the replete.

Dougal was silent. He had been silent for some time and felt no requirement to say anything. He was small, neat and well put together. 'Built like a nippy little five-eighth,' said Nelson with envy, neither of whose sons had inherited his legendary rugby skills. Nelson had played hooker for the Bay in the twenties, the golden days of Hawke's Bay rugby, when the invincible Magpies took the Ranfurly Shield on tour and the wheels of their supporters' train sang the victor's score all the way home from Wellington: 48–8; 48–8; 48–8.

Dougal leant back on his hard chair, one foot supported sideways against the other knee, the calf and thigh forming a flattened triangle as he inspected the sole of his polo boot with the concentration of someone hunting for a thorn. Attracted by the classic pose, Sarah winked at him. He blushed, wondering if she had guessed his lack of interest, his longing to get down south and begin his life in the real world where the sky was endless and you could stand outside the musterers' hut at black midnight and snatch the stars from the sky. He glanced at Jack's jutting jaw, his flashing eyes. This was the man who'd flagged away a half-share in Glenfrae, one of the sweetest holdings in the Bay.

Dougal yawned a jaw-stretching gulp and groped for his handkerchief. His hand encountered a small jar. He pulled it out from his pocket and inspected it for leaks before handing it to Sarah. 'Mum sent this as well,' he said. 'Horseradish sauce.'

'What a bit of luck,' said Sarah. 'We'll have it with the snapper.' Her eyes blinked at Jack's sulky face and Charles's tight pale one.

'The fish lady's Italian,' she babbled. 'She's a lovely lady. She goes round Eastbourne selling fish and it's so fresh. She's a lovely lady. Italian like I said. All her sons are fishermen, she's got five. Mrs Dossi.'

No one said anything. 'Last week,' cried Sarah, 'during all that rain, she said, "We had the sum. We had him last week."'

Jane swung her right leg once more. Her sandals were bronze-coloured, her feet small, her toes orderly and without blemish. 'Sum?' she said.

'Summer. She meant summer.' Sarah was getting desperate. 'That's why it was so funny. "We had him last week. The sum." That's what she said.'

'Oh.'

'She leaves bits off, see. "Sometimes he full, sometimes he empt," she said the other day when she'd run out and I wanted some hapuka.'

'Italian is jolly difficult,' Jane told her big toe.

'Oh, I'm sure it is. I don't mean that. I couldn't speak a word of it. She says she'll let me draw her soon. She has the most wonderful head!'

Jane was thinking hard. She continued to think when Sarah retreated to cook the snapper and the smell seeped in in fishy waves through the cottage. Jane had decided early in life that there was no sense in having brains if they did not achieve the results you desired. She desired Charles. Charles, she felt, did not desire her as much as he used to. Jane was puzzled by this problem.

Charles, she thought, listening with one ear to a conversation about New Zealand writing to which she would normally have contributed, if not dominated, is serious and intelligent. I wish to marry Charles and sleep with him, to wake beside him each morning. I have no objection to any aspect of the man. His looks have always excited me, especially now. Jane moved slightly, wondering with surprise if she was slightly damp. Likewise his intelligence and I see no impediment in the fact that he is the only son of a wealthy landowner. His seriousness I share, if not his commitment to life's multitudinous underdogs and chronically disadvantaged, but he doesn't need to know that at the moment.

'Did you know,' asked Charles out of nowhere, 'that Wordsworth had a daughter called Dora?'

Jack laughed. 'We'll change it immediately.'

'No,' said Sarah. 'No, we won't.'

'There's a lot of nonsense talked about Wordsworth,' said Jane, rolling slightly towards Charles.

He glanced at her new proximity but didn't move. 'In what way?'

'In every way,' yelled Jack and they were away again, the three of them, the men shouting, Jane calm. Dougal, completely excluded, watched unperturbed from the shore as they floated out to sea on an ice floe of words.

Sarah stuck her head round the door. 'Come and give me a hand, Doug.'

Dougal relaxed in the little hutch of a kitchen. He passed things, told her news of their parents, especially Laura, all the gossip from the Bay. They were happy together. Dougal gave a quick backwards chuck of his head. 'Do they go on like this all the time?'

'Not often.' Sarah felt a quick stab of affection for him, his compact body which had once been so clumsy, his unclouded eyes. She felt very old.

'You'll have a great time down south, Doug.'

'I hope. Yeah. But I'm not a cadet or anything, just a shepherd. Hard yakker for a thousand years and eventually a manager's job if I'm lucky.'

'Still.' She shoved the fish-laden plates at him in turn. 'Here. Deal them round, would you?' She grabbed a pot of mashed potatoes from the stove. 'I'm coming. Where's the horseradish?'

Dougal beamed at her, a steaming plate in each hand, glad that one person in the place had some sense. 'Yeah,' he said. 'Still.' He turned at the doorway. 'Are you still painting and that, Sal?'

They were now onto Dorothy Wordsworth's devotion to her brother. '"We walked,"' mocked Jack. '"William composed." What a sweet life.'

'Why shouldn't he compose?' demanded Charles. 'That's what William was for.'

'But what about Dorothy?' demanded Jane. 'What about her life?'

Charles was irritated and showed it. 'What about her? She loved him. Admired him, worshipped his art. What's wrong with that?'

'I would've expected better than that from you,' she laughed, accepting her snapper from Dougal with a nod.

Charles's eyes were grey. Dark grey. 'In what way?'

'I would've thought an intelligent man like you would understand.' Her hair swung as she moved her head, teasing, following her argument away from him, dancing beyond his reach.

Her hair was rather a beautiful colour, shiny as a new-peeled chestnut. Charles held out his hand, palm upwards. 'I don't. Tell me.'

Revelation descended upon Jane, a mantle of wisdom slid about her shoulders. He would never give up anything until he understood it. His passionate desire to know, to understand things that most people have always known or can't be bothered finding out, would include her. Jane placed one small hand on his leg.

Charles watched it. It seemed to have no weight, this hand, to have drifted down to rest upon his thigh through mere lack of updraught. He found it agreeable, this gentle thing which had come to rest upon his person.

'Tell me,' he said again.

Her teeth were white and even. She dared him to disagree. 'No one should devote herself, body and soul, to providing a serene environment for genius to thrive in. Any genius.'

Jack and Sarah were watching each move. Dougal, who had

almost finished his fish, stretched an arm across the sofa for more horseradish. He quite liked it with mashed potatoes.

'Why not?' Charles looked genuinely puzzled. 'If that's what she wants to do.'

Jane was certain. 'She shouldn't want to do that. To live vicariously.'

'A cop-out you mean?' asked Jack.

'I have no intention of dwindling into a wife,' said Sarah.

Jane acknowledged the quotation and the back-up from her best friend with a quick dip of her head.

'What if it was a man?' said Charles. 'A man devoting his life to a woman of genius?'

Jane's laugh was merry. 'Name me three.'

'I'll work on it.'

'Do that. And let me know.'

'Yes, yes I will.' Something seemed slightly easier. The tight band of loss and self-hatred around his chest had slackened slightly. Charles saw Granny Bremner's tiny body in the deck chair beneath the pepper tree in Hastings. Heard her describing how she had felt as a young girl when she had unlaced her whalebones. 'It was an expansion of the soul, Charles,' she said. 'A beautiful easing. I had the same feeling when your uncles came home safe from the war.'

'How long are you staying?' asked Charles.

'Till Monday.'

Jack winked at Sarah who turned away.

Jack slammed his hands down on his thighs and sprang to his feet. 'Did I tell you I've finished the final draft of *Ultima Thule*?'

Surprise and enthusiasm were expressed. Dougal shook Jack's hand.

Sarah was also on her feet, seizing plates, sliding them together, moving with speed and grace and hidden panic.

'Isn't it great?' she said. 'And I'm working towards a solo exhibition. Mr Becker says he's sure the lady at the coffee shop in Eastbourne will leap at it. Mrs Staunton her name is.'

Dougal was shocked. What a pair of skites.

8

Dougal's marriage to Tim Potter's eldest daughter Felicity surprised no one. Tim had no sons and it was a suitable match. He had eyed Dougal through the venetian blind in his office the day the new hand first climbed from the truck five years ago. Tim was noted for his stockman's eye, his ability to pick quality. What's bred in the bone . . . Tim couldn't remember the rest but it didn't matter. Dougal fulfilled his early expectations; hard-working, decent, he would do for Flicka. They were married in 1957. And less than a year later his sister Sybil did equally well for Tim's nephew, a large friendly Potter with the spring-heeled lope and alert puzzled expression of a boxer pup. Humphrey Potter's father, before he was killed at Alamein, had farmed a skelp of the original Lookout Point land beside Tim. His son had recently taken over the farm from the manager and was in want of a wife. He met Sybil when she was eighteen, a bridesmaid at her brother's wedding. She enchanted him, she was so pretty and so happy and so funny and so adorable. The strength of his passion surprised him, he'd never been much of a one for girls. But she wouldn't, not till they were married. Humphrey quite understood but the months of waiting till the house was ready were torment. He masturbated nightly and writhed with shame. Their wedding night astonished them both.

Jack was not pleased at the news of Sybil's engagement.

He looked up from Dora's adding game (Dora was not good at numbers) as Sarah put down the telephone. 'Oh God! Now there'll be dozens of boring little Sybs and Humphs and Humphs and

Sybs. They'll be one hundred per cent fecund. Start a dynasty, two dynasties. What a thought. What a balls-aching thought!'

He held up a plastic 2 and a 4. 'How much is four and two?' he asked Dora. Doubt engulfed her, creased her forehead and squeezed her eyes shut. 'Six, honey. See it's six.' Jack held it up. 'Six. Like you.' He glanced at Sarah, who was scrubbing potatoes above his head. 'I know what he'll give her for a wedding present. A phial of his champion bull's semen so she can start her own stud.'

Sarah ignored him. 'Aunt Sybil wants you to be a flower girl, Dotty. How about that?'

'White gloves!' yelped Dora.

'Jesus Christ.'

Sarah flapped an anti-profanity hand.

Dora leapt up from the table, tugging at Sarah's skirt. 'And pink eh Mum, pink frock and pink shoes and . . .'

'You bet your sweet life you'll be pink. The whole flaming thing'll be pink. It'll be pink from here to Wanaka, it'll be the pinkest fucken thing you've ever seen,' snarled her father.

Sarah glanced at him. He had always been dismissive of the values of their mutual relatives, reducing their inability to lie to naivety, their compulsive work habits to neurosis; but lately his acerbity had increased, his wit lessened. And what did he offer instead of solid virtue? Freedom, of course. Sarah, whose work was going well and who had every intention of leaving her husband to mind Dora for a few days while she went to see some pictures, put her hand on his groin. He grabbed the hand, startled. Lust and work. A beautiful combination. The only combination in the world.

Ultima Thule was still unpublished. Five years of rejection slips lay in a drawer of Jack's office alongside the MS of his almost finished second novel. He had tried to make it more conventional, accessible was the word editors used, but it kept taking off, delighting him and alarming them.

People tried to help him; intelligent, serious men and women who recognised his ability and wanted him to succeed invited him to stay in their houses and talked with him through the night, begging him to let them help him. 'Unpublishable,' they said. 'In its present form. Completely unpublishable. But the talent is there.'

After a few years Jack stopped accepting their invitations. He could no longer think of anything to say. He had no words to make them understand, to explain that even if he allowed any changes, which he wouldn't, there was still no solution. He didn't know how to change it. Hell yes, of course he wanted to be published, but he didn't see how he could write any other way and say what he wished to say in the words he wished to use, couldn't they understand? He could no more alter the way he wrote than change the colour of his skin, add a cubit to his stature, all the rest of it. As they tried harder he felt more trapped, more inadequate at not being able to help them achieve what they all, including apparently a waiting world, wanted. He retreated to subterfuge, to hopeful lies. Absolutely. Yes, yes. Certainly he'd try and rewrite it. He saw exactly what they meant. Anything as long as they would shut up and leave him alone. Their helpful words clanged in his hollow head. He felt phoney, as devious as Oscar Wilde locked in his cell with his square of blue sky, telling lies day after day to his elderly solicitor.

Jack declined their invitations. He thanked them all for their help. He would put the book away for a while.

'Like Titian,' said Sarah, tugging on her secondhand boots.

'What?' It irritated him, the way she could always punt up some painter in response to any statement he made about his writing.

'That's what he did. He'd turn the canvas to the wall for months before looking at it again. Gave it time to cook.'

'I do look at it. I look at it all the time. And it's good.'

Otto and Olga's newest plan was ambitious. They were travelling to Auckland by car to see an exhibition of paintings from the collections of Charles Brasch and Rodney Kennedy, Olga driving as usual. They would be away four days, staying in Takapuna with friends.

'You must come,' cried Otto. 'You must see this man McCahon. Mrs Dossi,' he waved a carefree hand, 'will mind Dora after school till Jack gets home.' Sarah's toes clenched. As a child her double-jointed toes had been an indicator of delight and still were. 'Where could I stay?'

'Charles and Jane live in Takapuna, do they not?'

'Yes. No.'

Otto looked at her but did not pursue the subject. 'Nevertheless you must see them. This man's pictures.'

Otto and Olga were cordial to Jack but puzzled by him. Did he not know how talented his wife was? They discussed the matter often and in some detail. Perhaps he didn't. That would explain his lack of insistence that she see good paintings whenever possible. But then, had Olga considered, Jack was only twenty-five. No more. Perhaps later, would he not become more aware of his wife's remarkable talent? As he became more mature? More rounded? Olga doubted it. 'People are the people they are by the time they are twenty,' she announced. 'They just become more so.'

Sarah described the plan the following evening. 'Otto and Olga have offered me a drive to Auckland. Otto wants me to see this man McCahon he's so keen about. See his work.'

Jack held up a 3 but Dora had retreated into a pink haze of excitement since last night's telephone call and refused to play.

'Is he any good?'

'Very. I've never seen Otto so excited. And Olga.'

Jack didn't care about Olga. He held up a 4. No one took any notice. 'Who's going to mind Dora?'

'Mrs Dossi and you.'

His defeated smile was endearing. 'OK.'

'But the thing is,' Sarah continued, 'I've nowhere to stay.'

'Charles and Jane.'

She changed the subject. 'Otto thinks I should work towards an exhibition.'

'Uh huh.' His hand tightened on the red plastic number. 'I had a letter from Charlie this morning. He's read *Ultima Thule* again. He's sent me the money for the air fare to Auckland next week to

135

discuss it. Baron bloody Bremner.' His hand opened. The point of the 4 had marked his palm. 'He's bought out the man in Totara Press.' Jack sucked his palm, his eyes careful, staring at her above his hand. 'God, it'd be great to have money like Charlie.'

'But that's great! That he wants to read it again.' I can stay with them if Jack's there. Mrs Dossi won't mind. I can *go*.

'It doesn't mean anything.'

'It does. It will. He's always liked it.'

'You could come too. He'd pay for you.'

'No. I'll go with the Beckers. Share the driving with Olga.'

He shrugged. 'Just a thought.'

Charles respected his wife, he always had. He liked Jane's quickness, her ability to cut through, to get there, to spike the severed head of her opponent before he'd felt the blade. Jane's combination of advance and retreat, of warmth and cool pleased and satisfied him. He was proud of her intellect. Her depth. She was well read. Conversant with different cultures. She seemed to take both the present and the past personally; East and West alike were her stamping ground. Sarah would have expected such range to have made her more tolerant, but a fool, of no matter what persuasion, was still a fool to Jane. Regrettable, and to be treated with tact if possible, but still a fool.

She was a source of life to Charles and only occasionally of disappointment; for example when he expounded on the rift between the industrial and political wings of the labour movement and she looked at him blankly. Her lack of concern at the Labour Government's suicidal 1958 Black Budget depressed him.

Charles knew that although women liked him, men like Jack (and God knows what he meant by that) thought him a dull dog. Jane un-dulled him. She wouldn't have a dull dog in the house. Charles had put away his ache for Sarah. It was wrapped up, put away and forgotten.

Charles and Jane had lived together for some time before their wedding, which was a simple ceremony. Prudie, scrupulously polite, her heart awash with grief, made conversation to the guests at the reception at the Hawke's Bay East Coast Aero Club. Frank Bremner drank steadily. The Atwoods beamed on one and all. Jane had done the right thing again. The bowling club's reaction danced before Cyril Atwood's eyes. 'Jane's a doctor now. No, no. English, ha ha, English. Married a Bremner, one of the Waikeri lot.'

Jane offered her husband an asparagus roll after the speeches. 'No thank you, darling,' said Charles.

Sarah and Jack sent their wedding gift, a large pottery platter, up by Newmans. They couldn't get away at the last moment. Unfortunately.

Jack and Sarah had not seen their gift since they sent it off three years ago. Tonight they had admired it with the discerning eyes of the ex-donor. The platter, a strong piece now aglow with persimmons, sat on a pine table overlooking the beach at Takapuna.

Charles and Jane had both been pressing in their enthusiasm. Of course the Macalisters must stay with them. Apart from anything else they hadn't seen the house yet.

Charles had bought the section with money inherited from Granny Bremner when he first moved to Auckland to work for Totara Press. He chose a Group architect. A long, low wooden house crouched on the cliff staring at Rangitoto across the channel. 'Why don't you cut down the pines?' people asked. 'They break up the view of the sea.' At first Jane thought she would have to wear dark glasses inside, but her eyes became accustomed to the dazzle. They were proud of their house and stood unsmiling at the top of the steps, Jane's hand on Charles's shoulder, as their guests clambered from their cars below them. There were no children and they had begun collecting New Zealand art early.

Charles handed the manuscript of *Ultima Thule* to Jack, who lay slumped on the leather sofa, his head cushioned by kilim. 'I'll take it,' he said. 'I want to publish it.'

'As it is?'

'Yes.'

Jack's heart began beating again. Steady, sure, pumping away for ever. 'Great!'

He stared up at his host's thin face, the glasses, the dark shirt. A few more years and he'll look like a clapped-out old missionary. All he'll need is one of those hats.

'I've always wanted to publish it. You know that. I can now that I'm a free agent.'

Jane's eyes slipped from one face to the other. 'I think it's excellent.'

She'd read it too, had she?

'So do I,' said Sarah. She had said little all evening.

Jane expounded about *Ultima Thule* at some length. Jack wondered what she was on about. Redemption figures, expiation imagery, phallic symbolism dripped from her lips. A white breast gleamed as she moved. She must have one of those push up half-bras. Yes, she had.

'Tell me about the sexual symbolism,' he said.

'Well it's so obvious, isn't it.' She offered her sacrificial throat, her head back. Jack had often wondered about her. He was still wondering.

'Not to me, it isn't.'

'All those towers. Lighthouses.'

'They *go* to a lighthouse.'

Jane smiled.

'Even Freud said that a cigar is sometimes merely a cigar,' said Sarah. 'I read it somewhere.'

'It won't make any money, of course,' said Charles.

'Oh, I know that,' said Jack, his gut tightening with disappointment, his smile bleak.

Charles watched him. He did know what he meant by men like Jack. They are rare in New Zealand. Men like Jack hide behind hedges while some other fool changes the wheel of their girlfriend's car, then reappear in time to be sighted by the departing deliverer. That is part of the fun. Charles smiled. A wry smile, but still a smile. It didn't matter. *Ultima Thule* must be published. He jumped to his feet. His wife's hair gleamed in the spot which lit a pale cubist study of blues and greens and pale ochres. His feet were loud on the polished rimu.

'Let's have a drink,' he said. 'To celebrate. A brandy?'

Jack was pleased. 'Thanks.'

Charles dropped to his heels, one hand groping at the back of the cupboard in the kauri sideboard. He swivelled on one heel, squatting with the brandy bottle in his hand. 'It's time we asked Mum to come and stay.'

'I don't get the connection,' said Jane.

Charles stood up, his face stern. Worse, far worse, than Jane's lack of interest in the Labour Party was her condescension towards Prudie.

Jack was still deep in the sofa, looking forward to his brandy. He watched as Charles poured, lifted the glass, a balloon for God's sake, and poured again. He felt expansive. 'How's your old man?'

'I don't know,' said Charles, handing him his drink. There was a pause. The brandy in Jack's glass moved, tawny and filled with light.

'Look what I found!' Jane was on her feet, head down, her hands groping in a vast fold-over bag. She extracted a magazine and waved it at them. *Decor New Zealand* screamed the title above the white painted furniture, the tiles, the canvas umbrella, the spikey pot plants and the sea. 'Someone left it on the ferry.' She riffled the pages. 'Listen to this. "Sybil and Humphrey Potter's North Otago dream house." This is the best bit.' The tip of Jane's tongue flicked her lips and disappeared. '"The lounge. Here soft pink reigns supreme. Sybil prefers the use of single colours through the living areas of a home. She saves her dramatic statement for the bathroom or perhaps a dining room."'

Jane tossed the thing at Sarah in triumph. Sarah's smile was uneasy. I have slept with your husband, though he wasn't then, therefore I can no longer laugh at my sister with you. I trust you understand this, because I don't. She sighed.

Jack picked up the magazine from her lap, scanned it briefly and dropped his head in his hands.

Charles's eyes were on Sarah. He understands my loyalty to Sybil, if you can call it that. How extraordinary. And he approves. Sarah stared at her elderly boots. 'I'm looking forward to tomorrow,' she said, 'seeing the pictures. Tell me about them. The McCahons. How many are there?'

'About seven, I think.' Charles reached for his briefcase beside the sofa, fiddled about till it opened and handed her the catalogue. 'Yes, seven. Keep it. I'll get another.'

'No, no. But I'd like to borrow it tonight. What'd you think of them?'

'I liked them.'

Sarah smiled into his eyes. How typical of you. How restrained, how honest you are. But not phlegmatic. It is not that. You have not yet worked out this man. Possibly, my love, you never will. But you are working on it. You like his work. You have just said so.

'Which ones did you like best?'

'The two kauri ones. See here.' He wriggled nearer so that they could share the catalogue. 'He talks somewhere about "something logical, orderly and beautiful belonging to the land and yet not to its peoples". OK, you can see the cubist influence but . . .' Charles's head moved in admiration. 'A visionary.'

She nodded.

'You're going in the morning?' he asked.

'Yes.'

'I'll meet you for lunch. Check your reaction.'

'I'll be with the Beckers.'

'Ah. Ah yes.' He stowed the catalogue away in disgust, then remembered she wanted it and removed it again. 'Yes of course.' The briefcase snapped shut. 'I'll have to wait, then.'

There was no point in suggesting he joined them.

'It's very kind of you to have us. And to publish the book. It's so lovely here,' bleated Sarah. Worse and worse. The only comment was silence.

Charles stood, drank a mouthful of brandy. Swigged it in fact. 'How's your own painting?'

She stared up at him. Far above her, his face in shadow, he waited.

'Quite well, thank you. Yes. I mean, yes. Good.' What on earth is the matter with me.

'I'd like to see what you're doing next time I'm down.'

Jack was on his feet, his brandy finished, his attempt at stifling a yawn half-hearted. 'Bed,' he said. 'Come on, Sarah.'

Bernard Long was in full cry in the tearoom. 'Of course you've got no conception of what things were like then. We existed on a shoe string!' He flipped a dismissive hand at the tea urn, the white cups, the wobbly table. 'This is positive decadence.' He leant forward, his beard jutting at Jack. 'Do you know, when I started at the Correspondence School we had to do our own birdcalls for radio?'

Jack's smile loved him. 'No!'

'I assure you. I do rather a good morepork.' Bernard sat up, straightened his shoulders. 'More pork. More pork.'

The two syllables, plangent, resonant and mysterious, echoed around the charmless room. Jack was four years old, alone and awake in the dark, hearing them call; wondering, were they near or far? Were they really just birds? More pork. More pork. Again and again. He shivered. 'What'd you mean you had to do them?'

'They wanted them for radio sessions for the Correspondence School kids. There were no recordings. Not then. None of this archival stuff then. None of these fellows crouching in the rain at Milford for months on end to catch a kakapo booming. My boss Athol Saxon said, "Can you do a morepork?" so I said, "I can try," and I could, so he said go further down the corridor and do it again. So I went and he said further again, so I went and he said a bit nearer. "Stop! Once more." So I tuned in and away we went and Athol said great, now this one's for real and recorded a morepork for the kiddies.'

Jack stretched his arms high. He was more relaxed when he and Bernard were alone in the tearoom than anywhere else on earth. Except occasionally in the pub or after a good fuck with Sarah. He felt as though some coiled spring inside him had unwound, unravelled, unfolded itself backwards like a ponga frond.

He liked Bernard, admired his poetry, its toughness and its rough spots. 'You must have them, the rough bits,' Bernard told him. 'Otherwise the whole thing'll just slip off the page like that man said. Useless!' His hand creamed sideways following the slide of words. He was now back to birds. He could tackle anything, snatch a subject from the air, expound on it, toss it in the air and throw it away. He knew everything and everyone and used most of them. Only to the young, talented young men, was he generous and compassionate as he led them by the hand, showed them the way, did what he could to help them.

'All birds imitate,' he said. 'People think it's just a few.' He shook his head, his eyes closed briefly with astonishment at the stupidity of the world.

'Starlings, for instance.' His eyes shot open. 'Starlings, which of course are introduced, they imitate Californian quail—also introduced as the name would imply. Know Californian quail?'

Jack nodded. Mother quail had often motored across the tennis court at Glenfrae followed by a line of chicks, bumble-bee fluffs of down on wheels. Jack had rejected Glenfrae completely, he didn't want a bar of its calm, the sleepy afternoon beauty of the homestead, the grinding brutality of much of the work, but he thought about it continually.

'And of course the whiteheads in Wellington are completely different from whiteheads in Kapiti,' continued Bernard.

'I didn't know that.'

'Oh God, yes.' Bernard damped his mouth with cold tea, dragged the back of his hand across his pink lips. 'They have regional accents.' He smiled. 'Nice, isn't it?'

'Very.' As usual Bernard made him feel good. The man was an itinerant word seller. A hobo adventurer poet at rest. A man who knew the land was essential to all, who loved it and its inhabitants as much as he lambasted the latter, who had wandered the narrow length of the country not because wandering was a way of possessing but because he needed to search for echoes. The memory of Bernard's excitement at Charles's acceptance of *Ultima Thule* ('A masterpiece, don't change a word. Not a word!') was better even than Sarah's reaction. He knew more about words. He was an expert witness.

'The whole subject of birdcalls is not all sex, mating calls, stuff like that.' He shook his head sadly. 'No. Most of it is territorial. Boys defining the limits of their patch. It seems a pity.'

'Sweet way to do it though.'

'Don't be coy. The pathetic fallacy makes me toss. Talking of which. How would you like the job, how would you like to be,' Bernard snapped his fingers at the empty air, 'shall we say *entrusted* with the task of driving a drunken over-the-hill colleague through the South Island? I mentioned it before, I seem to remember. When you first joined School Pubs. Yes? I want to combine country pubs with a few readings at universities where I have contacts. Maybe the odd library. I won't make a penny, of course, but it might be fun.'

Jack hesitated.

'Oh you won't be out of pocket, dear boy. Well not much. You drive. I'll pay for the car and your board and we can chip in for meals. I was thinking of a week in May. I think we could fiddle time off. Research, culture, there must be something.'

Jack was flattered, delighted. 'I'd like it.' He tried harder. 'Very much. Very much indeed. Great.'

'Carry your bag, sir?' cried Bernard. 'No, no. Let the old girl walk.'

They rinsed their cups in silence. The saucer of one slid from its supporting cup onto its face and lay on the damp bench spurting an occasional bubble from its rim. 'That's the sort of thing that makes me wonder. About the numbering of hairs on the head, sparrow falls, things of that nature.' Bernard's bright eyes stared at the conundrum. 'Why, do you suppose, would God bother to make that saucer slip?'

The pub near Wanaka was large and square; a verandah encircled the upper storey. A man leant from an upper window and gazed across the empty flats. He could see for miles; the ravine cut by the river bisecting the plateau, the hanging valley of an extinct glacier, the mountains.

Bernard climbed stiffly from the Holden and lifted a hand to the man. The man spat on the verandah thoughtfully and with care, not in rejection. Bernard was pleased. 'Lonely man in shirt-sleeves spitting out of window,' he murmured. He reached for a battered green suitcase from the boot and headed for the bar.

At first Jack had had a few surprising qualms of conscience about his role. Should he attempt to keep Bernard sober for his poetry readings? He soon gave up. It would have been impossible and the students seemed happy. None of them had ever seen a live poet actually doing it before. The one or two readings at libraries where Bernard had contacts were not so successful. Elderly women in woolly hats fell asleep, one man leapt to his feet to shake Bernard's shaking hand, to tell him that he'd been at Cassino and that he was spot on in that one. Poetry and farce teetered together throughout the south. A librarian enthused about the work of Bernard's rival, Anton Samuel. 'But then people are so interested in *young* poets these days aren't they?'

Bernard stared at the collection of bookmarks retrieved from Returned Books with glazed eyes. 'I like the Saint Sebastian one,' he said. 'May I have it? As a memento of the Bluff?'

One or two nervous young men handed Jack wads of poems with their names and addresses clearly marked on the upper right hand corner. They had tried to shove them at Bernard and been waved on to his assistant.

'You'll get him to look at them later?' they begged. 'Sure,' said Jack. 'Sure.' And did so.

Jack was enjoying himself. Last night in Southland had been surreal. Bernard knew a marvellous pub he was determined to revisit. So far off the beaten track it scarcely existed. A must, a definite must. 'But we can't get there till after six,' said Jack. 'Not a show.'

Bernard looked genuinely astonished. 'But they've never heard of six o'clock closing in this part of the world. They have a system.'

'What?'

'Leave it to me, lad. Leave it to me.'

Jack shrugged. Bernard was paying, he was here to drive. Jack continued to bump the hired car over back country roads. He was hungry as well as thirsty.

The small building on the crossroads was in total darkness. Bernard, completely unfazed, climbed out of the car and marched to a bell outside the Public Bar. He leant on it for a very long time. The silence, the still flat darkness, remained unbroken. Bernard tried again, his finger on the bell once more for an inordinate length of time. Again there was no response. Bernard was displeased. 'This is ridiculous.' He set off around the corner of the wooden building to the car park behind. Male figures melted behind towers of beer crates, slid into cars or disappeared into a concrete bunker labelled 'Men'. 'What's going on here?' demanded Bernard, who was also thirsty.

'Bernard!' A tub-like man rolled towards him, shook his hand with vigour. 'Terry Slade!' he cried. 'I'd recognise that voice anywhere. Shut up for God's sake. The cops are here.'

'Where?'

'Didn't you see Lance round the front? He's just given his long warning blast on the bell. That's why we're all farting around here.'

'That was me.'

'Bernard.' Terry was deeply saddened. 'Bernard, how could you forget that? Our after hours ring is three shorts, man. Three fucken shorts! Back we go boys,' he cried, heading for the door. 'Old Bernard's made a fuck-up.'

They drove on next day along good empty roads past the silver sheen of tussock towards the mountains. Bernard opened his eyes. 'I wish I'd thought of it first,' he said.

Jack's glance was brief. 'Hunh?'

'Jim Baxter. "In this land the mountains crouch like tigers."'

Jack had not let Sarah tell Sybil of their excursion.

'Sarah's sister lives near here. She's married to a high country run holder,' Jack told Bernard as he handed him his drink in the square pub near Wanaka.

Bernard had been drinking fast, faster even than usual. Double whiskies had appeared, been inspected briefly and drunk with speed. He was leaning back in his chair, his face benign, his beard dark and lustrous. 'We all make mistakes,' he intoned with closed eyes.

Things were hotting up in the bar. It was Friday night, party night in the Public. The men—there were no women—were convivial, their eyes sparkled, they slapped each other on the back, shouted each other, told endless and involved stories, loved each other. A circle gathered around Bernard, attracted by this exuberant talker, this colourful character. 'I am being plied with drinks,' he told Jack happily. He tasted the word again. 'Plied.'

Jack was not listening. He was watching the barmaid. Dark with long straight hair, thin as a whip, not a joke in sight, she was twice as efficient as the two sweating barmen beside her. She was a barmaid body and soul, doing the job she was paid to do. Jack watched her stretching arm, the lift of her breasts as she reached for the Creme de Cacao, of all things. She caught his eye. Her chin lifted, she glared at him then dropped to her heels groping for clean glasses. Programmed, fierce as a ferret, desire nipped his groin. 'Tonight's the night,' sang the man beside him. Jack gripped the back of Bernard's chair and nodded. 'Yes.' And again. 'Yes.'

Bernard was singing hymns to a delighted audience. 'Yield not to temptation,' he roared, 'for yielding is sin.' He stopped short. 'There is a lot of nonsense talked about sin.'

'There's a lot of it about,' said a young man with yellow hair.

'It depends what you mean by sin. Adultery now. How do you go on adultery?' Bernard's face was very serious. 'Is adultery a sin?'

The brown face was also solemn. 'It says so. We had it in Bible Class.'

'Yes but *who* says?'

'God.'

Bernard's hands flung apart in rejection. 'I can't see frankly that he'd fuss. The one sin is cruelty. We are against that, both of us. And you too, sir, I presume. And cruelty is a lot easier to arrange than flagrante delicting around.'

Jack had abandoned his beer and moved behind the bar. He infiltrated without a word, with hardly a glance he had moved in when one of the barmen had retreated to the Gents clutching his gut. 'I'm a pro,' lied Jack. 'No problem.' The remaining barman, sandy-haired, blank-faced, made no comment. Any help was better than nothing on a Friday. Val ('What's your name?' 'Val.') gave him a long look but said nothing. Jack worked hard. Bernard, now surrounded by loved ones, appeared not to have noticed his absence. Jack was rewarded by proximity, by fleeting contact ('Oops! Sorry!'), a brief grin and the yeasty smell of her. His hand brushed her breast. She backed off angrily.

'Coming,' she called to a shouting face. 'Keep your hair on.' Jack regrouped, worked harder, dealt faster with the endless insistent demands. There would be time later, he could wait.

An hour later she swung against him, a dripping glass in each hand. Jack kissed her mouth. She tossed the beer at him in outrage. The drinkers roared with approval as the end wall of the Public Bar concertinaed in on itself to reveal a startled group of diners in what had been until that moment a separate dining room.

'Six o'clock,' yelled the barman. 'Time please. Hotel guests only. Time gentlemen please.'

The waiter in the dining room retied his apron. They had a dining licence but in his experience it was hard to get rid of the casuals on Friday nights.

Over the top of Val's head Jack's eyes met those of the heavily pregnant Mrs Humphrey Potter, the spellbound Mr Potter and friends, agape at their table.

Sybil was on her feet, surging forward, a galleon with topsails and gallants set. 'What on earth are you doing here!' she cried, stepping over Bernard Long who had subsided at her feet as he breasted the bar. 'How dare you! How *dare* you! In front of the Bader-Bouwmanns!'

Val, the elusive chilly Val, smiled. 'Get stuffed,' she said.

Jack, his face plastered with Coral Tango, his hair drenched with beer, tightened his grasp on his true friend's breast. 'Bugger the Bader-Bouwmanns,' he advised in a moment of anarchic bliss before reality iced over.

*

147

Sarah was working, as she acknowledged to Otto, against time.

He snapped his fingers, '"An antagonist not subject to casualties." Why did you tell Miss Pearson you would take her April slot?' He looked at her in despair. 'Foolish, foolish girl.'

'It's the only one the Gallery had left until the end of the year.'

Sarah fitted up extra lights in the bedroom, shoved the bed against the wall and worked through the night. Jack's absence was a lifesaver, a hand stretched out from a raft with a gift of time.

Dora still slept on a camp bed behind the green sofa. It was not good enough, as Sarah told Jack frequently. 'No,' he said.

'Children have rooms,' she said.

'Not all children.' He kissed his daughter's head. 'Do they, Dotty?'

'No,' said Dora.

The telephone rang at ten-thirty p.m. Sarah leapt to the kitchen, brush in one hand, to seize it before Dora woke.

'Yes?'

'It's Sybil.'

'Oh, hello.'

The story came pouring out; tumbling down the line, sobbing and sighing along the wires from Wanaka came the saga of humiliation and betrayal, the importance of Herr Bader-Bouwmann, their horror, the awfulness of it all. 'He's a top German woolbroker,' moaned the disgraced hostess. 'Top!'

'Why on earth did you take them to a country pub then?' snapped Sarah.

'Oh you know what they're like, these people. Especially Germans. They all want to see the real New Zealand. And we'd heard it was a *nice* little pub.'

It took Sarah some time to sort out the fact that her husband had been kissing the barmaid *behind* the bar.

Her instinctive rejection of Sybil-induced doom was as strong as ever. 'Worse things have happened at sea.'

'But you don't know what it was *like*. He was covered with lipstick and beer and his hand . . . I can't tell you where his hand was.'

Oh yes you can. And soon will. Rage at Sybil and Jack, at Jack and Sybil, rage at all deceivers, all informers glued to the face of the whirling world stiffened Sarah's back.

'It was on her *bust*.'

Sarah replaced the receiver gently. She sank onto the kitchen stool, her eyes staring past the brush in her hand. So. I can't trust him. I cannot trust him with any available out-of-town busts. Grainy tears pricked the back of her eyelids. And he can't trust me. It is six years since the Bechsteins' party. If I had had the chance while we were in Auckland would I have lain again with Charles, kissed him where he wished to be kissed, enjoyed him, been enjoyed? Yes. So what are you on about, you fool?

It was no good. Grief drenched her, slackened her shoulders, screwed her with pain; grief for lost trust, for the rock-like faith of other marriages, possibly boring marriages, marriages like Nelson and Maggie's, her parents', probably her siblings'. And the Beckers'. The Beckers. The Beckers.

After some time she stood and drank a glass of water. There was still work. Half-trust. Something else beside sex. A respect for the mystery of the other. A different sort of something which perhaps could be called love. It didn't have to be all the same. She glanced at her watch. Midnight. Time was the thing. She returned to the floodlit bedroom, her eyes dry, her brush still clamped in her right hand. Time.

9

'His unity! That is why he is so exciting, this McCahon man. One of the reasons.' Otto, seated at the table in Eastbourne, patted the book of Giotto reproductions open in front of him. 'Like this man.'

Sarah shifted her weight to her other foot. 'Yes.'

Otto flapped the catalogue from last year's Auckland exhibition in her face. 'And neither of them is tied to lines running back!' His hands were in mid air moving diagonally towards each other on a collision course as he demonstrated perspective. His face became portentous, pregnant with truth.

'McCahon,' proclaimed Otto, 'has burst the chains of perspective.'

'So have a lot of people.'

'Yes, yes, yes.' Otto's behind huffed about on the hard chair, jigging from one buttock to the other in irritation. 'He is not the first. In 1959, how could he be? But still.' His finger traced the loving shape of Giotto's Joachim as he enfolded Anna in his arms outside the Golden Gate. 'But still. It is interesting, is it not? The strength of simplicity, seeming simplicity.'

'And Giotto's colour.'

Olga entered the front door. A grey hand-woven carrier bag hung from her shoulder, two bulging string bags trailed inches from the floor. She looked exhausted. Sarah sprang to unload her, to kiss her soft crumpled cheek. 'Sit down,' she said.

Otto's glance was brief. He lifted one hand in greeting.

'Colour, of course,' he said. 'But colour is not so important,'

150

the Auckland catalogue flapped once more, 'to this man.'

'It is to me.'

'So you say, so you say.' Otto's behind shuffled once more. 'But there are other things.'

'I still think that . . .' Sarah moved the chair slightly in invitation, glancing at Olga, who remained weighted by bags, staring at them.

'If you're going to be a great painter . . .'

'I am.'

His hand slammed down on Joachim. 'You are cock-a-hoop, cock-a-hoop already, is it, because one silly little exhibition at the bottom of the world is a success. Yes, a big success.' He paused. 'Here.' He paused. 'In Wellington.'

'You told me I had to know I was good!'

'Yes, yes, yes. But . . .'

Olga shook her head at the still-proffered chair. 'No,' she said and moved towards the kitchen.

'And anyway,' said Sarah, carefully not shouting, 'I live here. This is where I see. Where I paint.'

'You are happy to be,' Otto's mouth moved, a quick sideways tug, 'a regionalist?'

'Yes,' shouted Sarah, who had never given the matter a thought. 'What does it matter? What on earth does it matter? It's the *pictures.*'

'It matters.'

Olga appeared at the entrance to the kitchen. 'Otto.' One hand clutched the wooden bench, the other her head. 'Come, please, Otto. I am not well.'

It was inoperable, the thing which grew inside Olga's head. That was the word they used, speaking slowly and clearly to Otto, who stood in front of them with his mouth open. Both hands clutched his funny hat, his eyes never left theirs as he begged for mercy. There are complications, they explained. It is just a matter of time, they said. Not long.

There are words that everybody knows for this too, thought

Sarah. Universal words and phrases to echo, to mouth at others so they too will know them and can pass them on. The registrar tugged at the lapel of his white coat. He had been working till three a.m. last night and had come on duty again at eight-thirty. 'We will keep her here for a few days for further assessment,' he said. 'Then she can go home. She would be better at home, wouldn't she? Have you any help in the home? Any assistance?' The large hopeless head shook briefly. 'Family?' Otto fumbled behind him for a chair. The young registrar grabbed a reflex hammer from the seat as Otto subsided.

'There's me,' said Sarah.

She had driven him around the harbour in the Beckers' car. He had never had a licence, Olga had done the driving. She was a good driver, attentive to smooth gear changes and minimal use of the brake.

The sharp young face slackened slightly. The worst was over. 'There is a lot of domiciliary care available in cases of this sort, Mr Becker. Mrs Newbury, the social welfare lady, will fill you in.' A loudspeaker sounded, insistent and urgent; an emergency. 'Excuse me,' he said. He turned at the doorway for the final words. 'And we will do what we can to keep your wife pain-free, Mr Becker.'

'Thank you,' said Otto.

Olga lay in a ward with three other women. Her springy hair was upright, her eyes calm. She had been told. The doctor had been very nice. But there was Otto. She put out her arm to him. He snatched at the hand so clumsily he almost missed it as he sat down. She touched his hair, murmuring.

'I'll go,' yelped Sarah. Neither of them glanced at her. She pulled the curtain behind her with clenched hands.

'Hello dear,' said a thousand-year-old woman in the next bed. Drifts of straight grey hair lay across her face, the beak nose was crimson. She was skin, and bone. There were no visitors.

'Hello,' said Sarah.

'And what's your name dear?'

'Sarah.'

'That's nice.' She tried it. 'Sarah.'

Coyness flicked across the parchment face. 'Mine's Gertrude.'

'Oh. Hello Gertrude.'

'Hello. What was it again dear? The name?'

'Sarah.'

'Sarah. I had a terrible night dear. Terrible,' said Gertrude, her gums wide. She leant forward. 'How many people are there in Japan?'

Sarah shook her head. She sat on a padded stool. 'I don't know. I'm sorry. I just don't know.'

'They say it's my head but it's my leg,' continued Gertrude.

'Which leg, Gertrude?' Anything, anything to distract from the muffled sounds behind the curtain. Sarah leant forward, ignoring the plaster cast suspended from an overhead pulley a foot from her nose.

'I'm ninety-nine!'

'No!'

'I am,' crowed Gertrude. 'No one will believe me but I am.'

An elderly Asian woman, her face expressionless, detached herself from a swarm of relatives around the bed of a young woman with a shaved head and shuffled across the ward. She stared at Gertrude in silence. Gertrude's gums grinned back at her. The old woman stared at the pulley for some time, poked the cotton blanket draped over the plaster cast, lifted it, peered at the plaster, poked that, replaced the cover and shuffled back without a word.

'Sarah,' called Olga, 'Please join us now, Sarah.'

Gertrude started upright on her pillows. Her hands tugged at Sarah's, the nails digging. 'Don't go! Oh God. Oh God, please don't go. Tell them. Tell them . . .'

'I'll come and see you again, Gertrude, I promise.'

Gertrude shook her head, her eyes blank. 'My feet are purple,' she whimpered and dropped the heavy useless hands from hers. She turned her head to the wall. 'Purple,' she said once more.

'You're mad.' Jack wound a piece of paper into the Olivetti on the kitchen table and glared at her.

'Who else is going to look after them?'

'What about your work? Your exhibition?'

She smiled. 'You can take over in the weekends.'

'Very funny.' He had been circumspect and caring for several months after the Wanaka incident, suspecting with accuracy that part of Sarah's distant tolerance stemmed from her refusal to be patronised by anyone, least of all Sybil, who had since produced an heir and referred to herself frequently and with reverence as a young mother.

But now he was distracted and worried. *Ultima Thule* was still not out. He'd sent the corrected galleys back to Charles months ago. What was the bugger doing? His new novel *The Judas Sheep* was bumping along most nights and every weekend but there was no room to hide in the cottage. Little girls came to play, hopped, skipped and chanted feet from the kitchen table where he wrote.

'They'll suck you dry,' he spat at her. 'Those two.'

She turned her wedding ring round and round, remembered Prudie and stopped quickly. Leaning against the kitchen sink, she tried again.

'Would you do their lawns? Just occasionally?'

'She's dying, not him.'

'He just sits and cries. He loves her, you see,' explained Sarah.

Jack's hands slammed the table in defeat.

'Oh God yes, I'll do the fucken lawns. The great New Zealand male gesture. When in doubt do the lawns.' His sigh was half sob.

'Wash the dishes, dry the dishes, turn the dishes over,' chanted Dora and Janice and Colleen, their voices high and true. The flick of Colleen's pony tail appeared and disappeared at the window as she jumped.

'One, two, three, four.'

'You tripped,' squealed Dora. 'Your rout.'

'I am not.'

'You are, she is, isn't she, Jani?'

'Yeeas,' squeaked Jani. Dora was usually the boss. Last week Sarah had found her standing on her head against the sofa, her face scarlet. 'Where's Jani?' she said, righting herself. 'She's gone home,' said Sarah.

Dora was not pleased. 'But I hadn't finished with her.'

Olga lay in the double bed propped by pillows and swathed in homespun shawls. A dark grey one knitted on number one needles guarded her shoulders. A silky white merino hung around her neck. She poked her fingers through the large holes of the grey one.

They had tried to bully her in hospital. 'But Mrs Becker, you must get up, keep moving.'

'Why?'

'You must get up and dressed.'

'No,' said Olga. 'I do not wish to.'

'Well,' she said smiling at Otto on her second day at home. He perched at her feet on the patchwork bed cover. 'Perhaps we should work out a system.'

'Otto will do better soon,' she told Sarah later. 'It is just rather a shock for him at the moment, my not being well.'

Otto did do better. He erected an old army camp bed beside the double one and helped Olga to the bathroom during the night. He followed her meticulously printed instructions each day and wrote a neat red cross beside each completed task. Everything had to be written down by her before he could accept which button to push on which contrivance.

He quite liked doing the washing.

'Do you know,' he told her, 'it talks, the washing machine.'

'Talks?' Olga stroked the coat of the tortoiseshell cat which until recently had been a lean and ravenous stray. She could feel the vibration of its purr on her stomach, which had also let her down; another part of her anatomy which had never until recently made a murmur, had been content to fulfil its role in life with silent competence.

'Not only "g' dunk, g' dunk," which is its usual sound. If something gets entangled it becomes angry. "G' g' g' dunk, g' g' g' dunk." It is a cry for help. I must stop and untangle the pyjama legs, then it is happy again. "G' dunk, g' dunk," once more it says.'

Olga smiled and stole a quick glance at her watch, wondering how long until the district nurse arrived with her injection. She had told Olga she was worried that she might become addicted but Mr Cumberland had prescribed the dose so she supposed it must be all right.

'Don't worry,' replied Olga. 'I promise I'll die quickly.'

'Oh,' cried the nurse, 'I didn't mean that.'

Then what did you mean? What did you think you were saying, my harassed handmaiden, deliverer and friend?

Otto became more and more efficient as Olga sank further into her pillows. As long as she wrote it down, he could do it; oven temperature, remove outer covering before heating, remember oven cloth, turn off oven. He couldn't of course use Olga's own recipes. Not all of them were written down and many of them required long slow attention to detail. Sarah showed him how to heat fish fingers, cook a sausage, peas, open a tin of sheep's tongues. He heated the casseroles and soups she brought him. He was grateful but wondered vaguely what had gone wrong with them.

Olga ate virtually nothing except a little soup brought by her friends. 'Look,' said Otto, opening the refrigerator to show Sarah twelve tightly stacked jars of chicken broth. 'It is good for you,' he explained. 'It makes you well.' He removed one and realigned the others neatly. 'Olga has good friends also.'

When he was not attending to his tasks he sat with her. Sometimes he lay beside her in silence, his head flat on the bed, his eyes closed, his hand holding hers against his chest. He read to her. He brought her his discoveries for her inspection.

'Have you found, liebchen, that pot cleaners roughen your hands?'

'Yes,' said Olga.

Sarah kept the house clean and sat with Olga while Otto walked Flops and Peter on the beach each day. Mops and Cotts had demised last year within weeks of each other, overtaken by age and decrepitude. Olga had had to lift their emaciated forms into the back of the car for months before they died. They waited, their eyes damp with mute appeal as their unconcerned offspring leapt in, jostling for position on the sheepskin as usual. Their parents never learnt to accept the certainty of Olga's assistance. She nursed each dog till it died and grieved for them deeply. Otto buried the two corpses side by side beneath the lemon tree.

Sarah had always liked Otto and Olga's bedroom. The walls, unlike the living area, were plastered and painted white. Wide windows framed the tangled garden, a high recessed one ran the length of the wall which faced the road and the sea beyond. The sea was hidden but cloud shapes sailed by, dissolving, reforming, melting again to nothing. The sunsets were long slabs, oblong sections of changing colour. The white walls, the cool light and the quiet reminded Sarah of a monastic cell which she had never seen. There was little colour except for the bright patchwork quilt and two paintings, a watercolour of a flowering tree by Rita Angus and a small jokey Klee to which the Beckers opened their eyes each morning. The only photograph was of Olga's lost younger brother, an intense young man with a savage haircut, who stared into your eyes and would not let go.

Flops and Peter were not allowed in the bedroom. They never had been and had accepted this ruling long ago but Olga's absence worried them. They stood at the open door to the bedroom whining with loss. Flops quivered endlessly. It was tempting to think he cared more but he had always shivered. It was a nervous condition, not dangerous, the vet had told Olga. At first Olga murmured at them from the bed but their frustration increased. They made little jumping movements, stood on their hind legs, gave quick little yelps of agitation. Sarah and Otto agreed. It was upsetting for Olga. They tried to keep them out of sight.

The cat Werther had never had it so good. He lay deep in comfort, his purr a muted thunder. Olga spent a lot of time with the cat on her stomach. 'I have always had a good lap for a cat.' She held his head in her hands as she gazed into his pale translucent eyes. 'Cats' eyes,' she told Sarah, 'are the most beautiful in the world. You could gaze into them for ever. You could learn the secrets of life. Of eternity, if you believed in it. Beyond eternity.' She kissed Werther's head and lay back. 'Their eyes operate on a different system from ours. Or so I understand.'

'What is it?'

'I don't know.' Olga's hand, pale and speckled with large brown spots, still lay on Werther's head. 'And probably now I never shall.'

'Dying is very interesting,' she murmured. 'It is very strange. One minute you are alive and, shall we say, kicking, the next you are under sentence. I am not afraid of death. There was a man on the radio. He said that those who die best have either a strong faith in some religion . . .' A small indentation of mirth appeared each side of her mouth. 'I gather it didn't matter which. Or else they have no faith at all; they know we live and then we die. *Tant pis.*' A small sound, a failed snap of her fingers, lingered in the silence. 'I am of the latter persuasion. But what does puzzle me, disappoints me, is the knowledge that this is it. There is no more. All I have learnt, all I have studied, my *lebensweisheitslehre*, the playfulness of my lifetime's wisdom, will be snuffed out. There is no second chance.' She seized Sarah's hand in her soft little paw and squeezed it. 'So do what you have to do now. So paint.'

Sarah nodded.

A regrettable smell lingered in the air.

'Pardon me,' murmured Olga.

'It doesn't matter.'

'Oh it matters. It matters.' Olga's eyes closed for a second and reopened. 'Do you know,' she said, pointing at a cushion on the end of her bed, 'that cushion could be a mile away.'

'I'll get it,' said Sarah, leaping to her feet. The indentations appeared again. 'No, no. I am just saying. I don't want it thank you.'

Sarah was still on her feet. Otto's unironed cotton shirts hung in her mind. 'I must do the ironing.'

'No, sit down a moment, child. There is something else I must say.'

'You're too tired.'

'No, no. While Otto is not here. Otto,' said Olga, 'has been very good to you.'

'I know.'

'And when I am dead you must be good to him.'

This was it then. There would be no end to the grief, the

dependent agony of loss. 'Yes,' said Sarah, staring into Olga's brown eyes which used to snap with excitement at a new fleece, a shared treat, the wonder of her world shared with her friend Otto.

'You must look after him.'

'Yes.'

'It will not be easy.'

'I know.'

'You will not want to, perhaps?'

Sarah opened her mouth.

'But you will?' said Olga quickly.

'Yes.'

Olga smiled. Relief flooded her small half-buried face. 'I knew you would. You may not want to. Why should you want to? But you will. Thank you.'

The three of them settled into a routine. The doctor came once a week. 'Courtesy call only, I'm afraid,' he muttered as Sarah opened the front door.

'They are always very grateful. Very glad to see you.'

'I know. It's odd, isn't it?' He was a kind man. A really kind man. 'And the district nurse comes regularly?'

'Yes.'

'Good. Good.'

'Husbands are marvellous when you're dying.' Olga handed Sarah her lunch tray which Otto had prepared before departing to walk the dogs. 'It brings out the best in them.'

She seemed to be shrinking. Getting smaller day by day.

'Sit down, Sarah. I have something else to say.'

Sarah put the tray on the kauri chest of drawers. It was several days since her promise and she hadn't told Jack yet. She sat down gingerly. Werther stirred, kneaded the eiderdown with his paws then burrowed deeper.

'You are a good woman, Sarah.'

'No!'

'But you must learn to cook.'

Sarah snorted with laughter, caught unawares by the ridiculous release of tension. She shook her head. 'I don't want to,' she said.

'But you must.'

Sarah continued smiling. Her head moved in negation.

'Is your mother a good cook?'

'Every woman in the Bay is.'

'Then why not you?'

'Because it takes so much time.'

'Yes. It takes time. But it is time well spent, one of life's great joys. You cannot,' insisted Olga, 'nurture with a fish finger. To nurture is more than to cook.' She struggled upwards on her pillows. 'Friendship. How can you have good friendship, good fellowship without good food, how can you know rare people unless they are happy, relaxed, well fed?'

Sarah smiled. 'What about the dish of herbs where love is?'

Olga smiled briefly. Her hands moved. She was too tired to argue.

Sarah tried again. 'I don't know any rare people except you and Otto. And Jack of course. And fish fingers are Dora's big treat.'

'Pap.' The voice was infinitely sad. 'I will teach you. Go through my books. Explain.'

Worse and worse. Sarah tried again. 'Last week you told me I must paint, Olga. Now you tell me I must cook.'

'You must do both.' Olga smiled her small secret smile. 'It is perfectly possible to do both.' There was a brief silence. 'To see a thing takes time. To nurture friendship takes time. You will land up,' Werther's head lifted for a moment as her hand chopped above him, 'lop-sided.'

'I want to be lop-sided.'

'I think perhaps that is a mistake.' The old spark flickered briefly in Olga's eyes. 'But then I would say that, wouldn't I?'

She died a week later. Sarah took alternate night watches with Otto as she became weaker.

'There are professionals for that job,' muttered Jack but said nothing more.

The camp bed was stowed away and replaced by a small chair

160

deep with cushions. Otto was exhausted, locked in his helpless concern. He refused to let Olga go to hospital. His wife did not wish to, he insisted. He had promised her she would die at home. Thank you, but he and Miss Tandy could manage quite well. No. Thank you. He flapped the doctor out of the house with both hands and nodded at Sarah. 'That's got rid of him,' he said.

His main concern was that Olga should not die without him. 'You must wake me,' he insisted each time Sarah took over. 'Anything. Any change, you must wake me at once.'

'Yes.'

But there was no change when Olga died. She just stopped breathing. Sarah, who had been secretly hoping that she would not be present when it happened, was startled by the nothingness. The ragged uneven dragging in and pushing out of air ceased. Nothing else changed. There was no sound, no brushing wings, nothing. Olga had died. Sarah rose stiffly from her chair, shivered violently and went to wake Otto.

She came to see him two days after the funeral. He met her in the garden by the lemon tree. Spade in one hand, he peered at her with myopic eyes. He was puffing slightly. 'I have just been burying Flops and Peter,' he said.

'What!'

His smile was a slight wobble of face and chin. 'Fortunately I could remember where the other two lie.'

'But why?'

He jammed the spade into the ground, brushed his hands together and wiped them on the seat of his trousers. 'Come inside and I'll tell you.' They climbed the wooden steps slowly, stopping halfway for extra puff. The leaves of the lemon tree glinted beside them, sparkling in the afternoon sun.

Otto sank into his blue rep chair. 'It was her wish,' he said. 'She asked for them to be put down. I took them both to the veterinarian this morning, held them one after the other in my arms for the injection.' One hand smoothed his floating hair. 'Yes.'

'But why? Wouldn't they have been company . . . ?' Sarah

stopped. What on earth was it to do with her?

His smile was broad now, his large hands gripped the chair arms firmly. He was in control. 'She knew that I did not love them enough.'

'I thought you did.'

'I am sorry she guessed. I certainly never said anything, never "let on" as you would say. But perhaps it is better this way. She thought of everything. Her will was very straightforward.' He blinked and stared out the window. 'She left you her jewellery. There is not much. A nice fire opal ring. You remember?'

'Otto, you can't give them to me!'

'I am not giving them to you.' Again the blink was overlong. 'And who else is there?'

'I'll make a cup of tea,' said Sarah, leaping to her feet to escape.

'No. No.' Otto dragged himself up and headed for the kitchen, his head well in front, his body blundering along behind. 'Yappy little things,' she heard him mutter.

He came back with the familiar tray, the pottery mugs slashed with blue, the pottery teapot Sybil had thought was mad. (Whoever saw a teapot with a sticking-out handle like that?)

'What do you do if someone gives you a hideous eggcup?' Sarah had asked Olga years ago.

'I dispose of it. Someone will love it. At some white elephant stall someone will fall on a plastic pixie eggcup with glee. There is no good and bad. Only different. Sometimes,' said Olga, scratching the back of her hedgehog head, 'artists forget the wildness and the wonder of other people's lives.' She sniffed. 'They become insular. They miss a lot.'

Sarah followed Otto with a plate of *vanille kipfels* made by Clara Bechstein. He placed the tray on the table between them and straightened. 'Ah,' he said. 'One moment.' He padded back to the kitchen and returned with two casserole dishes and handed them to her. 'Your vessels,' he said. 'Thank you.'

'I'll bring some more next week.'

'Thank you,' he said. 'But I have much already. Clara, all our friends.'

'I'll wait a bit then.'

He nodded.

They drank their tea in silence. Otto put down his cup. 'Did you paint her?' he said suddenly. 'When she was dying?'

Sarah did not move. 'Yes.'

'Good. Good. You must let me see them.'

'I have them here.' Her hands shaking with relief, Sarah reached in her bag for her sketch book. There were two pen-and-washes and one pencil sketch.

He stared at each one for a long time. 'These are very good,' he said finally.

Sarah said nothing.

He looked at each one again and held up the better of the pen-and-washes. The shadows on the face were stronger, the colouring more subtle. 'May I keep this one?'

'Of course, of course. All of them.'

'No.' He stared at them again. 'Did I ever tell you how we met?'

She heard the story once again. It had been quite by chance. Olga had been waiting at a bus stop in Vienna, her friend hadn't come. The bus was late. It was very cold. Snowing. They had talked. It was a 'pick up'. A 'pick up', chuckled Otto. His hand-kerchief mopped with vigour. 'Na ja. There is something impor-tant I must say to you.'

Not again. Sarah braced herself.

It was about her work. She knew, did she not, that she was a good painter, that she had real potential. Yes. 'Good. Good. But there are other things I must tell you.'

A small unfinished oil of Sarah's stood on Otto's easel by the French doors to the back of the garden. Otto lurched to his feet, picked it up and shuffled back to subside once more in his deep chair. Bands of vertical colour swam down one side of the canvas. Nacreous hidden colours, mother of pearl, pinks, violets and blues melted together. A vague hill shape was backed by cobalt blue. A dark smouldering form burned in the foreground.

'I have forgotten its name?' said Otto after some time.

'*Burn Off*,' said Sarah.

He nodded. 'Gauguin told Van Gogh that the reason the Mediterranean sky was so blue was because a large space of blue is bluer than a small space.'

'Mmn.' Another much-told story. It occurred to Sarah that she loved Otto dearly. She jumped up and kissed him. He seemed pleased but not surprised. 'It is the same in this country.'

'It's the only sky I've seen.'

'And a very nice one it is too.' He stared again at the oil in his hands. 'Abstract?' he muttered. 'Semi-abstract? What does it matter?'

'I don't see that it does.'

'No, child. But you will puzzle people. They won't,' said Otto crossly, 'know where to put you.'

He had always liked her slow smile. Olga's smile had been quick, busy, taking in the whole world. Sarah's was more selective.

'And you have another problem.'

'Oh dear.'

Werther padded across the room, high-pawed and disdainful. Otto's pale eyes followed his exit to the kitchen. 'Would Dora like Werther?' he asked.

Dora would, but what about Jack?

'Don't you like cats either?'

He shrugged. 'Yes. But not now.'

'All right,' she said after a pause.

'Thank you. As I was saying. Your other problem is that you are accessible. For a serious artist in New Zealand in 1959 this is not necessarily an advantage. People, silly people, will say, "She is seduced by colour, she is not serious." Even sillier people may see your work,' his arm waved, 'and think, "Ah pink. And blue."'

Sarah was outraged. She blushed scarlet, astonished at her fury. 'Well, let them!'

'Oh, yes,' said Otto. 'I agree, but people are prepared to overcome their terror of abstraction for colour. They do not see the thought, the balance, the quality. Some fools,' his voice dropped, 'may describe your work as decorative.'

Sarah was on her feet. She could kill him. 'Rubbish!'

His air-patting gesture was identical to hers when curbing Dora. 'I know. I know. Sit down.'

Sarah sat fuming. 'At it again, you two.' She heard Olga's murmur as she shuffled in with the shopping. 'At it again, I see.'

'I'm not going to fuss about what people say!'

'No, no, no. But register it. The answer is . . .' Otto's bulk rolled forward. From behind a cushion he dragged a small blue book. 'I was reading this to Olga. It made me think of you.' He handed it to her. '*Four Vital Years*, by Arthur Howell. It's about Frances Hodgkins's career. This man was her dealer. He managed her career for those years. He would not let her exhibit until he thought she was ready. He controlled her market.'

'But my pictures are just beginning to sell.'

'Forget that.'

'But we need the money.'

'Are you a serious artist?'

'You know I am!'

He nodded. 'You *must* have a dealer with integrity.'

She turned the book in her hands. Eventually she put it down and gazed at him. 'But you'll tell me what to do, Otto. You'll advise me.'

'Yes, yes, yes,' said Otto, huffing about in his nest of cushions. 'But you must know, yourself. Paint, paint, paint—the more the better but don't release it all. It is so tiny here, the market, and you paint with speed. Nurse yourself, liebchen. Nurse yourself, is all. Your talent will last. Only release the ones to which you cannot add a glance.' His hand moved. 'A flick.'

'All right.'

A few days later impractical, non-mechanical Otto attached a rubber tube to the exhaust pipe of the Morris Minor, climbed into the driver's seat with a bottle of whisky and Sarah's sketch of Olga, shut the windows tight, stuffed the dogs' sheepskin around the entrance of the tube and started the ignition. He remembered to use plenty of choke. Olga had complained frequently about the amount of choke the Morris Minor required. It was in need of something, she had said. Some technical adjustment or cleansing which would correct this failing.

He left a copy of his will, which was recent and in order, on the dining room table addressed 'To whom it may concern'. The police opened it. Otto Heinrich Becker left everything of which he was possessed to Sarah Frances Tandy Macalister of Mahina Bay, Wellington. His entire estate, including all his paintings, he willed to her with affection. There were no other bequests except one to the RSPCA.

He chose a day when he knew Sarah was not coming. A neighbour, attracted by Werther's yowls, rang the doorbell and telephoned several times before calling the police, who later rang Sarah. A young policeman handed her a sealed envelope addressed in Otto's black spikey writing, *Sarah Tandy*. She opened it in the sunny room, sitting in his deep chair. The policeman perambulated about the room cap in hand, pretending not to watch her.

September, 1959

Sarah,

Something I must tell you so you will not feel guilty in your funny New Zealand way, which is also our way. I do not wish to live without Olga. That is why I choose to die. Nothing you, with your loving kindness and charity, could do for me would alter that.

I hope you do not feel I have deserted you but I do not think you will. We have been painting together for seven years now and there is little else I can teach you. And you are a strong woman. And a good painter. And I am an old man. You have given me and my Olga much pleasure, Sarah. I would like to say auf wiedersehen but I do not believe that we shall meet again. Nevertheless we have enriched each other's lives, I think.

My love, Liebchen,
Your affectionate friend,
Otto.

*

There was little sound; her head was hidden on her lap as she rocked backwards and forwards, backwards and forwards. The young cop was quite startled.

Eventually he touched her shoulder. 'Was he a relation, then? The old man?'

She looked at him; uncomprehending, blinded by tears, she shook her head.

10

They moved in a month later. Their lives flowed into the Beckers' house and took it over. Jack, after the first uncontrollable yelp of joy, the first clenched punch of liberation, had been grateful—almost, for him, humble—at their good fortune. He comforted Sarah, rationalised the astonishment of the legacy. 'People like to have someone to leave their lives to, Sal. Some people really fuss about it. They want a face to put to it.'

Dora was delighted. She walked about the house touching things: a smooth stone, a Chinese ivory carving of a mushroom gatherer, an Iron Cross won by Otto's German cousin at the Somme. She sat on her bed with her legs hanging and smiled. After some time she picked up a reluctant, stiff-legged Werther and carted him around as she explained the wonders of the house to him. She didn't have to catch the bus to school any more. She had her own bedroom, see, and her own wardrobe even and chest of drawers and her own bathroom with its own lavatory and a rubber mat in the shower so you didn't fall over because Olga and Otto had been old. Dora had not visited the Beckers' house much recently. When she had begun to crawl Sarah had 'approached' Mrs Dossi. Would she, could she, how much would she be prepared to accept to mind Dora for one afternoon a week while Sarah had a painting lesson? Mrs Dossi wept for joy at the beauty of her life and clasped Dora to her heart. She welcomed the tough little dinghy of Dora's love and gave it another haven from the rips and squalls of Eastbourne Primary.

Sarah sold Olga's vast loom. She watched as the carrier's men handled the cumbersome thing down the path. She refused to be like Maggie, who flung half-dead flowers onto Nelson's bonfire and turned away, sensitive and shuddering. 'I can't watch! Don't let me watch.' 'Don't worry about my fire,' muttered Nelson, poking his fork at the sputtering pyre.

After they had lived in the house for six months Jack excavated the bank behind the garage to make himself an office. He hired a skip, stripped to the waist and hacked at the rotten rock after work and every weekend; his khaki shorts low on his thighs, the cleft of his buttocks exposed, his body drenched with sweat. He had a dream. To switch to part-time at School Pubs; to write at home on the other days. In his office, at his own house.

'He can work when he wants to, can't he?' said Tony their neighbour approvingly one Saturday morning as they watched Jack struggle with his laden barrow along the plank crossing the mud to the bin.

Sarah smiled meekly. She had come to borrow some milk from Alison ('Again dear?') and was not in a strong position. Jack lifted an outraged face from his skip and roared at Tony. 'Is this your bloody ngaio in my bin?'

'Certainly not!' yelled Tony, 'What do you think I am?'

'A bloody bin-bludger!' Jack looked as though he was going to cry.

Sarah lifted her cup of milk in thanks and ran down to him.

He hired a jobbing carpenter to build the office but worked as builder's mate in the weekends. Sarah could hear their curses and occasional bursts of laughter as they hammered beneath her feet.

She was working for her next exhibition. Jean Pearson was enthusiastic, almost insistent.

'I'm not ready. I won't be ready for a long time. I can't make a time yet.'

'It would be a pity at this stage of your career,' said Jean, who was small and grey-haired and had a good eye, 'to leave it too long.' She fingered the chip on the rim of the terracotta pot which housed a Hen and Chicken fern. Sarah's eyes followed her fingers, wondering why the chip made the whole thing look better.

'It's different now.'

'That is rubbish.' Arms akimbo, Jean stared at the fool across the counter. 'Otto would be disgusted at such nonsense. Go away,' said Jean, 'and try harder.' She patted the behind of her trousers with both hands searching for her handkerchief. 'And soon.'

Sarah did as she was told. Blankness stared back at her from the canvas. She had done the first sketches weeks ago and thought about the picture for months. She wanted every one of the sea tones, the colour behind the storm cloud, the darkness. She seemed to spend hours staring at it for each brush stroke she made. It was not that she was dependent on Otto. For years they had painted side by side. 'Do it your way. No one can tell you. Think. See. That is all.'

It took a long time. Eventually she turned the canvas to the wall like Titian and went to the beach.

'That is one of the reasons I regret no longer believing in God,' Otto had said to her one day as they walked the dogs beside the surf. 'It is sad not having anyone to thank.'

A year later, Sarah was working for her exhibition when the telephone rang, shrilling through the empty spaces and breaking the calm. She stared at it vacantly for a second before answering the thing.

It was her father. His story was garbled. Laura had been staying at Waikeri, she'd gone out on the paper-car, she didn't like shingle roads, Sarah knew that, didn't she, and Prudie was bringing her back and they went into a skid. Laura was in hospital. Prudie had disappeared.

'But Mum, tell me about Mum!'

'She's very ill.' The voice paused. 'Head injuries.'

'I'll come up tomorrow.'

'Thank you. That would be nice. Yes. Thank you, dear.'

Sarah sat motionless with the telephone on her knee. She had scarcely given her parents a thought since Olga and Otto had died. They were just there. Delighted to have Dora at any time.

'Of course, darling,' her mother's voice would call down the

170

telephone. 'We'd love to see her. Put her on Newmans tomorrow. The driver will look after her.' Sarah, Jack and Dora made quick dashes up to the Bay now they had transport; when the good pears were in, the best apples, the cheap tomatoes. They went up for Christmas dinner cooked by Laura, the Highland Games, the Show, when Dora had insisted on a doll on a stick with a stiff halo of skirt, which Sarah had never seen the point of at her age. 'It's so beautiful, Mummy,' she breathed, one finger tracing the spikey circle of the skirt with reverence.

Laura was always the same; non-judgemental, interested in their lives and enjoying hers. Last time Dora stayed in Hastings they had driven up, presumably so they could load the returning car with loot.

'Stop!' cried Sarah as Jack backed the Morris Minor's replacement down the concrete strips of the drive.

'What the hell?'

'Look.' The living room curtains had not been pulled. Dora and her grandmother were dancing together. Round and round they circled, their clasped hands held high, their faces filled with joy in each other and their merry dance.

Sarah wept for shame, for the way things fall on your head, for being too late.

She went up next day by Newmans. Jack couldn't get away till Friday. Mrs Dossi would mind Dora after school and he'd drive up after work. 'Of course I'll drive carefully, you nutter.'

She stared into his chameleon eyes. They were gold, pure gold. 'I feel if I haven't told people they won't do it. Told Dora not to drown, say.' He kissed her hair. It smelt of bonfires. She had taken a running jump at the garden in the weekend. 'Why is everything always your fault?'

'Oh, I don't mean that,' said Sarah quickly.

Nelson rang. He and Maggie had a plan. Sarah, silenced momentarily by the familiar phrase, said nothing. 'Are you there, dear?' he yelled.

'Yes, yes.'

Nelson would meet the bus in Dannevirke, that would be no trouble at all, in fact it would be his pleasure at this sad time and he could whizz her straight up to Hastings in no time at all because by the time you get to Dannevirke, by crikey, you feel you've been sitting long enough if your behind's anything like mine. Not that we use Newmans much, not now, though don't get me wrong, they're a great firm. Maggie had left her new coat on one once when she was going to Hawera and it was at the depot in Hastings waiting for her the next day, which was what Nelson would call service.

'Thank you, Nelson. That'd be wonderful.'

She walked into his arms at Dannevirke. It was like being enfolded by a large and friendly bear. Hot stupid tears fell down her face. He hugged her again.

'There, there, love. There, there. Never say die,' said Nelson.

She gave a short yelp of hopeless laughter and mopped her dripping nose. OK, Nelson. Don't let's.

He drove extremely fast, arms out straight like Jack but a better driver. He glanced at her. 'Not scared of the speed, are you, dear?'

'Not with you.'

If I went tiger-shooting with you, Nelson, and something went wrong, I wouldn't be scared. You would tell me what to do. You would shoot the tiger, you wouldn't let me shoot the tiger. Nelson's girls don't shoot tigers. Would I go tiger-shooting with your son, Nelson? Who wants to go tiger-shooting. Sarah clenched her fists, blinking back hysteria.

'Maggie doesn't like it when I go fast. That's one of the reasons I said, "No, don't come," today.'

Good thinking, Carstairs.

'She wanted to, of course. But I said, "Look you've got all this cooking you want to do for poor old John and the family. I'll run you into town tomorrow if you like. Sarah'll understand you not being there today."' He gave her a fleeting anxious glance. 'You do understand, don't you?'

'Yes, of course.'

'I knew you would.' He changed down as they cornered and

sped up the hill by Norsewood. 'Where did you have lunch?' he said suddenly.

'Palmerston.'

'Palmerston. Yes they do now, don't they? Palmerston. Clean?'

'Not bad,' said Sarah, who hadn't the faintest memory of the place.

'You should see Maggie at it.' He chuckled. 'She marches straight into the Ladies and if that's not perfect we're up, on our feet and it's off, out. We shoot through like a robber's dog. Though usually of course she makes a picnic.'

'Yes.'

Those picnics. Delicious curried-egg sandwiches, their crusts trimmed guillotine-straight, stacked neatly in tins lined with lettuce leaves.

'Where's your favourite place to stop, Hastings to Wellington?' continued Nelson.

'Well, Dora loves milkshakes. We usually go to a milkbar.'

We don't have enough structure in our lives, rituals, stopping places visited time after time and remembered with affection.

'We like the Woodville domain, ourselves,' said Nelson.

Could the Dannevirke milkbar become a hallowed-oasis memory? Why not? Stop fussing. The Woodville domain, the Aokautere primary school. Why not the milkbar?

'Nelson?'

'Mmn.'

'Can I talk to you while you're driving or do you like to concentrate?'

His glance was faintly shocked as though she had impugned his masculinity. 'No no, love. Fire away.'

'Nelson, what happened? And where's Prudie? It's all so weird.'

'Ah yes. Well, I'm glad you asked. I can fill you in there. As I understand it,' his voice droned on, his eyes never glanced from the road. As Nelson understood it, Prudie had gone into a bad skid at Kereru and gone off the road. She had limped two miles to the nearest house for help and insisted on walking back to the car after she'd rung the ambulance. The men at the farm were in town with

173

the truck and there was no other transport. She had thanked the lady very much and explained that she must get back to her friend.

Sarah made a small indeterminate sound.

'When the ambulance men arrived she was sitting in the dark with your mother's head in her lap.'

'She moved her!'

'Oh I don't think so, dear. Prudie wouldn't do that. Not with her training.'

'But where is Prudie?'

'Yes, well, that's rather a mystery at the moment. Now don't you worry about it,' he said, as Sarah moved beside him. 'That's not your problem. Charles is looking after that side of things. And Frank, of course,' he added after a pause. 'Though frankly, Prudie and Frank . . . Yes well, things change, don't they? But seemingly Prudie went in the ambulance with your mother and she was interviewed by the police and that and then she said she wanted to go back to the hospital to be with her friend and she walked out of the police station and, er, disappeared.'

Sarah's head moved. 'Wasn't she covered in blood?'

The way they come out with things. 'She had a coat in the back seat of the car. She'd brought it in with her.'

Sarah nodded and stared out the window.

An ambulance shot past them, lights flashing, siren wailing.

'Ambulance,' said Nelson.

'Yes.' Sarah stared out the window. Leafless willows hung by dark streams, sheep trailed in single file along terraced hills. The light was fading. Soon it would be dark and Nelson's red Holden would change to khaki.

'Nelson?'

'Mmn?'

'Tell me about when you were young.'

'Come again, love?'

'Tell me about the time when you caught three crays in one dive off the rocks. About the best wool clip Glenfrae ever had. About when there was no road when you were a boy and the year's clip had to be rowed out through the surf to the lighter. Tell me about all that.'

So Nelson told her. Sarah listened, calmed by old sagas. After some time her head slipped forward and she slept safe as a child in the right arms until they drove up the drive in Hastings.

Sarah and John came back from the hospital together. John drove the Buick up the twin concrete strips divided by drifts of white alyssum.

He turned off the ignition and sat still.

Sarah opened her door. 'Come on, Dad. There's some soup, isn't there? We can have some soup. Brandy. Something.'

'When she planted it,' he said, 'they were all colours. Mixed. Pinks and purples as well.' He turned to her, his hands still splayed on the wheel. 'The alyssum.'

'Oh.'

'But the whites took over. They've all gone now. The pink ones.'

She touched his arm. 'Come on, Dad.'

He steadied himself against the rounded lid of the dustbin at the back step and smiled briefly in apology.

Several flies followed them inside, cruising about in the evening light. One did a handstand on the table.

'I must get a fly door,' he said.

'Yes. They bang though.'

'Yes. Yes, they do bang.'

He sat on the painted stool at the kitchen table, his hands held loosely in front of him.

'They say,' he said after a while, 'they say you should cry. It's a good thing to cry, they say. The only thing is, how would you stop?'

Sarah took her father in her arms and held him. She was the wrong one. Sybil, warm cuddly Sybil, would have been more use but she couldn't get here till tomorrow.

'You see,' he said eventually, 'it wasn't only that I loved her.' He glanced at Sarah's hand. 'Don't you wear a wedding ring?'

'No.'

'Why not?'

'It was a Woolworth's one. It broke last year.'

'You must have your mother's.'

'I'd like that. Thank you, Dad.'

He nodded, pleased with his decision-making. That was one thing settled. 'Yes. What was I saying?'

He is grey all over. Hair, face, suit, tie. Grey on grey.

'Something about not just loving Mum.'

He blew his nose and nodded. 'I don't mean she took over or anything. She didn't turn me into what she wanted. Not like one of those awful fungus things,' he gave a hideous gasp of mirth, 'that, you know, live on caterpillars. Vegetable caterpillars, they're called. A fungus, like I said. There was a specimen in the Zoology Lab with a fruiting body on top. I don't mean like that.' He shuddered. 'It's funny the things you remember. It's just that she told me what to do, that's all. Not my work, I don't mean that. But everything else. She told me what to do. Always. So lovingly. Not bossy, ever. I won't know what to do, you see, without her.' His desperate grey eyes held hers. 'Do you see what I mean?'

'Yes.'

'She didn't, you know. Henpeck. I don't mean that.'

'No.'

'It was just, love, she told me what to do.'

'Yes.'

Dougal and Flicka and Sybil and Humph flew up for the funeral. People were very kind. Women arrived with food, casseroles, cakes, a City Councillor's wife ran over with a leg still warm from the oven. Cook something and pop over. When people die, make a cake. It's not a bad idea, thought Sarah, staring at the mounds of food on the kitchen table. It is a very good idea. People will still eat and people will pop in and food will be needed. Sybil took over; smiling and efficient, she thanked, sorted and labelled and told her father where to look for what in the deep freeze.

'See Dad, I'm putting Enid's soup in this end. Celery. That'll be nice later on.'

'Thank you, thank you.' He lifted his head, his eyes glazed with terror. 'Which Enid?'

*

176

Dougal and Sarah accompanied their father to the undertaker, Kevin Pately. They drove past the saleyards, now renamed the Livestock Retail Centre. Or probably not renamed. They had not been called anything before, as far as Sarah could remember. Everyone knew what they were. The saleyards. What else could they be with their large wooden pens empty for six days a week and crammed on sale day with fidgety cattle beasts and vacant-eyed sheep and men peering at them and the auctioneer's high-pitched spiel heard three sections away or more depending on the wind. Nelson had often called in to 'wet his whistle', as he called it, before the long drive back to Glenfrae. He sat drinking tea with Laura in the kitchen where he insisted on sitting, banging the seat of his pants to demonstrate the dust in the yards. He liked Laura, her bright eyes laughing at him above her Taurus mug, her dark clipped hair, her ease. Why she had married that dry stick was beyond him but there you were. 'It'll drag you further than gunpowder'll blow you,' muttered Nelson to the lavatory during his pre-drive-home pee.

Frank Bremner always went to the Hastings Club.

John turned into Heretaunga Street, which passed straight through the town to leafy Havelock North where many farmers and their wives went to live when their sons took over the farm. Kev Pately's holding paddock, Nelson called it, but Maggie was looking forward to a manageable house and a nice little garden.

The car passed Rush Munro's Ice Cream Garden. It was just the same, the flowers, the colours, the paint job on the chairs, a cool haven in the hot heart of the Bay.

'Sunrise Meats,' screamed a sign with a jolly cartoon butcher brandishing a cleaver.

'Beds, beds, bedz; beds, beds, bedz,' cried the shop next door.

John drove carefully over the railway line which bisected the town. Sarah glanced at the Centennial clock beside it. There had been a competition for its design, which had been won by a young local architect. When Sarah was a child a street photographer had danced in front of it snapping the passers-by. Lots of the results were very good. They were more natural, people said. Identical sized snaps of Grans and Grandpas in hats, of nieces and nephews and cousins and aunts sat in countless homes and were cherished or otherwise.

It is only nine years since I left. This is where I was born. Where my mother first loved me. My home.

Home is where the heart is. A poem in a childhood *New Yorker*, forgotten for a thousand years, resurfaced in the front passenger seat of the Buick.

'So that you may enjoy your meal in a more home-like atmosphere we have provided a hat-rack under your chair,' announced the management of the restaurant. *The New Yorker* replied,

> Home is where the hat is
> Underneath the chair.
> Cosy custom that is
> Some in fact declare
> Welcome on the mat is
> Never needed where
> You may know your hat is
> Underneath your chair.

Sarah gave a loud guffaw.

'Sal!' said Dougal from the back seat. John gave no sign of having heard. Sarah turned to smile and shake her head at her brother in some sort of explanation. 'I just thought of something,' she said.

Dougal liked Sarah but she was different and probably getting more so. You never knew quite which way she was going to jump. Yesterday she had been either sobbing in Jack's arms or comforting Dora, who had loved Granny T dearly but was soon beguiled by the drama. 'More presents,' she yelped each time the doorbell rang. Sarah had been precious little use to poor Syb with the food, though she had dealt with the flowers. And here she was. Well. Laughing.

They drew into the generous concrete parking-apron in front of Pately's Funeral Parlour and Chapel in silence.

A blonde woman in overalls was washing her car from the

outside tap, lathering and sluicing at her task, her feet encased in white rubber boots. She glanced at them nervously, turned off the hose and backed inside with an embarrassed smile.

'Caught on the hop,' muttered Dougal.

'She's probably the lady embalmer,' said John. 'Kev told me he had a lady one.' He paused slightly. 'I wonder where she got her operating boots.'

Sarah clutched his arm. 'Dad. It's OK, Dad,' she said fiercely. 'It's OK.'

They sat in Kev's neat office. A ray of sun from a high window caught Kevin's shining head in a pool of light, illuminating it, making it the focus of their hypnotised stares. Kevin and John had been to primary school together in Otane. They agreed that it was a long time ago. 'More years than I care to mention,' said Kevin and did so. 'It'll be well over thirty. Forty more like.'

'Yes,' said John.

'Yes, well.' Kevin leant back. 'Perhaps we'd better sort out a few details at this sad time. Lovely woman, your wife, John. Lovely in every way.'

John nodded. 'Yes.'

Kevin picked up his pen. 'I've made the booking at St Matthew's. That's all right, all teed up with the vicar. He's happy about Tuesday afternoon, as I'm sure he will have mentioned.' He paused. 'The next thing'd be the casket.'

John stared at him. Kevin's polished head, tanned and burnished by weekend golf at the Club, swam before him. There were two Kevins mouthing at him. 'The casket?' he gasped.

'We have a range,' explained Kevin, shoving a shiny blue book across the desk at his childhood playmate. It looked as though it should have 'Our Wedding' stamped on it in gold or silver. It contained large colour photographs of the merchandise available. The price list was at the back.

John reared back in his chair. It had arms, unlike those for the lesser mourners.

'We want the cheapest one possible,' he said.

Kevin's expression did not alter. 'The cheapest?' he said.

'Yes.' John glanced at his startled offspring. 'That's what she used to say, your mother. She used to laugh. "They hold you to ransom," she used to say. "Take advantage of your grief. Don't have a bar of it."' He shook his head, baffled by the impossible complexities of the situation, his wife's face laughing up at him as she shovelled compost. 'She wanted cardboard!' he yelped.

Dougal leant forward, his brown hand pressed his father's knee. 'No, Dad, not cardboard.' He glanced at the undertaker. He was a customer, a well set-up man, a man of substance, previously unacquainted with grief. 'What's the next one up, Mr Pately?'

'Pine,' said Kevin.

'OK. Pine it is. Pine OK, Dad? Sal?'

They nodded. The blonde head of Kevin's lady embalmer, transformed by bubble glass, bobbed along the passage.

'And no tarty handles,' continued Dougal.

'Simple as you like.' Kev sketched a meagre oblong in the air with his hands. 'Basic.'

Sybil, who had cleaned out the deep freeze and restocked it, was deeply shocked.

'Pine!'

'That's what she wanted,' said Dougal.

'She didn't. Not really, I bet. That's the sort of thing people say,' cried Sybil, tears of mortification welling in her eyes. Dougal hugged her. She was good to hug. You never banged into unpleasing angles of chin or cheekbone when embracing Syb. She leant against his chest sobbing. 'Pine,' she sniffed. 'No one could want *pine.*'

Charles flew down as soon as his father rang. Jane couldn't come, unfortunately. She was marking exam papers. Charles stayed at the Hastings Club. Frank Bremner had given his son a life membership on his seventeenth birthday in the days when he regarded Charles's aversion to taking over Waikeri as puerile nonsense out of which the fool would soon grow.

Charles had offered to pay the money back. 'Don't be so bloody insulting,' snapped Frank, his face tense above *Straight Furrow,* the smoking-room leather chair at Waikeri sighing away excess air as he ground himself into its depths. A Goldie hung on the wall above him, a tattooed kuia with sad eyes, labelled in English.

Frank and Charles stood side by side at Laura's funeral, Charles's head six inches or more above that of his father. They stood side by side afterwards as people approached them nervously to express their concern for Prudie. Yes, they said. It was a worry, but they were sure she would turn up soon. Temporary amnesia, they murmured, the shock, yes, undoubtedly the shock.

They made small gestures with their hands, clasped those of John and his children, murmured phrases. What could they say? What could anyone say, let alone Prudie's husband and son. They had already written to John, and Charles had written to Sarah.

They declined to join the mourners for tea and whisky and food at the Tandys' house afterwards. Frank drove his son around the corner to the Club. Charles had bitten back his instinctive 'No thanks, I'll walk'. They sat side by side outside the white-painted pile.

'Come in and have a meal, Dad.'

'No, no, I think I'll get back to Waikeri.'

'We'll find her.'

'Oh God, yes.' The fierce eyes flicked at him for a second. Rage? Hatred? Despair? How could you tell? They had always looked like that.

'We'll find her all right,' Frank sighed. 'The thing is though . . .'

'Yes?'

The lined face, burnt and reassembled by sixty years of wind and rain and sun was puzzled. 'I've no idea what I was going to say.'

'I'll keep in touch, let you know as soon as I find anything.'

'Yes, yes, do that.' One gnarled thumb and forefinger squeezed the bridge of Frank's nose. There was a time when Charles was little, before anyone had noticed he was blind as a bat, when he thought all real men had thumbs like that; that misshapen, hooked, split or scarred thumbnails were a badge of honour like the war medals for which Frank had longed.

'Do you have any idea where she will have gone?'

'No,' lied Charles. 'Not at the moment.'

They sat in silence. 'Well, I'd better be on the road,' said Frank.

'Yes.' Charles climbed out of the Humber and walked round to the driver's side. Frank wound down the window. Charles stood for a moment then put out his hand.

'And thanks for this, Dad.' He gestured at the Hastings Club behind them.

Frank's smile was grim. A wry smile, perhaps.

Prudie had discovered Charles aged eight, flat on his stomach beneath the billiard table reading a murder trial account in the *Dominion*. The prisoner had just left the dock with a wry smile when Prudie snatched the paper away. It was in the days of capital punishment. Charles remembered that.

'Glad it's been some use,' said Frank. He turned on the ignition then leant out the open window. 'I've remembered what it was. Her jewellery's gone. Yes.' His father nodded and drove away.

Charles went up to his room, lay on the bed and closed his eyes.

The next morning he rang the Tandys' number and was answered by Sarah.

'Sarah. It's Charles.'

'Oh. Hello.'

'Sarah, would you come into town and have a cup of coffee with me?'

There was a pause. 'Now?'

'Yes. I want . . . There's something I want to tell you. Talk to you about.'

'I could come now. Jack's taken Dora to Cornwall Park to see those smelly old parrots. She loves them.'

'Is that right?'

'It's not the parrots that smell, of course. It's the lysol.'

His laugh rumbled down the line.

'I'd like to see you,' said Sarah. 'Where?'

'There's some sort of coffee place round the corner. I've no idea what it's like.'

'It doesn't matter what it's like. There are plenty of cars here. Ten minutes?'

'OK.'

'The Camelot: Living Decor, Coffee and Craft,' announced the board at the entrance. A cut-out cardboard owl was propped against the board. 'Be wise. Eat Podge's Pies,' said the balloon issuing from its beak.

African violets fought for shelf space beside plywood sabres for small boys. A ladder fern drooped beside hefty-looking toy push-chairs made of wood, too heavy surely for all but the sturdiest of small girls to lift. Meticulously depicted English robins and tomtits in baroque metal frames encrusted with glass rubies and sapphires peered from behind a cascading fern in a macramé plant-hanger emblazoned with wooden rings, pottery beads and things that looked like rope pulleys. There was a good deal of sludge-coloured pottery thrown by an apprentice hand on a bad day.

'This place is unbelievable,' murmured Sarah. Charles looked quite ill. He had kissed her when they met but said nothing.

He smiled. 'Wait till you see the Olde Tea Shoppes in the UK. And the coffee's not bad.'

'Thank you for your letter,' said Sarah.

'Thank you for coming.'

'Of course I'd come.'

'Oh yes. I hoped you would.' He shook his head in angry rejection of uncertainty. 'I knew you would.'

'How's Jane?'

'All right. Thank you.'

'Give her my love.'

He nodded.

She took his hand, turned it over. She still didn't know which was Life or Fate or whatever. 'What did you want to tell me?'

'I think I know where Mum might be.'

She blinked. 'Where?'

'She always loved Piha. Her parents had a bach there. She grew up in Auckland.'

Sarah knew that. Everyone knew where everyone came from.

Where their baches were if they had them.

'Dad refused to go there.' His finger moved against hers. 'Probably because she loved it too much. And then she couldn't bear the thought of him being there and then it was sold.'

'I didn't realise . . .'

'She tried to like him. For years. In the end,' Charles's shrug demonstrated defeat, 'she gave up.' He was silent for a moment. 'I think she may have told your mother she was going to leave him.' He stirred his cold coffee, put the spoon down, picked it up again and examined it. 'Her jewellery's missing.'

'But that's good!'

He smiled at her again. 'Yes. I haven't told anyone else about Piha. Especially Dad. She may not be there of course.'

He collected two more cups of coffee from the frazzled blonde behind the counter.

'What will you do?'

'Go to Piha. Find her.' He stared at her. 'It's a million times worse for you.'

She shook her head. Not in negation, in not knowing anything, in not understanding anything ever again.

They sat holding hands for some time in silence. 'Just like *Brief Encounter*,' hissed the blonde to the sandwich lady in the kitchen. 'Go and have a shufti.'

Jack was using his boot to lower the level of neatly wrapped garbage in the rubbish bin when Sarah arrived home. Dora was clumping around the back yard in a bright red pair of gumboots.

'Unfortunately, Mum,' she said, 'they're not working. I suppose they're too big.'

'They're Granny's,' said Sarah, kissing the top of her head.

'She won't want them in heaven.' Dora set off across the concrete to the defunct henhouse instituted by Laura in response to her daughter's delight in the beauty of hens, their padded behinds, their beady eyes, their tearaway action when released to wider worlds.

Sarah raised her eyebrows at Jack. He inspected his boot and replaced the rubbish tin lid. 'Heaven?'

'Well, what would you say? I had to think of something. And anyway,' Jack brushed his hands, 'you don't have to believe in it to know that some people'll go there.' His foxy eyelashes blinked in the winter sun. 'How's Charlie?'

'Terrible.'

'Did he tell you that he's taken *The Judas Sheep*?'

'No!' It was the first time he'd seen that conspiratorial grin for days.

'Really the man's a weirdo. Fancy not mentioning it.'

Sarah propped her behind on a large square piece of concrete. It served no purpose, being all that remained of the dining room chimney which had been demolished after the '31 earthquake as a safety measure. She stared up at Jack and chose her words with care. 'His mother is responsible for my mother's death and has disappeared. He doesn't know where she is. He has other things on his mind.'

Jack's teeth were clamped together, his jaw prognathous as Neanderthal man's. He nodded. 'Sure. But you'd think he would've mentioned it.'

'Mum,' called Dora, who was having problems standing on her toes in the gumboots. 'Come and tell me what sorts you had.' Sarah strode across the suburban back yard which had once been a whole world. 'We had White Leghorns, which are good layers but not much fun, and we had Black Orpingtons, which aren't good layers but have brown eggs which are nicer . . .'

'Why?'

'Prettier. Don't you think they are?'

But Dora wasn't sure. She would have to work on it.

Sarah stared through the wire-netting at the empty henhouse and shuddered with loss.

Charles was right. Prudie was at Piha. He had booked into the guesthouse and started looking immediately. The first thing was to put a notice on the board in the store. He wrote it so she would recognise his handwriting. 'Mum—Please ring me at Piha 1. Charles.' She rang that night. She had rented a small cottage near where the family bach had been. Charles drove straight round. She greeted him with joy, amazed that he had gone to such lengths to find her.

Jane also had been surprised. 'Put a private detective onto it, why not?'

'Because *I* want to find her.'

'Why?'

Charles thought. 'I suppose because I love her.' He looked at his wife's face. 'Is it odd to love your mother?'

Jane shrugged and returned to her Stage II essays.

'As flies to wanton boys, are we to the Gods / They kill us for their sport.' Discuss the theme of poetic justice in King Lear *with particular reference to this quotation.*

She had been appointed a junior lecturer at the beginning of the year and her pleasure was obvious.

Prudie was calm despite her heartbreak. She knew she would have to face charges. 'That's not why I ran away.'

'No.'

'I was leaving. I knew if I stopped, went back to Waikeri, I'd be there for life. And I'd told Laura I was going.'

'I thought you might have.'

'I'll ring the police in Titirangi tomorrow.'

He took her long bony hand in his. She wore no wedding ring.

'I'm lucky I have a bit of money of my own.'

'I can't think why you didn't leave him years ago.'

She smiled at him. 'What did I do to deserve a son like you?'

'Married Dad.' They rolled back in their brown vinyl chairs and laughed. Tears of absolution fell down Prudie's face onto the hooked rug in front of the dusty two-bar heater at Malcolm and Philly Jones's bach at Lion Rock, Piha.

John Tandy remarried within six months. His second wife was a brisk Sister at the private hospital named Muriel Dench who collected miniature teapots, which she packed away when Dora was in town.

'Though of course I wouldn't mind any grandchild of yours, Johnny, you know that.'

'Yes,' said John.

He picked her up after duty and they slipped out to the links for a quick trot round the back nine each evening after John finished surgery, which happened earlier and earlier as the long hot summer continued.

Sybil was outraged, huffing and puffing down the telephone at her sister.

'Don't be nuts, Syb,' said Sarah, wishing she could tell Sybil not to ring her in the morning and anyway it was twice the price. 'Mum would be pleased. He's got someone to care for him. Mind him. Love him.'

'All ankle socks and dirndls, taking Mum's place!'

'She's keeping Dad sane. I've been up every week since Mum died. At first he sat around like a lost soul, poor man. Told me about the nasty taste in his mouth and the maggots in the dustbin and how lonely he was.'

'He wouldn't have maggots in the dustbin if he wrapped the bones properly,' huffed Sybil.

Sarah said nothing.

'He loved Mum! How could he marry again so soon?'

'Of course he loved her. What do you want the poor man to do? Ring Lookout once a week and tell you about his maggots? He's found this lady all by himself. Bought himself a trousseau, new suit, shirt, everything. We should be on our knees with welcome. And,' gulped Sarah, 'I am.'

'You don't sound like it.'

'I am.' Grief and loss, selfishness and despair clutched Sarah and shook her rigid.

'The wedding's on the twenty-fifth. I'll ring you later. It's all for the best,' bleated Sarah. 'I promise.' She picked up her brush and clenched her jaws together to stop her teeth chattering. The paint had hardened.

II

The Judas Sheep sold 523 copies, which Charles insisted was not bad for a local author in 1960, especially one as challenging, experimental and difficult as Jack.

'Why does everyone go on about my being difficult?' Jack muttered into his beer at the Midland. 'What's difficult about me? I just say what happens. I don't fart around.'

'You know what happens, why you use which word,' said Charles, opening his filled roll and discarding a slice of gherkin. 'The reader has to work for it.'

Jack ate the thing and licked his fingers. His meat pie had disappeared long ago. He refilled their glasses at the bar and returned. The pub was not the ideal place to talk business but he couldn't very well take his publisher to the tearoom at School Publications and Eastbourne was too far away.

'What happens is that a man leads another man to destruction and escapes himself and that's what I say happens,' he continued, shoving a full glass across the table at Charles.

'It's the way your mind works.'

'I can't help that,' said Jack, who had no intention of trying.

'I realise that. It's your strength.' Charles wasn't going to give him any better than that. Jane had used the word genius, had tried to interest the Common Room at Auckland University with mixed success. Genius was not a word Charles used. He wouldn't publish the man unless he was good. 'How's the next one coming along?'

'OK. Too many words, though.'

'Any name yet?'

'*Down to Earth*.'

Charles raised his eyebrows but made no comment. He leant back in his chair. 'How's Sarah?'

'OK. She's got an exhibition on. Just round the corner.'

Charles could have hit him; picked him up, kicked him out sprawling onto the pavement beneath the scaffolding and the painters overhead and the lunchtime office girls tip-tapping back to work in their high heels. 'Would you have told me if I hadn't asked you about her?'

'You did ask.'

Charles left him drinking in the pub and walked around the corner to Pearson's Gallery. Care had been taken with the mounting and framing of the watercolours so they hung successfully with the oils. Jean Pearson had done well and the light was good. Charles had never seen so many of Sarah's pictures in one space before. He spent the next two and a half hours staring at them with mounting excitement. He bought two small oils, a still life of pumpkins and kumaras and an abstract entitled *Colour Scheme* and left for the airport with his heart thudding and his hands clammy. He lay back in the taxi and tried to calm down. He rang Sarah from the airport to share his enthusiasm but there was no reply.

What kind of a man, though, would not mention such things created by his wife unless prompted? A man like Jack Macalister. Why publish him then? Why the flaming hell should I publish the sod when I despise him? Because he's good, because he's good and he must be published and I can afford to and not many people can. Charles felt balked, defeated, frustrated by his self-inflicted altruism from his desire to reject Jack Macalister, to stop the swine in his tracks, to fling him just once in his selfish shitty life against reality and rub his nose in other people's lives. He wished to refute Jack in the way Dr Johnson refuted Bishop Berkeley's theory of the non-existence of matter. He wished to kick something hard. The vision in his left eye blurred and danced in the zig-zag lines of incipient migraine. And Jane couldn't pick him up because there was some Staff Party thing on and it would take him hours, bloody hours, to get home to the North Shore from the airport by public transport and bugger everything.

He rang his mother from the Auckland airport. He had been away a week and it would be too late by the time he arrived home. Prudie was cheerful, full of plans for refurbishing the Jones's cottage which she had recently bought. He told her about Sarah's exhibition, how he'd bought two paintings. She was pleased, would look forward to seeing them. Perhaps Charles would bring them over to Piha soon?

He leant his throbbing head against the wall of the telephone booth. Thank God he didn't have the car. 'You must come and see us, Mum. You haven't been for ages.'

'Yes.' There was a slight pause. 'I'd love to but the road's a bit rough for my little car at the moment.'

'OK, I'll come soon. We'll both come.'

Sarah's exhibition was a financial success but Otto had been right about the critics. They mentioned her opulent colour. They were pleased by her tonal values. But they were more interested in the work of another woman painter exhibiting at the same time whose strong canvases reflected the frustrations and despair of housewives trapped in suburbia. Sarah kept her head down and worked hard, as did Jack. *Down to Earth* was published in 1963, sold even fewer copies and sank without trace. The *Landfall* reviewer, an Australian male academic, did his best with strong images of post-lapsarian Arcadia but no one was interested.

Jack, who was now writing part-time at home, wriggled his behind into the woven cushion on the chair in his office and continued his next book. He loathed them, all of them. He despised the limp gods who smiled on mediocrity and dismissed him as difficult. He wanted to kill them, he wanted lion-pits to trap, stakes to impale and jaws to crunch, but he controlled his rage and channelled it.

The Killing Shed was published two years later and did much better. The *Landfall* review, this time by a Canadian male academic, managed to be both muted and enthusiastic. It spoke of cultural resonances unknown to an outsider, which nevertheless had echoes for the reviewer in the self-consciousness of much colonial literature. The reviewer was also interested in the self-preoccupation of the text with its own story. There was an exuberant richness of texture and extended virtuoso prose flights. *The Killing Shed* was a powerful, difficult work, the subtext of which spoke strongly of death.

It sold 600 copies and was granted an Award for Achievement by the State Literary Fund.

Charles was pleased. He arranged a few interviews.

'What the hell do I say?' said Jack, masticating his lower lip.

'Just leave out the fucks,' said Charles.

'The ultimate aim of writing is discovery,' Jack told the young woman from the *Evening Post*, who wrote it down. 'My wife is a painter and I think she would agree that the desire to create works of darkness is shared by both painters and writers.'

'Why on earth did you say that?' demanded Sarah. 'What does it mean?' Her hair was now swept onto the top of her head and anchored by a rubber band before it fell downwards again. It looked faintly Grecian and left the back of her neck exposed, which pleased him.

'I thought you'd understand.' Jack gave a quick sniff reminiscent of Nelson. 'And I think it's true. That's why I said it. And anyway you have to say something. It's difficult to make any sort of sense with them sitting there with their ballpoints poised and their knees close together and their mouths open. You've got to say something.'

Nigel Macalister rang from Glenfrae. Nigel had married Betsy Gale from Gisborne just when Maggie had begun to fear that perhaps one grandchild would be her lot. Like John Tandy with Sister Dench he had found Betsy all by himself and wooed her and won her and brought her home to Glenfrae in triumph. They moved into the shepherd's cottage, fortunately empty at the time, and immediately started a family, which they did beautifully. 'It's one of the compensations of marrying a Macalister,' Jack had told Sarah when he first sighted Dora twelve years ago. 'We all have beautiful babies. But we don't necessarily last.' He was right, as baby and toddler photographs of himself and Nigel at Glenfrae demonstrated.

Nigel's telephone call was a request for help. Mum and Dad were leaving Glenfrae and retiring to Havelock North. Dad had seen just the place in Tauroa Road last week and snapped it up, though not of course until Mum had seen it and given it the OK. They planned to move in soon and could Jack and Sarah and Dora come up over Easter and help with the sort out and pack up and maybe some of the move, even, though Dad was getting Ashfords in for the heavy stuff.

Four days lost. 'OK,' said Jack. 'We'll be there.' He sat down at the kitchen table, reached behind himself with one hand for the cheap red wine and filled his glass.

Blue mist rose from the raupo swamp at the Glenfrae turn-off. The air was crisp; the late autumn sun, golden and Bellini as ever, poured over the bare hills. Mauve shadows defined them, the small limestone hummocks and the drumlins. Except for a few stands of bush in the valleys there were few trees. It was grazing land, a land flowing with milk and honey.

Glenfrae also was at its best. Stripped of curtains, denuded of Maggie's knick-knacks and Nelson's gizmos, the bones of the house showed more clearly; strong, plain and built to last. The fourteen-foot stud gave them room to breathe and the wide verandahs welcomed them.

Betsy was upended over a tea chest when they arrived, two blond infants tumbling at her feet. Maggie, her face scarlet, tottered past them with a box of thirty-year-old *Auckland Weekly*s for the bonfire which Nelson had had burning all week. Jack seized them from her. 'You can't burn those!'

'Whyever not?' Maggie's eyes were glazed with decision-making. 'I've cut out the wedding photos of all the people we know.'

'They're priceless, those things. I'll take them back to Wellington.'

'Well, if you want them, dear.'

Discard and resnatch in endless combinations continued all over Easter.

'One man's meat is another man's poison,' Nelson told Dora as she retrieved his ancient wide-skirted leather coat from among the oilskins in the back cloakroom and clutched it to her budding breasts.

'I can't think why they wanted us,' muttered Jack as he and Sarah lay in the twin beds of the spare room that night. No flowers this time. Maggie's hospitality was pared down and stripped for action.

'The whole flaming Road's here packing themselves silly. Betsy's doing her Lady Boss routine. Dad's got his burn-up and Nigel's got the rubbish organised. Why drag us up here?'

'Of course we had to come. How could we not come?'

'Nigel and the Lady Boss are going to be living here. Let them do the work and I can write my book.'

'Don't you feel anything about the place? About your life here?' Sarah turned to watch him, her hand on the bedside light switch. He lay on his back, his eyes on the centre light and its decorative plaster surround.

'No.'

He walked over next morning to check on Ernie's whare. Dora came running across the home paddock and took his hand. It was one of the nice things about Dora. Her affection for him at almost thirteen was as spontaneous and physical as it had been when she was six years old. She sat on his knee, draped him with her shiny black hair and embraced him.

Her hand was smooth and warm, a child's hand. 'Four today, Dad,' she said.

'Eggs?'

'That's jolly good for six hens, you know, at this time of the year.'

The door of the whare was not locked, but warped and bleached by the sun. Jack put his shoulder to it and fell sprawling on his knees as it gave way. The place was completely empty as he had known it would be, so why had he come? He and Dora sat side by side on the wooden step. Even the sheep were silent except for an occasional cough from an ancient ram nearby.

'What was Ernie like?' asked Dora.

He supposed her eyes were grey. They seemed to have no colour at all, to transmit nothing but affection, but he supposed that was a trick of the light. He had never lied to her unless you counted Granny T and heaven.

'Honest. Funny. Never moaned.'

'Why did you love him?'

He shrugged. 'Why does anyone love anyone?' He stood up, held out his hand. 'Come on.'

Nelson was still poking and feeding his bonfire on the concrete square by the laundry. He lifted his fork and called. 'Here a minute, would you, son?'

Son. Oh Christ.

Dora departed with the eggs. She wished to continue refurbishing the leather coat with dubbin.

Jack hunched his shoulders and ducked across the drying green, his head bent beneath a red-checked tablecloth and two damask ones which Betsy had decided might still be useful at Christmas, you never knew.

Nelson straightened himself. Red-faced, covered in ash, his working trousers tucked in his gumboots and a pitchfork upright in one hand, he looked ridiculous but he knew what he wanted to say. The pitchfork waved. 'Sit down, son.'

They sat on the steps leading up to the top level of the green. Jack could see Maggie's ironing machine through the cobwebs of the laundry window.

'Are Florence and Sidney still around?' he asked.

'Who?'

'The two magpies who used to hang around here.'

'No, no.' Nelson wiped his forehead with a soot-streaked handkerchief. 'Gone long ago.'

'Did Mum bag them in the end?'

Nelson's blue eyes blinked with irritation. Here he was all set for a serious conversation . . . 'No. Yes. I don't remember. What does it matter?'

'I liked them,' said Jack simply.

Nelson glared at the irresponsibility, the betrayal, the sheer bloody-mindedness of a farmer's son pretending he liked magpies.

'How do you and Sarah get on for money?' he muttered after a pause.

Jack's behind shifted on the concrete. 'Not very well.'

'Tell me.'

Jack told him: his salary, his pathetic royalties, the money he would get for organising a WEA weekend study group in May.

'How much?'

Jack told him. Nelson was silent.

'Of course we're lucky with the house.'

The large head nodded in quick impatient affirmation.

'Yes. Yes.' He paused. 'You'll be getting some from us soon. From Glenfrae.'

'What?'

'Well, of course.' Nelson's face was redder than ever. 'You didn't think we'd let Nigel and Betsy have the place just like that and you and Sarah get nothing?'

'Christ, Dad. Thank you. Thank you very much.'

'It won't be much, mind, not with the Havelock house and that, not at the moment, though when Mum and I snuff it that'll be a different thing again but I've got all that sorted out with young Townsend in McLaren Thompson and Speight. Your mother and I never wanted you to lead this half-cocked hand-to-mouth life in the first place, the two of you, but that's your decision and we respect that decision, like I said.'

Jack shook his head in wonder. Empathy enabled him to ask the forbidden question.

'Have you ever read any of my books, Dad?'

Nelson's eyes, bluer than ever in the smoke-grimed face, blinked again, this time in shyness.

'I've tried. Every one of them. But somehow . . .' A hand the size and shape of a nearby spade gripped Jack's knee. 'They're not easy, you know, son.'

Jack laughed; a liberating belly laugh of pleasure echoed around the drying green. 'Let's have a drink.'

'You'll be coming to communion with us tomorrow?' said Nelson. 'It's Easter Sunday, remember.'

Jack had switched some time ago from beer to cheap red wine or sherry which he bought in flagons and hid about the house at Eastbourne. Not that he hid them intentionally. They were just there, a bottle perhaps among his shoes at the bottom of the wardrobe, another one in his office, always one on the bench in the kitchen. Sarah didn't know what to do. She had gone to the Lower Hutt Library, rather than the Eastbourne one, to see if there was a book called, perhaps, *Does Your Loved One Drink Too Much?* There was. The advice given was that the worst possible thing the partner of the drinker could do was to criticise and nag. This would immediately put the drinker on the defensive and make him/her feel guilty whereupon he/she would drink more. And what was more and what was too much and what was 'all right'? Jack seemed fuddled at night. He wasn't obviously drunk, but he often tripped slightly as he undressed. He lost things. His attack was less sharp. Sarah tried to discuss the situation with no success because according to Jack there was no situation. He could always win with words. Not the easy slang of his unconsidered everyday speech but when he wished he could marshal them, group and deploy them, accurate, fast and deadly. His delivery also was timed for maximum effect; when other people were present and Sarah's guard was down, or flung across the room at her when she was exhausted. Sarah lacked his finesse, his twist as blade brushed bone. She stumbled on, her verbal blows clumsy but cumulative in their effect as lead poisoning. He drank too much. Why hadn't he come home last Thursday? Where had he been? What did he do with his money? Who did he think she was to put up with this drinking and whatever else he was doing night after night? The nagging phrases appalled her: slimy toad words flopping from a bottomless pit of complaint and each one justified.

Sarah was glad to get to the fresh air, the space and the sweep of Glenfrae, to watch the changing light on the hills and Dora's pleasure as her father showed her once more the best rocks for crays, or they hunted down the old grave in the bush. Sarah enjoyed the treasure hunt and trove of other people's discards. She and Jack were both working too hard, that was part of the trouble. It was good to be here with amiable people and not to have to think about food.

She picked up her cardboard carton laden with half-empty pickle jars and sauce bottles which Maggie had eventually decided she could live without in Tauroa Road and headed for the trailer parked by the kitchen door. This was what Nelson called Nigel's part of ship. His elder son ran a shuttle service to the farm tip and rattled back, the empty trailer bouncing behind the Land Rover as he shouted the number of the recently completed expedition to anyone within earshot. 'Eight!' 'Nine!' He was already up to ten. He reckoned at this rate he might get up to twenty.

The storeroom door was ajar. Sarah shoved it open with one hip, intent on more expendable and sticky jars. Jack stood with his back to her, his head flung back, a whisky bottle upended to his mouth. He swung around in horror, one hand slamming the bottle on the bench.

Dora was beside Sarah, her eyes wide.

'Dad! What are you doing?'

'Sarah!' called Betsy. 'It's your father on the telephone. In the hall.'

Jack had been surprised at the invitation to run a WEA Study Weekend at Piha. Why anyone would want to attend a series of lectures on 'The Novel Today' tutored by someone as lacking in popular appeal as himself was beyond him. However, that was the organisers' problem. (They had hoped for M.K. Joseph, he learnt later, but he was unavailable.) Jack accepted. He noted that alcohol was forbidden at the course but doubted if they would search amongst the supervisor's socks. He had cut down since the apocalypse at Glenfrae. He still woke sweating in the night at the memory of the stricken faces, the puzzled half-comprehension on Dora's, the disgust on Sarah's.

He suggested they both accompany him on the course. It lasted from Friday to Monday and they could stay an extra day or so, why not? It was to be held at Piha in some sort of trampers' hostel place. It sounded a bit basic but would they like to come? They were pleased, smiled at him, rewarded his attempt to organise a treat for the rest of the family while nobly working himself.

Sarah had stayed at Piha as a child in Prudie's family bach and loved the Waitakeres and the wild iron-sand beaches. Dora had never seen them. The ever-blessed Mrs Dossi promised to feed Werther, they packed the car and set off.

The hostel was a disappointment. They had expected bunkrooms and spartan ablutions block but not decay. Slimy buff and coral-coloured mould trekked down the tongue-and-groove of the showers. Dora produced a pallid toadstool from the floor of the washroom; the drying room was hung about with unclaimed single socks, a couple of bras and unappealing rags which presumably had once been underwear.

There were signs everywhere. Fiercer, more peremptory notices than the yellowing parchments recently removed from the walls of Glenfrae instructed the guests to shower quickly, not to loiter in the dining room, not to smoke, never to drink, always to stack their used plates and cutlery after each meal as indicated. Knives! Forks and Spoons! Plates Large! Small! There were only two notices in the women's bunkroom. The management was not responsible for guests' private property and no, there were no more blankets.

The writer of these admonitions was Arthur, the caretaker. As Jack said, you could have guessed from one glance at his eyebrows. Enraged quivering thatches of hair leapt about his forehead and sent single spies across the bridge of his nose. He was a very angry man, faced with the endless labour of knocking fifteen bemused men and women into shape week after week and year after year. His wife did the cooking and was seldom seen.

More boring for Sarah than the decay and Arthur's bad temper was the attitude of the members of the course, who seemed to resent the presence of the tutor's wife and child. This puzzled Sarah. They had paid for their accommodation, they met the students only at meals and in the evenings. What were they on about? She soon found out. All of them, especially the women, wanted Jack. Everyone, except for an angry young woman called Penny, seemed to want him soul and possibly body. They wanted him to sit beside them in the dining room ('No Loitering Please!') and talk to them by the hour, preferably about their own literary efforts. They wanted him to love them and to give them his all. Some of them virtually insisted on it from the moment they arrived, inviting him to bring his disgusting coffee and sit by them on the verandah among the wetas, glancing up with ill-concealed annoyance at Sarah when she came to say goodnight to her husband before she and Dora passed 'No Men Beyond this Point!' on their way to bed.

Sarah was amused, or hoped she was. Dora was unhappy. She couldn't understand what was going on, why everyone looked at her like that when she draped herself on her father's knee and told him about things.

Sarah made a good story out of their awkwardness, their unnerving feeling of being de trop, when she and Dora visited Prudie on Saturday morning.

'It's not much fun though, Mum,' said Dora.

Prudie was serene and gentle behind her pink-framed spectacles. She had always loved Laura's elder daughter and was grateful that Sarah had sought her out. She leant forward and poured more tea from her plain white pot. There was nothing visible from Waikeri. Prudie had found everything for the cottage in elegant junk shops; single cups and saucers from the thirties, for example, each one a different pattern, which pleased her. She liked her strange old wooden-armed chairs, her cane rocker and her narrow bed.

'Come and stay the next two nights here, Sarah,' she said, 'You and Dora. I'd love you to come.' Her thin hands demonstrated her pleasure at the thought.

Dora and Sarah came immediately. Jack agreed it was probably a good idea. He found to his surprise that he was enjoying the course. He had much to tell his audience about things which interested him and they wished to hear. He was so busy he couldn't see much of Sarah and Dora anyway and if they'd prefer it, why not? He wouldn't wish Arthur on anyone—let alone the ablutions block.

Sarah rang Jack that night. Camelot was getting more bizarre by the minute, he said.

She was back with Charles beneath the macramé plant holder. 'What?'

'Work it out,' replied the tutor.

Dora was pleased with the white hailstone muslin curtains and bedcovers of the spare room, which Prudie had bought en bloc from the previous owners. She liked Prudie, was happy to stand on one stork-like leg or sit at her feet talking by the hour while Sarah sketched. Prudie was a good listener and interested in the alarums and excursions of the Third Form at Hutt Valley High.

Sarah also enjoyed talking to her, especially about Laura. Prudie was now very thin. She wore cotton trousers, faded Aertex shirts and tennis shoes. Her long hair had been cropped and fell about her face like an elderly but personable Christopher Robin. Sarah found that she was one of the few people she could talk to about painting. They sat on the verandah drinking coffee next morning in silence, their eyes on the haunches of Lion Rock and the white frills of surf beyond, endless, repetitive and satisfying. There were one or two surfers, their wet-suited bellies flat on their boards as they waited for the big one.

'Hear the bellbird?' said Prudie.

Sarah nodded, enjoying the sun on her legs. 'Mmn.'

Prudie pointed to a stool with a woven seagrass top which lay discarded on the verandah. Beside it sat a blue plastic bucket and a scrubbing brush. 'Tell me. When you see those, do you see stool, bucket, brush, nothing more, or do you see the spaces between and the shadows?'

The bellbird's limpid song fell about their ears.

'I see the shadows. I think I see the shape of the spaces between, but I'm probably kidding myself.'

The three of them went for walks together. Prudie flung hefty sandwiches and lemon drink into her minipack and led them to signposted tracks, all of which she had explored. They climbed up through the bush to the site of the old logging dam and on to the icy pool beneath the waterfall. They hiked over the hill to Karekare and ran wild on its lunar landscape beach chasing spinifex and hunting for interesting driftwood. There was scarcely a soul in sight despite the school holidays.

The course was due to finish at lunchtime on Monday but Jack had suggested he pick Sarah and Dora up early on Tuesday morning for the drive home.

On Monday afternoon Prudie and her red minipack bobbed ahead of them on the steep pull up the hill to Anawhata. There were one or two baches at the top. Hidden and secret, they waited with drawn curtains for their owners, or possibly a would-be intruder with a jemmy.

The drop down to the beach was also steep. They walked in silence. They had left Prudie's house late and must soon be heading back before the shadows lengthened and the evening came. Prudie and Dora jumped down to the beach and flung up their arms to run shouting in victory. The beach was empty. It was theirs alone.

Sarah retreated from the wind to pour the lemon drink. She stepped through a small gap between two gigantic rocks and came within inches of the faces and buttocks of Penny Broad and Jack standing barefoot in the sand. They stood upright and absorbed, stroking each other. Penny gave a low moan, flung back her head, opened her eyes and yelped.

The open plastic bottle fell at Sarah's feet. Rage and shame engulfed her, clinging and repellent as the stuff on her ankle. Shame for herself and for them. Astonishment of course at their mutual presence, but almost equally that it was Penny Broad. The encounters between them that Sarah had witnessed at Camelot had all been hostile. Penny's bushy head shaking, her stocky little body swinging away from the lecturer in what looked like disgust, must have been storm signals of desire.

They dressed. They hid. They followed later.

Sarah and Dora returned to the hostel that night. Charles, who had an appointment with one of his authors in Titirangi, planned to stay the night with his mother and must now be avoided at all costs. This was difficult to explain to Prudie, but Sarah was adamant without giving her reasons. Charles at this moment was unthinkable. How could she meet him and greet him, behave like a rational being at this time?

Penny had departed by the time they arrived. Sarah said little to Jack. Dora was delighted to see him.

They packed in silence next morning, received a dour farewell from Arthur and departed. The long drive back to Wellington was endless, made worse by lack of communication and three near-lethal pies at Turangi. Even Dora was quiet.

The row did not erupt until late the following evening.

Jack, who had caught the last bus home from the pub and decided that the best defence was attack, struck first. Sarah was selfish, she was cold, she was obsessed, she was a suspicious nagging bitch, she didn't give a man a chance. Had she any idea, the faintest idea in the world, what it was like for him struggling on as he did day after day, week after week? He wrapped his arms round his head and sulked.

'Oh shut up!'

He raised his head. 'What?'

'Shut up!'

Deliberately, slowly, he reached one arm for the bottle of red wine behind him and poured himself a glass. 'Would you like one?'

'No.'

'No, thank you.'

Sarah exploded. Giving as good as she got but with less finesse, with no finesse at all, with brutal honesty, she told him what she thought of him. In words of one syllable she told him, her eyes flashing, her fists clenched.

He was on his feet, the kitchen chair upended, its legs raking the air behind him.

'Right. That's it! I'm leaving.'

'Do that!' Sarah felt as if she had run a mile. The betrayals and humiliations heaped around her heart, impeding its function.

'I will. Now!' The sandy eyelashes blinked. '*And* I'll take Dora.'

Her heart stopped. For a second she almost screamed. Then she lifted her head and sank into another chair in Olga's wood-lined kitchen. She put her chin in her hand and stared up at him.

He was panting, his legs braced.

'Right,' she said. 'Do that.'

His jaw dropped. His face was a picture.

12

Dora was adamant, her eyes wide, her fingers clasped in anguish. How could they possibly expect her to go with them? OK, she wouldn't mind going to the UK some time but not now, see. Great for Dad getting a Literary Fund grant, she didn't mean that, not for a minute, but how could they possibly expect her to go? Each of her fingers led its own existence, bony and explicit as a self-portrait by Schiele.

Sarah removed the cap of her new tube of sap green and squeezed. The coil of colour lay on her palette, untouched by human hand, shrieking at her. 'We don't,' she muttered. 'Not if you don't want to come.'

'I'm going to be eighteen in a minute, for God's sake.' Dora's eyes glinted. 'Next week.'

Party. 'I know,' said Sarah.

'You can't expect me to leave all my friends. What about Max? Everything. I'm not going to work in Hurdleys for ever, you know.'

Sarah nodded again. 'No.' She dragged her eyes from the palette, frustration tugging at her fingers.

'Just let me do this bit?' she begged. 'Ten minutes? Please?' She smiled, nervous, placating, intent on keeping the whine from her voice, her brush from the sap green. 'Then we'll talk about it. I promise.'

The result was predictable. One of Olga's woven cushions arced across the room to land huddled by the door to the kitchen. 'It's always the same!'

'Don't *do* that,' snapped Sarah.

Dora, achieving a flounce in a miniskirt, made her exit.

Sarah's tongue damped her lips, guilty and grateful for her stolen minutes as Jack for an unobserved swig. She'd worry about it later. Her brush stabbed the virgin paint.

Dora appeared an hour later with yards of wet hair around her shoulders. She sank into Otto's chair with crossed legs, her eyes averted from the easel and the thinking face in front of it. 'It's always the same,' she repeated, her tone now flattened and resigned.

Sarah gave up and cleaned her brushes. It is nobody's fault. It is how it is and I am extremely lucky—am I not?—and we are going to England and I can see the paintings which previously I have studied only in Miss Pritchett's five-by-three smudges in History of Art in the Upper Sixth at Hastings High School with the windows wide and the magpies yodelling. She leant over the back of the chair, put her arms around Dora's neck and hugged her. Dora, who was five inches taller than her mother and had arms to match, responded with a headlock.

Sarah had thought in her sneaky scheming heart that when her daughter grew up she would be able to paint uninterrupted, undisturbed by the essential claims and rosy delights of childcare. Fat chance. Fat fucken chance, my sweet one, moon of my delight, my possessor, my guilt extractor. It infuriated her that she, who had parked her baby in coalsheds without a qualm and picked her up smiling when she was ready to do so, should now be brought to heel by words and the language of movement. She remembered Dora aged three months lying on her back in the carrycot, her face submerged beneath one of Maggie's woolly hats, which had slipped forward. She had made no objection, her arms continued their amiable waving; no one had told her that sudden darkness was unexpected, that there was any cause for complaint. Maggie, who was staying and couldn't tear herself away from the baby even though she knew she must get back before the shearing as it was a busy time for Nelson, was astonished. 'Why doesn't she cry? She won't always be like this, you know. She'll kick up bobsy-die later, poor little pet. Mark my words.'

Jack understood Sarah's need to work. It was one thing which united them, grew stronger through the years, remained the steel reinforcing, the matrix which strengthened and lay beneath the pitted and cock-eyed structure of their marriage. Again it had been easier when Dora was little. Occasionally Jack had volunteered. 'I'll get her out of your hair this afternoon.' Dora had regarded these expeditions to the beach, the local library, occasionally the long haul by bus around the harbour to the zoo, as gifts from on high, as had her mother.

Sarah and Jack had had few rows in those days. When they did occur they were brief, explosive, fuelled by the accelerant of knowing that they would probably end clutching each other, breathless and horizontal, their rage transmuted to passion in the best Hollywood tradition. Once when they were in full flight Dora, aged about eight, had appeared at the doorway of the living room in her pink footed pyjamas. She stared from one to the other and disappeared. They discovered her curled beneath her bed clutching Olga's sheepskin.

'We must never fight again,' gasped Sarah, as she extracted the stricken heap.

'Never,' said Jack.

They were still united by this semblance of understanding, by passion and rectitude. He knew as she did to keep away from the danger area of the other's private self. 'Stand clear of the vent in rear,' he muttered to his daughter occasionally after a glance at Sarah's face. Dora never did.

Unlike her father she took personally Sarah's despair when she couldn't get the damn thing right. His wife's absorption while working left Jack unscathed, as his silences did her. They shared throughout their lives the same unease, the same sense of work unfinished. They knew they hadn't finished their homework nor ever would. They respected each other's judgement, which was not given until asked for, when the end product of this obsessive behaviour was in existence.

'No one, ever, will see my first sketches for a painting. The first thoughts,' she told him one day, shovelling glutinous rice onto his plate.

Jack looked at it thoughtfully. Sarah's cooking had not improved but Maggie's feasts were distant dreams by now.

'They are my secrets,' she continued.

He nodded. 'Itches in the mind.'

They lifted their tannin-laden red wine to each other and smiled.

They laughed at pomposity and themselves and were serious to the point of tedium about their work. Jack's infidelities and drinking habits had scarred their marriage but not, so far, destroyed it. They shared the tunnel-vision selfishness of those who know that what they are doing must be done. Sarah acknowledged this was tough on Dora and tried to compensate. Jack regarded her efforts in this regard as oakum-picking woman's work and was rewarded by his daughter's deep and steady love.

Charles had suggested last time he was down from Auckland that Jack apply for a Literary Fund grant. 'You're thirty-six. Never been overseas. They send other people away. You're an established writer, whatever that means. Four interesting novels under your belt. Very interesting,' he said as he paid for their beer.

'I don't want to be interesting,' said Jack. 'I want to be good.'

'That's been said before,' said Charles, who would spend the next two days wondering where and by whom, looking it up and not finding it, resenting the need to know.

'Not by me,' said Jack, dismissing the matter. He dipped one finger in the spilt beer on the wooden counter, drew a five-petalled daisy alongside, centred the dot and licked his finger. 'Nobody buys them, the novels. Not that it matters,' he said firmly, a proud wallflower who didn't want to join the dance, who preferred the wall at the back, the dignity of disregard.

'That's an exaggeration. And look at your reviews. Here and there. People are sitting up over there. Taking notice. What about that *TLS* review of *The Killing Shed*?'

Jack nodded. The *Times Literary Supplement*'s review of his last book lay buried deep inside him, warming the cockles of his antipodean heart which didn't give a damn what they thought.

'It's high time you went overseas,' continued Charles, who'd already been twice and was off again next year to be followed by Jane when she had finished her marking.

'I like it here.' Jack bit a hangnail on his thumb. It parted with a sharp crack, was inspected and discarded on the floor. 'I belong,' said Jack, eyes shining as he sent up his own pomposity, but how else would you say it, 'to the Pacific Basin.'

'You only find out why you like it here when you've been there. Quite apart from everything there is to see.'

Jack sighed. 'I know. It's just that I hate bloody travel.'

'How do you know? You've never tried it.'

'No.' Jack's face was truculent as he lit another cigarette. 'But I could've gone somehow, if I'd been mad keen.'

Charles felt the old irritation licking around his feet. He was probably standing on the damn hangnail. He shuffled, moved slightly. 'What on earth are you on about? It's not only getting away. Don't you want to get away from School Pubs for a bit?'

'Yes.'

'And Sarah'd love to go,' said Charles, his eyes on a large colour photograph of the 1967 Auckland Regatta, the sparkling harbour alive with a myriad of yachts unexpectedly trapped on a dark Wellington wall. He moved his head to avoid the smoke. 'It would help her career as well. And people *fly* these days. It doesn't take weeks.'

'Then I'd better slap in,' said Jack, his face blank except for a single twitching muscle at one side of his mouth.

'Do that,' replied his publisher.

Dora went with them to England. Parents for whom children are not the whole world often have loving offspring. It is a fact of life, as is the reverse.

Jack's grant was generous, given the time and place. They could survive nine months, perhaps a year. They packed up, rented the house to Jack's replacement at School Pubs and departed. Now they were going Jack was angered by his previous lack of initiative.

Why had he stayed home so long? Why hadn't he knocked off Abroad before? Got it out of his system? He was bad-tempered for weeks. Sarah, ecstatic beyond words, treated him with the consideration he deserved.

They left behind a lump of gift-wrapped coal given them by Nigel and his wife Betsy to ensure survival during power cuts in London, which she had heard were imminent.

'Typical Betsy,' said Jack, staring at the shiny black planes, the sharp facets of the fossilised joke lying in his hand.

Betsy was Maggie's favourite daughter-in-law. Which, as Jack said, was not surprising. She made mustard with black seeds and yellow seeds and honey and spiced vinegar and gave it to her friends and relations at Christmas in jars frilled with gingham hats of red and white. Jack and Sarah donated theirs to the tenant as well as the lump of coal. 'But I didn't want you to open the coal! It was meant to be a surprise when you arrived,' Betsy wailed down the telephone. There was nothing wrong with Betsy. A good mother. An agreeable wife. She was all right. Except for her jokes, which invariably fell about her feet, stale discards from the table of wit, to be brushed from sight and memory as quickly as possible.

'Air travel is what Granny Douglas used to call a good sit,' said Sarah, peering out the window at the sun setting over some continent. 'Why do people fuss about it?' she asked Jack, who had also been reading for the last twelve hours and enjoying the drinks.

'Which one is that?' she asked a passing stewardess with an interesting tiered hairstyle.

'India, madam.'

Of course. There was a delta. Sarah picked up *The Female Eunuch* again.

Jack put his finger between the pages of his Patrick White and flapped it in front of her nose. 'You'll have to read this, it's about a painter.'

'Male?' He nodded. 'One of those all for art and stuff-the-loved-ones?' Sarah fiddled with the blowhole above her head, diverting the stream of air away from her right ear.

'The woman survives because she's an artist too.'

'That's nice.'

'A musician. Uncompromising. Intransigent.'

'All for art?'

'Mmn.'

Sarah nodded and went back to Germaine Greer. The cover was arresting: a naked female torso, equipped with hand-pulls on the hips, grey and rubbery as a wet-suit, hung from a coathanger. You would look at this cover. Pick up this paperback. 'Jane gave it to me,' she said.

Jack returned to *The Vivisector*. He could have guessed.

Dora left her seat behind them to saunter up and down the length of the economy class each hour. Someone had told her it 'helped'. The first time she did it heads lifted, mute eyes glazed as heifers trapped in an overloaded truck had followed her progression up and back, up and back. Dora enjoyed the sensation of showing off in the cause of holistic medicine and continued to give mild pleasure to several every hour on the hour. Her legs were too long. They twitched with confinement but she enjoyed the plastic meals.

'What's a "roman-fleuve"?' She was now leaning over the back of Sarah's seat.

'I don't know,' said Sarah, 'and do stop kicking my seat.'

'Novel about a family. Saga. That sort of thing,' said Jack. 'Why?'

Dora held C.P. Snow's *Last Things* between two fingers. 'This is one.'

'Don't touch it!' yelped Jack. Heads lifted from their pens.

'Charles gave it to me.'

'He must be mad! The thing's so leisurely it's horizontal. All the man does is drift around commenting on the claret and being restrained. It's crap, absolute crap. Don't read it. Or rather, do read it and tell me what you think of it like a good girl.'

Dora kissed the top of her father's head and reassembled her legs. It was time for her to undulate.

*

Heathrow was a shock, the sensation of exclusion from the informed members of the tribe almost overwhelming. The three of them appeared to be the only ones among the scurrying figures, the purposeful queues, who had no idea where to go or what to do; three worker ants without a password, unbriefed and ineffectual, they stood close together, staring at symbols, hoping for a sign. Sarah, to her astonishment, was useless, and Jack not much better. Customs had been all right, the herding and drafting had not perturbed them. It was when they hit the main concourse that Dora came into her own. She saw notices they had missed, she used her wits, she kept calm. Sarah leapt out of the way of a man pushing a trolley loaded with three-foot-high Father Christmases, their pink plaster faces rigid with 'Ho Ho Ho's. She couldn't see their feet, perhaps they had none. The noise seemed to have got louder. A white-haired woman in a purple trousersuit pushed a laden trolley straight at them, her mouth a rictus of effort. Behind her tottered a very old man, his legs wobbly, his eyes damp. There were too many people, far, far too many people.

Two luggage trolleys stood abandoned against a wall beside them. One of them had lost a wheel and leant in drunken exhaustion against the other. Sarah ran to disengage them, to secure the operational one for their use. The impaired one floundered, flung itself at her feet, clanging to the ground in cacophonous despair. No one glanced or broke step. Sarah dragged the whole one free in time to see Dora wheeling a laden trolley in the opposite direction. She swore briefly, abandoned her prize and scuttled after them to catch the bus to dear dirty old London.

Everything fascinated her, sharp images of important and trivial differences greeted her each day. The petrol stations were different, the corner shop selling tinned soups, exhausted vegetables and Billy Bunter iced cakes swathed in plastic bore little resemblance to the dairies at home. The hoardings were better; gay with toucans, pelicans and bright pebble sweets for merry children. They did a good job. Beneath them bus queues shuffled in silence, over-familiar with such delights.

Sarah felt for the first few weeks as though a film had lifted from the mundane, dissolving like mist from a bush valley to reveal a sparkling new world, a land transfigured, unseen except by her. This unique excitement withstood grime and the surge of people, the troglodyte world of the flat and the bleach-scented boredom of the launderette. Even the pink pig landlord who lived above them.

This one-skin-less sensation, the quivering sharpness of her impressions, lasted about a month. It reappeared briefly when she returned home, and had nothing to do with her usual visual awareness.

The mechanics of existence also differed. Even to attempt cleanliness required effort, guile almost. Freshness had to be paid for, as in vegetables. Beetroot was precooked. A large woman, her legs encased in something resembling amputated cardigan arms, handed the shopowner a weeping crimson globe.

'I'll cut off the mould for you, dear,' he said, his cap on backwards, his eyes kind.

'Don't worry, Danny,' she said. 'I'll do it when I get home.' He wrapped the thing in white paper and gave it to her with a smile, heaving his collapsed trousers up with the other hand.

Sarah and Jack knew they were lucky to find the flat. Bernard Long had a friend who had a friend who was going to New York. It was a basement in Notting Hill and had its own entrance down the area steps, a fact impressed upon them by the porcine landlord as a point in its favour.

'You mean for us?' asked Jack with attentive interest.

The pale eyelashes fluttered. 'Yes.'

'Why?'

'You don't have to enter through my house.'

'Aah,' said Jack. 'Traipse.' He turned the central heating thermostat up to 64 when the man had ascended upstairs to wider vistas, cleaner air and his new red Magistretti dining chairs.

At first the truncated, disembodied legs trudging past at eye level were rather fun but their attraction palled. The flat was small, dingy and smelt of gas and sour dish clouts, their ingrained stench seemingly impervious to the slaps and tumbles of the launderette Bendix. Also, of course, it was dark.

Jack, who could write anywhere, brushed the toast crumbs from the kitchen table onto the red-tiled floor each morning, set up his portable Olivetti between the roll-topped breadbin labelled 'Bread' and a tin tray labelled 'Tray' in Gothic letters and began the first pages of his saga, his hands-across-the-sea salute to home. He wrote doggedly as he had always done, getting the words down, stopping frequently to rewrite, to scratch for the exact word he needed to show him what he meant, what he had to say, to capture the boredom and the beauty, the sunburnt decent banality of small-town life at home; the cheerful crassness, the tensions, the wonder of it all. Charles was quite right. You had to get away. Not for nostalgia, Jack didn't mean that. Nostalgia was not what he wanted. Jack slammed his palm on Tray in rejection of sentimentality, in gratitude for his smug conviction that he could do it. He was alone, attent and anonymous in his cave. All he had to do was to get it right. To show what it was like where he was a lad.

The local library, he was surprised to find, was useless. Even the drab spines of the tight-crammed books looked bored. There were few people and no old newspapers. Jack tried further afield and was rewarded by treasures he had not dreamt of. He showed them his letter from Charles (my publisher). They let him fill in forms, request things, wait for things and finally handle and read things, original manuscripts in the author's hand, which made him aware of his heartbeat as he traced the working of his man's mind. Crossed out 'O'Bloom a man of intrepid heart', did you? Yes, I see that. But why change 'heavy uddered, treading kine' to 'hoofed kine'? I rather like 'heavy uddered, treading'. Jack sighed. He would have to stop this self-indulgence. He was not here to salute heroes. The next day he trailed out to the Newspaper Library by tube to search nineteenth-century issues of the *Ayr Advertiser* and take notes for later use. Background verisimilitude was required for vol. one of his antipodean saga, which was coming along slowly between Bread and Tray, far below the eyes of the dismembered legs.

The *Ayr Advertiser* of Jan 1853 gave details of ploughing matches, General Meetings of the District Farmers' Society, of cattle and sheep markets. A black-faced ewe had been found straying. Its owner could have same etc, etc. The back of Jack's neck prickled with déjà vu. He could have been reading the *Herald-Tribune*, flung from the paper-car twice a week into the open mailbox at the Glenfrae cattle-stop. No wonder the Ayrshire 'agricultural labourers, citizens and others accustomed to work with their hands' granted assisted passages made Good Settlers, hardworking Pioneers. 'Everyman his own doctor, or common sense on common subjects,' an advertisement said. It all sounded very familiar.

An editorial was firm. 'We are sorry we are forced to admit that musicians are almost proverbially drunkards, but it is not music that makes them so.' Jack wrote it down.

He was drinking less, which surprised him. No one could be tempted by English beer and Spanish sherry was not for swigging. He must investigate cheap reds when he had time.

Sarah had applied for a term's painting course at a school of art in North London as soon as she heard they were coming. She had sent off her folio and slides, her references from Charles and Jean Pearson and waited for her letter of acceptance. The fee absorbed the entire profits from her last show. The place had better be good. The course did not begin till late January. Each morning Sarah ran up the area steps and headed for the waiting world. She hopped over the collapsible black umbrella which lay feigning death like a broken-winged sea bird outside the tube station, she stepped politely into the gutter at Notting Hill to avoid groups of young black men showing their muscle. Once she smiled. A mistake, as Dora told her. 'Don't be daft, Mum. Keep your head down.'

The tube pleased her. Why was there no monument to its creator? Who was the genius who had designed the map? Sarah searched each face in the rush hour hunting for clues to the endless patience, the calm acceptance of life nose to armpit and hip to thigh, noting the flare of red-haired nostrils as seen from below, the crisp chiselled beauty of a black man's ear. A middle-aged woman in a white crocheted hat with stiffened brim and a bobble stood in front of him. Her conversation with her friend in red was animated. She moved her head frequently, the bobble brushing the end of the nose above her with every happy nod. The man moved his head from side to side in resigned evasive silence. It was hopeless. His every move was anticipated by white fluff. Sarah caught his eye. Still completely expressionless he dropped one eyelid.

Sarah headed for the National Gallery. At first she rushed about like a demented hen distracted by excess but she soon calmed down. You are going to be here for a year. These places are your resource centres. Study those paintings, you fool. She made sketches, dreamt of shapes and colours each night and went home to start work in the murky flat. The bathroom had a skylight. Sarah put a stool in the bath, her shakey easel in front of her, and got on with it, attempting to imitate the strokes of pure colour, the streaks of rose and gold laid side by side on the brown shoulder of the coat of Rembrandt's *Old Man in Armchair*, signed 1652; the dribble of white paint transformed into the highlights gleaming from Belshazzar's jewels. How had the painter achieved the concentration on his mistress's face in *A Woman Bathing in a Stream*? Hendrickje Stoffels's eyes were downcast, her attention focused on the water in which she paddled, her shift held high. She would slip if she wasn't careful. How did he show you that thought? Hendrickje's chubby knees blurred before Sarah's eyes. She continued sketching.

After a few weeks she moved on to the Tate and while hunting for Frances Hodgkins came face to face with Winifred Nicholson's small painting *Windowsill, Lugano, 1923*. Paint had been applied quickly and vigorously with the fingers; the resultant impasto was almost sculptural. Five flower-filled pots stood on a windowsill, the landscape beyond receded in alternating bands of blue and white. Sarah stared with her mouth hanging. This woman knows what I'm trying to do. This woman has copied me. Who *is* this woman? No one seemed to know, least of all the bored and adenoidal young woman in the bookstore and why should she?

It was not the subject matter. Sarah had no particular wish to paint flowers but the subject was incidental. This woman was painting colour and light, she knew they were the same thing, the essential preoccupation. Sarah saw Otto in his characteristic position at one end of the table in Eastbourne, his hands flattening a fat paperback of Delacroix's *Journals*, heard him murmur about light and yearning and desire. Who was this woman who was prepared to experiment with speed, to be fast and furious with her fingers in 1923? 'Fingers were made before forks!' She heard Nelson's voice boom above the crashing surf as he tucked into crayfish caught minutes before and cooked on the beach in a kerosene tin.

She searched periodicals and art books. Ben Nicholson was always there, Winifred very occasionally. Sarah found several of her paintings in a private gallery and studied them, noting the weight of colour against colour, the balance. This is what I am going to do. This is how I am going to paint for ever. She began deliberately to copy. The results were bad, bad beyond bad peculiar. Sarah sat for hours on her stool in the bathroom staring at her attempts in despair. She longed for the painting course to begin so someone could help her, point in the direction of her opponent so she could fight on—a bare-knuckled boxer blinded by blood, obsessed by victory against all odds.

The amount of psychological setting-up exercises she seemed to require to enter private art galleries depressed her. She hated herself, her shy glances, her nervous intimidated smiles, her jittery behaviour when signing the Visitors' Book. Only her conviction that Winifred Nicholson could tell her something she had to know overcame imminent failure of nerve when a young assistant shimmied past her on the stairs bearing a tray of sandwiches and champagne.

'Are you joining them?' she asked when he reappeared. 'No, no,' he said, dragging his hair back with an anguished hand. His cufflinks were golden cloves. 'That's for them. Up there. How can I help you?'

Dora had no such qualms. She strode into any gallery, however

216

rarefied, with her head high. She was now driving a 2.9-ton pick-up truck for Biba and enjoying life. She and her new pair of bell-bottomed jeans from The Emperor of Wyoming could take on the world. She had been delighted to find the shop fitted out as a replica of the saddle-shed at Glenfrae, complete with bare boards, saddles on racks and tastefully draped bridles. 'They've *made* it like that,' she told Jack, who was not surprised.

'How do they know we're not eccentric millionaires?' she said, striding into the warmth and muted reverence of a Bond Street exhibition of Edo brush paintings. Sarah felt they had their methods.

A tall man pushed open the heavy glass door behind them with a well-heeled elbow. A stream of air sucked inwards around Sarah's ankles. 'Very alien culture,' he murmured over his shoulder. His companion, who was smaller, nodded. The door closed.

Sarah and Jack queued in the melting sleet for gallery seats for *The Wild Duck*. It was Jack's birthday and Ibsen excited him. He danced from one foot to the other expounding on the man's harsh humour, his sardonic insight.

'Have you seen it before?' asked Sarah, wondering if they'd get in before she wet her pants. It must be the cold. Surely not a chill on the kidneys like Granny Tandy. The results there had been disastrous.

'Of course not. I've read it.'

The doors opened. Sarah raced to the women's lavatory and queued again. A small woman in a yellow bun hat nodded at her. 'Before the war,' she muttered, 'you could spend a penny at the drop of a hat. Now look at it.'

'You know what he's on about,' said Jack as they strode through the dead sodden leaves of a nearby park on their way home. Sarah pointed to the naked illuminated branches of the plane trees above them. 'Trees at night are pure drama. Look! Made up. Invented.'

Jack was a yard in front, his face sectioned by yellow streetlight. 'That play is about home, don't you see? Provinces, cities, the terrors of small towns.'

'Terrors?' she said vaguely.

'Culture handed on from on high.' He was angry now. 'People ruining themselves. Trying to absorb ideas despatched from some metropolis to its hinterlands. Bugger it!' He stopped so suddenly she banged into him. His cheek was icy.

'Why don't you care!' he insisted.

'I do, I do.'

'Let's go and see Aunt Mary in Camberley on Sunday,' she said later as they lay in bed clutching each other for warmth.

'Whatever for?'

'She's your mother's sister.'

'So?'

The three of them went by bus, past 'Bagshot welcomes careful drivers' to the peremptory 'Camberley and Frimley Districts—No accidents please!' Aunt Mary ('Not Auntie for goodness sake, child') met them in the Rover. She had never met anyone from a coach before, she told them. But all went well. Dora and Aunt Mary developed an instant rapport. They were both elegant women with a vested interest in their own beauty. They appreciated it, nurtured it, gave it houseroom and anointed it with oils. They were aware of themselves and their impact upon their fellow men. They were flirts. This interested Sarah, who had never tried it. She had watched her daughter's reaction when a large man smiled at her in the bus. Her smile had stayed serene. Look me over, her eyes signalled. Dora at eighteen and Aunt Mary at sixty-five had a great deal in common. They recognised quality when they saw it and relaxed in mutual trust. Within an hour of their meeting Aunt Mary had taught Dora the Maori version of 'For he's a jolly good fellow', which she had learnt up the Coast as a girl and had not uttered since because you never knew what Camberley might think. It was different from home.

Like all flirts she treated men with positive discrimination. The boys got the breast when Aunt Mary carved. Her deceased husband Angus had been a happy man. She had nursed him to the end, missed him, but life, as she often said, must go on and did so very comfortably. She glanced around the munching faces of her relatives. They were all presentable. She might advance her sherry party a little.

'I understand you're going to attend some painting course, Sarah,' she said, placing the wishbone carefully on the side of her plate to be dried later on the latch of the kitchen window. There was no one to pull them with now. It was one of the times when she missed Angus. She had invariably won the wish bit. Not the wish always of course, but it was nice to dream of some treat. An extra week in Rapallo perhaps.

'Yes,' replied Sarah, slicing a Brussels sprout.

Aunt Mary touched each side of her mouth with her napkin. 'Why on earth do you want to do that?'

'I want to paint even better.' She is very like Maggie, thought Sarah. Better-looking and no one could call Maggie a flirt but they were the same vintage, from the same feminine gene-pool who peered with disapproval over the fence at the non-ministering females of the herd.

'I just love the penguin on your bath mat, Aunt Mary,' said Dora.

Aunt Mary's shining pink lips parted with pleasure. She'd just had an idea; she could pull her wishbones with Dora. She had another thought. 'Colonel Weatherley has a daughter who runs a gallery in London,' she said. 'Letitia.' She paused. 'Charming girl. Really. Though perhaps a little . . .'

Sarah sat up straight. 'Where?'

Jack was bored. He remembered his father ripping a bird poster from his bedroom wall twenty years ago. 'The Kiwi,' said the caption, 'eats roots and leaves.' The thought cheered him and Aunt Mary could cook. He handed up his plate at her request. Aunt Mary had not forgotten. Men always had seconds on the Coast.

Letitia Weatherley was different. Definitely different. She was lean, hungry and ill-favoured. Her hair was lank, her skin sallow. She wore unrelieved black and smoked continuously, scowling at the cigarette's glowing end with loathing. Her voice was the most pleasing Sarah had ever heard, her courtesy a physical attribute.

'Daddy,' called Letitia down the carpeted stairs of her West End gallery. 'Would you like to come up here a moment, please.' Daddy appeared, manfully attempting to hide his puffs as he progressed up the steep steps.

'What, darling?' he asked, proud of his clever daughter, his darling, the joy of his life. Letitia introduced them and went back to Sarah's portfolio. 'Miss Tandy is from New Zealand,' she said.

'New Zealand,' cried the Colonel with delight, his puff now restored. 'Do you know that we have a most unusual tree from New Zealand on the south wall of our house. A kowhai.' He told Sarah all about it, his pale eyes leaked with excitement, his hands shook. A forebear, naval man, brought it home in the nineteenth century. Sailing ship. A captain. Captain Nicholas Dukes. Really quite a curiosity. You must see it. A New Zealander! And Mrs Pepperwell is your aunt. Well, well, well. Next time, next time you are in Camberley. No, no, I insist. Edith will be delighted.

Sarah was in torment. She liked him, he was kind and probably generous but the effort required to keep her eyes fixed on his mottled face, his excited hands, when her real world was being judged two feet away, was excruciating. She suspected Daddy had been wheeled on by Letitia to keep her in play, to enable his daughter to concentrate and judge in silence. Letitia had ground out her cigarette, stabbing it with rage against a heavy glass ashtray before she untied the portfolio. Her fingers were gentle as she turned the unframed watercolours, the gouaches and bright oils. She laid them out one by one, giving each its gift of space on a long white table behind her desk. She scratched her black-leather-clad behind and stared.

Colonel Weatherley ran out of steam. Sarah said nothing. My heart is in my mouth. It is banging in my throat and I am unable to breathe.

She leant against the cool white wall. Stared at a Hepworth on a plinth. A *Hepworth*.

'Why did you come to me?' said Letitia, her voice gentling the fierceness of her gaze.

'I, I . . .'

'Because of Mrs Pepperwell,' boomed Daddy. 'Contact, a contact wasn't it, my dear? Any contact is better than none. Certainly so in my day. Aldershot. Whitehall. Ask anyone.'

Oh dear God. Sarah gaped in misery. 'Shh, darling,' crooned Letitia, lifting one mantis limb. 'Have you taken your work to anyone else, Miss Tandy? Any other gallery?'

'No.'

'Will you leave it with me for a day or two?'

Sarah nodded, speechless.

'Now,' said Colonel Weatherley, 'we can have a cup of coffee. I'll go and put the kettle on.' He headed for the stairs and descended carefully, one hand clutching the hand rail, his right foot testing each step before giving it his full weight. Letitia's hand gestured towards the stairs. Sarah went in front, followed by Letitia clutching the portfolio against her flattened chest.

Letitia telephoned next morning when Sarah was in the bath. Dora, booted and spurred for work, yelled from the hall as she ran up the area steps. Sarah leapt up, dislodged three wisps of bikini knickers from the towel rail into the water and ran to the telephone.

'Miss Tandy? Letitia Weatherley speaking. I think I might be able to offer you a place in a Group Show at the end of the year, in September.' The words sang, melted, soared upwards through the stale air.

'Are you still there? Miss Tandy?'

Sarah was shivering, her nipples tight with cold, a puddle soaking the carpet square beneath her toes. Jack, who was passing with a piece of toast in one hand, watched with interest.

'Yes,' whispered his wife. 'Yes. Yes, I'm still here.'

Jack reached out one hand for a towel and handed it to her. She waved it away in quick rejection. He kissed one nipple, leaving toast crumbs, and moved to the kitchen.

'Thank you,' whispered Sarah, one hand clutching her breast which seemed about to explode. 'Thank you very much.'

'I like your work very much. I'd like to talk to you about it. Would you be able to come and see me please? Later in the week?'

'Yes, yes. Any time. Thank you.'

'And my father sends you his best wishes. He enjoyed meeting you very much.'

'Thank you,' said Sarah yet again. 'Thank you.'

Jack was delighted, generous with his praise. She sat naked on his lap. They were thrilled with themselves and pleased with each other.

'I told you, didn't I,' said Sarah later in the bathroom, 'that Jane's arriving soon.'

'Here?'

'In London.'

'Where's Charlie?'

'In France. For months, apparently.' Sarah paused, her toothbrush clutched tight. 'I got the impression from her letter . . .'

'You talk about me and Dad! Your father's always "getting the impression".'

'Well, how else would I put it? I don't know, do I?' Sarah's hand rocked this way, that way. 'I just got the impression that things are a bit shakey on the Bremner front.' She loaded her toothbrush with a slab of peppermint-striped dentifrice. 'Why are they travelling separately?'

Jack shrugged. Gossip interested him but this seemed a bit tenuous, lacking in meaty substance. Not gamey enough.

Sarah looked up from the handbasin, her mouth ringed with froth. She spat, rinsed and spat again. 'And why does Jane want to come to Italy with us in August? It seems tough on Charles.'

Jack had lost interest. 'Charlie is a big boy now. The salt of the earth. A dead bore. Italy'll be enough without Charlie on board for laughs.'

Sarah banged a towel against her mouth, transferring a trace of toothpaste to its brown depths.

13

Travel, thought Sarah, gazing out the car window at a man with a white stick shouting at his wife in Arezzo, does not broaden the mind. Travel narrows the mind, reduces it to a survival course of where and how; how to get there, where to eat, how to communicate. It demonstrates limitations, it exposes weakness, it reveals.

'Though of course I'm mad about it,' she said. 'I wouldn't have missed this for worlds.'

Jane swung round from the front seat beside Jack, her sentence to him left hanging. 'What?'

'Abroad,' said Sarah. 'I like it. And Italy.'

'Good,' said Jane and turned back to her in-depth conversation about the Italians. She had read quite a lot of the Italians. In translation, of course.

Jack, who hadn't, was interested. Jane told him about them. He nodded, his hands gripping the wheel of the hired Fiat as they bounced along the country road to Monterchi. Sarah studied the back of her husband's neck, the quick movements of her friend's hands as she demonstrated the wisdom of Alberto Moravia, his depth, his humanity. 'He's unique,' she said. 'Quite unique.'

'One horse,' said Sarah.

The glance from the front seat was brief. 'What?' said Jane once more.

'That's what unique means. One horse. Uni equi. Uno horso. I read it somewhere.'

'Balls,' said Jack.

'It's all there. Everything,' said Jane after a pause.

'I wish we had some liquorice allsorts,' Sarah murmured to an old man on the roadside who was drinking Coke beside a pile of rubble. His face was seamed mahogany, shiny as a polished nut. He lifted the can to Sarah and grinned. She waved back, reassured as they sped on through dust.

'Is it much further?' she asked. 'Monterchi?'

Jack shoved the map at her over his shoulder. The car swerved.

'*You* find it,' he snapped. 'You're the one that wants to see the guy's stuff. That's why we hired this clapped-out . . . *You* find it.'

Sarah squared her shoulders. He was quite right. She was not pulling her weight. She was dragging her anchor, freeloading and being a colonial sponge. But there must always be one who susses things out, who finds the way, hops into, out of, across, before the others. Who carries the banner, the banner labelled 'Onward'. It is never me, certainly. But why should it be? What does it matter. I am not a fool. Why then do I behave like a petulant child? Because the lids are lifted when travelling. Quickness and sharpness shine forth, weakness is exposed. And of course Jane has the language— which is just as well.

I must, thought Sarah, try harder. They are doing this for me. I am the one who wishes to see as many paintings by Piero Della Francesca as possible. Not my husband or my best friend. I have wanted to see the frescoes of the *Legend of the True Cross* in Arezzo for ten years. I have seen them this morning. So shut up.

She leant back. The monumental shapes of the figures, the colours, the calm certainties returned to her mind, restorative as a blessing bestowed upon the devout.

She felt the brush of Jane's hand across her arm once more as she pressed a button on the illuminated guide into which Sarah had inserted 500 lire. 'You had it on Italian,' she said gently.

'I meant to,' lied Sarah.

'Why, if you can't understand it?' Jane moved away. She had a theory about a newly discovered fresco. 'I think it might well be by Piero,' she said to Jack, who was mooching down the nave with his hands in his pockets.

Anyone would think she owned him. He is mine. Sarah laughed aloud at her remembered flash of rage, her idiocy.

Jack's eye caught hers in the rear vision mirror. 'What is it now?'

'Sybil's teddy was called Mine,' said Sarah, giving up on calm serenity and cataloguing her frustrations into an orderly, self-indulgent and reprehensible list.

'It'll be cheaper if we share. You pay by the bed, everyone says so,' Sarah had told Jack in Notting Hill Gate.

Jack sniffed a lime-green sock, pulled it on and groped beneath the bed for its partner. 'I haven't any pyjamas,' he said, resurfacing.

'There must be some somewhere.'

But the mechanics had worked well. Buses had been caught, pensiones had been basic or spacious, tempers had been kept. Jack had no objection to sleeping with two women.

He watched Jane from beneath lowered lids. She pulled her pants on before her bra and dropped forward into it more slowly than Sarah, which was interesting. In Florence the only room available had a bathroom attached. When he blundered in in the middle of the night for a piss he discovered Jane flaked out on a duvet in the bath with one arm flung above her head, sleeping with the abandon of an exhausted child. He watched her for a long time, his hand on the flush button, then pressed it. Her eyes opened, brown, calm and smiling. The ribbons at the neck of her nightgown were pink.

'You snore,' she said. She stretched, yawned and turned her back to sleep again.

She was good at sleep, another talent required by the complete traveller. Whenever and wherever they waited, on cavernous railway stations or at country bus stops, Jane put her head on her pack and catnapped, to awake restored and pink-cheeked as Churchill.

They had travelled from Florence by bus, thundering along through heavy mist to Arezzo where they were to pick up the car.

'It's so romantic, so melancholy,' said Jane, staring out the window.

'I wouldn't mind seeing what it looks like,' said Jack.

'Do you know about Courtly Love? As a concept?' she said, changing tack.

'No.'

She told him about it. It was her special interest and had been so ever since she was an undergraduate. Her PhD thesis on a particular aspect of Courtly Love as a manifestation of the play element in culture had been well received. 'Of course it's part of the whole concept of chivalry. You have to remember that. *Morte d'Arthur.* All that.'

'Mmn,' said Jack, who was interested in every aspect of human behaviour but thought this one sounded a bit Pom. And anyway, what about Launcelot?

The bus shuddered into the station. Jane and Jack seized their packs and leapt down the front steps.

Sarah climbed out the back door, which sighed and sucked behind her in farewell.

'Stop,' cried Jane, leaping to bang on the driver's window, knowing that Sarah had got it wrong, would be driven miles in the opposite direction, would mess up everything yet again through incompetence and lack of attention to detail.

'Here she is,' said Jack, indicating the enterprising wife beside him who had got off the bus all by herself without being told to by either of them.

'Oh,' said Jane and marched towards the queue outside the Bureau de Change which she had spotted across three platforms.

It was while they had waited in the endless shuffling pack-kicking queue, sandwiched between Bart from Arizona and a small silent Turk, that Sarah had first decided that her attitude was in need of correction. She saw herself lying half-naked beside Jack after a swim at Glenfrae. The fleshy under-arms of Cousin Kath beside them had wobbled as she shook two small snivelling blond boys with vigour. 'I've brought you here to enjoy yourselves,' she hissed at their shivering faces while dispensing towels and rub-downs. 'Now get on with it!'

Exactly, thought Sarah, beaming at the Turk. His smile was hesitant. He doesn't trust me and why should he?

At last I have the chance to see the work of this man, which I have admired for ever. I am beyond postcards, reproductions, slides. I am *here*, with the originals. Her eyes pricked with gratitude as she watched Jane and Jack who were being so accommodating.

Jane was speaking, Jack was still nodding in concentration and agreement, his mouth clamped tight. Still Courtly Love, perhaps? Sarah's hand itched to slide into the back pocket of her husband's jeans, to claim his right buttock with a quick nipping desire. He had a beautiful arse, but so do most men till they droop.

And that resolve, not to nip the marital buttock but to buck her ideas up and improve, had been made less than twenty-four hours ago and once again she had failed to relax and revel in each moment. 'Enjoy!' Bart had instructed her in farewell, lifting his wad of lira to her in salute as he left the Bureau de Change. Yes indeed. Enjoy.

'The mind is its own place and of itself can make
A hell of heaven, of heaven, hell.'

Sarah clenched her fists in brief self-reprimand, executed a few mental press-ups and clambered out from the back seat as the Fiat stopped outside the tiny garage-sized chapel at Monterchi.

It was closed.

It should have been open.

'See,' said Jane, one finger demonstrating on the appropriate page of her green Michelin.

'Yes,' said Sarah and Jack.

Jane swung off towards the cemetery beside the chapel, the toes of her sandals pointing outwards with purpose, her arms swinging. Jack and Sarah trailed behind her.

Jack dropped one eyelid at his wife, a gesture shocking in its complicity and beautiful as well.

The cemetery was unexpected; a busy scene in a vast filing system for the dead. Pigeon-holed coffins were stacked row on row, immured and sealed behind concrete. The front of each grave bore an inscription giving details of the occupant. Several displayed glass-covered photographs of the incumbent. There were at least six similar structures ranged behind the front row and on the opposite side of a wide path. It was difficult to avoid thoughts of unimaginative housing estates, of concrete jungles of the worst sort, but they tried.

The flowers helped. Each grave had a vase attached in which women were arranging flowers, snipping off dead heads, climbing ladders to the upper rows with agility to top up the water from long-snouted cans, chattering and laughing as they refurbished the drooping bounty delivered to honour the departed on All Souls' Day a week before. There were many chrysanthemums, bronze, yellow and white. Mop-headed as Beatles and good lasters as well, they stood stiff and proud in remembrance.

Jane was questioning a woman on the top level. Her claret-bottle calves swung round at a dangerous angle to the ladder as she pointed at an old man far below.

'Grazie,' cried Jane, advancing on the old man. He replaced the large watering can on the path, beat his gums together like Gertrude of the purple feet and glared at her. Yes, his wife was the custodian of the chapel. No, he didn't know where she was or when she would appear. He turned his back on Jane and lurched up the wide path between the rows, spilling water on the dust at every rocking step.

'Sometimes,' said Jane, 'they can be as bad as the French.'

The custodian was in situ when they returned to the chapel. She was dark, and angry with them because she was two minutes late only and why had the Inglese not waited as they should have done? How could she have been in two places at the same hour, she demanded with wide-spread palms. All this was translated by Jane. They shook their heads at their own absurdity. Jane apologised for them all, Sarah and Jack nodded shamed assent. Eventually the custodian smiled, a crooked snatching movement of the left side of her mouth. Her hands forgave them.

'Grazie, molto grazie,' they said.

'Prego.'

Jack was thirsty. Very thirsty.

He kicked a large stone as she unlocked the door. It lifted and soared down the ruts of the dirt road as they entered. *La Madonna del Parto* gazed down at them.

The God-given wonder of people who can do it. Who can create an image which transcends both beauty and time, an image which has already lasted five hundred years and will, with luck, continue to exist, tough and enduring as the bones next door, though of course it's not. Humility and wonder, joy beyond serenity and shame at the ease of her existence reduced Sarah to silence. What on earth was she *fussing* about?

Her fingers gripped the altar. One port and one starboard angel held back the canopies of the small fur-lined tent to reveal the Madonna, her face expressionless beneath the flattened plate-like halo, her drooping eyelids heavy above downcast brown eyes. The lips were full, the strong right hand lay across her belly, its fingers spread across the white chemise beneath the gaping blue robe.

Acceptance and numinous awe stood flanked by solid angels, their red and green hose planted on the crackled white of the fresco floor.

'OK?' said Jack beside her.

Sarah nodded. 'OK,' she said.

She had seen it. They sped on through the mist to Urbino where they planned to spend the night so they could knock off the Pieros in the Ducal Palace next day. Fog is hell to drive in, both Sarah and Jane knew this, but they had insured the Fiat in Jack's name only to save money. They sat quiet and helpful. They were solicitous with maps and comforts.

'Shall I light you a cigarette?' said Jane.

Jack shook his head. 'Just tell me the directions in *time*. Don't leave it till we're practically past the bloody signs.'

'But we can't *see* them in time in this mist,' said Sarah from the back seat.

'Well try!'

'OK.'

They stopped in a small nameless village to buy the makings for lunch. A large white banner flapped across the width of the street announcing *Mostra de Tartufo Bianca*.

'What's that?' asked Sarah.

'Mushroom show. Truffles.'

'*Mushrooms?*'

'They're big here. *Porcini*, all that.'

'Oh.'

The butcher's shop was closed. Flattened cardboard boxes piled in the doorway leaked a rusty puddle of blood across the pavement.

'Look,' said Jane, setting off towards a hole-in-the-wall café filled with hawk-eyed old men with walking sticks.

Sarah, imbued with strength imparted by the Madonna, found the lavatory, nodding and beaming at the owner with multiple thanks for her directions.

She returned with speed.

'Didn't you go?' said Jane, glancing up from her espresso.

'She's been,' said Jack, who was enjoying his wine.

God in heaven! Sarah bit her lip. Madonna, madonna, madonna. And tomorrow there will be *The Flagellation* and *The Madonna of Senigallia*. She smiled down at her friends.

'I'll get the lunch,' she said, facing up to the counter and the woman behind it with sinking heart, her eyes on the inexplicable floppy things to take away.

She smiled and pointed and smiled again. Eventually the tired sad face smiled back as she handed over the steaming paper bags. Sarah offered her money. The woman shook her head and muttered something. Sarah tried again, flapping the notes slightly in insistence. She could feel the silence behind her as the voices and tapping sticks of the old men stilled.

The woman was bored. She gesticulated once more towards the wall-eyed man behind the till.

Give it to your *husband.* Of course! Sarah turned to place her lira onto the man's open palm.

'Give it to the *man,*' screamed Jane in her ear.

'I *am* giving it to the fucken man,' yelled Sarah back into her teeth.

She apologised, of course. It was ridiculous, she couldn't think what had got into her. Jane was dignified but not pleased. Jack said nothing. The mist grew worse as they crawled through the gorge to Urbino.

'The only one they've got left has a bathroom,' said Jane, slipping back into the front passenger seat. 'But he'll let us have it at ordinary rates.'

'Great,' said Jack, grinding out his cigarette with relief.

'Yes,' said Sarah, staring at the towering walls of the Ducal Palace far above them. 'Clever old you.'

Jack dragged the heels of both hands across his eyes. 'God, I'm tired,' he said.

You must be, they told him. Yes indeed, they said. That mist.

The room was bare, thick-walled and whitewashed, the only furniture other than the beds a three-drawered chest. There was no rug on the wooden floor.

'I suppose people pinch things,' said Sarah.

They fell into their beds soon after Pensione Famiglia Steiner's doubtful *spaghetti all'aglio e olio* and local wine.

'Thanks for a wonderful day,' called Sarah, but they were both asleep.

She shot bolt upright in the darkness, tense as a starter on blocks. There was no sound. She peered at her watch. Unreadable. She groped her way to the bathroom, avoiding the two other beds with care, and pulled the light cord.

Jack and Jane lay naked on a crumpled duvet in the bath. Jack was on his back, the knuckles of one hand trailing on the floor like David's Marat in death. His mouth was open, small incipient snores whistled in and out, in and out. Jane lay motionless on her side, her sleeping head on his arm, one hand curved against her breast, the other hidden.

Sarah watched the tableau for a moment, her heart thudding, her body rigid with shock. She leant across the bath, one arm outstretched for the shower control, and turned the cold on hard.

The row was short. Sarah was incandescent, shaking in reaction to the double betrayal. Jane returned her fire but it was of a different calibre and her range was inaccurate. They were adults, for God's sake. Couldn't Sarah behave like one or was that completely beyond her? She seized a towel and rubbed herself vigorously. Like most people with good bodies she had no objection to being seen naked but she was cold and showed it. Her bush was golden red. As Jack had told her in the bath, she was basically a redhead.

Jack, who was also shivering, wrapped the towel around his waist and tried to jolly them out of it which was a disastrous misreading of the situation and a bad error of judgement.

Sarah and Jane surged back to the stark empty bedroom. Jack followed them after a pee to discover Sarah now half-dressed in jeans and jersey rummaging about in her pack, digging in pockets, checking on passport, traveller's cheques, lira. She held out her palm to Jack. 'Give me some lira.'

'Why?'

'Give me some.'

He felt colder than ever. 'No, I won't.'

She sprang across the room, seized his jeans, emptied the contents of one pocket into her money belt and put it around her waist.

'Sarah!'

Jane climbed back into bed in her towel, pulled the meagre blanket round her shoulders and watched them. She had the air of a concerned spectator, a confidante in the dorm, a counsellor even, one who would do what she could but was not intimately involved and certainly in no way responsible for the situation.

Sarah continued her packing. She was breathing deeply. Consumed by rage and transmuted by fire, she was getting out of here.

'Sarah, talk to me.'

She lifted her head from her pack. Her tousled night-messed hair fell about her face, her eyes glittered. When she was little he used to tease her, called her Lily because her eyes were dark and dreamy as the house cow's. 'How many times,' she gasped, 'how many times am I expected to find you with naked women and still, and still . . .'

Jane's interest heightened. She sat straighter, leant forward.

Sarah's voice choked, refused to come. She leapt up and pulled on her parka. 'I'm going.'

'You can't walk out into whatever this bloody place is called . . .'

'Urbino,' said Jane.

'In the middle of the night!'

Sarah was now dragging a brush through her hair. She was still shaking, she thought she would shake for ever. Damn them both. Damn their eyes and blast their buttocks.

'I am not leaving this place. I am leaving this room and you fuckers.' The accuracy of the obscenity pleased her. 'Fuckers,' she said again. 'In the morning I'm going to the Ducal Palace because there is something there I wish to see and then I am going to fuck off.'

Jack was still staring. 'Leave you,' said his wife. She was beginning to feel faintly pleased with herself. A bad sign, rage was the thing. 'I should've left you years ago.'

He seized her wrist. 'What about Dora!'

Sarah glanced at the ex-friend's face above the blanket.

'You've got another playmate now.'

'I don't want her.'

'Thanks very much,' said the face.

Sarah walked out.

She knew it would not be easy travelling by Eurail on her own and it wasn't. After missing the train from Florence to Basle she discovered a great truth. There is always another train. With no one to organise her she organised herself, worked things out. Her sense of achievement did not dull the ache of betrayal but it had its place in her mind. And the joys of solo travel were genuine. Freedom from other people's time clocks, gallery boredom or tempers was compensation for occasional moments of panic and the approaches of amorous men. 'Je ne comprends pas,' she murmured sadly with downcast eyes at advances which would have been obvious to a slab of wood.

She arrived at the Gare de l'Est early in the morning with the address of Charles's pension in her pocket. He was in Paris for a month in August. He had some work to do and anyhow, Jane had shrugged, he said he'd skip Italy this time. Weird. Jack had winked at Sarah, who had not altered her expression.

She did not examine her motives. She was not going to descend on Charles, to fling herself at the man. She was going to see him and then go back to London and tell Dora what had happened. Her stomach churned at the thought. How do people do these things? It was no help that Dora was eighteen and a grown woman. What difference did that make?

She would not mention Jane to Charles. She probably would not mention that she had left Jack. She would see her friend Charles who happened to be in Paris, France, where she was for a few days and then go back to bloody art school and bloody London and work things out.

The taxi driver could have taken her to the other side of the moon but didn't. He delivered her to a small street on the South Bank lined by dusty chestnut trees. 'Pension du Bon Chat' read the sign on the door. Sarah walked in with head high. The man behind the desk did not lift his eyes.

'Excusez-moi.'

'Oui?'

She explained that she wished to see Monsieur Bremner who was staying here.

'Non.' He was not here. He had never been here. The man riffled the register in demonstration. No Monsieur Bremnair had ever been, nor ever was going to be, here. He himself, the hands flung apart, was very busy. 'Excusez-moi.' The head bent.

And to you too. Sarah pointed at an open letter in Charles's small neat script among the papers on the desk. 'Ici se trouve sa lettre,' she said gently.

The man shrugged, a gesture of painless and honourable defeat. 'Nombre dix-neuf,' he muttered.

Sarah climbed the spiral staircase and knocked on the door. 'Entrez.'

Charles was sitting up in bed eating a boiled egg. 'Good God!' She smiled, delighted to see him.

He was about to spring out of bed then remembered he was naked. There was no chair. He dumped his tray on a tiny bedside

234

table and patted the bedcover. The chestnut candles were at eye level.

Years of living on the ground floor or below had wiped the tree-house memories of sleeping upstairs from Sarah's mind. She walked to the open window. She could almost touch them. 'Nice.' She turned and glanced at the tray. 'Finish your egg.'

'I've finished.' He hadn't stopped smiling since she walked in. The lines at the side of his mouth had deepened. He was wearing his spectacles, presumably so as not to miss any egg.

'What on earth are you doing here?'

'I'm in Paris for a few days to look at pictures. On my way back to London.'

'Where's Jack?'

'I don't know. I've left him.'

His legs moved beneath the duvet. 'I think I've left Jane, or she's left me.'

There was a knock on the door.

'Entrez.'

A man in the shapeless black suit of a junior-ranking French waiter entered. He was old and small and sad.

'Ah.' Charles rubbed his hands. He would like two cafés au lait and two croissants, please. 'Black cherry jam OK?' Sarah nodded. 'And cherry jam.'

The man murmured something and reached for the egg tray.

Sarah pointed at the remains of the egg. 'Oeuf à la coque,' she told him.

The man's chuckle was unexpected. 'Oui,' he said. 'Oeuf à la coque, madam. Vraiment à la coque.' He departed, still chuckling.

They were lying side by side on the bed, the young woman on top of the duvet, when he returned. They thanked him profusely and Charles's tip was generous.

They spent a lost week in Paris looking at pictures together then drove down the Loire Valley in a hired Renault. Some days they said little but they were at ease together and the sun shone. Large raw-boned French cows peered at them through cow parsley as they picnicked deep in Corot landscapes. They visited chateaux hand in hand. A woman flapped Sarah away from her stall, which sold plaster replicas of Chenonceau. Sarah was beautiful but would she please move. Sarah leapt away, realising with delight that the woman was telling her in French that she was a better door than a window. They stayed in small country inns which varied in quality but all provided a bed. Sarah sent postcards to Dora, who was staying with Aunt Mary, wondered how to sign them and realised this was ridiculous. She had never obtained Jack's permission for the countless tokens of parental affection, the love and kisses she had signed on his behalf throughout the years. 'I am in France now,' she wrote from Blois. 'We love you, Mum and Dad.'

They ate that night in a large brightly lit restaurant in the centre of Tours which someone had told Charles was the place for shellfish.

She didn't care what it was the place for. She was glad to be here with him at this wobbly table. She looked at the mouth she had sucked last night, the useful fingers which clutched the menu. She had put Jack and Jane away. They were somewhere else.

A man entered the restaurant, a dignified man in a dark suit and brown hat. The back of his neck was red, his moustache drooped, his eyes were dark-ringed. He hung up his hat and sat down at a central table beneath an overhead light, placed his hands flat on the table beside a curiously shaped water bottle labelled Ricard Anisette, nodded to the waiter and ordered without a glance at the menu. Contained, self-composed, he waited, detached from the cheerful babble, the three-generation parties, the lovers. A regular customer at his regular eating house. A mountain of steaming shells was placed in front of him and a half-bottle of white wine.

'What on earth is that,' murmured Sarah.

Charles glanced to his left. The plate contained an incipient midden of pipi-like shells, mussel shells, cockle shells, winkle and oyster shells, prawns, a miniature langoustine.

'*Fruits de mer*.'

Without a glimmer of change in his expression the man tucked his napkin beneath his chin, picked up his implements and began his job of work. Winkles were extracted, prawns denuded, oysters extracted with practised ease; a twist of the wrist, a stab, a levering at the base of the foot muscle of a bivalve. There was no impression of speed, no apparent pleasure, no coarseness; any more than a bulldozer is coarse or a mechanical shovel enthusiastic. There was work to be done and the man did it with rhythm and despatch. He rinsed his fingers occasionally, he sipped his wine. He ate the langoustine last and lifted his hand to the waiter. He was gone in forty minutes.

'Stop feeling sorry for him,' said Charles.

'I wasn't,' she lied.

'Yes you were. It's patronising. He's probably the happiest man in Tours.'

'Stop analysing me,' said Sarah, concentrating on her *moules marinière.*

They lay in the hammock-like bed next morning while bells invited them to pray and Charles read the local paper, which impressed her. They stopped for lunch on a side road near Chinon in what must once have been an orchard. The bank sloped gently to a slow-moving stream which brushed the tips of the waving grass beside it.

'We don't have streams like that at home, do we?' said Sarah, her eyes on the slow drifting water, the shallow banks, the half-drowned grass.

'No.'

'Why not?'

He kissed her. 'I've no idea.'

'Probably because we're a young country.'

'Don't be daft,' he said, before he realised it was half a joke.

A fat man with shirt sleeves rolled up to expose ham-like arms, his waistcoat straining across his back, sat on a stool beside the stream; presumably a folding stool but it was invisible, overlaid by his vast behind. He was fishing; a red Jeremy Fisher float bobbed in front of him in the water. He had turned when they arrived, lifted one papal hand in blessing and forgotten their existence.

Madame, also large, sat with her back against a lichen-encrusted apple tree tatting. Her fingers moved so quickly they too were invisible. She was slower to grant her permission to stay but gave it finally in one unsmiling nod. Later she prepared lunch. She spread a cloth, she searched and found in deep baskets. She made several trips to their ancient Peugeot and returned. A chicken, sausages, something *en croûte*, five or six different dishes plus cheese, red wine and fruit awaited Monsieur. A *déjeuner sur l'herbe* such as Sarah had never before seen, not even in the back of Nelson and Maggie's Holden at the Hawke's Bay A & P Show. Monsieur came eventually after attaining the vertical with considerable effort. They ate with energy, tore baguettes apart, banged napkins at their faces, revelled in each mouthful and reached for more.

'Now don't start thinking it's different because there are two of them,' said Charles, lifting his cotton hat to laugh at her.

'I wasn't.' She pulled out her sketch book. 'I asked you to stop analysing me.'

She worked quickly, trying to define what it was about them which moved her so much. Two old, fat peasants tucking in on their day off.

After an hour or more Madame cleared away the remains of their feast, shook the cloth and stowed the boxes in their car. She returned. Monsieur patted the grass. She lay down beside him and they closed their eyes.

Sarah was still staring at them. 'We don't know how to relax, that's the trouble. Not properly. Look at them.'

He rolled over onto his stomach. 'You romanticise everything.'

'I do not.'

'It's because it's foreign. If they came to the beach at Waimarama,' she noticed his avoidance of Glenfrae, 'they'd look at us and think, "Now that *is* the life . . ."'

'We'd all be playing bloody cricket or heaving balls around.'

'Not me. I can't see, thank God.'

Not Jack either.

'It wasn't only the melodrama of *The Bride of Lammermoor*

238

Donizetti liked,' continued Charles. 'Scotland was exotic, romantic, far away.'

She knew what it was now, the memory nagging at the back of her mind. They, the old man and his wife, lay side by side like Otto and Olga. The thought shocked her, not the thought but what it meant. They were married, these two. They fought possibly, indeed probably from her glimpse of Monsieur's choleric face and Madame's sour one. They had reared children together, shared grandchildren. And now they lay together side by side in peace.

She sprang to her feet. 'Let's go somewhere else.'

He opened his eyes. 'I like it here.'

'Well, I'm going.' God in heaven, she must be mad.

He sat up slowly. 'Sarah, what's the matter?'

She was still on her feet, packing the remnants of their minor picnic. Charles clamped his fist around her ankle. 'Sarah?'

'Let me go.'

The old couple sat up, turned around and watched with interest, the man's napkin still at his throat.

It was two days before Sarah could convince him that she meant it, that she couldn't stay with him. It was her fault. She should never have come to him for comfort.

His face twisted with outrage. 'Comfort!'

'I'm sorry, I didn't mean . . . I've got to go. Now.'

'Why? You see two old peasants stuffing themselves and you . . .'

'It's nothing to do with that. You romanticise me. Bore into my brain.'

'Don't be insane.'

'You have every right to hate me. I know that. I've always known that. But not to pretend I'm something, someone, else. Someone gentle. Loving.'

'For Christ's sake!'

'If I stay with you I won't be able to paint.'

'What the hell are you talking about!'

'My painting is me.' Her eyes were fixed on his, her fingers plaited together in her intensity. 'I'm not what you want. You've got it all wrong. I'm not like your mother!'

He banged his knee against the iron bedstead as he leapt at her in rage. The pain was excruciating.

She tried to be rational, to explain her unease, but he refused to listen. They fought bitterly, hissing things at each other which they would never forget, their faces distorted, their eyes blinded by their spiralling self-destruction.

Eventually he shouted in despair, 'Are you going back to him?'

'I don't know.'

'If you leave me now, I'll never see you again. This is it, by God. He can kill you, the sod, kill you and I won't lift a finger.'

'I know.'

'Why! Why?'

She stared at his agonised face, his shielded eyes. 'It wouldn't work. It wouldn't work for you either. You want to be too close to me. Too married.' She gasped, a shuddering intake of breath. 'And I don't.'

14

It was money, or lack of it, that brought her back. Sarah didn't have any. None of the considerable amount left by Laura to John Tandy had as yet filtered through to his children. Sarah had sunk all the proceeds from her last exhibition in the art school fees and in so doing had lost both her freedom and her 'float'. She couldn't get herself and Dora home. And would Dora come, 12,000 miles away from her crowded life and the pale hands of her new boyfriend Henry, even if her mother could pay her fare?

Sarah walked out of Notting Hill Gate tube station on an airless August evening feeling sick. Her pack was heavy, the straps bit into her shoulders and her neck ached. The Channel crossing had been rough.

She was almost knocked off her feet by two young men who cannoned into her. They wore suits and ties and well-polished shoes and carried retractable white sticks. Their hair flopped over their foreheads as they apologised. They couldn't be more sorry, was she hurt? No, no, not at all. Well thank God for that, Simon, you blind fool. But Simon wouldn't play. If Rupert hadn't been talking so hard he could've seen disaster ahead. I do apologise, let me rephrase that. What was his stick for anyhow? They laughed at each other, their faces alive and teasing, their eyes blank, their white sticks silent as they spoke. Please would she let them buy her a drink? They couldn't be more sorry once more. They introduced themselves. 'You see, that's the trouble,' said Rupert, 'we get a bit cocky. Sometimes, just occasionally. You will forgive us. Now what about that drink, Sarah, is it? Sarah. There's a pub round here somewhere. Where do you come from, Sarah? Ah, New Zealand. I couldn't place that, could you, Simon?' Simon couldn't either but that wasn't surprising. They didn't think either of them had met anyone from New Zealand before.

Sarah would have liked to drink with them, talk to them, watch the discrepancy between their eager faces and damaged eyes. She stared from one to the other wondering whether she would have sketched them, been sneaky enough to attempt the contrast. She felt sicker than ever. She thanked them, explained that she had to get home to her husband (dear God). No, no, she was quite all right. She shook hands with Rupert and Simon and left them striding ahead, their sticks tapping, their faces still alive with pleasure at Simon's, no no, Rupert's, balls-up in B company.

It was late August, dusty, dry and very hot. Another rubbish collectors' strike must be in progress. Reeking black sacks leant against each other in doorways and split. A plane tree sighed, almost crackled, above her head. Even the few elegant gardens in Notting Hill Gate were parched. It was difficult to keep the colour going in late summer, an attendant gardener confided to Sarah as she stopped beside his railings to adjust her pack, but Madam didn't fancy dahlias. She had taken against them three years ago and that was that. There was nothing he could do.

Sarah walked down the area steps and opened the door with her key. Her neck was more painful than ever. Jack was sitting in the gaseous kitchen in his underpants, his typewriter centred as usual between Bread and Tray.

He looked up as she entered, his face glistening with sweat. The hand about to slam the carriage back paused in mid-air. 'Good evening,' he said.

Cold-eyed, expressionless, they stared at each other. The smell of gas was stronger than ever. Sarah dumped her pack and sat opposite him. 'Good evening.'

They sat in silence. A cockroach made a dash for it from beneath the gas cooker. Jack's leg stamped. He hobbled to the door with the toes of one foot poised in mid-air and scraped the remains onto the Victorian boot scraper. He grasped the door, waved it back and forwards a few times in a futile attempt at draught production and left it open. 'Well,' he said.

'I didn't think you'd be home.'

'I am.'

'Yes.' She paused. There was no air. None. Not a breath. 'Have you rung Dora?'

'Yes.'

'What did you say?'

'Nothing.'

Sarah's shoulders relaxed, her breathing slowed. She rubbed the back of her neck with her right hand.

Jack padded around the table, his bare feet slapping the tiles. He stood behind her and took over, his hands kneading her neck, digging, easing, probing deep into the pain. Sarah rolled her head backwards and sighed.

'When's she coming home?'

'On Friday.'

'Good.' She smiled. 'That's good.' She would tell him about Charles later. He would presumably tell her about Jane. His fingers kept digging, relaxing and digging again.

The sensation was unexpectedly sensual. 'I'm not going to sleep with you,' she said, her eyes fixed on the boot scraper, the ex-cockroach and the steep area steps.

Dora arrived home having had a happy time with Aunt Mary, though why they hadn't let her stay in the flat by herself she'd never know. Aunt Mary had shown her all her furs. 'I don't like furs, though. They're so dead.'

Sarah smiled at her daughter, enjoying the sight of her in her sale-price Quant. 'No deader than your coat. But I know what you mean.'

Dora strode around swinging London in her grandfather's leather coat feeling good. She was at ease among the miniskirts and the leather and the pot-scented boutiques, the Beatles and the rock.

Her immaturity, her chameleon-like qualities, kept her happy;

her ability to slip from Aunt Mary to her friend Henry, from Camberley to Carnaby, without skipping a beat was an asset. Her enthusiasm for the kimono Sarah had bought for her in Paris had been muted until she learnt it was second-hand and found in a flea market.

She and her friend Henry now worked for a catering firm in Soho. Henry was pudgy and pale; his hands, the whitest Sarah had ever seen, had faint traces of grime in the cushions of the knuckles. Sarah found his local accent difficult to understand but Dora had no trouble. He was proud of his purple lovebites and held his head high beneath his Canadian Mounted Police hat.

'Dora,' said Sarah.

'Yes?'

I cannot say, did you bite Henry's neck, so help me God, I cannot say it. 'You and Henry,' she said.

'Yes?'

'You are using some form of contraception, aren't you?'

Dora's pitying disbelief was both reassuring and depressing.

She arrived home next night shaken and unhappy. She had been stopped by a police car as she walked home from the tube with a sack over her shoulder containing vegetables discarded by the catering firm. Her eyes were wide with fright.

'They stopped me. They wouldn't let me go. It was awful.'

'Sit down,' said Jack. 'Tell me.'

'They wanted to know what was in the sack, and I said, "That's my business," and the older one said, "Watch it," and any more of that and I'd land up at the station, and the big one grabbed me and the other one looked in the sack and said, "Where'd you get this lot then?" and I told them and they sort of sniffed. And they asked me where I lived and I said, "Over here," and they said, "Prove it." They just stood by the car and watched, I'm sure they didn't think I really lived here. They didn't believe me! It was awful, Dad, awful!'

Jack found himself telling her she must be careful, the cops had their job to do. It was a tough area in parts, and it would have been a lot worse if she'd been black. He shook his head in surprise at himself and hugged her, soothed her and reassured her. It was all right. It wouldn't happen again. And consider yourself lucky you're not black. And male. And unemployed. He was beginning to sound like Charlie.

'Henry says that's why he doesn't wear a tie. Even if he wanted to he wouldn't. The cops grab them and throttle you.'

Jack shook his head in what Dora thought was sympathy and concern. Did he believe Henry? He didn't know. There were many things he didn't know and more over here.

The art school in North London was a disappointment and had been since the beginning. It was months before Sarah would admit this even to herself. She had been so sure, so determined that a formal environment with expert guidance would enable her to paint better, to dig deeper and to see more clearly. These wise men, these strong women would show her the path upwards from the arid plateau on which she was stranded.

She had produced, as required with her application, 'a mature and committed body of work', and demonstrated by so doing her 'ability to be self-motivated' despite her lack of 'formal art training'. They were lucky to have her and the fees were high.

She had waited with impatience for the course to begin. She had longed for her own studio space, the teaching access, the regular staff of visiting artists, the wide range of facilities and theoretical studies, the lectures and seminars and use of the library. It had seemed a dream and proved to be one. For months Sarah struggled to convince herself that it was her fault, she must try harder to gain value from all the course had to offer. She must work on her ciphers and crack their code. It *must* help her. She had always been self-critical. Otto had insisted on that, telling her in the next breath that she must know she was good; deep in her heart she must know it. But this self-doubt since she left home, despair almost, was new. The thought of the Group Show, of the Colonel's eagerness and Letitia's fierce expectations, appalled her. Normally she would have discussed it with Jack but not now.

He was working night and day in virtual silence. There was little point in Sarah taking an outraged tone about not allowing him in her bed. There was nowhere else for him to sleep. He fell onto the lumpy mattress hours after Sarah. Occasionally she woke to find him aroused with clutching hands, mumbling words of devotion into the back of her neck, but not often. The three-vol. saga was exhausting him mentally and physically. He looked haggard and unkempt; his frown of concentration was now permanent. He sat in the smelly kitchen and worked, which was the only thing left and lost to Sarah.

The work Letitia Weatherley had praised had all been done in New Zealand. Sarah tried painting from memory, which was another failure. All her abstracts began with a sharp visual image and memory was not enough. She had left their sharpness at home.

Sarah had high hopes of Sebastian Rivers when the course began in January. Beaked and severe, he would show her the way. He found her work interesting, stood behind her as she worked in her own studio space, murmured something about her lower foreground and moved on. He reappeared, his shoulders hunched in his denim jacket. 'But then Cézanne wasn't interested in foregrounds either,' he whispered.

Stephanie Hodwell, foursquare and forthright, wanted Sarah to get right back to basics. There was something wrong with her fundamental handling of paint for God's sake. 'Show me. I'll watch, you paint. Show me.' She hoisted one buttock onto a nearby table and watched in silence while Sarah worked on a still life. Once or twice she moved nearer, peered at the canvas and retreated to the table again. 'It looks all right,' she said finally, 'but there's a flatness.' She picked up a jar of water abandoned by a previous student and squinted through it as through a prism. 'You know what I mean?'

'No.'

Ernest Limpour was the one who sliced her hopes of external help off at the knees. His eyes gleamed behind his horn rims, his face was smooth and scrubbed, he smiled on the world, told jokes of breath-catching obscenity and was reputed to be depressive.

Sarah admired his work more than any she had seen of the rest of the teaching staff. He painted the unlovely streets of the Midlands town of his childhood; strong lonely images, their bleakness sometimes relieved by a red sign swinging, a child at play. 'Frankly,' Sarah heard Sebastian murmur to Stephanie in the corridor after his recent exhibition, 'Worksop and Ernest's angst in tandem are too much. All those drear disconnected *shapes*.'

Sarah confided in him: her self-doubts, so sudden and inexplicable, her gratitude at even a glimpse of her former confident attack. She made no mention of course of her private life: the uneasy basement truce with Jack, who she feared was drinking again, her concern at Dora's passion for the slob-like Henry. Her eyes begged his for help as they sat facing each other in the Life Room, alone except for Jason, a short-arsed barrel-chested model who stood combing his dark curls in a corner. He adjusted the collar of his pea-jacket, lifted a hand to them in farewell and departed.

Ernest tipped back his chair. He liked gossip, soul-searching, appeals even.

'You have a place in Letitia Weatherley's Group Show in September I understand, Miss Tandy.'

'Yes.'

'I know Letitia. She has a very good reputation. She and her gallery.' He considered the situation. 'An unknown colonial. Not even from Australia. It's quite a coup, you know.'

'But how am I going to do it!' Her hand flicked upwards at her easel. 'She won't take this stuff.'

'Does she want oils or watercolours?'

'Both. She wants eight or nine to choose from.'

'Well, work. Get on with it. Forget all this. Listen.' He leant forward, he had something to tell her. She liked his short As, his chances and his dances. He put his hand on her knee then snatched it away. 'Impotence is often transitory, and despair very cruel while it lasts. But this flat period won't last. And much, much better than impotence because you can work your way out of it.' He clasped his hands, loving the anxious face before him. 'Whatever sort of mess your life is, and I'm sure,' he added hurriedly, 'that it's absolutely splendid, you can *work* your way out of this Grimpen Mire, this Tandy flat. No one can do it but you. I suppose you came here,' the neat, well-barbered head bobbed in accusation, 'I suppose you came here thinking these bastards are experts. They can put me right. Didn't you?'

'Yes, but . . .'

'I know, I know. You're going to tell me you've been trying for weeks.'

'Months.'

'Months, then.' His fingers snapped the wasted time away. A small black shape lay by the door. Jason had dropped his comb. He would be sunk without it.

'Months. So? There are plenty more.'

'Not enough. Not till November.'

'You still have the New Zealand ones?'

'Yes.'

'Well then, you still have a chance. The mistake you made,' one finger demonstrated, stabbing her error back at her, 'was in thinking that anyone here could fix your *malaise*. We can help, we can teach, we can explain and advise. But we all have periods of inertia, of self-loathing even. Determination can help, plus of course talent, let's not forget talent. No one else can do it. Only you.'

She knew this already. Otto had told her. Her hand touched his briefly. 'Thank you. Yes. Yes, I see what you mean.'

She worked on.

Jack's agent was responsible for the thaw in the basement. Jack had assumed that it would not be difficult to acquire a literary agent and been disheartened to find otherwise. His work, three firms told him in different words, lacked publisher-appeal. In the fourth firm he was interviewed by a bland man submerged by typescript who found his work interesting. He could say no more than that at the moment. What was Jack working on at present? Could he see it? Thank you. The agent rose, cleared his throat and sighed deeply. Jack blundered out of his office, went the wrong way and reappeared. The man glanced up in resignation. 'Right,' he said. 'Turn right. No one can ever get out of this place. Thank you. Yes. Right.' His hands shuffled through piles of manuscripts, his head ducked beneath his desk and reappeared, pinker and less bland. 'Oh Christ, don't tell me I've lost it.'

Sarah strained the slithery strips of pasta in a colander with one hand and reached for the telephone with the other. She held it out to Jack, jiggling it slightly to emphasise the fact that she had only two hands. 'It's your agent.'

'I haven't got an agent.'

'That's what he said.'

His agent had sold the rights of the three-vol. saga. The publisher was quite excited. Could Jack see the publisher at ten-thirty a.m. on Monday?

Sarah watched her husband's face, the lift of his head, the exhausted slouch of relief. He was tired beyond words. She held out her arms to him and loved him. What did it matter? What did anything matter except this.

'We're a team, Sal,' he told her later.

'I don't know. I don't know anything.'

'You'll see.' His lips brushed down the side of her neck, paused to kiss a mole and carried on. 'You'll see.'

She lay on her back studying his face. 'What about your drinking? Your fornicating?'

'I've stopped.' He pulled back from her. 'And what about old Charlie?'

'At least we don't operate in front of you.'

He kissed her, lingering, taking his time. He had all the time in the world. 'No, I wouldn't like that.' He rolled on his back, his hand in hers. 'I wouldn't like that at all. I told you I had a letter from him.'

'No.'

'Formal. Typical Charlie. It's somewhere around.' He glanced briefly around the dark cluttered bedroom as though it might crawl from beneath something. 'He said he wants me to find another publisher.'

'Oh, no.'

'Yes.' He smiled at her, the brief arrogant grin of a man who is on his way. 'He suggested I try Selwyn Dempster.'

'Will he take you?'

'Of course he'll take me,' Jack lifted one hand to indicate Abroad, 'after this lot.'

He heaved himself back onto his elbows. 'Old Charlie will have missed out on something good.' He glanced across at her, his smile waiting for her reaction. 'That's what you get for screwing another man's wife.'

'You always go too far.'

'I know. I know I do. I mean to.'

They didn't mention Jane.

His reaction to her pregnancy astonished Sarah. She told him several weeks after the local doctor's sad dark eyes had confirmed her fears. The intra-uterine device inserted after Dora's birth had collapsed, ruptured, whatever the unspeakable things do occasionally. Sarah, who had been so appalled she couldn't even think, was outraged at his delight.

'It's terrible!' she insisted.

He seized her hands, held them, kissed them, held them tight again.

'It's wonderful!'

She snatched them away. 'How can you, how can you sit there and bloody . . . !'

'Look! Dora's wonderful. Right?'

'That has nothing to do with it.'

'It's everything to do with it. We'll have another one. It'll keep us young.'

'God in heaven! It'll kill me.' She spat it at him. 'I want to paint! And I'm thirty-six. It will kill me.'

'Mum was 104 when I was born.'

'Oh shut up.' She tugged off her boots and flung them in a corner of the room. They lay with their heels splayed apart, old, abandoned, worn out and tossed aside. 'Just shut up, will you.

Just when I'm starting to get somewhere. I'm painting again. Painting well. How would you like it if at this very moment you were landed in this. If your whole world collapsed around you.'

But he knew he was safe. She snatched her legs away from beneath his hands. 'You realise the child is just as likely to be Charles's?'

His pause was momentary. Within seconds he had examined her statement, rejected it and dismissed it for ever and ever. 'Balls. She's mine.'

'She?'

'It's a girl. We'll call her Emily. Brontë. Dickinson.'

Dora was appalled at irrefutable evidence that her parents did it. It seemed to her obscene that they could lie in some pale imitation of the abandon she and Henry achieved night after night in his squat and once in a doorway almost when they were desperate.

It was difficult not to feel shifty before her daughter's clear outraged eyes but Sarah tried.

'You're being ridiculous! What did you expect? It's bad enough being pregnant without your going on as though I'm some sort of fallen woman.'

'You're thirty-six.'

'I know I'm thirty-six. With my luck I'll probably be pregnant when I'm forty-six.'

'What about me? I won't go out with you when you're . . .' Dora couldn't say it. Her outstretched hands in front of her stomach indicated vast phantom bulk.

Aunt Mary was not pleased either. She had no children and no regrets. Angus had opted for a yacht. Bagshot, she told Sarah, was full of pregnant women. She also said that it seemed very unfair on Dora. Sarah's shamed head lifted. 'In what way?'

'In every way. I mean, what age is she now?'

'Nearly nineteen.'

'Such an impressionable age.'

Jesus wept. And not only Jesus. Sarah thought long and hard before writing to Charles. She had no idea where either he or Jane were. Nor had Jack. He refused to discuss them. They were not important. He had nothing to say. After several attempts Sarah sent a letter to Charles's office.

Dear Charles,
   I feel I should let you know that I am pregnant. Jack is convinced the child is his.
   Love,
   Sarah.

She knew he would be cold but had not expected ice.

What do you want me to do?
   Charles.

She replied: *Nothing.*

She slept badly that night and woke suddenly, her eyes staring at the dark and her heart thumping, surprised that her ankle was not swollen and painful as it had been in her dream. She had watched, floating above her own body in the theatre as the operation was performed, seen the muscles peeled back neatly from the ankle-bone to reveal the head of a tiny manikin with closed eyes, expressionless and calm as a gentle Noh mask. There was no blood, the head was excised by the scalpel in a rubber-gloved hand and the wound restitched. Sarah lay back panting with fright.

She became addicted to television, the more mindless the better. She watched doctors being concerned and clean as they made decisions about other people's lives and deaths in hospitals, listened to people discussing their most intimate concerns over pints of half-and-half and departing with 'T'rar's to reappear next night and carry on where they left off. They were reassuring. She could see why the lonely and the 'house-bounds' and the 'shut-ins' loved these people. They came when they said they were coming. They didn't leave exciting messages of promise and then not appear. They were reliable and you could turn them off. Or not.

She insisted on watching week after week an in-depth series on the lives of birds; dab chicks, hen-sized puffins, albatrosses with eight-foot wingspans, mute swans and pristine penguins pleased her. She wanted to know all about them, how they lived, how they survived, how they ticked. Nothing was too in-depth: regurgitation had its place, the drama of the eye-tooth held her, even the bedraggled newborn were interesting. The television in the flat was small and flickered. Jack took a break occasionally and slouched smoking beside her on the sofa.

The voice-over was being reverent about the life and times of the mute swan. 'They still have the egg yolk within them,' the hushed male voice murmured. Then lifted with excitement. 'The last of the chicks is dry!'

'Good on it,' yawned Jack. He paused. 'Where are we?'

Sarah glanced at him. 'What?'

'Which continent? England? Europe? The States?'

'I don't know.' Sarah stared at the screen, one finger coiling and uncoiling a strand of hair, her eyes fixed on an underwater shot of a female mute swan's normally invisible webbed feet dabbling like mad beneath the smooth gliding body. She was reminded of the Potter women's luncheon parties. The chicks milled about their mother trying to scramble aboard. Two of them hopped up with ease, one made several abortive rushes before finally succeeding and falling on its face. The female mute swan sailed straight ahead with head high. 'Embraced by Mum's wings the tired chicks can safely doze,' crooned the boy-like voice.

Jack filled the small blue hot-water bottle shaped like a rabbit which he had bought and handed it to her. Her breasts ached and he felt it was something he could do now the weather was cooler. She said it did help. And he was drinking less, as promised.

She thought about Laura. She wished she could tell her, tell her all about it, as if she could and what was there to tell?

'I'm pregnant, Mum.' The momentary pause on the end of the line. 'But that's lovely, dear.' 'It might be Charles's child, Mum.' 'Nonsense, darling.' She might even have said it would keep her young but Sarah thought not. She did not tell her father and Muriel. She would do so later. There would be plenty of time before next May for Muriel to sniff among the teapots, for her father to be startled but amiable. She felt mean depriving Maggie of even a moment of anticipatory pleasure but the thought of tiny garments winging the world made her physically sick. She would tell no one, no one. Not yet. It wasn't till May.

She was working hard. Ernest Limpour had helped. He had said nothing she did not know but he had said it and said it firmly. She had the strengths, the talents, to get on with it and he had told her so.

'It's not as if you were having a breakdown,' he told her. 'I certainly don't advocate the chin-up and buck-up approach for real depression.' He looked at her with interest. 'By the way, are you pregnant?'

'Yes.'

'Pleased?'

'No.'

'Ah well,' Mr Limpour trotted out a well-oiled phrase of comfort, 'perhaps you will be later.'

Sarah continued working. He noted the clamped jaw, stared at her canvas. 'You have both strength and originality, depth as well as colour,' he said and left her studio space.

The Group Show at Letitia Weatherley's Gallery opened in the last week in November. Sarah refused to go. Dora was torn between affection for her mother and shame at her condition, which was scarcely obvious.

'But are you *sure*, Mum?' The yards of black hair swung back. Dora, like sari wearers, had learnt her management skills early. 'It'll be so exciting. How can you bear to miss it?' The clear eyes blinked once. 'I don't mind, Mum, about, you know, not if you want to come.'

Sarah was pleased with her generous and loving child. 'It's nothing to do with that, I promise. I just can't stand exhibition openings. It's like standing around with no clothes on. I mean,' she said quickly to cover her unfortunate simile, 'I can't talk about my stuff and it's worse when other people try. You can't believe what it's like. Hideous beyond words. I don't mean I'm not pleased when people are interested, it's just that I can't think of a thing to say and openings are the worst thing in the world, that's all. I swore at the last one at home I was never going to another. You go with Dad and tell me every single thing about it. Everything, OK?'

'And Henry?'

'Of course,' said Sarah. The thought of Colonel Weatherley and Henry in conversation pleased her.

The opening wasn't quite as good as Dora had hoped. It was fun, of course. Champagne and stuff. There were lots of people there but they weren't all beautiful or rich or anything. Dad was about the best-looking, for heaven's sake, though not his clothes, of course. She really liked Colonel Weatherley and he was really sad not to see Sarah.

'I didn't tell him, you know, I just said you're not good at openings and he said he quite understood and he and Henry had a really good talk about motorbikes. The Colonel had had the same sort of one that Lawrence of Arabia was killed on but I can't remember which sort it was. No one else talked to us, well hardly, which was funny wasn't it, though of course we were all right, the three of us and the Colonel was really nice. Dad thought they were a bit, you know, but he had a nice time with somebody's niece.'

She can't be nineteen surely, even by a month. How was I so tough, so tough and so old at her age? Sarah kissed her beautiful child.

Sarah had spent a lot of time with Letitia before the Group Show, sorting and discussing her work. She trusted her, was grateful to her for the chance to be shown, for her clear-minded judgement, her conviction that Sarah was an artist who one day would have to be taken seriously. Letitia thought it ludicrous that people said nothing could silence a born artist. The wonder was, she snarled, how many remain unsilenced, and Sarah must be one of them.

'We'll have to wait and see how the reviews go,' she said. 'I think they'll be fine.' She lit an untipped cigarette and dragged deeply. 'I think. You never know. But with any luck.' She dragged again, a strip of biltong puffing smoke.

'With any luck I can start pushing you. There are one or two people who might be interested. One or two. We'll see.' She paused, her eyes squinting at the end of her glowing cigarette. 'You haven't seen Daddy's clever tree yet.'

'No, we haven't been down for a while.'

And won't either, till the Camberley Aunt calms down. And I haven't told Maggie yet either. Oh Lord.

Letitia's grin was half grimace. 'It'll probably still be there.' She made no comment about Sarah's increasing girth.

There were not many reviews of the Group Show but Sarah's name was mentioned in all of them. 'Sarah Tandy's work showed both vitality and originality and subtlety of tone.' 'Two of her watercolours were of remarkable ability.' The *Sunday Times* was pleased by her natural vision of things. A small art monthly agreed, adding that all art was abstract whether figurative or not, and that Miss Tandy's colour, though perhaps verging on crudeness in one or two of her tonal ranges, had a decided freshness. The magazine would watch her career with interest.

Two of her watercolours sold.

Sarah exhibited in the post-diploma show at the Art School End of Year and gave Ernest Limpour a small drawing of Dora asleep. He seemed pleased, shook Sarah by the hand and wished her well in her beautiful country. 'And when do you return? Go home, I mean.'

'After Christmas.'

'Ah well. I'll say goodbye then.' He didn't move. They shook hands again. He was the only member of the staff who had come to the Group Exhibition.

Christmas was not a happy time. Aunt Mary, threatened by their imminent departure, worked herself into a frenzy of wrapping, peeling, stuffing and tears. There was no room for anyone of Sarah's size in the kitchen, couldn't she see that? Dora took over, a willing helper and a better shape. Sarah departed in a rage to see

Daddy's tree but this also was a mistake. She should have telephoned first. Daddy, and presumably Mummy, had dropped off over the crossword after tea and the afternoon of Christmas Eve was, Sarah discovered, an inappropriate time to view anything. The kowhai was almost unrecognisable. Espaliered against the south wall of the house, it looked moth-eaten and despondent, its few tiny leaves clinging to the stone for comfort. Sarah and the Colonel (Mrs Weatherley stayed within) stood in the powdering of snow and stared at it. Sarah could think of nothing to say. Her longing to be home shook her, her need to be surrounded by golden trees alive with tuis belting their heads off was intense. She must get home. The child kicked. She thanked Colonel Weatherley. His eyes were sad above the icing sugar traces on his moustache. His tree had been a disappointment but he was a courteous man and said nothing to increase Sarah's confusion. They shook hands and Sarah stumped back to Furze End, her breath hanging in clouds among the traces of drifting snow. She had been surprised by snow. She knew that it drifted, Granny Tandy had had one of those paperweight things, but she had not expected such variable rises and falls, such gentle vagaries within the main thrust. Light snow lacked the directional blast of rain. A scud of flakes lifted by her hand, proving her point as she rang the bell. Jack answered, one finger keeping his place in the final draft of vol. one. He patted her behind. 'What was it like?'

'Pathetic.'

'Christ, it's cold. Shut the door.'

'And I should've telephoned. They were half-asleep. Mrs Weatherley was far from pleased.'

He took her cold hands, laughed in her face. 'Thicko! We'll be home in two weeks. Balls to Mrs Weatherley.'

Sarah found it difficult to say goodbye to Letitia. She stood in the beautiful uncluttered space of her gallery and tried to thank her. The Hepworth was still on its plinth. Still waiting, like the rest of Sarah's work. For the first time Letitia acknowledged the fact of Sarah's pregnancy. She jerked her head sideways in the general direction of her stomach, 'You won't be put off your stride now, will you?'

'No.'

'It's very important to keep work coming at this stage, when you have even half a toe in. And of course,' Letitia clamped her suede-covered arms around herself and scowled, 'it's a dead bore your being so far away.'

'I can send my stuff. There are boats, planes. We're the other side. Not off the edge.'

Letitia's smile came up through thunder. 'Well do that. And I'll keep at it too. Oh, by the way,' she continued, 'this arrived yesterday.' She patted her hands across the top of her desk, her fingers spread wide to trap the wanted letter. She held up the blue aerogramme. 'It's from New Zealand. A collector of yours wants something from the Group Exhibition. He's given his price. Wants me to choose. Would you like to?'

Sarah's hands clenched. How dare he hate me and not my paintings? Supercilious smug bastard, cold as a frog. Jack was right. Jack is always right, which is a lie. Rejection of me, the his-or-not-his child. Not interested. Do not disturb. The man's a bloody *collector* now is he. Not some peasant who buys because he buys because he must. A collector who buys and hangs and buys again. A patron of the arts, dear Lord; which of course is what I need.

Refuse to sell, then? No. Sarah rejected spite. Letitia's hooded eyes were still on her. 'No,' she said quickly. 'No. You choose one.'

Letitia shrugged. 'All right. A Mr Charles Bremner.'

Sarah nodded.

'You could take it with you, perhaps. We would pack it, of course.'

'No.' There was a touch of spite remaining after all. 'He can afford the airmail.'

'All right.'

They shook hands and wished each other well. They thought highly of each other.

*

258

Selwyn Dempster, Jack's new publisher, met them at Auckland Airport. He was small and bald and hot, waving a placard labelled 'Macalister' at them among suntanned men in towelling hats and women in jandals. He was delighted to meet Jack, delighted, and also of course the ladies.

He didn't know, he mentioned later in passing, he didn't know if they had heard. Not that he wished to gossip but as they were personal friends. Had they heard that Charles's wife, Jane, wasn't it, yes Jane, was now living in Australia? Sydney, he thought, though he couldn't swear to it. A very interesting job, so he had heard. Yes.

He had a great admiration for all of Jack's work. Yes indeed, all of it. He would enjoy working with him, a privilege. Growing overseas reputation, he understood. Jack, who had not met this approach before from a publisher, was unsure. Phoney? Not phoney? He discovered Selwyn had come originally from Clapham but didn't know if this reassured him or not. Time would tell and at least the man was affable and enthusiastic.

Sarah was drowning in sleep. 'Why didn't you wake me? I've missed Ruapehu, everything,' she said as the plane bucked its way into Wellington.

'I didn't know how,' said Jack.

Maggie and Nelson were there to meet them, wreathed in smiles, eager-handed in relieving them of bags and coats and ready to roll home to Eastbourne in the new Holden which had had a minor teething problem with the automatic choke but was fine now. Fine. Maggie could hardly contain her excitement over Sarah's bulk and the fact that Dora's hair was longer than ever and her skirt shorter. Her hands moved nearer. If she pats me, thought Sarah, I'll kick her. Through half-closed eyes she gazed at her harbour and fell asleep again.

Maggie took over for two days. The tenants had cleaned the house but while Sarah and Dora slept she cleaned it again just to be sure. But there were unexpected flutters of tension in the conversational gambits at Muritai Road. Maggie and Nelson wanted to know everything, everything, they said. But didn't.

Dora tried, told them about the wonders of the wine bars, the pubs, the excitement of it all. She didn't mention Henry, whom she had abandoned without a qualm. She had got sick of him and was looking forward to meeting up with Max again.

'Plenty of pubs here,' sniffed Nelson.

'Yes, Pop, but they're so lovely over there. Not booze barns. Each one's different and they're all so full of character and . . .'

'No booze barns here. Not in 1972, my word. Those days are gone. You're living in the past, Dotty.'

'And don't call me Dotty!'

'You like being called Dotty.'

'Not now, I don't.'

He gazed at her in astonishment. 'You used to. You haven't gone all funny on your old Grandpop, have you?'

'How funny?'

'You talk a bit funny too, doesn't she, Maggie?'

Maggie was at a tricky stage, picking up around the neckband. 'Eighty-four,' she murmured. 'Oh, I don't know.' She smiled briefly at Dora to indicate that even if she did talk funny she was still Granny's little girl.

Dora tried again. 'And the wine bars!'

Nelson was adamant. 'We've got wine bars here.'

'Where?'

'I saw by the paper. There's one just opened up in Auckland.'

'Well. *Auckland.* And I bet it's no good.'

'Why do you bet it's no good? You haven't seen it.'

'No, but in this country . . .'

'Don't you this country me, my girl.'

Dora gave up.

Praise was not always acceptable either. Sarah delighted in the freshness of everything, the fat tomatoes, the green peppers, the sweetcorn.

'They're wonderful. Just as good as Italy,' she said. 'Better.'

'It's not always like this you know,' said Maggie gloomily. 'It's only this time of year. Sometimes the tomatoes have no taste at all.

I said to you some time ago, didn't I, Nelson, I said these tomatoes are red mush.'

'Yes.'

Jack stood up. 'Red mush in the Bay! What's this country,' he snapped his fingers, 'the country, coming to?'

He had gone too far again. Their bewildered eyes groped for meaning. They were only trying to help, to love, to welcome home. What is the matter? they begged. Sarah heaved herself from the table and went to the lavatory once more.

Emily was produced by Caesarean section. Eventually. At the end of twenty-four hours Jack had had enough. He bailed the consultant up against the radiator in the maternity annexe corridor. 'Do something. There must be something. A Caesarean. Something!'

'There is no reason at this stage. Your wife is . . .' The man was puffing garlic fumes in his face. 'Excuse me, please, my buzzer.'

Jack snatched the creep by both lapels of his white coat and shook. 'Do something. Now!'

Emily was his, all right. He had always known. But still it was good. Jack gazed at the perfect face unmarred by trauma, the drumstick legs, the ridiculous-sized hands. He took his daughter from Sarah and held her tight. 'I told you,' he said.

Sarah was not listening. Her eyes were closed.

15

Emily screamed without cessation for the first three months of her life. She screamed in the morning, took a short nap in the afternoon, screamed in the evening and all through the night. She was either sucking her bottle or screaming. Sarah's lovely supply of twenty years ago had not reappeared or perhaps not 'let down'. Sarah moved in a daze of exhaustion. Her body had not snapped back, her mind had departed elsewhere. She could make no pact with this child, all she hoped was that she could stop short of physical injury to the defenceless scrap of humanity which was destroying her. She read with dry eyes stories of parents who 'snapped'. Did they get any warning? She walked for miles up and down, up and down, crooning and keening at Emily through her screams.

'It's real "fibre from the brain does tear", isn't it?' said Jack.

'Yes,' said Sarah.

He dreamt of sleeping on a safari bed in his office away from the uproar but Sarah insisted he take his turn. Whose child was it, anyway? They stared at each other in the middle of the night sobbing with despair and lack of sleep. Jack sang songs to the enraged scarlet face.

'Going to throw the baby through the plate glass window, going to leave the baby in the cold,' he promised the throbbing fontanelle, the minuscule balled fists.

The professionals gave up. There was nothing physically wrong with the child. 'Some of them,' explained the paediatrician they finally consulted in expensive desperation, 'just do this. For no apparent reason. They're what we call difficult babies.'

Dora capitulated from her decision to ignore Emily's existence and was loving and helpful but she was at work all day at Kirkcaldies' Interior Design Department and slept without blinking all through the night. Max had disappeared, he was reputed to have gone down to Central but no one was sure. Dora had in mind both a new boyfriend and some agreeable flatmates, preferably with a spacious apartment in Oriental Bay. She was nineteen, for goodness' sake, and, much as she approved of Emily, conscious of the dangers of becoming mother's little helper. She was aware that this sort of thing had occurred before.

Even Maggie's jiggles and soothings achieved nothing. She was defeated. The poor little mite must be colicky.

At four months Emily stopped screaming. Sarah was so relieved, so on her knees with gratitude at her reprieve, that she could deny her baby nothing. She played with her, gave her time and attention and ceased her painting at the first whimper. When Emily's woolly hat slipped over her eyes and she screamed with outrage Sarah leapt to straighten it.

'The squeaky door gets the most oil, eh Dotty,' said Nelson. Grandpop was sixty-six but he was a downy old bird and Dora loved him. It was a pity he and Granny were no longer at Glenfrae. Betsy was a pain, there was not much point in going there now, leafy Havelock left much to be desired after London and Muriel was beyond everything.

Dora decided to flag away the Bay except for Grandpop. And Granny. Of course.

Mrs Dossi was not getting any younger. Now over seventy, she had flung her apron over her face with excitement and scrubbed her hands with glee at her first sight of Emily. But her legs did play up. There was no denying it. Even Mrs Dossi found varicose ulcers and childcare an impossible combination. She sat grounded and alone in her cottage with her holy pictures and her snaps of innumerable grandchildren stuck alongside pink paper roses in the ornately carved frame of the mirror above her fireplace and apologised. 'Sometimes he OK. Sometimes pouff. I'm sorry. I'm so sorry Miss Macalister, I'll be better next week, OK.'

Brave, lifesaving Mrs Dossi was so sorry. So sorry.

Jack was still writing part-time. On Tuesdays and Thursdays he retreated to his office downstairs after breakfast and stayed there all day with his head down; finding the words, hacking away. He came up at lunchtime, greeted Sarah and Emily if they were present, made himself two cheese-and-gherkin sandwiches and went downstairs again. His afternoons were slightly less productive than his mornings due to his cache of flagon red. His comparative abstemiousness while Abroad had not lasted. Sarah had given up.

They saw few other people. Every Friday after work Jack drank in the back bar of the Midland and fell onto the last bus home. If he missed it he made alternative arrangements, which varied according to circumstances; a bunk down with one of his mates with a tolerant or resigned wife, a flop-house in Abel Smith Street, the railway station, once or twice in extremis the Night Shelter. It was not particularly pleasant even for copy. The drug addicts were a bore. Better a drinker than that spaced-out vacancy, those twitching hands. Any day, any day. Jack in his early forties had reached the stage where he never had a hangover—a source of faint pride for several years before it dawned upon him that it might be better if he did.

He would drink less now he had finished the saga. He owed Sarah that. Vol. three was with Selwyn Dempster, who was more enthusiastic than ever.

'You realise you are New Zealand's senior novelist?' said Selwyn.

'What does that mean?'

'Established, respected, admired.'

'All that?'

Perhaps one day he could write full-time.

Letitia's letters were insistent. Had Sarah nothing at all to send her? She had warned her, had she not? To stop now could be fatal. Sarah had no reputation, she was in no way established. Letitia could only do so much.

Sarah wrote back. She would send something when she could.

'Yes,' she told Jean Pearson. 'I am working. Of course I'm working. I'll let you know.' She refused to blame Emily. All babies are demanding though some are more demanding than others, except for a few sports like Dora. They were meant to be, it is part of them, like the pram-stopping appeal of their huge eyes and tiny features. They are designed for survival, if possible.

'I had a letter from Charles Bremner,' said Jean. 'He's very interested in your work. Anxious to see anything new.'

Sarah said nothing. The telephone rang as she replaced the receiver. Yes, she told Selwyn Dempster, Jack would be home tomorrow. She would get him to ring Selwyn straight away. Was it important?

'Very important, most exciting.' The man sounded as though he was jumping up and down. Vol. three of the Antipodean saga entitled *Five Hands* had been short-listed for the East-West Prize.'

'What's the East-West Prize?' said Jack when he rang back.

'Come, come. Established last year to promote serious literature in the Pacific Basin. The States, the Islands, Japan, Australia, New Zealand. Very prestigious. Very. And the money!'

'How much?'

'Fifty thousand dollars, US.'

Why had he never heard of it? 'Did you put *Five Hands* up?'

'Yes.'

'Well, well, well.' Sarah was watching him, her palette dipping in her left hand. The curtains stirred behind her, lifting in the breeze from the sea.

'Thank you.' Jack paused. 'Is it one of those ones where you don't know who's won?'

'Yes.'

'Look, I don't want to stand around while some other bugger gets the dough.' Jack lit a cigarette with his left hand, coughed as he tried to talk through the first inhale. 'My stuff doesn't win prizes. Why should I be butchered for their holiday? Tell them to send me the cheque.'

Selwyn's laugh could be described as silvery. Mirth slipped down the line. 'Come *on*.'

'It's barbaric, this second runner-up business. What do they think we are? A pack of failed Miss Pacific Basins?'

'You needn't worry. Winner takes all.' Selwyn laughed again, an infuriating sound. 'The East-West Foundation is a very wealthy foundation. Two or three nights in a first-class hotel in Sydney. For you and Sarah.'

They had not been to Australia.

Jack changed the subject to give himself time. 'Why not South America?'

'What was that?'

'Chile say, Peru. They're in the Pacific. Why aren't they in this Pacific rim thing?'

'They don't seem to crop up. Not in the East-West. I don't know why. The rules, I suppose. I don't know and frankly I'm not worried.'

They went to Australia plus Emily. Mrs Dossi was heartbroken but No. 'Look at him Miss Macalister,' she said as she demonstrated her ulcers. 'Look at him.'

'I'm too big for that,' said Emily kicking the pushchair as they climbed out of the airport bus.

'No pushchair, no koala bear,' said Sarah.

Emily considered, her eyes thoughtful beneath dark lashes. She was a beautiful child; Nelson's deep blue eyes, her father's hair and both her parents' determination. There was a pause. She wanted that bear with the ears. She climbed with dignity into the chair and waited for propulsion. She fell from it with shrieks of joy to embrace a toy dog, a fluffy white hydrocephalic thing which leered from the Duty Free. Its red velvet heart was embroidered 'I wuv you' in black.

'No,' said Sarah. 'No darling. Koalas are much more fun. No!'

This is insane. Why did we come? How on earth can I survive with a four-year-old heller on an occasion like this. But I want to see the pictures in Sydney, do I not? She comforted Emily, crooning her earliest lullaby. She would throw the baby out the plate glass window, she would leave the baby in the snow. 'Cold,' muttered Jack, his eyes on the selection of whiskies available. Sarah lifted Emily into his trolley with the grog. She liked trolleys.

The East-West Foundation was very generous. The hotel was grand, the domed ceiling of its foyer adorned with a huge bronze-armed mobile. The muted and quilted pastel bedroom was luxurious, the view of the harbour and the bridge spectacular. Emily inspected it and declared herself pleased, but mealtimes were not easy. No, she didn't like prawns, no, she didn't like avocado and where was the peanut butter? But she was pleased with the bidet and enchanted by the world of the harbour. The three of them hung over railings, dazzled by sun and sea, surrounded by voices as insistent as those of the local birds which hopped and preened in the scrap of hotel garden.

The bus driver had leant out of his cab near the ferry terminal at a Mercedes whose bonnet protruded beyond the Stop line. 'Going to back it,' he enquired, 'or do I drive through it?' Jack loved them. Australians were more honest, more fun—they had sloughed off the Brit thing years ago. This was their patch. They were here to stay. He was not interested in the Aborigines.

The East-West Foundation put on a tour of the Art Gallery for the finalists and their ladies. Jack, noble generous Jack, took Emily to Taronga Park Zoo. Sarah had already been to the gallery once but she was happy to spend every waking hour there. Their escort was a professional handler, a large friendly woman labelled 'Zelda' whose expensive jersey sported an appliquéd koala and silver leather gum leaves clawing at her bosom. She worked, she told Sarah, for a firm called Conventions Unlimited. 'We handle everything. Everything.' Her jersey was much admired. 'Poor wee things,' she said. 'They're not very bright. If there's a bush fire—you know about our bush fires? Yes? Yes well, they just sit in the trees and cry. They never try to skedaddle or clear off or anything. Sad.'

'No, no,' she said in answer to a question from the grey-haired wife of the American finalist, 'Australia doesn't have earthquakes. Australia is a very old and stable country. Not like New Zealand, ha ha. Anyone here from New Zealand?'

'Me,' said Sarah, proud of her youth and instability.

'Oops, sorry dear.'

'Not at all.'

The grey-haired woman was explaining something to the American finalist, her husband Ed Dellabarca. He was bald and reminded Sarah of President Eisenhower, the same loopy grin, the same sense of latent toughness. Jack said he could write too.

'Well, what would you expect?' she was saying. 'With her sun conjunct, Pluto in square aspect to Saturn and forming a triad with Jupiter . . . ?'

Her husband nodded. 'Yeah,' he said, 'Yeah.'

The wife of the finalist from Japan, who was sitting beside Sarah, laid one gentle hand on her arm. 'Excuse me please,' she said shyly. 'Perhaps you could tell me, Mrs *Mac*alister. Brissie? What is Brissie?' She was a zoologist, an expert in arachnid taxonomy, and had been here before. Yes, she liked Australia very much. Very much. Especially Sydney. Her favourite place was Mrs McQuarrie's Seat but perhaps that was because she had found a very interesting spider there once—a close relative of one she had found in Hokkaido. Her smooth face smiled at the memory. 'And you, Mrs *Mac*alister,' she said politely, 'do you have an interest?'

'I'm a painter.'

'Ah.'

Yes. And next time I'm here I will be showing at the Biennale at the Power Gallery of Modern Art. You see if I'm not, Mrs Sugimoto. Sarah nodded to herself. And Mrs Sugimoto, as you probably know, Hokusai said that he didn't understand working till he was seventy-three. I'm only forty-one, Mrs Sugimoto. Emily, whom I love dearly but who is not an easy child, is already at playcentre and next year she will be at Eastbourne Primary and then watch me go. By a hundred and ten, Mrs Sugimoto, Hokusai hoped to have discovered all. Me too, Mrs Sugimoto. Me too. I have not yet begun and the pictures I have seen here have given me a real blast, yes indeed. In fact, Mrs Sugimoto, I can't wait to get home and start painting again.

Mrs Sugimoto's eyes had closed. Eyelids pale and heavy as

magnolia petals covered them, her mouth drooped. After a few moments she opened her eyes and carried on without a pause.

'As long as you have an interior interest. Not many Japanese married ladies are able to have an interest.'

'Is that right?' said Sarah.

She excused herself from Zelda at the end of the tour. The docent guide had not been good, she was much better on her own. Thank you, she would walk back, get a cab, something. She would like to stay longer with the pictures.

'It's a long way,' said Zelda, one hand on her heart and the gum leaves. 'But just as you like, dear.'

It was a long way and it rained, suddenly, unexpectedly and very hard. Sarah was drenched. She trailed into the glittering foyer to collect her key, which was still in its pigeon hole. Jack and Emily must surely be beneath cover on the home-coming ferry by now. Surely. The man behind the desk handed her a telephone message slip. Ms Jane Bremner had rung. Please would Miss Tandy phone her as soon as possible at the given number.

Sarah went to their room. The rain was sleeting across the harbour. The land looked neither stable nor old. It looked more like work in progress, the skyscrapers clinging for dear life, the bridge a coathanger abandoned by a departing giant who was moving on, who had got sick of it.

Sarah ran herself a deep and steaming bath. It seemed an appropriate place in which to consider her reaction to Jane's note, who presumably would suggest a meeting.

She was still considering when Emily and Jack entered with his key. Emily threw off her clothes and climbed in with her mother. Jack put down the lavatory seat and sat on it.

'We saw a tapir,' said Emily.

'Was that the best?'

'I don't know if it was the best but it was there.'

'The wombat wasn't having much fun though, was it?' said Jack.

The blue eyes clouded. 'No,' said Emily finally, dragging her heart back from the shuffling hearthrug ploughing slowly through the dust.

269

'And a cassowary. We saw a cassowary too, didn't we?' Emily nodded.

Sarah picked up the damp telephone message from the floor and handed it to Jack in silence.

He handed it back. 'I'm not going.'

'Why not? And anyway, you haven't been asked yet.' A bit of hair had collapsed. She repinned it on top of her head. Emily sank eel-like between her legs and disappeared.

'I don't like her. And don't tell me it didn't look like that five years ago.'

'Five years?'

He was now blowing bubbles for Emily. He squatted by the bath concentrating, his middle finger and thumb forming a perfect circle, his hair curlier than ever from the rain. There is something arousing about a man's concentration. The challenge of exclusion.

Emily stuck her finger through his bubble.

'I won't play if you muck them up.'

Sarah leant back. Well well well. Five years. As long as that. 'I think I might go.'

'Great, I'll mind Em.'

'Even better.'

Sarah and Jane exchanged quick French pecks to both cheeks, which Sarah thought was daft for New Zealanders, but she was too feeble to back off after one.

'Well! Where's Jack?'

'He didn't come.'

'Oh.' Jane looked genuinely amused, or if she wasn't she wasn't going to let on.

The windows of her flat stared straight across the harbour at the sails of the Opera House. She could run out the door, she told Sarah, when the ferry passed that beacon and still catch it.

She looked good, her figure was better than ever, her tan smooth. Her hair still gleamed but it was longer; she had abandoned her Joan of Arc mode.

Her clothes were magnificent. Sarah, who maintained she had

no interest in clothes, could have snatched them from her back. Jane wore a heavy patchwork skirt crafted by an expert from fabric designer off-cuts; sharp pinks, blacks, purples and a sudden flash of emerald. Her shirt was black chiffon, the huge sleeves gathered from a shoulder dropped by a Shakespearean hero in tights. Romeo, say, or possibly Hamlet. Sarah almost licked her lips.

'Where did you get those *clothes*?' she yelped, which was not how she had planned to begin the conversation.

Jane took her coat. 'Oh, a little woman near here.'

Balls. No little woman, near or far, could have created that skirt or shirt. Jane, Sarah saw to her sorrow, was now in the Wearable Art league. 'I hope she's gone off,' Jack had said as he kissed her goodbye. Which had infuriated Sarah. As she told him, anyone you fucked in a bath was entitled to some shred of loyalty.

Jack laughed. 'Wave, darling. Wave to the mother figure.'

Emily waved politely, her eyes on the coffee shop in the foyer. She had discovered pink and green balls of ice-cream in high glasses with tiny paper umbrellas which worked.

Jane led the way into the living room. Another surprise. Sarah had always assumed it was Charles who had his finger on the art and decor pulse at Takapuna. And look at this place. It was a cool shell, a pale husk, its walls lined with modern Australian paintings. 'I think it's a myth about white walls,' said Jane. 'Dark green or apricot are much better for hanging. I'm going to get them re-done.' Sarah nodded, her eyes on a small erotic sketch by Brett Whitely.

'I'm thinking of getting rid of that,' said Jane as she sank onto white leather. 'The only people here worth collecting since 1950 are Tucker, Brack and Fairweather. And Fred Williams of course, though I sometimes wonder about all those disparate squiggles.'

Sarah opened her mouth and shut it again. At least Fred had made it. 'Isn't that a touch exclusive?'

'Well of course. What else can one's taste be?'

Sarah hadn't heard the impersonal pronoun spoken for years. At school Mrs Balfour (English) had insisted on it. Jane and Sarah picked it up, kicked it around a little, waded about knee deep in their own ones. 'If one does what one can that's all one can do,' murmured Sarah. 'What more can one do?' sighed Jane.

Now even Princess Anne had dropped it. Sarah had heard her youing away on television the other night just like the inhabitants of her mother's dominions beyond the seas.

'How did you find out where we were staying?' she asked.

'Rang the East-West Foundation. The man wasn't too keen but I gave them the old pals spiel.'

How simple one's life is if one uses one's loaf.

Sarah sipped her wine. It was cool and delicious. Even she could tell that its aftertaste was fruity. 'Which are you going to have? Dark green or apricot?' she asked, trying to visualise the alternative effects.

Jane stared at the wall, her chin cupped in one hand. She wore no jewellery other than one enormous jade ring. 'I haven't decided yet.'

Sarah, who was relieved that indecision on anything was still possible, said nothing.

'How did you become so knowledgeable about Australian painters?' she asked after a pause. 'You've only been here five years.'

'One can learn a lot in five years,' said Jane.

'I suppose one can.' It was still catching. 'But how did you start?'

'I was a docent guide for a couple of years at the gallery. They have quite a good training scheme here. I sucked it dry and then left. I couldn't stand all those hordes of pearl-strung middle-aged females another minute. Over-dressed, eager, all scribble scribble scribble and licked-off lipstick. God!' Jane leant back, ran her finger round her glass and sucked it. 'And the other docents weren't much better. Mad keen. All of them running around with, you know, the briefcase and the slides, swotting their heads off. Instant experts. A few lectures on "Manet, Baudelaire and the quest for a painter of modern life" or somesuch and they're in business. And not all the lectures are good. I went to one the other night.' She grimaced at the memory. '"French portrait painters 1860s–1870s."' Jane's competent face crumpled. She was distracted and useless and overwrought, her hands fussing at an invisible slide carousel.

'"Don't know who that general is. I meant to look him up. Sorry the slides are not in order. Oh well, it doesn't matter. I had a better one, but I forgot to bring it." Who do those dumb bums think they are? Give them a captive audience and they melt. Incompetent wimps.'

Sarah laughed. As Olga would have said, Jane was the same but more so. Her lack of charity was now fearless, her tongue sharper. Whatever vagary or imperfection you wished to hide, Jane would pounce on it, Sarah could see that. Gone was the teenage burbler of Rush Munro's, the restraint of Charles's unspoken censure was no more. She was still good company as long as you remembered that you too would be tossed, gored and discarded as soon as you left the room. Nelson had some old saw about supping with devils and needing long spoons. Like several of Nelson's received maxims, Sarah was not a hundred per cent sure what it meant but she was reminded of it as she laughed and sipped and laughed again.

She leant forward. 'Tell me about your life.'

'Lovers or lectures?'

'Both.'

Jane placed her neat patents together and dorsi-flexed them. The gesture was so familiar, so evocative of exchanges of confidences throughout the years, that Sarah blinked. Jane was going to tell her the lot. Lectures were OK. The usual thing of course, fighting the male hierarchy for promotion, a decent room, a bearable workload. And as for getting a minute for one's own research!

'What are you working on?'

'Piero.'

'Oh.'

'Not his work. I'm not an art historian. I'm trying to tie him in with Italian literature of his time. There's a particular angle. I won't tell you what it is.'

Sarah rose to the bait. 'I'm quite safe. It wouldn't mean a thing to me.'

'No. But one thing one does learn. Never discuss one's research with another living soul.'

They sat in silence. They had always sustained each other with occasional draughts. Unlike many women they were not afraid of lack of sound. They could subsist for some time without the confetti of words, even interesting ones. And anyway, they were both waiting.

'As to lovers,' said Jane eventually.

'Yes?'

'I've just ditched an astrophysicist.' Sarah's snort of laughter was uninhibited and crass. She mopped her eyes, still hiccoughing. The pale gold in her glass trembled.

'Well, how would you describe him?' enquired Jane mildly. 'That's what the man does. One of Australia's foremost. World class.'

Of course. 'Was he, was he difficult to dislodge?'

'Very.' Jane's yawn was neat. 'All he would eat was steak or corned beef. And prawns of course.'

The meal Jane produced was beautiful. Two yabbies in their coral carapaces peered over the rim of white bowls half-full of chilled green soup. Smoked trout fanned with avocado slices lay basking in lime-green sauce; the wine was cool bottled sunshine, there was no other phrase.

'Tell me about Charles,' said Sarah out of nowhere. 'Do you see him?'

'Occasionally. He rings me when he's over. Charles,' said Jane, refilling their glasses, 'is the perfect gentleman.'

Which is something. Which is something. Which is something, let us not forget. Sarah felt an unexpected stab of longing for Charles's decency, his generosity, his concern for the heterogeneous multitudes of the world tidied by Maggie into one vast all-embracing corral labelled 'Have-Nots'. Charles, thought Sarah sadly, is a good man. Charles did not deserve Jane. Or me.

'What's the matter?'

'Nothing.'

'And what about Jack?' Jane had moved into the kitchen to make the coffee. Her back was towards Sarah.

'He's very well.'

'A finalist in the East-West at forty isn't too bad.'

'Forty-two,' snapped Sarah, over-reacting as always to the faintest whiff of condescension.

The coffee was served in tiny art deco cups. Jane stared at Sarah over a white octagonal shape decorated with drops of pure colour, red, black and palest blue.

'You know he wanted to dump me in Urbino?'

Sarah could feel her ribcage moving. She was breathing deeply. 'No.'

'Not at all the perfect gentleman and I told him so. "Just because your wife has left you," I told him, "that's no reason to abandon me."' Jane leant back remembering with apparent calm the chaotic room, the three unmade beds, the emptiness. 'He was furious but I insisted. Yes. I don't think he liked it at all but that didn't fuss me in the slightest. I wasn't going to let him ditch me there.' She laughed. 'I hadn't realised that he really does love you.'

Sarah said nothing. It was her heart now. It felt rather odd.

'Oh God, yes. I was amazed. Leaping into the bath one minute and then abusing me for destroying his life the next.' Her sniff was overdone. 'Men,' she said. 'I must say it wasn't very pleasant. He stormed out to get drunk the moment anything opened.' Jane paused. 'I didn't know he was a drinker.'

'He's not often. Not like that.' Sarah centred her elegant little cup with care. 'I think I'd better go soon.'

'Nonsense. We haven't begun.' Jane tucked her hair girlishly behind her left ear. 'Are you still painting? Or have you chucked it in for, who is it? Emily. Yes, Emily.'

'I'm still painting.'

'Good.'

They moved back to the living room, and the view.

'What on earth is this?' Sarah held up a piece of sewing which lay beside the white leather sofa. It was the front of a little girl's Liberty lawn dress, smocked from yoke to waist in complicated many-coloured zigs and zags, in whorls and bouillon roses. It was exquisite.

'Oh, I make those to order. For a chichi kids' shop in Double Bay. They cost the earth.'

Of all the unlikely images. Jane sitting with her beefy lover in her luxury flat in her luxury clothes and her Art smocking her head off night after night. These things take endless time. Sarah peered at it.

'They pay me very well.' Jane leant back, lifted her floating, tightly cuffed sleeves above her head and laughed. 'And I enjoy perfection. There aren't many things you can make in which patience will give you perfection.' The sleeves drifted downwards as she leant forward dismissing the subject. 'Thank God,' she said, 'we're finally getting away from all that hagiography of the Heidelberg chaps.'

'I like them.'

'You can't! All that yellow. Streeton and Conder are just Australian Whistlers and always have been.'

It was the fearlessness that was so stimulating, Sarah decided. You didn't have to agree or disagree. It was still interesting to hear Jane Atwood, ex St Aubyn Street, Hastings, giving her fearless authoritative burst on any subject beneath the waning moon. The Heidelberg School were now ducks on the wall.

And her range. She was now onto someone of whom Sarah had never heard. 'You must have.' Jane's brush-stroke eyebrows climbed her forehead.

'Never.'

'But Seuffert is really famous here, tremendously sought after. Museum quality. New Zealand nineteenth-century cabinet maker. Lovely stuff; kiwis and kangaroos in marquetry. Native woods. Moas. They're worth a fortune.' She sighed. 'I suppose they've been chopped up for kindling at home.' She saw Sarah's face and waved a placating hand. 'It's just as bad here. Worse, possibly, or has been, but they're waking up to their heritage now just in time to watch it disappear. As for the poor old Abos.'

'Don't call them that.'

Jane raised her eyebrows once more. Her left foot swung back and forward, back and forward. 'And the kitsch is just as tooth-jerking. I saw some home-made soap at a craft fair the other day painted with koalas.' Her voice dropped. 'Home-made painted soap. That's worse than home.'

Sarah's anger was mounting. 'Why do you stay then?'

'Because I love it.' Jane's eyes were on the Opera House sails floating across the sea. 'It's the only place in the world.' She leant to pick up the telephone purring beside her and held it out to Sarah. 'It's for you.'

'Me?'

It was the reception desk at the hotel. The housekeeper on the sixth floor had found Mr and Mrs Macalister's little girl wandering in the corridor. She had been rather distressed. Sarah's hand tightened on the ivory plastic. 'But my husband is minding her.'

'No one can find him,' said the voice. 'The kiddy was looking for him. We thought it was worth trying this number. On your dressing table it was.' Sarah saw the scribbled message with Jane's number. 'The kiddy said you were there.'

'Thank you, thank you. Yes. I'll come right away.'

'There's no point in leaving till the ferry passes that beacon,' insisted Jane. 'None at all.'

Ignoring her comments, Sarah ran all the way to the ferry. Jane had even, she thought as she waited, made some comment about McCahon being a painter of discovery as she showed Sarah to the lift. Sarah wanted to sweep away these strangers, these humped shapes who waited beside her. To weep from frustration at the time it would take to reach her child and kill Jack. What kind of man? What kind of man? She wanted to turn her face to the wall like Gertrude. To give up in despair.

Emily was asleep, her thumb in her mouth, her koala to hand. Sarah sat down suddenly. 'Thank you,' she said to Lynne, the attendant housekeeper. 'Oh thank you so much.'

Lynne gave her a graphic account. Her hands waved like Mrs Dossi's, her sense of drama was strong. She demonstrated how she had rocked and crooned the sobbing child, sung to her, put her on the toilet and bedded her down. Sarah, her eyes full of tears, handed her all the folding money she had in her bag and ushered her out, one arm loving Lynne's wide shoulders.

Jack was unrepentant as ever. What was she on about? He'd gone to have a few drinks with the other finalists. That was the sole point of this sort of thing. Fraternisation was important, exchange of views, shop talk, were stimulating, essential if any attempt was to be made at maintaining sanity in a situation as weird as this. Emily had been sound asleep before he left. He'd been in the house bar. Why hadn't the fools paged him?

'They did page you! Endlessly.'

He was thoughtful. Yes, well, they had slipped over the road to Sugimoto's pub but only for a moment.

He swung round at her. 'Anyone'd think she'd been napalmed! Just shut up about it. I want to write my acceptance speech.'

She flung her hands to her face for a second at the mistiming of the joke and ran from the room.

Emily was in Lynne's room folding face flannels. 'They're my size, Mum.' Sarah seized her reluctant child by the hand and stormed off to the Art Gallery.

'I'm getting sick of it, Mum,' said Emily from her pushchair.

'I'll buy you a big fat bun with currants and icing and everything, I promise.'

I have measured out my life in bribes. Big bribes and little bribes and lesser bribes between them. Striding along, her head high, Sarah's rhythm faltered for a moment. 'Or an ice-cream,' she said firmly.

Emily was good. Very good. The adventures of last night must have tired her. Her head fell back on the cushioned comfort of her golden sheepskin and she slept, her eyelashes dark cusps, promises of time given Sarah to look and learn and stare again. To recharge. Sarah stood surrounded by the Heidelberg Boys, in front of McCubbin's *Lost* and thought of Jane.

I don't think I shall ever see her again. I wish to be with nourishers. I need to be with people who extend, not cut down. I need to be with people who are fascinated by differences, not those

278

who slam every aspect of life and art into tennis-ladder slots ranging from received excellence to useless trash. I am not strong enough to resist the seep of toxicity. I need, thought Sarah, bereft among the Heidelberg School, my mother.

She stood forlorn and foolish for a few moments then concentrated on the McCubbin, the shimmering cloudy heat, the subdued blue-green and grey of the bush, the warm ochres of the clearing where the child stood weeping. Bother Jane, bother all dividers and separators. Who are they to decide what I may not enjoy? It is a good painting. I like it.

Charles's first instinct was to turn and leave the Heidelberg Room with speed and stealth. He had never been good at chance encounters, never yarned in the streets or chatted in foyers after concerts. Once, to his shame, he had pretended not to see a man he knew and liked in a taverna in Athens. Had scuttled away in fact. And Sarah he hated. Had hated for five years. Almost.

He moved behind the dividing wall and spied on her. She stood motionless, her back to him, one hand on the handle of the pushchair. He inspected Jack's sleeping child, the hair, the pouting lips, but it was Sarah who interested him. He watched till she turned to move on then, inaudible in rubber soles, walked quickly across to her.

'Hello.'

She leapt in the air, her hand at her throat. 'Don't do that!'

'Sorry,' he said cheerfully.

No one will ever believe they have startled you. 'You know I can't stand suddenness. What are you doing here?'

'Looking at pictures.' He smiled. 'What are you? The thing about narrative art,' he continued, 'is that it can't tell a story you don't already know. That one, say. You have to know the Lost in the Bush mythology before it makes sense.'

Her heart was still racing. She nodded in silence, then tried again. 'I saw Jane last night.'

'Did you?'

'Yes.'

279

He took off his glasses and held them to the light. 'How was she?'

'Put them on,' she said quickly.

He grinned down at her. 'Why?'

She shook her head. Because you look so vulnerable. You can't go round looking like that.

Emily woke up demanding cake.

'This is Emily.' There are some situations which are impossible, say what you like. Sarah had not blushed for years but did so now, though Emily's obvious resemblance to Jack was some help. As Mrs Dossi said, she featured her Dad; she lacked only the foxy upward glance, the guarded expression. Emily was candid, even for a four-year-old. Charles looked into her eyes, his face expressionless.

'Hello Emily.'

Emily removed her thumb. 'Hello.'

The tab at the back of the neck of his jersey was upright. A straw in the wind, indicative perhaps of a life lived alone.

'I must take her to the coffee shop. I promised her,' muttered Sarah, irritated that she seemed the only one experiencing any emotion whatsoever. 'Would you like to come?'

He glanced at his watch. A busy man. A thin, almost gaunt man, a man with appointments, promises to keep. 'Thank you. Yes, I'd like to.'

The coffee shop was not cosy, even the potted ferns were smart. They fell from huge pseudo-marble urns on top of fluted columns. The chairs were mushroom pink tweed and steel. They bounced slightly when you sat.

They talked carefully at first. About the paintings. Had she seen the Stella? Yes. What did she think? Yes, yes, he agreed. He moved on to her work, where she was going, her strengths, the pleasure her painting had given him for so long. How well she was doing. In the UK as well, he had read recently. And what about here?

Emily was playing cake games. She divided the Black Forest confection into six pieces and recarved each one. She herded and sorted and spooned and occasionally ate. She was busy and happy.

'Mum,' she said occasionally. 'Look, Mum.'

'Yes, darling.'

'You look very well,' said Charles suddenly. 'Are you happy?'

He will still look good when he's old. Thin men with big noses do, like eagles. They don't crumple, turn into Dylan Thomas podge. He still excites me, does Charles.

'Look, Mum.' The cake was now a castle.

Sarah nodded, smiling in wonder at the dark mess. She turned to him once more. 'What a question.' Especially at this moment in bloody time once again but I will not mention that.

'I don't see why.' He smiled at her. 'I am. Happy.'

'Good,' she said. 'Good. I'm glad.'

Jack and Sarah shared a taxi to the award ceremony with Ed Dellabarca and his wife Celeste, who was obviously a professional finalist's wife. From the moment they climbed into the taxi her face assumed an expression of ossified interest. She was dressed in some glittering silver and black shiny stuff which fell in toga-like folds across her stomach. Her silver-grey hair rippled backwards then fell halfway down her back. You don't see many women with long grey hair; they are haunted by images of witches and doom.

'Look at the old buzzard,' she muttered to Sarah. It took Sarah a moment to realise she meant her husband, who was sitting beside the driver looking imperious.

'What's your next project, Ed?' Jack asked him. He must be nervous. He never asked about other people's work.

'I'm working on a lean little play about well-tanned people on the West Coast.'

'You can do that stuff?'

Ed nodded gravely. 'Yeah, I can do that stuff. I can do that stuff like shit.'

The taxi swept into the forecourt of the Cultural Complex. The building was interesting. New Brutalism with a touch of Palladian about the columns and the pediment. Two tramps, territorial as blackbirds, were working the public telephones in the foyer, one down each side. They pressed the return button, fumbled with hopeful fingers for uncollected change and passed on with sham-bling speed to the next one, their eyes wary for trespass, their faces outraged. An official followed at a distance making vague shooing gestures. The Governor General would be arriving soon. And someone would have to remove the cigarette packet still floating in the shallow pool surrounding the base of a kinetic sculpture unexpectedly labelled *Mother and Child*.

'Shoot!' gasped Celeste, eyeing the table laden with the finalists' books. 'Don't tell me there are going to be *readings*.'

'Do stop fussing, sugar.' Ed too was nervous. He was sweating slightly, his skull shone.

Celeste hooked her mouth up at the corners. Her nose was aquiline. 'My God, the readings I've put in.' Her hand clutched Sarah's arm. 'If I had a dollar for every reading I've stood through, I'd be loaded. And they will not *shut up*. Ever noticed that, honey?'

Sarah dragged her mind from Emily's tear-stained farewell and Lynne's endomorphic daughter, who was baby-sitting, and smiled. She was beginning to like Celeste.

The Japanese finalist, Mr Sugimoto, and his wife appeared. East-West officials greeted them and introduced all the finalists to each other yet again. The ladies cooed at Mrs Sugimoto's kimono which was indeed beautiful. All the finalists in the East-West Prize from the Pacific Basin and their spouses had arrived, were all present and correct.

The Governor General entered, a path opened before him.

The wine flowed.

Sarah glanced at Jack. She had uttered scarcely a word to him all day. She looked at his nervous blinking face, his untidy hair, his tight mouth. A man in need of care and attention. She thought about Charles and smiled.

'Poets are the worst,' continued Celeste. 'You ask four poets to read for ten minutes each and two, at least two, will read for twenty so the thing never ends. I guess they can't add up. I guess they failed grade school math.' She smiled her three-cornered smile at Sarah, one claw hand snatching another glass of passing wine. 'Never miss a chance,' she hissed.

The room was large; a dais at one end covered with deep red carpet supported two throne-like chairs, presumably awaiting the Governor General and his consort. A table alongside was equipped with a carafe of water and a glass. 'Bad sign,' muttered Celeste. 'Believe me, honey, I know.'

A chandelier hung from the centre of the large room. Sarah stared at it, trying to remember which Janet Frame novel had a chandelier collapsing on someone. Several people, wasn't it? Jack would know. She turned to ask him and remembered she was not speaking to the irresponsible swine who had abandoned his child to go drinking.

Matching miniature chandeliers were placed at intervals around the walls. They must have come with the master one as part of a set. Against one wall two half-columns of Ionic appearance and no obvious function were linked by a false pediment. The colour scheme was egg-shell blue and buff, the curtains shiny and stiff, their pelmets swagged and draped like those above the stage of the Hastings Municipal Theatre. There were many mirrors.

The room was filling up. There was undoubtedly an air of expectation. One person was going to win a great deal of money and several more were not and the wine was good, first rate in fact, and so was the food. Any moment soon Jack would start biting his nails. He lit another cigarette and glared at his wife. Sarah turned her back and bent to Mrs Sugimoto, whose serene good manners were soothing to bystanders. No matter what inner tumult they might conceal, Mrs Sugimoto would continue to stand nodding and bowing above her orange juice until her husband told her where to move next and when, if ever, to stop smiling.

The television team milled about in Adidas and jeans alongside Mrs Sugimoto's brocaded silver cranes and pale chrysanthemums. The cameramen were hung about with bandoliers filled with what appeared to be cartridges but probably were not. All the men wore identical sensitive tough moustaches, the lone woman carried a boom microphone in a sheepskin cover. Something that looked like Davy Crockett's coonskin cap hung from her pocket. She looked hot and cross; her exciting unisex job was arduous and getting to her.

Jack was being moved almost imperceptibly nearer the dais and the still empty chairs. Not consciously, he made no attempt to do so, but something resembling Brownian movement taking place among the particles of the crowd was propelling him forwards. A young woman laid her hand on his arm. 'I must tell you,' she said. 'You are my favourite writer. Bar none.' Her eyes dropped, lifted again to his. 'In the whole world.'

This was what he needed. A lot of this was needed as an antidote to Sarah's frozen mitt, her hairy eyeball, her arsehole attitude. The misty grey eyes still clung to his.

'Thank you,' said Jack. He took her hand in his. 'Thank you, that's great to hear, especially . . .' he tossed his other hand sideways at the crowd throbbing around them.

'I know. It must be hell. I'm Nicola Bristowe, by the way. I work for East-West. They're sending me to Wellington.' Her shudder was almost imperceptible.

'You'll love it.'

'Perhaps we could get together some time,' murmured Nicola. It was her only hope, he could see that.

'Why not.' He reached for pen and paper. Halfway through the process his head lifted, his eyes stared. Something was going on. He stood very still. Nothing moved in his blank face except his eyes, which took it in, worked it out and made a decision.

'Excuse me,' he said and left her standing.

He moved his way through the crowd, who didn't care, who didn't know, who were irrelevant and unnecessary. He stood beside Sarah and smiled at her. He had something to impart, something of interest to tell his wife. His smile became broader, more loving, he seemed grateful to her for something. Sarah watched him in silence.

'Come nearer the front,' he said eventually.

'Why?'

He bent his head. 'I've won,' he whispered. 'Consider yourself kissed.'

'What?' His smile was infectious. 'How do you know?'

'The television cameras, the way they're angled. They haven't left me. Not once.' He took her hand. 'Come back to the front. Come on.'

16

Jack sat on the wide verandah at Lookout Point and decided that, as always, Shakespeare had got it right. Life was undoubtedly cyclical and none more so than his own. It was nearly thirty years since he had driven Bernard Long, that self-confessed drunken over-the-top poet on his cultural sweep from Blenheim to the Bluff and points east and west. Now Tom and Hemi, two poets in their twenties, escorted him. The differences were that this trip was funded by the Arts Council and that he was neither drunken nor over-the-top. A drinker yes, undoubtedly, but there was a difference; and no doubt at all about the writing. Jack still woke occasionally, his mouth dry as a Russian horse doctor's valise (Bernard Long), with the sensation that something good had happened. Then remembered the East-West Prize ten years ago followed recently by the Commonwealth Prize. And no one could take them away. Ever. And the sales had boomed and the monographs had been written and the modest fame had arrived, if you were interested in such things. Extremely modest.

And here he was sitting on wide bleached boards near Wanaka with a glass of whisky instead of tea at four o'clock, gazing across paddocks as Grandfather Macalister had done for most of Jack's childhood, with Sybil fussing at his side with teapots instead of Maggie in the Bay. He lit another cigarette, ignoring Sybil's pursed lips. She wouldn't allow them inside. His smoking life also seemed destined to be cyclical. At this rate he would end as he had begun, puffing furtively behind hedges, though at least Sarah didn't have unctuous signs all over the place thanking him for not smoking. He lifted his amber glass to Tim Potter and nodded.

The sensation of life repeating itself was ridiculous, almost alarming, as he flipped back to the last tour. The country pubs remained comparatively unaltered by the change from six o'clock to ten o'clock closing. TV and a few regrettable jukeboxes were in evidence but the atmosphere was much the same. A Labour Government had been in power both then and now. He thought of Charles Bremner's youthful idealism, his conviction that the sole justification for the existence of the rich was to provide jobs and pay large taxes to alleviate the condition of the poor. Where had it got him? Or the poor? Charles and the other rich had got richer, richer than ever before, under this Labour Government, and the poor poorer. There was still a strike every five minutes, nothing had been achieved. If the man felt like that he should have become a politician instead of bleating on. Jack inhaled, smiling. He could take a bet on Charlie's nuclear stance.

Charles had sold Waikeri as soon as his father died and given half the proceeds to his mother, which was ridiculous. And still the man must be rolling. Rolling.

Why was he thinking about him, anyway?

They met occasionally at book things, shook hands if necessary and disliked each other even more than they had in childhood, which was understandable. But neither of them was a good hater. They preferred avoidance to the cut and thrust of active antagonism. Charles had not remarried after he and Jane divorced. He was reputed to live with a personnel manager called Bronwyn who had trenchant views on the New Zealand literary scene. She certainly never appeared.

And the twenty-year cycle between Dora and Emily. Emily had even called her recently acquired kitten Werther after Dora's long-deceased pet. Jack's pleasure in Dora had been repeated at every stage by his reciprocated enthusiasm for Emily. He realised with a small secret shock that Charles had surfaced in his mind because he had been thinking of Emily's birth.

'Got your lovely hair though, hasn't she?' the checkout lady had enthused last week as the two of them stocked up on Coke and windy waters, her eyes on the red-gold tangle of pre-Raphaelite exuberance falling down Emily's back.

'Sure has,' replied Jack smugly, leaping out of the way as Em charged him with the trolley.

And soon, no doubt, Dora would have a child and he would be a grandfather, sans teeth, sans eyes, sans taste, etc. And very nice too. The grandchildren, not the rest.

He felt positively benign as he stared across the valley to the mountains. He was glad on balance that he'd accepted Syb's invitation to stay. The Commonwealth Prize following on from the East-West had finally buried Sybil's regrettable memories of his last visit to North Otago and he liked Humph and Tim. Tim and Helen Potter now lived in the cottage originally refurbished for Humphrey and Sybil. By rights Flicka and Dougal should have had the Lookout Point homestead but they had only a meagre four children compared with Humph and Syb's seven. The move had been made when the twins Nigel and Nigella were babies. A complicated three-way exchange of houses had been arranged to everyone's satisfaction except possibly Dougal's, but he knew his secret dream of drinking his sundowner on the Lookout verandah was unworthy considering how lucky he had been. Flicka was as pleased to escape being chatelaine of the rambling dark-panelled homestead as Sybil was to tear it apart and redecorate. Flicka was a spinner and weaver. The old schoolroom cupboards bulged with her fleeces. She had made their stowage at Lookout Point her one condition for the house swap.

Tim reappeared at Lookout most afternoons for his glass of whisky at teatime, leaving Helen head-down bottom-up among her roses. Helen couldn't live without her roses, she had explained at the time, as long as Syb was sure she didn't mind her taking them. Sybil didn't mind at all and the cowman-gardener transplanted them to the cottage in a flash and grassed over the empty beds. This upset Helen. As she said, 'To think of Lookout without a single *Souvenir de Malmaison*! Not even a climber.'

The wide view bore some resemblance to that at Waikeri but

none to the enclosed stillness of Glenfrae, Jack moved his legs in the winter sun. The feel of it through his jeans was agreeable.

'Yes,' he said apropos of nothing, his eyes on the snow-covered peaks. 'Yes. Well, this is the life.'

Humph appeared for a cup of tea. He thanked Sybil politely and sat on the steps, his head against the post. He had grown out of his boxer pup stage long ago. A tough, intelligent man, Humph. You had to be to survive as a farmer in 1987. Everything was on the farm computer: the Beef Plan, the Sheep Plan, the spreadsheets. Everything.

He took a large swig of tea and smiled at his weirdo brother-in-law. 'Watching the wool grow?'

'Something like that.'

Sybil was now banging on about how hard Humph worked and the havoc caused by boarding school fees for seven. Jack refrained from telling her that you would expect seven children to be more expensive to raise than one or two and that no one had had an electric cattle prod on either her rump or Humph's as they herded their offspring into private schools.

She was now onto Extras. Everything was an Extra! Piano. Ballroom dancing. And now *gamelan*, for goodness' sake.

Jack stopped listening. He raised his face to the sun in imitation of his brother-in-law and continued his thoughts on the cyclical life: the affectionate teasing admiration of Hemi and Tom repeating his for Bernard; the audiences and the lack of audiences. The differences were there of course: the Arts Council funding for a start, the barnstorming of remote Memorial Halls, Settlers' Halls and schoolrooms, the knowledge and enthusiasm of the people who did come and the marked increase in the number of wads of poems handed over shyly for them to 'glance at later'. But the fellowship of the country pubs remained, the boozy evenings with good talk deteriorating as the evening wore on. He could drink far more than either Tom or Hemi with none of the ill effects they suffered next morning.

'You're probably half-shot all the time,' Hemi had explained to him, his eyes on the Pigroot as they swept through Central. 'The booze doesn't make much difference to you, eh.'

Jack had said nothing. His face was thoughtful as he watched two Merino rams, their horns curled in Woolmark coils, high-stepping their way around clumps of tussock. Monolithic slabs of rock lay on the dozing hills. No, not dozing. Jack's head moved, his eyes still closed against the Lookout sun as he remembered. People had got it wrong all those years ago. Jim Baxter, Bernard, himself. Those mountains were not sleeping tigers. They were tigers playing possum, heads down, paws outstretched, the hollows of their flanks deep purple.

A pair of paradise ducks had lifted from the wide gravel river-bed beside the road, the female leading, white-stockinged neck and head thrust beyond her bright chestnut body, the drab male following behind.

'They mate for life,' said Jack.

'The female's prettier too,' said Tom. 'You don't often see that. Not in birds, you don't.'

Jack still missed his friend Bernard who had died of cirrhosis of the liver two years ago. The wonder was he had lasted so long. He had lived alone in a flat in Abel Smith Street and, as he said, he did for himself. At the end of the tour thirty years ago Bernard had made a pass at Jack. They had both been drunk, blind drunk, in Nelson on the last night, the night before he and Jack and his bust-clutching hands returned to Wellington. The barman had tipped them out of the hotel bar when it closed and shovelled them into the lift. He had even pressed the button for the fifth floor. Jack leant against the brown carpet on the wall of the lift. 'Even the carpet's going up the wall,' he moaned. They laughed, they giggled, they fell about, they were delighted with each other. 'God, I love you,' said Bernard, his voice suddenly clear and firm. His beard brushed Jack's cheek as he kissed him. Jack leapt into the corner, appalled, maidenly, both hands barring access. 'For Christ's sake!'

He handled it badly, very badly. He could still see Bernard's hunched shoulders, hear the sounds coming from the figure sitting on the bed in the anodyne pink and grey room. He had always known Bernard was gay. It had never been a secret. How could he have let himself get into such a ludicrous situation? But how could he have avoided it? He got Bernard to bed finally, both of them still apologising. Jack fell into his room nearby and locked the door. He was asleep in five minutes.

Next morning Bernard did what he called his Mr Darcy. He handed Jack a sealed envelope and invited him to read it at his leisure. 'Not now, dear boy. Good God no, not now.' He picked up the menu. 'No. Not fried eggs today I think, thank you, Glenys,' he said to the smiling young waitress, who thought he was a scream. 'Or sausages. No.' He handed the menu to Jack and stared straight ahead at a particularly fine royal mounted above the glass doors to Reception. 'A stewed prune, perhaps. Or two.'

The letter was a moving document. It was a love letter, an apology, a last testament. It concluded,

It was my mistake. (I nearly wrote cock-up.) Only you can alleviate the situation. Try to forget it. It won't happen again. Drunkenness is not a valid excuse but it is the only one I have to hand for making a fool of myself with anyone as irredeemably heterosexual as yourself.
My love,
Bernard.

Jack read it many times and put it away carefully. He would have to wait till Bernard was dead, of course. But still. He thanked Bernard with feeling. Their friendship continued. It was probably stronger than ever, though Jack had never analysed the situation; what was the point.

Tim and Humph were now onto blood lines. Syb was silent, her head on one side, attentive as any good wife to her men's shop talk. A farm truck spun the gravel on the circular drive behind the homestead. The sheep dogs chained to their kennels in the plantation nearby burst into uproar. Humph unfolded himself, roared one indecipherable word and sat down again. The noise cut in mid-bark. Jack looked at him with interest. Why was it necessary to stand? Nelson had always stood to quieten his dogs. Authority? Breath production? He glanced across at Tim's thoughtful face. Perhaps he could ask him later.

Jack began listening again. Genetics interested him. Look at his daughters, for example. Dora, who had been living with a mad scientist called Eddie for years, was taller than both her parents, her eyes and skin colouring her mother's but where had those sheets of black hair come from? Emma was also far too tall for fifteen or whatever she was but resembled him in every possible way. Jack lay back smiling in the sun.

Humph picked up the smile, smiled back. 'Yes?'

Jack rubbed a hand on his warm denim thigh. 'Nothing. Forget it. Tell me. What's the thinking on sports these days? Can you still have a completely rogue animal? Not necessarily useless. Not things like two-headed calves. But something different suddenly appearing from two proven lines. A throwback?' He thought again. 'Maybe not a throwback but something with unexpected characteristics. Completely unexpected.'

Humph and Tim both leant forward to assist the seeker after knowledge but Sybil was too quick. 'Oh no,' she said, her hands clattering among golden saucers. 'Not if you're a good stud breeder like Humph,' she dipped her head at his uncle in gracious inclusion, 'and Tim. You cull them out.'

'It's not quite as easy as that, Syb,' said Tim slowly. He explained why, lucidly and at some length.

But Sybil had lost interest. She waved a letter from Bindy, the fifth-born. 'I told you she wants to learn the gamelan. *Gamelan!* Does she think,' moaned Bindy's mother, 'that money grows on trees? Not one of them ever seems to think, ever gives a thought to the fact that there are *seven* of them.' Sybil's head waved in amazement.

Why the hell would they? It was satisfactory in a way that Sybil was still such a fool. A dolly-bird turned matriarch, a grisly metamorphosis. And she didn't, from the evidence available to Jack on his brief visit, seem to long for her expensive offspring,

292

who sat around in silver frames smiling in the withdrawing room. Every letter or telephone call received from boarding school, university or overseas was pounced on and torn apart for defects. She reminded Jack of those hard-eyed owners of large dogs endlessly snarling and belting their best friends to heel, the animals' tails permanently between their legs, keen to get it right but forever circling just out of range with nervous eyes. Jack looked up into his hostess's face and smiled long and hard. 'You should've planned things better.'

'You can't talk about planning,' snapped Sybil.

Warmed by sun and afternoon whisky, Jack agreed, still smiling that infuriating lop-sided smirk. If there was one thing Sybil couldn't stand it was a *smirk*. 'Frankly,' she said, tossing her butternut curls, 'I can't understand how your marriage has survived, what is it . . . ?' She ticked off the decades on her left hand, her rings flashing blue ice at the sun: 'Ten, twenty, nearly forty years. Frankly,' she said once more, 'I'm amazed. Considering how it started.'

Her husband lifted his large head to stare. 'Hang on, Syb.'

Jack's head, which had been bent over yet another cigarette, also lifted. The smirk was gone. The voice was soft, silky even. Sybil had seen the word only in books but it was easy to recognise when heard. 'What has my marriage got to do with you, Sybil?'

Got him. Sybil gave a little bounce on her plaid-covered behind. 'You seem to forget it's my sister's marriage as well. Naturally I take an interest and frankly . . . Well, I mean, you seem to lead completely separate lives. Humph and I do everything together, don't we, Humph?'

Humph nodded.

'Even after seven children! We go for picnics, even. Farmers hardly ever go for picnics. They say they haven't got time. But we go for picnics, don't we, Humph?'

Humph, his face troubled, nodded once more.

'We know it's important, see. And we go for swims and we play tennis and *everything*.' Sybil was warming up. 'Why isn't Sarah with you on this tour thing or whatever? You'd think she'd be proud to come.'

And sensible, she almost added. Her pause was thoughtful. Val's well-formed fondled breasts hung in the lambent air. Sybil restacked the recalcitrant golden saucers yet again and emptied the teapot on the geraniums below the verandah, which she never allowed her young to do because it was lazy and mullecky-gullecky and simply not good enough.

He had never fucked Val. She had kissed him with enthusiasm and run. Lean and hungry, *troublante* and close at hand she had made a bolt for it, outraged by the smug cream bun bouncing about on her bottom in front of him.

'I told you,' he snapped. 'Sarah is in Australia. She has been invited to exhibit at a Biennale in Sydney, at the Power Gallery. A tremendous honour. You know how bloody avuncular the Aussies are. How many New Zealanders do you know who've been invited?'

Sybil gaped at him. Poor, innocent, cuddly, put-upon Syb. 'None.'

Jack was silent. His slicing contempt would be wasted on this butter pat. He put his elbows on his knees and stared hard at the mountains. Rage had given him indigestion.

Humphrey stared at his boots.

Tim inspected the dregs of his whisky.

Sybil heaved herself out of her cane chair with its hole in the armrest originally designed for a gin sling or a *chotta peg* and headed laden and wronged for the kitchen. In her own house, too.

'And,' called Jack at her retreating Black Watch behind, 'if she was here she'd be painting, not farting around after me. Your sister's an artist. Remember!'

'Now hang on.' Humph reassembled himself upright. 'Don't you talk to Syb like that.'

Tim held out the whisky bottle in silence. He only ever had one. Jack took it as Dougal appeared around the corner of the house to crush his right hand in greeting. 'Welcome to Lookout! Great to see you, man. Great. And how's Sal? Why didn't she come with her old man? And Flicka's expecting you all for dinner, you know that, don't you? Three ducks, more maybe. Well hung.' He rubbed his hands to convince them, his smile embraced the world. 'Shot by me and stuffed by her. Remember Nelson and Maggie's tuck-ins, eh Jack? Great to see you. Great.'

Maggie had died in her sleep in 1985, a few weeks after Bernard. She had confided to her neighbour Brenda as they hung their papery hydrangea trusses to dry at the back of the garage for their dried arrangements later that she hadn't been feeling well for some time, but she didn't want to worry Nelson. Nothing you could put your finger on, nothing at all really, just a little breathlessness; you know how you get going up stairs sometimes. Not always. Brenda, christened the *Tribune* by Nelson for the speed with which she disseminated local news, had nodded. Indeed she knew. Her doctor was up two flights and didn't even have a lift, would you believe? In this day and age.

Maggie had tidied her drawers that week with particular care. She wasn't morbid or anything but you never knew. There were other little worries as well. Things too silly to mention even to Brenda. She had fallen over her electric blanket cord a couple of times lately. Why on earth do that? It had always been there with its little red eye of comfort and its white cord lying and its dual control because Nelson liked his cooler. Sometimes nowadays when she made the bed in the morning and checked to make sure the blanket was off she felt quite wistful. It seemed such a long time till bedtime when she could sink once more into the warmth of its welcome. Why start falling over its cord now? Quite a heavy fall it had been last time, though of course she hadn't told Nelson. Apart from anything else he would have laughed, slapped her on the rump, called her Old Girl. Well yes, she supposed she was, but four years younger than he was and look at him. Seventy-eight last birthday and fit as a fiddle. There had been a song when they were courting; hiding in dark corners behind wool bales to clutch each other at Woolshed Hops. Or perhaps they were just married, the first year, before Nigel was born. She knew there were only two of them. Nelson still whistled it occasionally. Something about being fit as a fiddle and ready for love. Maggie saw them on their first night in the Bridal Suite at the Masonic Hotel in Napier, so shy, so hopelessly shy, and so excited. Nelson had been the one who was breathless that night.

He was still a fine figure of a man, thinner than he'd been thirty years ago. His stomach didn't hang over his belt like most of them, which was unfair considering the way he ate, as though he was still doing a full day's work at Glenfrae; cooked breakfast, smoko, lunch, afternoon tea and dinner. At least she didn't have to make a pudding every day now. He was quite happy with ice-cream as long as it was Hokey Pokey. But he still liked something home-made in the tins. He would come into the kitchen and rattle them expectantly just as the boys had done when they roared home from school every weekend, piling off the paper-car at the gate, charging up the drive to fling their bags in doorways, glad to be at Glenfrae for two whole days.

And another thing. She had bitten her tongue twice lately. Quite badly the last time. It had bled and been sore for two days. How could she have done that? Her tongue certainly hadn't moved. It was such an *old* thing to do. She slid her tongue around the cavern of her mouth, touched its roof, felt it testing the contours like some slippery chained sea mammal, normally quiescent but occasionally probing for escape. The ridiculous mini-accidents worried her. Life was enough, in all conscience, without self-inflicted wounds. She felt muddled, muddled by life, muddled by tiredness and her wish to lie down. She had never had lie-downs after lunch like some of the town girls. Never.

But even if she had wanted to tell Nelson, to confide in his strength, how could she? How could she possibly explain her gormless unease to a man she had lived with for over fifty years?

'Come and look,' Betsy said to Sarah after the funeral. She led the way into the rose-decked master bedroom. The only evidence of Nelson's share in its occupancy was an ancient grey flannel dressing-gown hanging like a moth-eaten pelt from a hook on the back of the door. The double bed was covered with mourners' coats and jackets. There had been quite a frost that morning but the sun had come out for the service.

Betsy touched one of the smoothly running drawers of the built-in unit. Maggie's underclothes were revealed, a pastel symphony of neatly folded pants, pressed petticoats and pale pantihose rolled in on themselves nose-to-tail like new-born leverets. Maggie had never worn those nasty hot brown ones. Or, of course, black.

'She would hate to have been a bother, you see,' murmured Betsy. 'Left a mess for us to sort, I mean.'

'Yes.' Sarah was hypnotised, her eyes on the paean to order revealed within the drawer.

'Do you think . . . ?' Betsy was awestruck at the thought. 'You don't think she *knew*, do you?'

'Of course not.' The back of Sarah's throat was damp, the pastel parcels swimming before her eyes. She was very firm. 'How could she possibly?'

She must get out of here. Find Prudie, who had driven down from Piha. 'All by herself,' as Betsy whispered, her lips damp at the courage of the geriatric. 'I mean, when you *think*. Why didn't she fly if Charles couldn't come?'

Nelson was marvellous. Everyone said so. He spent some time at Glenfrae but only when he could be useful, during docking, say, or crutching, or over the longer period of shearing.

He kept the house spotless, ignored Maggie's rows of glossy illustrated cookery books and resurrected Whitcombe's *Everyday Cookery for Every Housewife*, which had been given to Maggie years ago by a friend in the Road. It was minus its cover and you could tell the most-used recipes by the splashes on the pages. Nelson read it from beginning to end and worked his way through Meats. He cooked Spanish Steak and French Steak and Swiss Steak and Spiced Flank Steak. He liked the sound of Scotch Collops but they turned out to be mince. He invited people for meals. Two at first, then four, then six. 'I have to, you see, dear,' he told Sarah. 'People are very kind and I don't want to be a freeloader. And I quite like trying something different. It's not worth it for one.'

He served excellent local wines. As everyone said, he was marvellous.

He apologised to Sarah last time they were up for not inviting John and Muriel Tandy. 'I'm sorry dear, but somehow. I can't seem to get alongside her somehow, know what I mean?'

Sarah had hugged him. 'Forget it. Dad's happy. Forget it, darling.'

He looked at her, surprised, even faintly shocked, by her use of the endearment. Darling was for night. For bed with your wife. Dear was for day.

'I do all right, considering,' he told Jack. 'I'll come out of it eventually, I suppose. Eventually. It's just that fifty-five years is a long time.'

'Yes, Dad,' said Jack. 'Yes. It is.'

He thought about Sarah. Sex was as good as ever, it was not that, but they certainly didn't repine, were as contented as Eliot's Sir Henry Harcourt-Reilly with the morning that separated and the evening that brought together. But even at their most obsessed there had been work, their two different jobs. That was how they had wanted it. He could not have survived with a clinger, or indeed a soulmate, whatever that was. Nor could she. But thirty-something years was also a long time. He would miss Sarah, without a doubt. He glanced across at her as she leapt up to make the coffee; mustard cotton trousers, a faded ink-blue shirt, a rust-red handkerchief at her neck. She looked good. He would drink less when they got home. She would like that.

He hugged Nelson goodbye, his father's shoulders tense beneath his arms as always during demonstrations of affection. The gallant old boot. 'Tons of bottom' had been Grandfather Macalister's phrase of approval for pioneer forebears.

Sarah came back from the Biennale on a glorious God-given high. It was not the occasion itself. She did not believe a fraction of the accolades the critics gave her work; the enthusiastic welcome

298

had alarmed her. But to have people whose opinion she respected not only studying her work but understanding what she was attempting filled her with delight. She could go on experimenting, trying to find meaning, space beyond space, colour behind colour. One critic or viewer who understood would have been enough but the Sydney enthusiasm had been almost universal. Could it possibly mean she was getting somewhere? On stream? Letitia was delighted with the reviews and said so.

Jack was also excited. 'Has it got a title yet?' asked Sarah, curled up in Otto's chair in her paint-stained dungarees. She peered at him over hideous steel half-rims, her hair a nest for birds.

'*Emotion on the Page.*'

'About?' A fool of a question as she knew. It had never been easy to say what Jack's books were about.

He paused. 'You. And others.'

Her smile was vague, distracted by the sight of Emily dressed in denim, Great Aunt Pat's bridge coat and nothing else. 'Em, for heaven's sake. Take it off, darling, it's so fragile. Sweat will rot it.'

'I don't sweat.' Emily removed the bridge coat and lay full-length in the sun, a gentle animal at rest, calm and sensual as a Gauguin Tahitian maiden in jeans. She had a beautiful shape, had Emily aged fifteen.

Jack stepped over her on his way to the kitchen to pour them a drink, his mind ticking with pleasure at the way the book was shaping. He wondered if he could bring it off. He wasn't at all sure.

'Turn the oven on, would you,' called Sarah. 'One-eighty.'

Jack handed her the first draft three months later. You're my best critic and it's not my fault it's been said before, he had told her years ago. She was intelligent, free of any preconceptions as to what a novel should be or do. If she didn't understand what he was trying to say she said so and he knew a great many other thoughtful readers wouldn't either, which was useful to know, if disheartening. She knew he was an honest writer, he didn't play games. She was prepared to work for what he had to offer because she found it worthwhile. She liked his words, images, what he had to tell. It pleased her. She would look up, waving the granny glasses at him in emphasis. 'Mad about the bit on the island. Particularly Milly. How did you think of the name? She couldn't be anything else. A fragile bitchkin.'

If she didn't like it she also said so, which was not so much fun.

'Nobody's going to get this convoluted analogy about Te Mata Peak.'

He never gave up a word without a fight. 'Why not?'

'(a) It goes on too long and (b) it doesn't work. It's too involved. Just because they find marine fossils up there doesn't mean . . .'

He didn't want to hear the rest. 'I'll have a look at it.'

He always said that. I'll have a look at it. This time was different. She came storming down the steep stairs to his office, her sandal heels clattering on the wooden slats, her hand shaking the MS at him in fury. She flung it onto his working table with force, upsetting a small papier-mâché jar Emily had made for him at Eastbourne Primary. Paperclips cascaded, spilling silver. 'Watch it,' he said mildly, his eyes wary as he rounded them up. It was a bad sign when she shook.

Sarah collapsed in the ancient sagging armchair he had bought with his first pay from the woolstore. She had always hated it. When she was really huge before Dora was born she used to get cast in the thing, could only get out by heaving herself upright with assistance from the nearest stable object.

Her face was scarlet, her hands all over the place.

'I'm used to you, I'm used to you using bits of me, words, gestures, things I've said, silly things I've done. I've always known, of course I've known. What the hell does it matter? But this!' She sprang to her feet and banged, literally banged her fist on his table, unseating the paperclips again. He kept his eyes down as he collected and restowed once more.

'Look at me!'

He looked at her, polite, enquiring, the serious novelist interrupted whilst at work in his book-lined retreat.

'Did you honestly think . . .' She was spluttering now. 'Did you honestly think for one moment that I'd let you publish this!'

Worse than he'd expected. Oh shit and bloody hell. 'Yes,' said Jack.

'Apart from anything else it's pornographic.'

'Sarah, you're being ridiculous.'

'*I'm* being ridiculous.'

'What exactly is your objection to the book?'

She changed tack, followed his lead, absorbed his spurious courtesy, abandoned obvious rage and substituted steel. He knew her so well. After almost forty years of studying her as the nearest female member of the species to hand how could he not. Beneath her pretence of calm she was breathing deeply, her breasts in their elderly slack bra rising and falling. He could see the very tip of her tongue. He was going to have to fight for this book.

'It is the best thing I've ever written,' he begged.

'I don't agree.'

'Of course you don't agree at the moment. At the moment you're being subjective about the content. But later, when you read it again . . .'

Her knuckles clenched, relaxed when she remembered how calm she was. 'I am being subjective about the content, as you so naively put it, because the content is nothing other than my husband's intra- and extra-marital sex life. In detail, in minute lubricious detail. Every squelch, ooze, lick. Even Werther features. God in heaven!' Her tremulous hands screamed at him, calm abandoned. 'Where did you keep your note-pad? Under the pillow?'

'Sarah.' His voice was pained. He stared at her across the space he had hacked for himself out of rotten rock. His mouth was dry. She must let him, she must let him publish this book. He begged harder. 'Sarah. Please.'

'Why–did–you–do–it?'

'Because I knew it was important. And I thought I could bring it off.' He leant back. 'And I have.'

'Apart from anything else,' she said again, 'it's so self-indulgent!' She made a small odd noise, a breathy little puff of disgust. 'Who cares about the details of a fifty-two-year-old's wide-ranging sex life? His richly documented goings out and his comings in?'

'You know I've had other women. Why . . . ?' He stopped at her reaction.

Her face was hidden flat on her knees, he had to listen carefully. 'Had other women,' she moaned. 'Of course I know you've "had other women".'

She sat up, her voice now very clear. 'I notice you haven't named these "other women".' She paused, something had occurred to her. 'I suppose wives can't sue for libel?'

He was silent. He didn't know.

'That was one part I did find quite interesting, working out which particular graphic detail fitted which extra-marital lark.' Something happened to the jokey wanton phrase as she spat it at him. He swallowed, his eyes on hers. 'I suppose you were scared that the whole gang might sue. What a thought.'

Her eyes, he was appalled to see, were swimming with tears. 'Worse than that is what you've done to us.'

Oh God. He watched her in silence.

'I thought that that was one part which was ours. Even after I found out about you, what you were like about women, I still thought . . .'

'What about you and old stick insect!'

It was no joke. 'I know. But I still thought that when you and I were in bed together it was equal. In what it meant to both of us.'

Words were no use to her, as always they skidded away from what she wished to say, immiscible as petrol scum on puddles.

His also seemed to have deserted him. He resorted to gestures, leant forward with elbows on his knees in loving reassurance. 'So it is. So it is. Better than ever. Sex. Everything. You know that.'

She leant back, her head, her untidy beautiful head, defeated, her eyes closed. He watched, waited, chewed the inside of his cheek. Eventually the eyes opened. 'No.' She turned her head away. 'You've ruined it.'

'No.' He was on his feet, leaping across the few yards between to squat on his haunches before her, his hands on her knees. 'No!'

The corners of her mouth moved slightly, pulled downwards in self-mockery. 'Whose tongue did you prefer?' she asked. 'Mine or Werther's? You didn't make it absolutely clear.'

Selwyn Dempster thought it was magnificent, spell-binding, superbly written. And a break-through. There had been such a paucity of serious erotic literature written in the Pacific area. It was timely as well as masterly. 'The timing's perfect,' he said, clutching his hands behind his desk. 'I can say in all honesty that I don't know when I've been so excited about a book. Not for a long time. And it will last, you realise that?'

Jack nodded. He felt ill.

Selwyn picked a small slab of unpolished greenstone from his desk and examined it.

'There's just one thing.'

'Yes?'

'What does Sarah think of the book?'

The indigestion pain was quite intense. Jack smiled weakly and said nothing.

'I couldn't of course publish it without her consent. Not a book like this. It wouldn't do,' said Selwyn, sternly replacing the greenstone. 'And I would prefer, just to be on the safe side, you understand, not of course that there would ever be any question of someone of Sarah's integrity reneging on her spoken word, but all things considered I would prefer her written consent.' He glanced upwards from beneath wiry eyebrows, his smile calm. 'All right?'

'Read it again,' Jack begged next day on his return from Auckland. 'That's all I ask,' he lied. 'Just try and read it objectively, notice the words, how I've used them.'

She scarcely lifted her eyes from the *Dominion.*

'I know what words you've used.'

'See how I've put it all together. It's all I hoped for, a work of art, a . . .' He stopped. It was not the moment to describe it as a celebration. 'It will last. Even Selwyn says so.'

'It's all been done before. Henry Miller, all those Americans.'

'Henry Miller! If I thought you were serious I'd burn it.'

A bad move, regretted the instant her eyes flicked to the MS. He clutched it to him in instinctive ridiculous panic.

'Make a list, make a list of the bits you can't stand and I'll go through.' He swallowed. 'Cut them out.'

'There will be nothing left and you know it.'

'I'll cut them. I promise. The bit about Werther's tongue for instance.'

Her mouth moved. Her mother had laughed at herself as well. 'Poor Werther. Now we'll never know.'

'I want to show you something. Wait here.'

She shrugged. She wasn't going anywhere. She heard his steps thudding down to the office and back. He reappeared panting, his hand flapping a yellowing piece of newspaper with torn edges at her.

It was a poem. A fragment.

> *How is it love arises from the heart*
> *And then torments the heart that bore it?*
> *Just think of rust and iron; rust's born from iron*
> *What does it do but gnaw it . . . gnaw it.*

She read it several times. It had been written by a Persian poet, Bu'lfaraj, in the eleventh century and translated by Dick Davis.

'Where did you get it?'

'Tore it out of an English paper. I can't remember which. At the library in town. Ages ago.'

'You tore it out?'

He nodded. 'I wanted it.'

So you ripped it out. There was no point in commenting on that. 'Why?'

'Don't you like it?'

'Yes.'

'Well then. It's not *meant* to be easy . . .'

She stared at his bony face, his topaz eyes. 'You've got it all wrong! I could have written this, not you. It's my heart that's been tormented, gnawed. When has yours? Yours for me?'

He lit a cigarette. Exhaled, reached for her hand. 'Once or twice. Once or twice. Why did I tear it out otherwise?'

'Because it's good.'

'Yes.' But that wasn't why. He was silent for a moment, his eyes on the smoke streaming across the room to the Expelair above the stove. 'Believe me. If I could have written it for you I would. I couldn't.'

'So you stole it?'

He nodded.

He altered the bits she insisted on. She read the manuscript again, made notes, discussed it rationally, insisted on a few more expurgations, none of which, as he admitted to himself but not to her, were damaging to the structure or impact of the book. Then gave her consent. He was grateful, extremely grateful, and told her so.

He went down to the beach, which unlike Sarah he scarcely ever visited. He lit a cigarette, sat on the sand, thanked, what? His lucky stars, whatever gods may be.

He reached for a couple of flat stones nearby, stood up to skip them as he and Nigel had done as boys when the sea was calm at Glenfrae. They must get Nelson down soon. Ask him to bring one of his famous steak and kidney puddings, which would please him. Jack dug in his pocket for another cigarette, smiling at his interesting thought. What would Nelson make of *Emotion on the Page*?

'I'm always amazed that the place stays upright,' said Sarah, peering through the rain at their original rented cottage near 'Penguins Crossing'. It was still occupied, still giving shelter to the impoverished. It looked much the same: less paint, more rust on the roof but the curtains were new, the ice plant as exuberant as ever. 'Nor'westers always remind me of it. Remember how the rain used to blow horizontally, straight into the letter box?'

Jack nodded, his eyes intent on the wet gleaming road. They were on the way round the harbour to meet Selwyn who had flown down from Auckland for a day's business. Sarah's written consent to the publication of *Emotion* lay folded in Jack's shirt pocket close to his heart.

Rain squalls scudded across the harbour, breakers crashed and tore at the black rocks. Occasionally a wave broke beyond the sea wall sending sheets of sea and spume across the road. You had to concentrate. You couldn't lift your eyes for a second.

They parked the car in the wind tunnel of The Terrace. Sarah tried to put up her umbrella, which was immediately blown inside out, black struts exposed as it tugged for an independent existence in the buffeting storm. They ran across the road, clutching each other for support, their faces wet and laughing, reached the down escalator to Lambton Quay, laughed again at the well-filled underpants and bra advertisements presented for eye-level inspection as they descended, were tempted by doughnuts and coffee on the ground floor but resisted. As Jack said, Selwyn might spring off his tail and take them somewhere for lunch, stranger things had happened. And anyway they had run out of time.

'At least the hick verandahs keep the rain off,' Jack yelled in her ear as they half-ran along the Quay. 'To hell with pure lines and no shelter.'

'Strong verticals,' Sarah shouted back, flinging a hand at the concrete heights around them. He looked puzzled, he could make nothing of it. The wind had seized the art school phrase and tossed it away. She shook her head, it wasn't worth repeating. She attempted to open her umbrella once more with the same result. Her recently shortened wet hair slapped across her eyes, blinding her momentarily outside the jewellers on the corner. The lights signalled Cross, the audio-signal for the sightless squealed in her ear. 'Run,' called Jack. 'Run!'

She ran, her head down, her eyes on the flooded gutter ahead.

She didn't see him fall. She jumped the gutter onto the opposite pavement and glanced about, her eyes seeking him among the scurrying sodden crowd. She turned and saw him lying still, flat on his back on the pedestrian crossing behind her. No movement. None. She screamed and ran back, screamed again as she fell on her knees beside him. His eyes were closed, his face yellow-grey.

A crowd collected, gaping, murmuring, pointing at the body.

Sarah glanced up to find her head a few feet away from the giant front wheels of a truck labelled ERF. The lights changed, cars streamed past them on the left, the truck remained. She could see the driver's anxious face, his woolly hat. 'Ambulance!' she shouted to the crowd on the pavement. A man in a red Swanni lifted a hand and ran away. Sarah began to untie Jack's tie, her fingers shaking and useless. Why had he worn a tie, he never wore a tie, never. 'Jack, Jack, it's all right.'

Two people appeared from the crowd, a young Polynesian man and a blonde in a hectic parka. 'I'm a nurse,' she said. 'Don't move him.'

No, no, of course she wouldn't. Sarah was crying now, tears of terror ran down her face. She whispered his name again and again and again.

'He's alive,' said the blonde, her fingers on his pulse. Of course he was alive. Sarah held his hand, bent to embrace him, to be near.

'Give him air,' said the nurse. Her quick efficient fingers whipped off the tie, loosened his collar.

The young man said nothing. He produced a striped pink and blue umbrella and held it over the three of them. Jack lay in a pool of water; water streamed from them all. Seen from this angle the truck was sinister, everything about it enormous and out of scale. The driver was two flights up. The insects trapped in the radiator were splattered monsters. The truck hadn't moved, hadn't crushed them, was probably protecting them. The crowds were foreshortened, their gaping faces miles above them. The rain fell.

Jack's eyes were still closed. Sarah began tugging off her old raincoat to cover him. The man in the Swanni appeared beside them with a blanket. 'The ambulance's on its way.'

The young Polynesian was still silent. Rain ran in runnels through his cropped hair as he squatted beside them with his fun umbrella, his eyes on Jack's face. He would stay for ever. He was crying, or else it was the rain.

Where was the ambulance? It should be here by now. Sarah

glanced upwards. Surely, surely by now it should have come screaming with help, with professional uniformed life-savers and hope and hope and hope.

Jack's eyes flickered, opened, found Sarah's. His head moved in the smallest possible negation. 'Not here, Sal,' he murmured. 'Not here.'

'It's coming. The ambulance. Any minute. Hang on darling.' She smiled at him, a mad rictus of confidence and joy. 'It's coming.'

Hang on. Oh hang on, my darling heart. Of course you won't die here.

He was saying something more, so softly she could scarcely hear. The nurse moved backwards into the rain as Sarah took his hand again and bent her face to his.

'Top pocket,' whispered Jack and closed his eyes.

He was declared dead two hours later after another attack in the coronary ward. There had been some hope after the first one. They had tried everything possible. They were very sorry.

Sarah and the registrar sat in the ward office. A comic graph pinned to the wall with red pins showed healthy weight levels. A skeletal cartoon figure skulked at the bottom, a dangerously obese one sagged at the top, a healthy pilgrim trod the middle way. Sarah was no good at graphs, she couldn't work it out, not exactly.

Dr Ali, the registrar, was still talking.

An orderly in blue overalls leant against the outer wall of the office and recommended the film *Death Wish* to a smaller colleague tugging a vast bag of laundry across the polished floor. His informant had already seen it four times. It was not to be missed. The registrar rose and shut the door.

'I want him at home,' said Sarah. 'We all will. His daughters . . .' She stopped in horror. Dora and Emily didn't even know yet.

'Of course.' Procedures were explained.

'And I want to know, I want to know what was in his top pocket.'

If Dr Ali was surprised he did not show it. 'Top pocket?'

She couldn't look at the immaculate head, the eyes, the beard.

Her eyes bored through the idiotic shape of the thin man in shorts, or was it a woman, at the bottom of the graph. They shouldn't have silly things like that in the office. Not when people were dead. Tears ran down her face, a welling over of excess silent and inevitable as overflow.

'It was the last thing he said. My husband. I heard him.'

'Well certainly, Mrs Macalister. All your husband's belongings will be . . .'

'I want it now.'

He said nothing more but rose to his feet again. 'Excuse me.'

He opened the door, spoke to the two orderlies who disappeared down the corridor after a quick ghoul's peer through the office window.

Dr Ali returned in a few minutes and handed her the contents of the top pocket of Jack's coat. His face was contrite. He had hoped to offer the stricken face more comfort than a piece of old newspaper and a poem.

But she knew what it would be. She took the scrap of paper from him and smoothed it against her still damp skirt, her hand stroking it flat, caressing it.

'Thank you,' said Sarah. 'Thank you very much. I'm glad to have that.'